The bird sat by the edge of the stream, its body huddled up against a rock. The bird's bright yellow feathers looked dull in the early morning light. Rather than offering a pleasant whistle, the bird was strangely quiet.

Alex knew something was wrong even before he stepped out of his apartment's back door.

Alex quietly approached the bird and laid down the bag of bread. He was only a couple of feet away from her when he stopped and bent down.

"You're sick," Alex said.

At the sound of his voice, the bird tried to fly away. She spread her wings and flapped them vigorously. Her motion was clumsy and all she managed to do was spin on the ground in an uneven circle. She gave up after a few pathetic flaps.

In that moment, Alex had his first clear view of her. He let out a scream and fell back.

The bird's eyes were gone.

Other Titles by E. R. Torre

Shadows at Dawn (Short Stories)
Haze

Corrosive Knights Novels

Mechanic
The Last Flight of the Argus
Chameleon
Nox
Ghost of the Argus
Foundry of the Gods
Legacy of the Argus

The Dark Fringe Novels

The Dark Fringe (with John Kissee)
Cold Hemispheres

GHOST OF THE ARGUS

By

E. R. Torre

Book cover design by ebooklaunch.com

All other interior artwork by E. R. Torre

Please visit my website:

www.ertorre.com

Comments or questions? Email me at:

atrocket@aol.com

ISBN 13: 978-0-9729115-8-0

1

THE SIGNAL – Year 4330, After Exodus

At the dawn of the era of space exploration, automated vessels carrying primitive Displacer units were sent to distant solar systems. When they arrived at their destinations following many years of travel, the Displacers were activated. It took only a few days for their signals to reach the Displacer web and, once they did, vessels carrying human crews were sent through the newly activated devices to explore those distant solar systems. Many of those automated vessels were lost...

She drifted past the gravitational pull of Eventho 3 and slipped through the solar rays of the Pegasus sun, her body luminous in the shimmering red ion energy field. Particles from a dust cloud beyond Eventho 3's lonely moon altered her path by a few inches, causing the automated ship's internal processors to awaken for the first time in two hundred years. The computers checked the Displacer she was carrying to make sure she was intact before focusing on flight corrections. Though the deviation in her course was minimal, when her destination lay so many light years distant, even the mildest of deviations could result in missing her target by hundreds of thousands –if not millions– of miles.

The internal processors calculated the thrust needed to adjust the ship's path. A miniscule sprinkle of accelerant, no more than a puff of smoke, was ejected from the craft's lee side. To outside eyes, there was no noticeable difference in the ship's movement, yet this small change ensured she was back on her proper course.

The craft's internal processors followed the course correction with a routine check of all remaining equipment before preparing to return to its dormant state. It was during that check the ship's sensors detected a very faint radio transmission. It was an electronic squeal that lasted only a few seconds yet the ship's processors recognized it as something other than ambient static.

The signal was a very old code and one universal to both Empires.

Distress.

The ship's processors, cold and logical, did not question the how or why of an emergency signal so very far away from any known civilization. They began the task of determining the general direction from which the distress signal originated and found it came from a solar system in the Elicia quadrant of the Phaecian Empire. The system had three planets revolving around a massive red sun. The ship's processors sent out a series of sensor waves while precision cameras took magnified images of the distant worlds.

It would take months for the sensor waves to bounce back to the ship and provide a fuller picture of that distant system.

While the computers waited for the response, obscure code hidden within the ship's processors was activated and the ship released a distress signal. It stated the robotic vessel was hit by a meteorite and was experiencing catastrophic failure.

This lie would be the very last signal the ship would send its distant masters.

The vessel then released another burst of accelerant, this one more than just a mild puff, and the ship's forward momentum slowed to a near stop.

Eventually, every one of the information rich sensor waves returned.

The distress signal's origin was the planet farthest from the red sun. It was a cold world, one covered in ice and snow. The distress signal originated from that planet's equatorial region.

This information was saved and, afterwards, the ship's internal processors returned to their long sleep. The vessel and its Displacer waited in place to be activated.

It would do so for well over a thousand years.

2

"**My name is...**" the man said and paused.

A confused frown appeared on his forehead. Though he awoke the day before, he still fought a deep mental fog. It was only now he tried to remember his full name and was very surprised to find he could not.

He sat on a metal bench and spoke into the small recorder he found earlier that day in one of the seemingly countless rooms on this enormous space craft. Behind him was a large window and beyond that absolute darkness punctuated by starlight.

"I was sleeping," he said after a while. "A very heavy sleep. It was almost... it was like death."

He pressed a button and the recorder stopped. He replayed the events of the recent past in his mind, of awakening on some kind of stasis bed. The mattress he lay on was very firm, with the consistency of a rock, yet he felt no discomfort. There were no sheets covering his body nor a pillow under his head. He lay on his back, staring at a gray ceiling. Flickering lights illuminated a section of that ceiling, revealing rivets and heavy metal panels.

The man reactivated his recorder.

"When I awoke, it took a while for my eyes to adjust to the lights. As confused as I was –and still am– I knew I wasn't home." He laughed. "Damned if I can remember *what* home was like. I know it wasn't like this. The walls in the room were metal. My bed was encased in glass. I was trapped inside that glass like a bug in a bottle. It took a while to get my bearings and be able to... be able to *think*. I lay there for a while, looking around. There was one door leading into the room. Otherwise, it was a perfect metal cube. I panicked. I tried screaming for help but barely had a voice. It took a while before I could really call out."

"When I did, no one answered. I kept screaming and banging on that glass cage, hoping to get someone's attention. I screamed until I lost whatever voice I had. I banged that glass until my fists were bloody."

He held his injured right hand before him.

"The lid held. Just like I knew it would. Even though I couldn't remember much, I knew that glass was made to withstand impacts far greater than those from my fists. I thought that was it for me. I was going to die a slow, painful death in a small glass coffin."

He put his hand down.

"It was only after I was completely exhausted that I noticed a computer panel behind and just above my head. It flashed lines of information but because of the way I lay I couldn't see them all that well. I spun around and got on my stomach to get a better look. The information on the panel passed too quickly to read, but I did catch one line. The 'final scrubbing,' the computer said, was almost complete."

"Then there were some noises. Machinery under the bed came to life and the glass panel slid away. I was free."

The man suppressed a shiver.

"I sat up. Too quickly. My stomach heaved and I tried to throw up but there was nothing to throw up. The room spun and I fought to keep conscious. Some random memories came back. I recognized the glass covered bed."

The man looked out the window and at the stars shining in the darkness.

"It was a stasis chamber. Back in the old days, when it took years for a starship to reach its destination, stasis chambers were used to keep a crew sleeping for those very long journeys. That was before the Displacer network was set up."

The man rose from the bench and walked down the hallway. It stretched in a straight line for what seemed like miles before disappearing into the far distance. Doors lined the right side of the hall, while windows appeared every twenty feet to his left.

"Even as I realized all these things, my body went numb and I blacked out. When I came to, I was on the floor. I was still very weak and felt something new. Hunger. In fact, I was starving. I sat back for a while and let my body regain its strength. Soon, I felt strong enough to put weight on my feet. I did so, carefully. After a few minutes I took my first steps. I walked from my coffin to the door leading out of the room. As I figured, it was solid metal and just as impossible to break through as the stasis chamber's glass. This time, I was smart enough to use my head rather than my fists."

"Beside the door was a dull green screen. There were no buttons or keypads. Just that screen. I placed my hand over it and pressed down. A green light came on and it mirrored my hand. A few words appeared and disappeared. It was some kind of security protocol. I must have passed the test because the metal door slid open nice and easy and I had my first look outside."

The man stopped walking. He faced the window beside him and the emptiness of outer space.

"Beyond the door was what looked like a medical lab. There were no instruments in it, only empty cabinets and two automated medical emergency machines. I left the med lab and found a hallway not unlike the one I'm in right now, only much, much bigger. I walked through several such corridors, each just as big as the last. This place was built to house thousands of people yet the only one here is me."

"After a while I found what looked like crew quarters and, at their end, windows looking out into space. Though I suspected as much, I now knew for certain I was on a spacecraft. But not any ordinary spacecraft. This one is much larger than any I've ever seen before... and I somehow knew I had seen many. The crew quarters, like the rest of this ship, were enormous. They could easily house an entire army... maybe even a *couple* of armies. And like the med lab, they showed no signs of habitation. There were spaces for beds but there were no beds. The bathrooms didn't have faucets or running water. What kind of madman created all this... and for what purpose? Why was no one here? Surely this incredible ship wasn't made just for me? Or was it? And if so, why?"

The man shook his head.

"I found an elevator. Once inside, a computerized voice asked me for my destination. I told it to take me to the ship's bridge. The doors closed. The elevator moved smoothly, up and sideways, passing many, many miles before reaching its destination. When the doors opened, I was there."

"That's when most of my memories returned."

3

The Planet Pomos – Year 5029 A. E.

His name was Alex. He was eight years old and an only child. His parents did their best to spoil him with a wealth of gifts while also enrolling him in the best schools available. He rewarded their attention by scoring in the top twentieth percentile in the Kirkas Achievement Exams. These tests indicated he had a high aptitude for the sciences, should he choose to pursue that field into adulthood.

Outside of class, he was extroverted and friendly. His laughter was infectious and he had many friends. Classmates and faculty were certain his future was very bright.

They were wrong.

Alex stood beside the small stream in his back yard. His parents and he lived in an apartment in Petersburg, the capital city and central star port of Pomos. At this very young age he wasn't entirely sure what his parents did, but he knew their job was important enough to allow them this lavish lifestyle which included an apartment with a beautiful back yard and a fully functional recycling stream.

Birds flew in daily and bathed in that stream and drank from its precious liquid. Day after day Alex watched them and, whenever he could, feed them leftover bread. At first the birds were weary of his presence, but in time they grew comfortable and, Alex thought, friendly with him.

In the early morning and before he went off to school Alex usually saw between twenty to fifty birds massing around his stream.

On this particular morning, there was only one.

Alex carried his bag of bread and was disappointed by his sole visitor. The bird sat by the edge of the stream, its body huddled up against a rock. The bird's bright yellow feathers looked dull in the early morning light. Rather than offering a pleasant whistle, the bird was strangely quiet.

Alex knew something was wrong even before he stepped out of his apartment's back door.

The air outside, fresh and pure thanks to the filtration machines located throughout the mega-city, today had a bitter metallic smell. Perhaps, the boy thought, the machines were offline. In a city this industrialized, any problem with them meant smog would quickly settle in.

But the bitter smell wasn't the result of smog, Alex realized. He never smelled this particular stench before.

Alex quietly approached the bird and laid down the bag of bread. He was only a couple of feet away from her when he stopped and bent down.

"You're sick," Alex said.

At the sound of his voice, the bird tried to fly away. She spread her wings and flapped them vigorously. Her motion was clumsy and all she managed to do was spin on the ground in an uneven circle. She gave up after a few pathetic flaps.

In that moment, Alex had his first clear view of her. He let out a scream and fell back.

The bird's eyes were gone.

Dried blood filled the hallow craters that once held the bird's eyes. Her right wing remained spread out, offering her some balance. She let out a pathetic shriek. It was all she had left to defend herself.

Alex got to his feet. He stepped away from the bird and, his mind filled with concern, walked to the heavy plexi-glass that made up the edge of the balcony. He looked around to see where the other birds were, fearful they too might be in trouble. As he walked, his mind filled with strange images and electric impulses. He couldn't quite understand them. He looked past the plexi-glass and at the city.

The bitter metallic smell was gone, replaced by the unmistakable scent of fire. Thick black smoke rose from several buildings around his. Tiny shapes, other dwellers of this concrete canyon, moved about on their balconies. Some ran back and forth like ants scurrying around their nest. Many were perilously close to the balcony edges. Some even climbed over the rails.

They dropped…

Alex heard a bloody scream and a body fell right past him. In the split second she passed, he recognized the jumper as Mrs. Kane. She was a rich elderly woman who lived five floors above his apartment and on the one hundred and twentieth floor of the building. There was no chance she'd survive the fall.

More thoughts and impulses filled Alex's mind. Impulses that were like voices screaming for him to act. He felt like slamming his body against the balcony glass, only to then want to run away from it. He felt like shouting, he felt like whimpering. He wanted to cry... he wanted to hit. No, not just hit, *kill*—

Abruptly, the voices were stilled.

Alex knew what he had to do.

He reached down and picked up one of the rocks by the stream.

He stared at it, his mind filled with a blood lust the young boy had never, ever felt before.

He held the rock tight in his hand and approached the injured bird.

This is what he needed to do.

Afterwards, he'd follow Mrs. Kane.

4

THE PLANET ONIA

The warship *Andora* exited the Displacer at a little past 0600 hours and approached Onian orbit.

She was a large ship, one of fifty owned and operated by the Saint Vulcan Corporation. Though a warship, her most recent missions almost exclusively involved cargo hauls. Her last port of call before arriving at Onia was the Vera Epsillon Displacer within the Phaecian Empire. While the relationship between the corporate Epsillon Empire and the religious Phaecians was cooling by the day, it wasn't frigid enough to hurt the robust trade markets.

Captain David Desjardins stood on the bridge of the ship staring at the enormous view screen before him. It had been many years –approaching ten– since he last gazed at his home world and he couldn't help but feel a twinge of nostalgia and regret, especially since his visit would be so very brief. The green planet below him was a shining gem, easily one of the most beautiful in the Epsillon Empire and destined, he hoped, to stay that way forever.

"Sir?" the first officer said.

"Yes?"

"We are now in orbit."

In the corner of the main screen the *Cantina*, one of several service vessels operating in and around Onia approached. During the next twenty four hours it would fully service his ship, removing all waste materials while simultaneously resupplying all food stock, personal equipment, and fuel.

David Desjardins pressed a button on the computer panel attached to his jacket sleeve.

"This is the Captain," he said. His voice echoed throughout the ship. "All shore leave requests have been processed. First shift shore leave personnel are permitted to board the shuttles now. Second shift personnel will have clearance for shore leave in exactly eight hours and following the return of all first shift personnel. Third shift be ready eight hours after that. Please enjoy your brief stay planet side and behave yourselves. Remember, you represent the Saint Vulcan Corporation. Negative incidents will not be tolerated."

A small smile appeared on the Captain's face. Hopefully, this very young crew wouldn't get too rowdy down below.

I was young once, too.

Though he normally stayed on board during these brief shore leaves, Captain David Desjardins was in the shuttle along with the first wave of officers headed planet side. He sat in the shuttle's front cabin, removed from the others, yet couldn't help but over hear their excited conversations. Like them, he too was eager to touch ground, even if his destination on Onia did not include bars, shopping centers, or brothels.

Unlike most Epsillon Empire citizens, Desjardins remained deeply religious at a time when those who shared his devotion were emigrating en mass to the theocratic Phaecian Empire. As a result of the emigration –or perhaps because of it– religious intolerance was on the rise in the Epsillon Empire. As the Epsillon citizens devoted more and more of their energies to the acquisition of wealth and worldly goods, their brothers in the Phaecian Empire devoted themselves to the Holy Texts and The Word of the Gods.

Given the divergent nature of the individual philosophies, clashes were inevitable. Verbal arguments had a way of escalating into something far greater and sides were being drawn daily. Segregation between the religious and the capitalist was the new norm. Some feared this bad blood would spread until it dragged the mighty two Empires into conflict and, eventually, Galactic War.

For his part, David Desjardins avoided confrontation. Though devotion to the True Light was his ultimate calling, he never felt the need to sermonize to others. Not even to family and friends.

Desjardins checked his watch.

The reason he joined the first landing party to Onia was because he was eager to attend the Day of Sacrifice mass at the Blue Church. It was pure coincidence the *Andora* –and Desjardins himself– arrived on Onia on this most holy of holidays. The mass would begin in an hour and Desjardins was determined to participate in it. Warm memories of past masses from his childhood and early adulthood, all at the Blue Church, filled his mind.

Coming back here on this holy day was more than a coincidence. It was meant to be.

Following a brief check at Onian customs, Captain David Desjardins and his security escort found themselves walking the busy Onian Starport. Desjardins stepped into one of the changing rooms and slipped into casual attire while his security escort waited. Afterwards, the two walked past the heavy crowds and to the pickup zones. There, David Desjardins looked up into the sky. He spotted a shadowy dot high above the port and barely visible in the midday sun. It was the *Andora*. Despite her distance, her massive size allowed her to be seen planet side.

The security escort hailed a cab and kept the door open while his commanding officer stepped inside. He then entered the cab and slid the door shut.

"Welcome to Onia," the driver said. "Where can I take you?"

"The Blue Church," Captain Desjardins said.

The driver's eyebrows lifted.

"The...?"

"You heard me," Captain Desjardins said.

The driver eyed the security escort and shrugged.

"Whatever you say."

It took only a few minutes to arrive at their destination.

Desjardins' security escort produced a credit chip and paid for the trip. Afterwards, the two exited the cab and stood before a set of large wooden doors, the Blue Church's entrance.

"Is there something wrong?" the security escort asked.

David Desjardins noted the building's rundown façade. Her paint was chipped and faded. Several of the glass panels on the front of the building were broken and boarded up with weathered planks of wood. Even though it was the Day of Sacrifice, few stood around the building and fewer still entered. Several Onian Security Guards were at the corners of this block. They carried heavy fusion rifles and kept their distance.

"Why do you suppose they're stationed around the church?" Desjardins wondered aloud.

"Protection, I imagine," his security escort said.

"For who?" Desjardins said.

The security escort said nothing. Like most of the crew of the *Andora*, he had little time for, and even less interest in, religion. The sound of organ music wafted from within.

"The mass is about to start," Desjardins said. He reached for his communicator and shut it off.

"If there's any kind of emergency, don't hesitate to come for me."

"And interrupt the service?"

"If the emergency is legitimate, the Gods will understand."

Without saying another word, David Desjardins stepped into the church.

There were only a handful of people inside.

David Desjardins slipped quietly into one of the rows of benches and sat down. He clasped his hands and closed his eyes, offering a small prayer of guidance. As his prayer ended, the organ music built to its climax. From behind a set of rouge curtains stepped a very old man. The few people within the cathedral rose to their feet as Father Osmonsis, the Onian church's leader for the past five decades, walked to his weathered lectern.

Captain Desjardins immediately recognized the elderly man. In the ten years since last attending his masses, Father Osmonsis had aged considerably. His hands and legs shook but he needed no help to make this short walk.

Nonetheless, it took Osmonsis a while to steady himself before the lectern. While he did, he surveyed the few participants in this mass. His usually bright blue eyes were dull. Desjardins thought they lightened up a bit upon seeing him and wondered if the elderly preacher recognized his one-time student.

"We gather each week at this time to give thanks to our ancestors," Father Osmonsis began, reading off a passage from the ancient tome on the lectern. "This week in particular is important and this day is a very special one, for today we celebrate the Day of Sacrifice. It was because of our ancestors' actions, and that of the Unknown Hero, that we live and thrive. All praise the Unknown Hero."

"All praise the Unknown Hero," the gatherers chanted.

"For it was the Unknown Hero who foresaw the great Apocalypse," Father Osmonsis continued. "It was he who made the ultimate sacrifice, giving of himself while humanity escaped its doomed world. All praise the Unknown Hero."

"All praise the Unknown Hero," the gatherers again chanted.

Father Osmonsis offered the parishioners a warm smile.

"We are five millennia past the time of the three arks. Five millennia past the time our descendants fled Homeworld, our lost Eden. Though our ancestors did not know it at the time, Homeworld was fated for destruction and it was the Unknown

Hero who recognized her fate. Despite all obstacles, despite all the ridicule and hardships and, yes, *suffering* he endured at the hands of nonbelievers, he fought for our survival. He fought for what he knew was right. For that one man had the wisdom of the Gods themselves and the Gods blessed him in his quest. It was because of their love and guidance that he built the three arks. Arks large enough to fit humanity in its time of Exodus. Arks large enough to take our ancestors to the stars. This one man, alone in a world of doubters and condemned to face the apocalypse on his own, saved us. All praise."

"All praise the Hero. All praise the Gods."

"The three arks embarked on their separate yet equally sacred journeys for our ancestors knew their path was perilous. Should one ark fall, the others had to survive. Praise their wisdom."

"We praise their wisdom," the parishioners responded.

Father Osmonsis raised his hands over his head and a bright yellow light bathed him.

"The first ark came to orbit around New Eden, and from there the first seeds of the holy Phaecian Empire were born. The people of the second ark settled Zethus and so began our own Epsillon Empire."

The father paused for effect.

"The third ark was lost. And it is on this day we also pray for those lost souls, so that they may one day be found, and our brethren returned to the fold."

"So we pray," the members of the congregation replied.

The father lowered his arms and closed the holy tome.

"In these trying times, we must always remember our origins and the sacrifices of others. Despite pressures and differences, it is our shared history that unites us. It was while our Empires were newborn that we helped each other through the pains of rebirth. Orphans we were in this strange universe, yet we shared our knowledge and grew from infancy to adolescence and today... Today..."

Father Osmonsis paused and the weariness on his face grew. He was silent for several long, uncomfortable seconds. Finally, he spoke.

"Many worry about our future. Our Empires are not unlike siblings that have grown apart. Brothers and sisters, we are not perfect... we harbor jealousies and pursue different interests. That should not push us apart. We must grow with each other. Perhaps I won't see it in my lifetime, but at heart I am optimistic our people will reconcile. We cannot, we should not, we *dare* not, let these differences rip us apart. On Homeworld, darkness grew and destroyed the planet. We must not allow that darkness to grow here. We escaped not by fighting but by uniting. By sharing our goals and realizing *this* was the path to survival. We did it once before, and we can do it again. While Homeworld, the planet our ancestors called Earth is gone, we can still unite our Empires and ensure our brotherhood remains strong."

5

The mass ended a half hour later.

It was a short mass, much shorter than was customary. Unlike the other parishioners who silently walked to the church's exit, David Desjardins approached Father Osmonsis. He was seated beside the lectern, surveying his now empty house of worship.

"Father Osmonsis, I wanted to thank you for your sermon."

The elderly man squinted his eyes.

"You've been here before, haven't you? I seem to remember… What is your name?"

"David Desjardins."

The elderly pastor thought about that.

"Ah yes. I remember your family. I remember the accident. I'm sorry."

"It was a long time ago."

"Back when our church had crowds."

"You'll have them again."

Father Osmonsis offered Desjardins a weary smile.

"The Good Book willing," he said.

"Father, there are sections of the stained glass in the front of the building that are shattered," Desjardins said. "Was it…?"

"I'm afraid so," Father Osmonsis said. "Intolerance blooms like weeds in the Epsillon Empire. Onia lies in the Empire's borderlands and it has taken a while for that brand of intolerance to find its way here. The Gods know I try to be optimistic and preach fellowship over hostility. Yet…"

He let the thought die unspoken and rubbed his hands together.

"Enough of my concerns. What have you done with yourself in the years since you last attended our church?"

"I've been busy. I joined the Epsillon Military. I became a Starship Captain."

"My my," Father Osmonsis said.

"I left the military five years ago. Since then, I've flown for Saint Vulcan Corp., delivering supplies and exploring the edges of known space."

"Ah, Saint Vulcan," the elderly man said. "If it was up to her, the universe would have no mysteries at all. Sometimes I wonder if that's a good thing."

"Isn't knowledge humanity's ultimate goal?"

"Perhaps, but that's a discussion for the learned, not the old and tired," Father Osmonsis said and chuckled. "Now that you're here, is it your intention to stay?"

"No," Desjardins said. "Our ship departs tomorrow."

"So soon."

"There is still much to accomplish."

Father Osmonsis nodded.

"I felt like that when I was younger. Now, as my journey nears its end, I am not so ambitious. I take stock of my life and remember the good times that were."

"You are comfortable?"

"I will be," Father Osmonsis said. "In the next month I emigrate to the Phaecian Empire."

Desjardins was surprised by the Father's words.

"You're leaving the parish?"

"Yes. Understand, David, there remains much good here, within Epsillon, even as its people turn their backs on the Holy Texts. Science and industry –though more of the later than the former– have become this Empire's ambitions and goals. There is precious little room for people like me."

"You sound frustrated, Father."

"I am," he admitted. "Stained glass can be replaced and buildings fixed. The threats... the threats are quite another thing."

"You were threatened? Why not call the authorities and—"

"Authorities surround the church day and night and yet the vandals still manage to do their foul deeds. What does that tell you, David?"

David Desjardins shook his head.

"Who will run the congregation?"

"I've made inquiries but have yet to find anyone interested in taking over my position."

"Then... you intend to leave the church abandoned?"

"It is only a building, David. True faith lies within. Maybe in the next generation or the one after that, we will see a return of our values. If such things don't happen, especially between Empires, I fear... I fear there might be war."

The words startled David Desjardins.

"My advice to both the congregation and to those who do not share my faith has always been simple: Do well, both for others and yourself. If you are a man of the Gods, David Desjardins, you might want to think about taking your skills to the other side."

"Abandon the Epsillon Empire?"

"There's a place for someone like you as surely as there is one for me."

"But I've sworn allegiance to the Empire and Saint Vulcan," Desjardins said. "To turn my back on my oaths amounts to treason."

"Open your eyes, David. See what lies before them."

The door to the church opened and David Desjardin's security escort stepped into the Church.

"Sir?" he said.

The elderly man leaned back in his chair.

"N... nice talking to you," David Desjardins muttered.

He stepped away from the dais and walked to his security escort's side. The two exited the church and were again on the streets of Onia's capital. The Epsillon Guards watched Desjardins and his security escort as they walked away.

"What is it?" David Desjardins asked his escort.

"I just received a communique from the *Andora*. They've received a level five emergency report."

"Level five?" Desjardins repeated. Such emergencies were catastrophic in nature. "Where?"

"Pomos."

David Desjardins' breath caught in his throat. Pomos was Saint Vulcan Corp.'s home world. It was where Saint Vulcan herself was stationed and where all the main laboratories and experimental facilities operated. It was where the *Andora* was headed after her stop on Onia.

Most importantly, it was where David Desjardin's wife and her family lived.

"What is the nature of the emergency?"

"I don't know, sir."

David Desjardins nodded. He clenched his fist and hastened his walk.

"Let's go," he said.

When they reached the star port they found many of their crew were already there, milling about. Most were upset at having their shore leave cut while others looked worried. Like Captain Desjardins, they too had families and loved ones on Pomos.

"Is everyone accounted for?" Captain Desjardins asked his security officer.

"No sir. We're still missing twelve."

"Was everyone told shore leave was cancelled?"

"Yes sir."

Captain Desjardins cleared his throat and moved to the middle of his crew. The crewmembers stiffened. All eyes were on their commanding officer.

"Ladies and gentlemen, we begin boarding now," Captain Desjardins said. "In exactly ten minutes our shuttle craft departs. Anyone not on board at that time will be considered a deserter and arrested and prosecuted as such."

Ten minutes later the shuttle was cruising through the Onian atmosphere.

Captain Desjardins and his crew, all but five members, watched as the Onian Starport disappeared below them. Once the pull of gravity lessened and the craft reached orbit, Captain Desjardins grabbed his communicator.

"*Andora*, this is Captain Desjardins," he spoke into the microphone. "Report."

"This is Communications Officer Talbot," a female voice replied. "All systems are green. We await your arrival."

"The Displacer?"

"We have it on standby, ready to send us to Pomos."

"Understood," Captain Desjardins said. "Have you determined the exact nature of Pomos' emergency?"

"Not yet, sir. We're receiving the same reports of a catastrophic event, but they carry few specifics."

"That's damn unusual," Desjardins said. "Is it possible there were coded messages within them?"

"No sir."

"Then what is going on?"

"Whatever it is, it's serious enough for Saint Vulcan to issue containment orders for the entire planet. She is not allowing anyone in or out."

"Sounds like a biological or chemical event."

"It is possible."

Desjardins' thoughts returned to his wife. Was she planet-side when this happened?

"Where is Saint Vulcan?"

"Indications are she's on Pomos."

"What exactly were her orders to the fleet?"

"All Class III and above ships were to report to the planet."

Class III, Desjardins thought. The *Andora* was Class I.

Every one of those ships was fully armed and designed for conflict.

6

From her seat she watched the monitors before her.

Her full name was Catherine Vulcan. She first emerged to the public at large on Pomos, a fertile world run by a liberal intellectual commune. The Corporations of the Epsillon Empire ignored this world and her products for years, until she created and released astonishingly sophisticated computers that took the Empire by storm.

It didn't take long for her community to grow into an economic powerhouse. In the intervening years Vulcan's company amassed a staggering forty percent of the computer market and she became the human face of modern technology.

It was during this time that she received countless awards and, eventually, bestowed the prestigious title of Saint. She maintained her operations on Pomos and from there greatly expanded her empire. All was going incredibly well.

Until today.

On one of the monitors was a satellite display of Pomos. That monitor, in the center of the others, held her favorite view of her adopted world. The planet was achingly beautiful. It was where she intended to work for many, many productive years.

That dream was over.

On another monitor were the familiar lines that made up the eastern coast of the planet's central land mass. There, built to the very edge of the impossibly blue Azure Oceans was Petersberg, the mega-city capital. It was a city so large that it was visible from orbit. It lay on the equatorial line, extending from the central hemisphere to the coast. The glint of metal, a reflection from the sun, made her shine like a precious gem. Still, Petersberg suffered like all big cities with her slums, traffic, and congestion. There was too much trash and far too much misery, yet Saint Vulcan knew those problems could be solved in time.

Over six billion people lived on Pomos and as recently as a few hours ago they were free to move about from city to city or off-world. No longer. A virulent virus had infected the planet and her population. The first symptoms were relatively benevolent: Coughs, mild fever, headaches. But the headaches and fever turned into crippling pain and dementia. For the elderly, mental faculties dropped precipitously. For the young and healthy, the infection made them violent.

Saint Vulcan sent her best minds in search of a cure but the infection spread far too rapidly to combat.

In a matter of hours Saint Vulcan knew all was lost. There was only one thing left for her to do: Contain the virus. Her solution was one she dared not think about using even three hours before.

Saint Vulcan used emergency precautions she set up in case of a disaster of this magnitude. The planet's Displacer and planetary star ports were sealed and security forces acted swiftly and without hesitation or mercy. She controlled every transport throughout the planet yet knew that control was tenuous. As long as her security forces obeyed her commands, she could contain the virus. The moment they rebelled...

Saint Vulcan issued a statement through the local media that a burst of solar flares crippled outside communications and caused a strain to the global computer network. She used this as justification for the cancellation of all transport flights. A few Captains of crafts resisted orders to remain in port. These ships were blasted out of the sky.

From there, things only got worse.

Saint Vulcan called in her warships, every single one of them, and twenty eight were now parked in orbit. There was only one ship left to arrive.

Then we'll be complete.

She closed her eyes and leaned back in the chair.

The computer panel at her side blared a message. The Pomos Displacer came to life. She waited for confirmation of the incoming ship's identity, though she already knew who it was.

When they broke through the Displacer's energy wall and entered the space around Pomos, the computers on board the bridge of the *Andora* lit up.

"Getting multiple signals," the Communications Officer said. "It's hard to get through the clutter. It's like being in a room filled with screaming people."

"What about other vessels?" Captain Desjardins asked.

"I'm detecting twenty eight Class III and above ships in orbit around the planet, sir," First Officer Santos said. "With us, that's the entire fleet of large crafts."

"Evacuations?" Captain Desjardins asked.

"None detected," Santos replied. She pressed a series of buttons on the computer before her. She sat back. "Sir, you need to see this."

Captain Desjardins walked to his officer's side. On Santos' monitor was a visual display of the planet. The camera zoomed in on the city of Miter, then zoomed in further to display the city's star port. It was in flames.

"What about the city itself?"

The view shifted away from the star port. The roads to the city were littered with debris and broken down vehicles. Small shapes –pedestrians– ran in all directions. Several of the tiny shapes clashed, their attacks against others brutal and inhuman. Bloody bodies lay everywhere. On another screen were images of little children herded off the streets. A man grabbed one of them. He smashed her into a wall before another shot him down. Another monitor showed an apartment building on fire. People jumped from the upper floors to avoid being burned. Many laughed as they fell. Still another feed displayed a group of soldiers armed to the teeth and firing into crowds indiscriminately. They too laughed as scores of people died before them.

"By the Gods," Desjardins said.

Chatter from the other ships around Pomos filled the radio's speaker.

"Sir, we're being hailed by... by just about everyone," the Communication Officer said.

The *Andora* was the largest vessel in Saint Vulcan's fleet and Captain Desjardins the senior most officer present among them.

"They want to know what to do."

Captain Desjardins drew a deep breath.

"Tell them I am assessing the situation and will contact them in sixty seconds," the Captain said. He faced his first officer. "What about the other cities? The other star ports?"

"I'm seeing much the same."

"Is this some kind of civil war?"

"If it is, it's localized. The military bases are locked down. I'm not seeing any movement of troops or vehicles from any of them. There are no missiles in the air, no fleets attacking other cities."

"No invasion forces?"

"I have detected no outside spacecraft at all. It looks like... it looks like mass hysteria."

Captain Desjardins walked to his communicator officer's side. Despite his calm exterior, his mind raced. Images of his wife, somewhere down there in the hell that was once Pomos, filled him with worry.

Keep it together. For your sake as well as for the crew's.
"Any word from Saint Vulcan?" he asked.
"None sir."
David Desjardins pressed a button on the computer panel in his jacket sleeve.
"This is Captain David Desjardins," he said. His voice echoed through the *Andora*. "An unknown catastrophic event has occurred on Pomos. Like many of you, I have family and friends below and I am just as eager to get information of what's going on down there as I'm sure you are. For now, we must figure out what is happening. We will not act until—"
"Captain Desjardins?"
Desjardins faced his first officer.
"Sorry to interrupt, sir," Santos said. "I've just received a high priority message from Saint Vulcan. She's calling a meeting among all Captains."
Captain Desjardins nodded. He again spoke into his communicator.
"You will be updated very soon. We'll get through this as long as we stay focused."

Captain Desjardins hurried back to his quarters.
The door closed behind him and his bed slid into the wall. He stepped into the room's center and the lights dimmed. A seat and a small table slid up from the floor and he sat down. Holographic images appeared around him of the other twenty eight star ship Captains. They were, as he was, in their quarters on their ships looking at the same holographic images. Each and every one of the Captains' faces was filled with great tension. In some this bordered on panic. No one spoke, though every one of them was ready to. All waited for one person, the only one missing from the meeting.
Her hologram materialized at the head of the virtual table.
"Saint Vulcan," the Captains' greeted her in unity.
Saint Vulcan was in her mid to upper fifties. She was skinny to the point of appearing undernourished. Her hair was brown with streaks of gray and pulled back into a tight bun. She offered the Captains a tense smile, revealing brilliant white teeth.
"Thank you for coming so quickly," she said.
Her greeting proved too much for Captain Menos of the *Vulcan VII*.

"Please excuse my impertinence, but what the fuck is happening down there?"

"The planet is infected," Saint Vulcan said.

"By what?" one of the Captains said.

"We're not sure. Near as we can tell, the infection originated in Petersberg and spread in a matter of hours throughout the planet. The infected..."

Saint Vulcan paused to gather her thoughts.

"As you've no doubt seen, the infected display irrational, paranoid thought processes which result is self-destructive tendencies. They attack without provocation yet retain their base knowledge. Those who pilot shuttles or operate complicated machinery are still capable of doing so even as they view all others –including family and friends– as a threat. They will attack anyone before them and not stop until their perceived threats are incapacitated and... and dead."

The room grew very quiet.

"What do you intend to do?" one of the Captains asked.

"I've drawn samples of the infected blood and have a basic understanding of this infection."

"What about a cure?"

"That may take days, weeks... perhaps even months to come up with."

"Should we start evacuation protocol?" another Captain asked.

Saint Vulcan shook her head.

"Going down to the planet at this point is suicide. Should any member of your crew be exposed to the infection and return to your ship, it will spread throughout your vessel. If you were to travel to other worlds, the entire Empire would be in danger."

There was muttering among the Captains. The muttering stopped when one of the Captains asked:

"Saint Vulcan, they're killing themselves down there. How long can we wait before intervening?"

"The contagion has already spread throughout the world. Even with all quarantines in effect, population survival can be measured in days, if not hours."

A great hush settled over the room. Saint Vulcan lowered her head.

"Ladies and gentlemen, we have to be realistic about our options."

"What do you mean?" another Captain said.

"Pomos is doomed."

The Captains digested this information. None spoke.

"There is only one action that will stop any further outbreak of this contagion," Saint Vulcan continued. "That action lies within the weapon systems of your vessels."

"You're not suggesting—" another Captain began and stopped.

"She is," yet another Captain said. Her face was red with rage. "You want us to put everyone down there out of their misery, as if billions of people were nothing more than a rabid dog. That's why you ordered the ships into stationary orbits around the major cities. You want us to torch Pomos."

The realization was too much to bear for several of the Captains.

"That... that's criminal," another Captain said. "We can't—"

"We won't!" several shouted.

The meeting threatened to turn into pandemonium. And then a voice louder than the others spoke for the first time. The voice was calm yet forceful, full of rage yet in control.

"There is no choice."

The room went silent. The words did not come from Saint Vulcan.

They came from Captain David Desjardins.

"You've seen the vids," Desjardins said, his voice threatening to break. "By the Gods, you've seen the violence and carnage. The citizens of Pomos are tearing themselves apart. My wife..." he faltered for a second. "My wife is down there. She's my... Holly's my life. I don't know if she's still alive, but I do know one thing: If she is, she won't be for long. If this infection spreads beyond Pomos, the entire human race will be at risk."

"You actually agree with that *bitch?!*" one of the Captains hissed.

"You have biotech labs all over Pomos," another Captain said. "Is this your doing, Saint Vulcan? Are you responsible for this outbreak?"

There were screams and accusations. Finally, the Captains yelled over each other until, in unison, they faced Saint Vulcan and screamed:

"We will not fire on Pomos!"

As the arguments escalated, David Desjardins pressed a button on his sleeve. He wasn't surprised to receive no response.

He looked up, at the arguing Captains, before looking directly at Saint Vulcan. She sat as before, passive, emotionless.

Darkness filled Captain Desjardins features. He raised his hand and spoke, but his voice was lost in the shouts. He balled his hand into a fist and rose to his feet. He slammed his fist against the table, startling everyone into silence.

"We have no choice in the matter," he yelled. A single tear rolled down his cheek. "We weren't called together to this meeting to argue about what's happening down there. We were called together as a distraction. Weren't we, Saint Vulcan?"

Saint Vulcan's expression remained as before.

"From the moment the meeting began, we were frozen out of communication with our ships," Captain Desjardins said. He again pressed the button on his sleeve. "I certainly have."

The other Captains examined their remote Comm buttons. None could communicate with their crew. David Desjardins shook his head and motioned to Saint Vulcan.

"You have control over our ships, don't you?"

Saint Vulcan nodded.

"The actions I undertake are solely my own," Saint Vulcan said. "Every one of you will be absolved."

"Fuck you!" a Captain yelled. He disappeared from the Holographic meeting.

Several others faded away as well. They returned to the bridges of their starships, to see if they had indeed lost control of their crafts and, more importantly, if they could regain it.

"The judgment against you will be harsh, Saint Vulcan," Desjardins said.

"I know," she said. "The bombings began at the start of this meeting."

The few remaining Captains looked at each other and eyed instruments not present in the holographic setting.

"You didn't..." one of them muttered.

The truth on his monitor, however, was clear.

"You'll fry for this," a Captain said between clenched teeth.

"My fate is sealed," Saint Vulcan said.

The holographic images disappeared and Captain David Desjardins was again alone in his small room. The computer monitor at the side of his desk flashed with urgent calls from the ship's bridge. David Desjardins pressed a button on the desk communicator.

"I'm back, Officer Santos."

"Captain!" Santos began, her voice filled with panic. "The ship's controls have been overridden. We're firing on Pomos! What should we do?!"

"Nothing," Captain Desjardins said. Despite the incredible sadness, he knew Saint Vulcan made sure none of the Captains could counter her orders. Not until the weapon bays were empty and the planet a wasteland.

"Did you...did you get in touch with your family?" Desjardins asked.

"What?" Santos said. "N... no sir. Communications remain a mess."

"I'm sorry."

Captain Desjardins sat silently for several seconds. Until it was over, there was nothing he could do.

"Sir, there's a message coming in."

"If it's one of the other Captains, I'm not—"

"It's Saint Vulcan."

Captain Desjardins eyed the framed photograph of his wife on his desk.

"Put her through."

The image that appeared on his desk monitor was grainy. Saint Vulcan sat in her office.

"You're the only one who agreed with my course of action," Saint Vulcan said. "You understood this had to be done. If I hadn't taken over your ship, you would have initiated the bombings yourself."

Captain Desjardins closed his eyes tight.

"I would have," he whispered. A tear ran down his cheek. "Don't you dare confuse agreement with acceptance, Saint Vulcan. If you weren't down there, I'd be the first to see you hang."

"Have you spoken with your wife?"

"No," Desjardins said. He took a deep breath and for the very first time felt he was about to lose control.

"I'm sorry," Saint Vulcan said.

"What exactly happened?" Desjardins said.

"What I told you. A virus was released."

"An accident?"

"It was done on purpose."

"On purpose?" Desjardins repeated, incredulous.

"Someone planted it here."

"But... but you have quarantine protocols that reach a microscopic level. How did—"

"At this point, what does it matter?" Saint Vulcan said. "It happened and I... I have to clean this mess up. In the end, people will think that I was responsible. In a way I was. But only because I was the target."

The grainy image of Saint Vulcan looked away.

"I'm sorry," she said. Her image faded to black. "Goodbye."

Captain Desjardins remained in his room for the next two hours while every missile in every ship in orbit around Pomos rained down on the planet. Even Solyanna, the planet's sole Moon, was not immune. A base on her surface was hit by a secondary barrage of missiles. The damage to the moon was extensive. The blast cracked her surface and sent chunks of rocks the size of cities in decaying orbit around the ruins of Pomos.

When the firing stopped what was left of Pomos and Solyanna was complete and utter destruction.

7

ONIA, YEAR 5058 A.E.

*"**The years pass** faster than you know,"* the old man thought. *"And old age is its own particular hell."*

He shuffled past the souvenir shops, his limp more pronounced with each step. His weathered hands trembled and his white hair stirred in the soft breeze. It was cold that morning and the dark clouds above the Onia Starport hinted at the first signs of winter.

At the height of the season, the elderly man dodged the masses of tourists but today, close to the end of the year and deep into the off season, there were very few people to avoid. Many of the shop owners waved when they saw him. They didn't bother pushing their wares, for they knew he was a local and had no interest in them.

The souls of his heavy shoes clicked against the azure cobblestones, the sound echoing through the narrow passageway he passed. A young couple several steps in front of him pointed at the surrounding architecture, marveling at the long abandoned but now restored Blue Church. It was no longer a house of worship. Like all the other buildings in this block, it housed shops selling Onian trinkets. The couple were amazed that a church – even one that no longer offered services– still existed in the Epsillon Empire. It was then they noticed the elderly man.

"Could you take a picture of us?" the young woman asked.

The elderly man smiled and nodded. This simple act of kindness, no more than a polite favor, was far beyond the routine of his daily life. The old man waited patiently as the young couple explained how the camera worked and were satisfied he wouldn't somehow screw up their picture. Of course he knew which button to press. There were few pieces of electronic equipment, even those still deemed top secret by Epsillon Military or the ruling Corporations, he couldn't figure out given a bit of time.

The couple posed at the steps leading up to the entry of the Blue Church and smiled for the old man and their camera. He pointed the device and took the picture.

"Much obliged, citizen," the couple said.

The elderly man handed the camera back to them and they moved on, now walking in the opposite direction and toward Onia's Old Town. The elderly man made his way to the food courts.

It was called Cheri's Cafe and it was a local fixture. Her original owners were displaced Sumerians who died over a hundred years before but what they started and left behind, a coffee house specializing in Onian sweet pastries, still drew strong business even in the off season.

The elderly man paused for a second at the Cafe's entrance. He always did that, for it allowed him time to peer through the Café's windows and make sure she was there.

She was.

Every time he saw her he felt a swell of mixed emotions. How could he not? She bore an uncanny resemblance to his late wife. Perhaps it was the way she walked or the way she attended to her clients. Most certainly it had to do with those very blue eyes and that achingly bright smile.

The elderly man composed himself before walking into the Café. He found a table at the corner of the room and approached it. The early crowds were sparse, although by dinner the place would fill. As the elderly man sat down, he found her already standing before him.

"The usual, Mister Desjardins?" she asked.

Seeing her so close gave him pause. Old emotions roared back, despite his attempts to control them.

"Please, Julie, call me David," he said.

"The usual?" she repeated.

"Yes please."

When she walked away, he couldn't help but stare. Her name was Julie Bishop. She couldn't be much more than twenty five years old, the same age his late wife was when they first met all those many years before.

Of course, the waitress didn't look or act exactly like his wife. Her hair was darker, her laugh more boisterous. In this line of work, she had to be patient and displayed far more of that than his wife ever could. At times, Desjardins wondered if the differences were more pronounced than he thought. Maybe his mind was tricking him into thinking she was more like his late wife than she actually was.

Inevitably, David Desjardins let those thoughts go for they mattered very little. He was a very old man and harbored absolutely no delusions that this very young woman would have any feelings for him at all.

In fact, it would worry me if she did!

Desjardins chuckled. No, it was enough to be close to her and allow himself the indulgence of re-living memories of his late wife. These days, it was the best he could hope for.

He leaned back in his chair while Julie worked on his coffee and, eventually, delivered it to him.

Just as Holly had done innumerable times before.

When he finished his coffee and sweet pastry, Desjardins offered Julie several credit chips. As always, he gave a generous tip. When he first met her nearly a year before, she engaged in small talk with him. Over time, their talks grew shorter and shorter, to the point where outside of greeting him and asking what he wanted, there was nothing else she said. Perhaps she had grown tired of this old man's attentions. Julie might have sensed his nostalgia and mistook it for something else.

David Desjardins felt a twinge of sadness at this realization. Maybe it was best he leave her alone and never return. He grabbed a napkin and pocketed it. Julie hardly seemed to notice as he rose from the table and shuffled off to the door.

He saw her reflection on the glass door's surface. Julie eyed him for a second before shaking her head.

Desjardins walked through the streets toward his apartment, ignoring the people that passed him by. A taxi slowed, hoping to snag a new client, but he waved the driver off.

It took him nearly a half hour to reach his apartment building. It was a modest ten story complex inhabited by a mix of local families, out-of-towners, and retirees. Desjardins didn't interact with many of them beyond exchanging daily pleasantries.

When he arrived at the building's outer gate, he displayed his identification badge to a security camera and pressed his hand against a scanner. After verifying his identity, the metallic outer gate clicked opened and allowed Desjardins entry. He walked past a small garden and to the building's lobby. No one was there. It was very quiet, almost eerily so, and Desjardins felt an inexplicable nervousness. He paused for a few seconds to look around.

Nothing was amiss, but the silence was awfully loud.

He walked past the lobby and to the elevator. Once inside, he pressed the tenth floor button. With the money he made during his services and insurance from his loss, he could have lived anywhere. Luxury, however, held little meaning after Holly was gone.

When he arrived on his floor, Desjardins stepped out of the elevator and walked down a narrow corridor and to the door at the far end. His was the only apartment on this floor and he neared the door leading into it. He stopped.

The door to his home was ajar.

Behind him, the elevator closed and her engine hummed as the device returned to the lobby. Desjardins stayed in place, unsure of whether to move forward.

"Who's there?" Desjardin called out.

He received no answer.

It can't be an intruder, he thought.

The building's security was very good. Apart from the entry system, monitors checked every floor and exit twenty four hours a day. Anyone unfamiliar to the automated facial recognition security system would be stopped at the lobby. The elevators and doors leading into the building would be locked down. Once inside the lobby, there would be no way to flee or advance.

Yet the door to Desjardin's apartment was ajar. *Someone* had managed to do the impossible.

Perhaps I left it open when I went out?

That too didn't seem likely.

You're old, but you're not that old. If it is an intruder, he's a very clever one.

After the Pomos disaster, there was a trial. The starship video logs from all twenty nine vessels involved in the destruction of the planet were poured over by an Epsilon tribunal. In the end, the Captains and crews were cleared. All blame for this massacre fell –rightly– on Saint Vulcan.

It didn't stop there.

Though the personnel were exonerated, there were many who could not –would not– accept the evidence. They blamed Desjardins and the other Captains of, at the very least, neglect.

Desjardins recalled the chants and taunts.

You should have done something. You let her kill an entire planet and its people.

The first few years after the destruction of Pomos were a horror. Several starship Captains and many more crewmembers were killed or died under suspicious circumstances. Some found they had bounties on their heads. Many changed their names and identities and settled in far off planets where those who sought justice –*revenge*– couldn't find them.

Because David Desjardins was the only man who agreed with Saint Vulcan's actions, he was in the crosshairs more than almost everyone else. Many attempts were made on his life but Desjardins evaded them all. With each passing year and the growing threat of intergalactic war, Desjardins found fewer and fewer of the fanatics tailing him. Eventually the citizens of the Epsillon Empire forgot about Captain David Desjardins even as they could never forget the crimes of Saint Vulcan. Time cures all.

Or does it?

Desjardins cautiously approached his door while old, almost forgotten instincts kicked in.

From the slight opening, Desjardins noted the entry area of his apartment. It was a small square space with a couple of seats lining the walls and a mat in which to clean your shoes. All appeared as he left it. Everything was untouched.

Someone's there.

Of this he was certain. He could *smell* the intruder's perfume. It was delicate, an odor that brought back memories from long ago. A chill passed through Desjardins' body. He felt a sudden, blinding rage.

Desjardins pushed the door open and stepped into his apartment. He walked past the entry, looking around for something to defend himself against –or attack– the intruder he knew was waiting for him. He reached over the kitchen counter and grabbed at a set of knives. He took one and hid it behind his back. He walked into the living room.

The intruder sat in the sofa, staring out his front window.

When he saw her, Desjardins feared he had finally lost his mind.

She was in her mid-forties to early fifties and had short brown hair. The expression on her face was serious. It always was. She wore a white outfit and sat very straight in his sofa seat.

After the initial shock wore off, Desjardins approached the woman. He was unsure if what he was seeing was a hallucination. She turned her head ever so slightly, the way she always did when receiving guests. Big blue eyes focused on him.

"How can this be?" Desjardins said.

She hadn't changed. The last time he saw her, he was a young man in the prime of his life and she was at least twenty years older than he. Today, he was an old man and, other than her shorter hair, she hadn't aged a day.

"How can this be?" he repeated.

The woman pointed to the chair opposite the one she sat in. Her attention returned to the window and the city below.

"S... Saint Vulcan?"

"Take a seat, David," she said. "We have much to talk about."

Desjardins stood still. The shock receded, replaced by rage. Despite his age, despite his frailty, he struggled with the urge to grab the woman by her throat and squeeze until...

"You can't be here," he said. "You're dead."

"Do I look dead to you, David?"

Desjardins said nothing. His skin grew pale and he had trouble breathing.

"Please, David, sit down before you collapse."

Desjardins reached for the chair before her. His eyes didn't leave Saint Vulcan while he sat down. He remembered the knife in his hand. He was so very close to her...

"You can't be here. You can't..."

"Yet I am."

"If they find out..."

"I've followed the news," she said. "My actions at Pomos made me the Empire's greatest villain."

"You murdered an entire world," Desjardins spat. "You... you killed Holly..."

Saint Vulcan's face betrayed no emotions. There was neither regret nor sadness nor pride.

"You, more than anyone else, know that what I did was not just proper, but necessary."

"Proper?" Desjardins shouted. "*Necessary?*"

Desjardins' head slumped down. Tears fell from his eyes.

"By the Gods," he said. For what seemed like the first time since that dreadful day so many years before, he cried. He cried for his wife and the billions who perished. And he cried because he knew, more than ever, that Saint Vulcan was right. The horrible images of violence and carnage within the planet's largest cities seared his mind. She could not allow the continued slaughter of all those countless people and the risk this disease would spread to the Empire itself.

She did what had to be done.

"I don't know why you came or how the fuck you managed to survive, but you have to leave. Please... Don't torture me anymore. Let me live out what little time I have left in peace."

"You were one of the brightest minds in my corporation, David," Saint Vulcan said. "I need you."

Despite everything, Desjardins laughed.

"I'm long past piloting ships," Desjardins said. "Even if I wanted to."

"I know you well, Captain Desjardins. Maybe better than you know yourself. That's why I came."

Desjardins wiped tears from his eyes.

"You belong out there, Captain, among the stars. Not here, at the dead end of the Empires."

Desjardins shook his head.

"After Pomos was destroyed we were... we were sent to holding cells. Arrested, though no one formally admitted it. Even with your last testament and the recordings of our final meetings, the people of the Empire found it difficult to take your word and let us go. It took a very long time before we were freed. By then our names and reputations were destroyed. There wasn't a single company willing to hire any of us to do any job, however menial. We were blacklisted. We were not allowed to fly."

Desjardins sighed.

"You're right," he continued. "There was a time I couldn't imagine not being out there, exploring new frontiers. After Pomos, they tied me down and made it impossible to fly. As the years passed I realized the... the *worthlessness* of my past endeavors. My entire life was one long trip to nowhere, doing nothing, accomplishing little. Everyone was doing just that, even you Saint Vulcan, and you've accomplished so much more than almost anyone else in recorded history. The day you die, it ends."

"You still have your faith?"

"I lost that along with everything else."

Saint Vulcan sat back in her chair.

"Pathetic," she said.

David Desjardins frowned.

"What?"

"You heard me."

Saint Vulcan brushed the folds of her dress and rose.

"I came here looking for the bravest Captain in my fleet and instead find a broken down old man. Would you like an apology, Captain Desjardins? Would that make you feel better?"

The knife hidden behind Desjardins' back felt very warm. Saint Vulcan stood over him, within reach.

"You're alive when you shouldn't be and after nearly fifty years you haven't aged," Desjardins said. "How did you do it? Did you have some impenetrable bunker built for yourself? A stasis chamber? Did you climb into that chamber and freeze yourself while everyone around you died? Did you wait until all the bad feelings blew over before sticking your head out of that rat's nest? If you think after all this time people have forgotten, you're wrong."

Saint Vulcan folded her hands across her chest.

"Are you done?"

The knife in David Desjardins' hand was red hot. He leaned forward. She was very close. Certainly close enough. The grip around the knife's handle tightened. It was now or never. In spite of his age, in spite of his frailty, she couldn't stop him. There was no way she could.

Without uttering another word, David Desjardins thrust the knife with all his might at Saint Vulcan's chest. His ancient muscles were pushed to their limits and screamed from the effort. He knew this would be his only chance to take out this devil. The knife moved forward, as if in slow motion. He could see it just inches away from her. Just as it was about to penetrate her black heart, he yelled:

"I'm done with you, *Saint* Vulcan."

Then, he witnessed the impossible.

The knife sank deep into Saint Vulcan's chest. For a fraction of a second David Desjardins felt triumph. It was short lived.

Saint Vulcan didn't react.

She didn't react *at all*.

Four inches of blade penetrated her chest and sliced her heart. Yet Saint Vulcan remained before him, the expression on her face unchanged. No sign at all of pain, or fear. Or…

David Desjardins released the knife. Its hilt stuck out of her chest. Around the wound was no blood.

A small smile appeared on Saint Vulcan's face. She calmly grabbed the knife's handle and pulled it out. The blade was clean.

"That's the fighter I was looking for," she said.

David Desjardins' head spun and he pulled back, away from this... this demon. The strain on his frail body was too much. He felt his heart pounding away, threatening to burst. Then, abruptly, the pounding stopped. The world grew black around the edges. His time was over.

Seeing him fall back in his chair, Saint Vulcan reached out. Her right hand pressed against Desjardin's chest. Her touch was hot and, incredibly, her hand glowed with an inner light.

"No," Saint Vulcan said. "We aren't done yet."

8

The young David Desjardins clicked the recorder off. He walked to one of the ship's elevators.

"Destination?" a voice inquired.

His last memories as an old man, of confronting Saint Vulcan back on Onia, were so very fresh. It was as if they happened only a couple of hours before. On Onia he was near the end of his life. When he awoke in the stasis chambers of this ship, he was a man of no more than thirty years.

How could that be? And how could she –Saint Vulcan– remain so young? Despite these new memories, he was still missing much. What happened between his collapse and now? Did his older self survive the heart attack?

Try as he might, David Desjardins could not recall anything more of his last encounter with Saint Vulcan. All he knew was that he tried his best to rid the universe of her. His efforts were useless and he was here, where she wanted him to be.

But...

Why did she want him here?

Where was this ship going? What mission could interest Saint Vulcan so much that she would risk emerging from her hiding place?

"Why me?" he said.

You're the only one who agreed with my course of action. The only one who understood this had to be done. If I hadn't taken over your ship, you would have initiated the bombings yourself.

David Desjardins felt light headed. He staggered back and leaned against the elevator wall.

She was right.

"The Gods damn us all," he whispered. "You were right."

David Desjardins slid to the floor and covered his face with his hands. In his mind he pictured his beloved wife. Had he been able to communicate with Holly one last time while over Pomos, he would have told her he loved her.

And then?

"And then I would have begged you to forgive me," he said. "To forgive me for what *had* to be done."

He cried and banged his hand on the floor, a new born in an adult's body. He cried until he could cry no more.

"Destination?" the elevator's computer repeated.

David Desjardins wiped the tears from his face.

Please forgive me. Please...

"Bridge," he said.

A loud hum was heard and Desjardins felt the tug of gravity. In less than three minutes he was over fifty miles from where he began. The elevator slowed before stopping. The doors opened, revealing a large room replete with monitors and view screens. The largest of these view screens displayed a star field.

Desjardins walked into the room and made his way to the Captain's chair. There was no one else in the bridge nor, he suspected, the ship itself. He was its sole occupant.

Desjardins sat down and activated his recorder.

"I'm in a space ship," he said. "Larger than anything I've ever seen. Larger than anything I've ever known was possible."

He eyed the various screens.

"Which raises several questions," he said. "While I remember things that happened up to shortly before my arrival, I suspect memories following that moment are purposely being kept from me. There has to be a reason for this, one I can't see at the moment. This craft could easily house an army of soldiers yet I am utterly alone. I won't starve. Food synthesizers are spread throughout the ship. I won't freeze, I won't burn. So far every door I've found opens and nothing is locked. Everything is available yet when I ask the computer what our destination is, I get no answer. When I request astrological charts they are not provided. And when I ask why I'm here, the computer tells me I don't have the necessary clearance."

The lights around him dimmed.

"I'm even provided a sense of time. Evening is coming, and the lights turn low."

He shook his head.

"I'm so damn frustrated. Whatever information I seek is buried either in my head or within the computer's memory banks. It all goes back to Saint Vulcan. Why did you do it? Why did you send me out here alone?"

The lights dimmed some more.

David Desjardins put away the recorder. He prepared for bed.

9

When he awoke, Desjardins felt as if he was back home on Onia, the elderly man patiently waiting for his life to come to a silent and lonely end.

Being young again... such a beautiful dream.

The light around him was bright and growing brighter.

Artificial light.

It took a while for him to realize he was lying beside the Captain's chair of the mysterious and enormous vessel he found himself in a couple of days *–is that how long it's been?–* before. He stared forward, at the ship's view screen.

So very far away in the distance was a bright yellow star.

My destination?

"Looks like it, even if the computer won't tell me."

Desjardins rubbed his face and reached for his recorder. He stopped and laughed.

"What else is there to say?"

The star lay many billions of miles away.

By the time this ship gets there, I may no longer be alive.

Desjardins' laugh died.

No longer alive... or a very old man.

"Again."

In his later years on Onia, he shed most human contact. His family was gone and he made no friends. He never re-married. He didn't dare consider doing so.

He became a solitary introvert.

Still, he made casual contact with those around him. It might not have amounted to much more than polite greetings, but they were contacts nonetheless. Trapped in this vessel, how would he stand years being alone with no one to talk to?

He suppressed a chill.

During the early days of space exploration and before the Displacer networks were active, the incredible time required to journey between solar systems proved daunting to explorers. Research and common sense suggested large groups of astronauts stood a better chance of success on long trips. The earliest attempts at exploration were therefore done with groups of people rigorously screened and trained for their sometimes decade long journeys. In spite of enormous levels of preparation, claustrophobia and psychotic reactions were not uncommon.

Traveling alone was considered a torture not unlike being kept in solitary confinement.

For the first time since his arrival here, David Desjardins felt the full weight of his loneliness and the accompanying despair. For several long minutes, he hoped and prayed the dark feelings would pass. They persisted.

Stubbornly.

I need to move.

Desjardins tried. He tried again.

He didn't. In the darkness that swirled inside his mind, he thought he would never move again. He would remain here as the passing seconds turned into minutes, then the minutes turned into hours and the hours days. He'd rot away here, decomposing in this bridge until there was nothing left of him.

What's the use? You're going to waste your entire second life trapped here, in this Godsdamned...

"Fuck you, Saint Vulcan," he shouted.

His words echoed through the bridge.

Not loud enough.

"FUCK YOU!"

He was on his feet, pacing the bridge and yelling those words over and over again. Yelling until his throat was raw. Yelling until his body hurt. When he was out of energy, he fell onto the Captain's chair.

He wept.

Afterwards, he was back on his feet. He stepped out of the bridge and lost himself in ship's endless corridors. He wandered for hours, until he was sweaty and his energy spent.

Desjardins slept in one of the rooms he passed, huddled against the wall and on the hard metal floor. He dreamed of his wife and of Onia. He dreamed of Pomos and the horrors inflicted upon her.

He dreamed of Saint Vulcan.

In the morning, David Desjardins felt better. He left the room he slept in and continued his journey through the ship. As he walked, his thoughts felt clearer and his emotions more in check. What he felt the day before was alien to him.

Must have been a reaction to the drugs pumped into me during stasis. They're finally wearing off.

It was easier for him to focus on exploring the ship. Desjardins wondered how long it would take him to reach every compartment within. How many mess halls and laboratories and med bays and—

He abruptly stopped walking.

How many landing bays are there?

Desjardins' face lit up.

There *had* to be landing bays –*several* of them!– on a ship this size. If there were, might there not be shuttles or transport craft parked within?

If there's only one, that's all I need.

With a shuttle he could escape this vessel. He could return home.

Desjardins was walking again. Fast.

Yes, you're far away from home, but if there's a transport craft, a ship this size might be towing its own Displacer unit as well. Returning home might not be such an impossibility after all.

The thoughts kept his spirits up for the rest of the day.

That night he found and slept in another empty room. It had its own food station and a working bathroom. Desjardins cleaned and showered before eating and laying down to sleep on the hard floor. As he was drifting away, he thought he heard noises. He sat up and listened.

He heard nothing more.

It's too early to be going mad, he thought.

The next day Desjardins felt even more clear-headed.

Memories of his past returned with great clarity.   He remembered breaking his arm as a child and of the intense pain it caused him. He remembered his first day in school, of his first crush. He remembered the day he graduated. He remembered the pain from that accident that took his parents.

He remembered meeting Holly in the academy. She was seated in the row in front of his. Her blond hair—

Enough.

—her smile. Her—

ENOUGH!

He fell against the corridor wall. His body shuddered.

Keep it together.

He breathed slowly.

That's it.

The emotions passed.

Move on. Move on.

Later that day he found a large fitting room. He changed into fresh clothes.

He continued his search.

"There has to be a reason I'm here," he said out loud.

It made no sense for Saint Vulcan to manufacture such a monstrously large vessel and send it to a distant solar system with him its sole occupant.

There most certainly had to be a reason he was here, but what could that be?

David Desjardins spent many hours thinking about that.

He hoped his continued exploration would offer some clues. Perhaps there were other people here after all. Perhaps he had to find them and together they'd figure out what Saint Vulcan was up to.

A day passed. Another.

There was absolutely no evidence of any other occupants, hidden or otherwise, within the ship.

Desjardins' frustration grew.

He explored countless levels. The places he visited blurred in his mind. One room was just like the other, one corridor led into the next. After a while the places he visited felt the same. Even worse, he lost track of time.

How long has it been? Days? Weeks?

A month?

He no longer knew.

One day, while eating, Desjardins looked out of one of the innumerable windows in the massive starship. In the distance he saw the tail of a comet. It glowed like a starburst before fading away.

He wished he could accompany it on her journey.

I have to keep a journal.

"Didn't I do that already?"

He searched his pockets.

"Where is it?" he said.

He no longer carried the recorder. He tried to remember where he left it. He couldn't.

You left it behind somewhere. Then you forgot all about it.

"Idiot."

Without a recorder, he'd have to write information down.

"By the Gods," he said. "Write things down."

He swore.

"Make a map! How in Hades are you going to figure out where the landing bay is without a map?"

It took you this long to figure that out?

"You're not as smart as you think you are," Desjardins said.

He laughed.

He kept laughing.

Desjardins stared out the window.

The comet was long gone. He looked down and tried to get a view of the ship's sides. It proved difficult. The ship was either oval or spherical and all the windows looking out –at least those he found so far– offered few glimpses of the vessel's sides.

The one thing that remained a constant was her enormous size.

Despite this, his most recent searches yielded results. He lucked upon some boxes and, within them, paper and a couple of pencils. The papers were most blank. Some were standard, unfilled requisition forms. All were yellow with age and the box and room they were in was dusty.

Desjardins spent the day mapping the territory around him. He did the same the next day and the one after that. By the end of the week he had a clearer idea of the ship's size. It was far, *far* larger than anything he had ever seen. Larger even than Epsillon Mega-Cities.

Could this be... an ark?

The thought bordered on blasphemous.

The first ark came to orbit around New Eden and from there the first seeds of the holy Phaecian Empire were born. The people of the second ark settled Zethus and so began our own Epsillon Empire. The third ark was lost.

The original two arks were stripped, their parts used to build the first Empire cities.

"Is... is this the third ark?" Desjardins whispered.

Had Saint Vulcan found it? Was Desjardins on board it?

"Can't be," he realized.

This ship lacked basic amenities. Rooms that were clearly meant for habitation had no furniture. Bathrooms lacked fixtures or running water. It was as if the ship was launched from her berth in mid-creation, unfinished or perhaps rushed into service. What amenities were here could take care of Desjardins or a smaller group of people, but not one third of all humanity.

If it isn't an ark, then what is it? When was she commissioned and created?

It was hard to imagine a ship this size could be made by Saint Vulcan in complete secrecy, especially after the events at Pomos. Following the ravaging of that planet, all of her remaining laboratories and research stations were seized by rival companies eager to claim –and steal– her knowledge. Some of them, like Octi Corporation, rose from the ashes of mediocrity to become true powers.

So eager were the companies to lay claim on everything Saint Vulcan left behind that they conducted extensive searches for any remaining intellectual properties in all corners of the Epsillon Empire.

How could the existence of a starship this large slip through their fingers?

"It couldn't," Desjardins said.

He continued walking.

David Desjardins passed several doors, barely bothering to look into the empty rooms beyond. Somewhere along the line, he realized he had walked a very long distance that particular day.

Desjardins looked back. He spotted the dark gray frame that surrounded the elevator doors. It was at least a mile, maybe more, away. Desjardins didn't feel tired. Not at all. Before arriving on this spacecraft, before turning young, he felt the icy bite of arthritis. He enjoyed his walks on Onia but was limited in the distances he could travel.

In the past weeks he walked on a daily basis several times those distances and didn't feel winded at all.

A smile worked its way onto his face. The corridor continued for perhaps another mile before eventually curving away.

"Why the hell not?" he said.

Desjardins stretched and cautiously ran in place. Years had passed since his last run. It took him a bit to remember the mechanics.

Desjardins stopped. The smile on his face broadened.

"Why the hell not?" he repeated.

He was off.

Desjardins ran as fast as he could for as long as he could.

His movements were awkward at first, but with each step long dormant instincts took over and his movements grew smoother. When he was a cadet, he ran some of the quickest laps in his class. When he graduated, he continued exercising. He loved to run but as he aged, that ability slipped away. It did so slowly and quietly until one day he could no longer do it at all.

The smile on his face was dazzling. He let out a laugh and stopped. Between deep breaths he continued laughing, delighted at what he accomplished. He looked down the corridor, back toward where he came, and couldn't see the elevator doors' frame.

How far did I go? He wondered. And then: *What the hell difference does it make?*

He wiped sweat from his face. The joy of the moment passed, leaving behind silence. He looked forward. He saw movement from the corner of his eye and the smile on his face was abruptly gone.

He turned. Slowly.

Standing some twenty feet from him was a woman. Her features were spectral, her skin translucent. He could see through her, as if she was a ghost.

Which in many ways she was.

"It's good to see you happy."

Desjardins approached the apparition.

"I was wondering when you'd show up," Desjardins said.

The spectral woman offered Desjardins a small bow.

"It was best to give you time to acclimate."

"Are you on this ship, Saint Vulcan?"

"No. What you see before you is an augmented holographic representation. I'm sorry, Captain Desjardins, but I could not join you on this journey."

"I'm not a Captain. Not anymore."

"You are the Captain of this vessel."

"I have no crew or control over my destination. By Hades, I don't even *know* my destination."

"That will be explained."

"When?"

"When the time comes."

"If you can't tell me where I'm going, can you at least tell me how long before I get there?"

"Fifty years."

"Fifty...?" Desjardins whispered.

"There are other things we need to talk about."

"Fifty years," Desjardins repeated. "I'm trapped in this ship for fifty years?"

"David, we need to talk about the nature of your being," Saint Vulcan said. "Do you know what you are?"

"A clone."

The hologram was quiet.

"I figured that out a few days ago," Desjardins said. "It was the only thing that made sense. What did you do, transfer the thoughts and memories of the real David Desjardins into this... this duplicate body?"

"We call it Project Geist. It does exactly as you say, copying and transferring David Desjardins' memories into—"

"This husk."

"There were controversies."

"There always are with your projects, Saint Vulcan."

"We kept the second part of the equation a secret."

"Second part?"

"Project Geist allows people to record their memories up to that point in their lives. We never revealed the fact that we could then *export* those memories into other bodies. In time, people will figure it out."

"What happened to David Desjardins? The *real* David Desjardins?"

"He lived the rest of his life peacefully on Onia."

"I'm to take your word for it?"

"No."

The hologram before David Desjardins changed. The feminine features blurred until a new image, that of an elderly man, appeared. David Desjardins recognized his older self.

"Hello, David," the hologram said.

"Shut it off," the young Desjardins yelled. He ran through the hologram. "Shut it all off!"

The hologram disappeared. Beside the young Desjardins reappeared the image of Saint Vulcan. Her body moved with him though her legs remained still.

"The message is for you," Saint Vulcan said.

"I don't care," Desjardins replied.

"Don't you want—?"

"How long have I –the *real* me– how long has the real David Desjardins been dead?"

"David Desjardins died two hundred and ninety six years ago, shortly before this vessel embarked on her journey."

Desjardins stopped. That information hit him with a force he could neither explain nor understand. He doubled over, hands falling to his knees.

"You are David Desjardins in every way."

"No I'm not. David Desjardins was an old man who lived his life and died lonely and unloved hundreds of years ago and I'm… I'm *nothing*."

The young Desjardins swung at the air. The Saint Vulcan hologram said nothing more.

Desjardins walked away.

10

David Desjardins kept to himself for the next few days. He ignored Saint Vulcan's hologram and it, as if sensing his need for solitude, kept her distance. Nonetheless she remained ever present. She was an electronic ghost haunting him from beyond.

Was Saint Vulcan still alive? he wondered when the despair was manageable enough for him to consider such thoughts.

She has to be dead.

Just like the real David Desjardins. Then again, everyone thought she was dead after Pomos.

David Desjardin's clone walked aimlessly around the empty ship. He continued mapping locations, more determined than ever to find the landing bays and a possible escape. Now and again the Saint Vulcan hologram appeared before him and asked how he felt or if he had any needs. The expression on her face never changed, even while waiting for a response David Desjardins was unwilling to give.

What I need is a way out of here.

Desjardins' latest maps made him more certain than ever there had to be at least one landing bay and, hopefully, transport craft on board. If he couldn't find one, he thought more and more about hacking the ship's central computer and gaining control over her.

In either case, then what?

If Saint Vulcan was to be believed and the ship was on the tail end of an over two hundred year journey, gaining control over her meant he faced another two hundred year journey returning home... or at least someplace close to home. He was better off continuing the fifty year journey to the ship's current destination.

No.

His only hope of escape within this lifetime lay in the possibility this ship not only carried a transport craft, but, even more importantly, its own Displacer.

"You should talk to me," the hologram of Saint Vulcan said.

David Desjardins ignored the electronic ghost and continued to an elevator. He stepped inside. The Hologram didn't follow him.

When the doors opened on a lower floor, the Hologram was there, waiting for him.

"Please," it said.

David Desjardins shook his head in disgust.

"Fuck *you*."

His anger was suffocating. His body shook so much he felt he was about to black out. He fell to his knees and took several breaths.

Finally, he laughed.

"David?"

His laughter continued. It bordered on hysterical.

"David?"

"I'm fine," Desjardins said. "I'm fine."

"You don't seem—"

"As fine as anyone could be arguing with a computer program. Might as well yell at the toilet."

"I'm much more than I appea—"

"And I'm much *less* than I appear," Desjardins shouted. "The real joke is that you and I aren't all that different. We're copies of the originals."

The ghost closed her mouth. All was quiet for a few seconds.

"I'm getting out of here," Desjardins said. "I will not be trapped in this... this *cell*... for fifty years."

"It would be better if you accepted your situation."

"The hell it would," Desjardins shot back. "You anticipated this, didn't you? You had to. No one in their right mind would accept this sentence."

"You are correct."

Desjardins' eyes narrowed.

"Is this part of some test?" he asked. "It is, isn't it?"

"Your reactions are logical."

"Did I pass the test?"

"Yes."

"What did this prove?"

"That your temperament is adequate. You display a proper emotional reaction and an even better adjustment after the fact."

"Will this trip really take another fifty years?"

"Yes."

"You can't expect me to sit around here all that time alone without going crazy."

"No."

"Then?"

"We'll talk again, David."

With that, his electronic ghost disappeared.

11

The papers David Desjardins found and used to take notes and make maps were soon used up. He found no other paper and resorted to scratching floor plans on the ship walls.

By his count, over a month passed since the last time he saw Saint Vulcan's hologram.

At times he appreciated the loneliness, as it gave him the opportunity to meditate and think. It was when he was at his most calm he reflected on the extraordinary peace around him. The loneliness would eventually drag him down, but at least for these moments he welcomed it.

Toward the end of the month, the good feelings turned sour.

He wondered if being trapped in this ship was a punishment for his inaction at Pomos. He felt the cold touch of despair and guilt.

How long can I go on like this?

Desjardins found hundreds of rooms designed for individuals and very large groups. There were sections built for storage and others intended to be laboratories. There were rooms built with heavily insulated sterilization walls, as if meant to house biological and chemical experiments or test weapons.

Maddeningly, not one of them carried any of their intended equipment.

After each long day of exploration Desjardins returned to the ship's bridge and spent the remainder of his waking hours working on the central computer. Again and again he tried to make it past the ship's security features and reach the heart of the system.

Again and again he failed.

He found an astonishing array of entertainment in the computer's databanks. There was music from all corners of the Empires as well as all eras. There were holo-vids, including features not yet released when he was an old man living on Onia. There were entertainments, from the simplest puzzles to elaborate first person adventures.

He could spend years entertaining himself with them.

But David Desjardins ignored these diversions and kept his focus on breaching the central computers.

In time he realized perhaps this too was part of the trial Saint Vulcan was subjecting him to. Maybe she expected him to break the codes and prove himself clever enough to control the ship on his own. While he worked the computers these internal programs were charting his progress, analyzing every keystroke and missed opportunity while judging the success or failure of each action.

Or maybe they just want to see how paranoid I can get.

After a while, he gave up for the night.

He suspected all he was really doing was wasting time.

A week passed and then another.

David Desjardins dimmed the lights of the cockpit lower than their already low evening setting and fell asleep. He slept soundly, his belly full and his needs met.

His frustrations, which reached their peak a week before, eased. Instead of focusing on either escaping the ship or gaining control of her computers, Desjardins began using the entertainment programs. He allowed hidden speakers in the ship's corridors to play soothing music while he explored. He read books. He played holo-vids. He had the food dispensers make increasingly elaborate meals.

After another month, he again felt restless.

Despite all the comforts, each night when he returned to the cockpit and stared at the central view screen and saw the same distant star before him, he couldn't help but be reminded of the many years left to travel.

One night he returned to the central computer and, for the first time in a while, tried to crack through its security codes. As the hours passed, his optimism grew. He was making more progress than he ever had before.

This time, I'm going to break in.

David Desjardins wasn't sure how long he worked, but at one point he realized the dimmed lights around him brightened. A full day and night passed and he remained on the computer. He discovered subroutines and minute coding sources and pushed past them and into what he hoped would be the central program.

The dim lights grew even brighter. Here, in the early hours of what was dawn, he was certain his hard work was about to pay off.

Desjardins couldn't keep a triumphant smile from making its way onto his lips.

He found a set of hidden subroutines. He loaded them up. They were long and would take a while to sort, but Desjardins had nothing if not time. He pulled up the very first file, eager to see what Saint Vulcan kept from him. The first words appeared on the screen. He read them...

...and then the computer shut itself off.

For several seconds David Desjardins stared at the blank screen. The smile on his face was gone long before his brain processed what just happened. When that realization hit, a rage built like a hurricane within him. He sprung from his chair, sending it crashing back, then stumbled away.

How could you?

This was Saint Vulcan's doing. She left him to his own devices and gave him the tools and opportunity to find the information he wanted. And just when it was within reach, she snatched it away.

She *fucking...*

The screens came back to life and David Desjardins froze.

Before him were images of the sandy white shore of a beach. The beach's water was light blue and crystal clear. The impeccable white sand was beautifully manicured and, like the water, too bright given the night sky above.

The night sky.

Desjardins stared at that sky and spotted that star, his destination, in the far distance.

The beach was an artificial construct. It was somewhere on the uppermost level of this starship.

"That's where you want me to go?"

David Desjardins rubbed his face and hurried to the central elevators.

When he got in, a familiar computer voice asked him where he wanted to go.

"Take me to the beach," he said.

The doors closed and the elevator was on its way.

12

David Desjardins' body trembled.

He could hardly wait for the elevator to reach the desired level and, when it did, he rushed out.

The view before him was breathtaking. He walked onto what looked like a genuine wooden deck. He reached down and felt it. It was a hard plastic replica that was smooth to the touch. To his right and left were bathrooms, automated towel stations, and food dispenses. The food dispensers were colorfully adorned to look like restaurants. There were seats all over the deck, ready for masses of people. People that were, of course, not here.

Desjardins walked past it and reached the deck's rear. Before him was a wide staircase that led down to the beach. He walked the stairs and, on the final step, hesitated a moment to look around. Rock formations lay at the far right and left of the beach. Though the formations looked natural, their surface was very smooth and formed stairs which led to three distinct levels meant to be used for diving into the deeper waters. To the side of the rocks was another café, this one dispensing drinks. The café was built in faux weathered wood and projected the image of a laid back tropical island paradise.

Desjardins removed his shoes and stepped onto the incredibly white sand. It felt very soft and comfortably warm. The smell of ocean water was pleasant and not overwhelming. If he didn't know he was on a starship, he would swear this was a real beach.

He walked to the water's edge. The water was dead still, though Desjardins was certain he could command hidden machinery under it to make waves and create turbulence. Above him, the stars shined down. He could barely detect the tinsel glass that covered this beach paradise. He was certain that if asked, images could be projected on it.

Blue skies, a sunny day.

With just a few words…

For the moment, David Desjardins didn't say them. Only on a ship as large as this one could such an entertainment structure be built for the many passengers meant to inhabit it.

He kicked at the sand and, after his initial incredulity passed, found the anger once again building up in him.

"Is this another test?" he said.

He was nothing more than a lab rat in an incredibly large maze.

"What am I supposed to do here?" he yelled.

The anger grew until he could no longer contain it. He ran into the water until it covered the lower half of his body. He smashed his fists against the still liquid.

"Waves!" he yelled.

The hidden machinery below the still surface come to life and the water showed mild ripples.

"Stronger!" he yelled. "Make the waves stronger!"

His commands were heard and obeyed. Increasingly larger waves crested around him, smashing into the rocks and the shore.

"Stronger!" he repeated.

Soon it was as if a heavy storm lashed out on this small piece of paradise. David Desjardins was battered around and his body pushed back toward the shore. He fought the waves and coughed after swallowing salty water.

"Is that all you've got?" he said. "Show me blue skies!"

The tinsel glass changed, hiding the stars and outer space and replacing it with a beautiful blue sky.

"Show me clouds!"

The skies darkened.

"More!" he demanded. "I want a storm!"

The skies grew darker still. There were flashes of lightning. The wind around him kicked up.

Desjardins took the fury of the waves and demanded more. His energy faltered. When one particularly large wave hit him, he fell under the water and was slammed against the sand. He was helpless and in danger of drowning.

Am I better off?

The waves crested and he looked up. He saw the cloudy sky and the storm overhead. He felt the last bit of air leave his body.

It's for the best, he thought.

For that moment, he welcomed the darkness.

When he came to, he lay on the sandy beach. The fierce waves were gone and the waters were calm.

David Desjardins moaned. He coughed and spat out water before pulling himself to a sitting position. He faced the artificial sea.

He was cold. Very cold.

Desjardins got up and stumbled to the café. Beside it was an automated towel dispenser. He removed his wet clothing and used a towel to dry himself.

You tried to kill yourself.

He stopped, dimly recalling being under water before reaching up and gasping for air. He recalled telling the computers to stop the waves.

You tried but you couldn't do it.

"No I couldn't," Desjardins said.

You're a coward.

"A prisoner and a coward."

David Desjardins walked away from the towel dispenser and sat before the shore. He remained there for over an hour, staring at the tranquil sight. His mind was a blank, yet in that emptiness, thoughts stirred.

You may be a coward, but you are no prisoner.

The realization proved startling.

David Desjardins' mind was suddenly filled with memories of being an old man on Onia.

His very last memory before awakening on this ship was his savage attack on Saint Vulcan. He stabbed her right through the heart and she displayed no pain.

What happened immediately afterwards?

He was obviously still with Saint Vulcan, and she obviously did not retaliate. Why did his memories end so abruptly? What did Saint Vulcan and he talk about afterwards? Saint Vulcan was alone in his apartment. At no point did she attack him or defend herself. If anything, she was passive throughout the encounter, waiting for him to let his emotions out before presenting her case, whatever it was.

She was there to recruit you for this trip and she gave you the opportunity to accept or decline. If she wanted to force me to take a trip I wouldn't agree to, it wouldn't have taken all that much to disable me. She could have spiked a drink or taken me by force while I was walking alone in the park. She could have kept me under and used my DNA and memories to create this clone without the real David Desjardins ever realizing...

No.

Saint Vulcan made herself known to him. She revealed the fact that she was still alive. She talked to David Desjardins before placing his duplicate –me– on this space craft. She was there because she wanted him to know her plans. And he heard what she offered him and he... and he...

He agreed to this. All of this.

"Show yourself, Saint Vulcan," David Desjardins said out loud.

"I know I –my elderly self– agreed to come here. You were waiting for me to figure that out, weren't you? I don't know why you couldn't put all my memories together, but you had to make me realize this for myself, didn't you?"

He waited for the ghost of Saint Vulcan to reappear.

It didn't.

He stood for a few more minutes. After a while, he picked up his clothes and walked off the beach.

When he returned to the bridge, she was there.

Ghostly eyes stared forward at the view screen and their destination.

David Desjardins walked to her side and followed her stare.

"Why are we going there?"

"Because we have to."

Saint Vulcan faced David Desjardins.

"This mission isn't punishment and it isn't an experiment," the ghost of Saint Vulcan said. "Living through this flight may well mean the difference between the survival of the human race or its extinction."

"I wasn't ready to hear it before. I am now. Please, show me what David Desjardins has to say."

13

Saint Vulcan's hologram nodded.

Besides her appeared the image of the elderly David Desjardins. He spoke.

"There's a certain irony to this situation," the Desjardins hologram began. He wasn't talking directly to his clone, but rather to the unseen camera before him. "When you see this, the 'real' me will be long gone. Yet you are an almost exact flesh and blood duplicate. You carry all my memories, up to a point. For all intents and purposes, you are now the one and only 'real' David Desjardins."

The elderly man paused. Sadness reflected in his eyes.

"Undertaking this action –the creation of another me– was not something done lightly," the hologram continued. "After Saint Vulcan explained the mission, I spent two full weeks agonizing over the choices that were mine alone to make. In the end, I made my choice and I –we– bear that responsibility. Your memories end with her visit to my apartment. This, too, was done on purpose. It was not our intention to confuse or keep things from you, but at this time Project Geist is in its infancy and there is only so much strain we can put on your system. From the moment you were awoken you were monitored. This was done to make sure you adjusted to your status and did not show signs of any number of potential problems, from depression to psychosis. The fact that you are listening to this part of the recording indicates you passed that initial test."

"What if I had displayed irrational thoughts or actions?"

The hologram froze for a few seconds. When it next moved, the elderly Desjardins said:

"This may sound cold, David, but there are enough security provisions within this ship to minimize any damage created by a single person."

"Would the mission be in danger?"

"There are alternate means of completing what needs to be done, but they would not be as effective without your presence."

"What is the mission?"

"We cannot tell you. Not yet."

"Why?"

"Because the tests aren't done."

"You still don't trust me."

"It's not a matter of trust. It's a matter of being absolutely certain you are me. In every sense of the word."

"Why is that so important?"

The ghost of David Desjardins did not say.

"Humanity rests upon the shoulders of a clone with another's memories," the young Desjardins said. "Quite the honor. Suppose I find an airlock and end this test?"

"You could," the elderly David Desjardins replied. "Since you exited the stasis chamber, we have exerted little to no control over your actions. Though you may not believe it, you are a free man."

"I may not be a prisoner, but I am in a prison. If that star is my destination, then I've got a *very* long time to kill. I may sound rational now, but have either you or Saint Vulcan considered the effects of prolonged isolation? What guarantee is there I'll remain sane a year or two from now? What if I decide, just for the hell of it, to figure out a way to sabotage the ship and fuck up your mission?"

"You cannot affect the craft in that way," the Desjardins hologram said. "The ship's controls are, until it is decided otherwise, locked. The computer consoles available to you are mostly for your amusement. You cannot use them to alter the direction or destination of the craft until it is determined you are ready to do so."

"When will I be ready?"

"It won't be long," the elderly Desjardins hologram said. "Good luck David. I hope things work out. Believe it or not, I envy you. I envy what's coming. I wish it was me there instead of you. Goodbye."

The hologram of the elderly David Desjardins disappeared.

"Why do you need me here?" the younger Desjardins asked Saint Vulcan. "At least tell me that."

"In time this vessel will require the skills of a veteran Captain of my fleet. Someone who will take action when it is needed."

"But... fifty years? What I'll have to endure until then is torture."

Saint Vulcan's stare returned to the view screen.

"Would it surprise you if I said that of all the regrets I had about Pomos, one of my biggest was what happened to you?"

"Me?"

"When I realized the planet was doomed and we had only one course of action, I was certain none of my Captains would agree with what had to be done to contain the virus. Like you, almost every one of them was about to lose family and friends. The price was unimaginable yet you were the only one who agreed with me. Even at the cost of your beloved wife. How you must miss her."

David Desjardins steadied himself.

"A minute doesn't pass that I don't think about her," he said.

The ghost of Saint Vulcan was quiet for a few seconds.

"There is no forgiveness for what happened on Pomos," Saint Vulcan said. "I'll live with that memory for the rest of my life. Those that vilify me do so with good cause."

Saint Vulcan's ghostly eyes returned to David Desjardins.

"But I've always wanted to do what was best," she continued. "This situation will test you, especially at the end. In the meantime, there's no reason for your continued suffering."

"What do you mean?"

"There are fifty years to go before we reach our destination," Saint Vulcan said. "Make good use of your time, David Desjardins. Go back to the beach. This is the last time you'll see me until then."

"What?"

The ghost of Saint Vulcan disappeared, leaving David Desjardins alone.

For a moment, he fought hard not to scream. The realization that he was truly alone was like falling into an ice bath. He spun around in the bridge, looking from monitor to monitor.

"Saint Vulcan?" he howled. "Don't leave me!"

He moved on. Frantically. He hardly noticed when one of the smaller monitors lit up. On it was the beach.

"David?"

The voice startled him. It was female, familiar. A voice he hadn't heard in years and yet a voice he recognized right away.

"David?" the voice repeated.

"By the Gods," David Desjardins muttered.

Very slowly, he turned. She was on the monitor behind him, standing on the ship's beach. She wore a bright red bathing suit and was calling out to him, as if he had only momentarily stepped away.

She was exactly as he remembered her. Her hair was blonde and curly. Her eyes sparkling blue.

"Where are we David?" she said.

David Desjardins ran to the elevator and ordered it to take him to the beach.

When it reached its destination, he ran past the deck and down the stairs before leaping onto the white sands. She was by the shoreline, her back to him. He ran to her, abruptly stopping just feet away.

"Holly?" he said.

She faced him and smiled.

"She told me you were here," Holly said. Tears welled in her eyes. "She told me everything..."

Desjardins looked her over just as she did the same to him. He reached out and took her hands. She was no hologram. She was flesh and blood. David Desjardins held back his own tears. He released her and, hesitantly, touched her cheek. Her skin was soft and warm. Just like it was, before...

"By the Gods," he repeated.

He remembered the day he lost her and the crushing vacuum he felt since. That emptiness killed him piece by piece until his soul felt like a void. How he missed not having her by his side, of not seeing her smile or hearing her voice. Of not touching her hands or the caress of her...

"She gave us a second chance," Holly said.

They hugged.

In the back of Desjardins' mind he knew he was a clone of a long dead man as surely as the woman before him was the clone of that man's lost wife.

It didn't matter.

Their shared memories were here. *They* were here. And if memories don't make a person, then what does?

"It's going to be all right," he told her as he cried. "It's going to be all right."

14

Erebus Asteroid Field. Year 5419 A.E.

Inquisitor Cer stared out the window of her quarters on the Epsillon battleship *Dakota*.

Large and small asteroids floated by the ship. Had anyone told her even as little as three months before she would spend time aboard *any* sort of Epsillon military star ship, she would surely have told them they were crazy. Either that or wondered how the heathens of the Epsillon Empire managed to imprison an Inquisitor of the Phaecian Empire.

Relationships between the Empires, even two hundred years after the abrupt end of their one and only Galactic War, remained in the most polite of terms "frosty". Yet the two sides nonetheless came together for a mission that, had it gone wrong, may well have resumed that ancient war.

The days leading up to today were filled with high tension, intrigue, and death, all in the search for the super dreadnaught *Argus*, a top secret Epsillon battleship that avoided the incredible destruction that befell the Erebus Solar System at the end of the Galactic War. The *Argus* was trapped in the ruins of this system, now a wasteland of radioactive decay and asteroids.

The enormous ship held dangerous secrets and it was Inquisitor Cer's job to make sure they weren't revealed. For the *Argus* was much more than the largest battleship ever created by the Epsillon Empire. It was a massive explosive *disguised* as a spacecraft, an explosive of such power that it was capable of wiping out an entire Solar System. The ship was intended to be set off in Erebus and take out the backbone of both the Epsillon and Phaecian fleets, thus ending the Galactic War just as it started.

But she didn't detonate.

A twin ship, the Phaecian Empire's *Luxor*, destroyed Erebus mere seconds before the *Argus* arrived via Displacer.

Almost all the others who joined Cer in this mission gave in to the temptation of controlling the derelict and using it to return the Empires to their old ways. With the *Argus'* destruction and their deaths, all was as before and the Empires could continue their uneasy peace without the threat of galactic destruction.

Inquisitor Cer's eyes strayed from the window and to her sparse room. She, along with Overlord Octo and his two person security staff, were the only members of the Phaecian Empire aboard this battleship. Her companions had separate rooms and it wouldn't take long before they left the *Dakota* and returned to the Phaecian Empire, never to return to Epsillon again.

Inquisitor Cer's thoughts drifted.

Given all she experienced, she found it difficult to get her mind back to where –and who– she was before this adventure. In the Phaecian Empire Inquisitors were representatives of the Church and maintained law and order. Joining the Inquisitor ranks was a brutal task. Extensive DNA tests weeded out newborn candidates. The infants that scored highest were removed from their families shortly after their tenth year. They spent what remained of their childhood and early adulthood training for their eventual position. Of the ones deemed good candidates, fully eighty five percent of each generation proved inadequate. Of the fifteen percent left, most settled into local peace work. A fraction of those left joined the ranks of those who worked alongside the twelve Overlords that ran the Phaecian Empire.

In her year, Inquisitor Cer was the only one offered this privilege.

Once she completed her training, Cer was given her first assignments and forced to work alongside cruel taskmasters. It wasn't until ten years later, when she reached full adulthood, that she was bestowed the title of Inquisitor.

Since then she proved those who allowed her to join these ranks made a wise decision. Her loyalty and skills were beyond question. Like the very best Inquisitors of old, she shut out pain as easily as pleasure, for the members of her Holy Sect were meant to neither enjoy or suffer through life.

Inquisitor Cer ascribed to this along with deep suspicions of all things related to the heathen Epsillon Empire.

That changed.

Her gaze returned to the asteroids.

Following meeting and working alongside the Epsillon Independent named B'taav, Inquisitor Cer experienced new, strange emotions. Emotions she knew were forbidden. At first she feared all those years of training were insufficient and that she had failed her masters.

Over a very short period of time the feelings evolved. She realized they were natural and, incredibly, did not detract from completing her mission.

How could that be?

Inquisitor Cer sighed.

Now, alone in her room and the *Argus* mission a success, she felt a connection to B'taav.

He was at her side for most of this time and proved he shared as strong a sense of duty and justice as any Phaecian Inquisitor.

Cer brushed back her yellow hair and abruptly rose from her cot.

Inquisitors were celibate and forbidden from forming intimacies. They were always on duty. Such feelings shouldn't, couldn't...

Inquisitor Cer shook her head.

It was impossible to keep the visions of the Independent, of his stony face, his pale white hair, and his deep black eyes from coming back to her. In a harsh light, his looks were imposing and, in others, might cause fear.

But when he smiled...

...that smile...

The speakers within the room came alive. A message was relayed through the ship:

"Arriving at *Titus* in three hours. I repeat, three hours."

Inquisitor Cer walked to the door leading out of her room.

Once the *Dakota* reached the *Titus* Space Station she, along with Overlord Octo and his staff, would depart Epsillon via the *Erebus* Displacer. It would take only a matter of minutes to fly from the *Dakota* and through the Displacer's energy field and then, near instantly, be sent hundreds of light years away and arrive at *Vera Epsillon*, Phaecia's Outer Fringe Displacer. From there, Cer and her companions would commence the circuitous route to Helios, the Phaecian Empire's intelligence center. Inquisitor Cer would be called to report the details of her mission.

Again the image of B'taav entered her mind.

By that point, he will be on the other side of the universe.

The door to her quarters slid open and she stepped into the *Dakota's* corridor.

She needed to clear her mind.

Outside her quarters and spread throughout the corridor were a half-dozen Epsillon Military Guards. They were there to make sure that while aboard the *Dakota* Inquisitor Cer didn't get into any mischief. Obviously, state of the art high tech Battleships possessed a wealth of closely guarded secrets. These secrets were greedily   kept   from   rival   corporations   and,   especially, representatives of rival Empires.

Can't blame them for checking up on me, Inquisitor Cer thought. *I'd be doing the same in their place.*

Cer walked past the Epsillon guards and down the corridors she was permitted access to. The guards didn't follow her. They didn't have to. Enough of them were stationed in strategic locations and could watch her movements without crowding her in. The higher ups within the *Dakota* gave Inquisitor Cer a long leash, but a leash nonetheless.

Inquisitor Cer spent the next hour walking the decks of the *Dakota* she was allowed to. The military officers around her, unlike her Phaecian military crews, displayed greater ease among themselves. At first she thought it was a sign of weakness. In time, she admired their ability to behave with such... humanity. With the mission successfully over, perhaps it was understandable the crew needed time to exhale.

Inquisitor Cer made her way to the central elevators. She no longer kidded herself. She wasn't walking the deck to clear her head.

She was searching for *him.*

The central elevators were on the bow of the *Dakota.* Inquisitor Cer stepped into the first one available and found a single woman in it. The woman wore a tan leather bodysuit. She had brown hair and pale green eyes. Those eyes were on Inquisitor Cer, her look probing. She was sizing her up.

For a moment, Inquisitor Cer thought she was about to fight.

"Location?" the computer voice inquired.

"Observation Deck," Inquisitor Cer said.

For several long seconds the two rode in silence. Inquisitor Cer's back was to the woman yet she felt her presence and was ready for an attack she was more and more certain would come.

And then the elevator doors opened. Inquisitor Cer hesitated for a second before stepping out.

"He's in the forward deck," the woman said.

Inquisitor Cer spun around. The woman's expression was a blank, though her eyes suggested more than a little mirth.

"Who?" Inquisitor Cer asked.

"The one you're looking for," the woman said.

"Who are you?"

"Latitia," she said. "Remember the name."

Before Inquisitor Cer could again speak, the elevator doors closed and the woman was gone.

Inquisitor Cer moved on, toward the forward deck.

B'taav was there just as the woman –*Latitia*– said.

He towered over the few people around him, his body athletic and muscular and his face an emotionless enigma. Inquisitor Cer noted his jet black eyes, the most alien feature on him. His eyes contained neither iris, pupil, cornea, nor sclera, the white of the eye. Instead, they were an inky black. In her brief stay aboard the *Dakota*, Inquisitor Cer overheard officers speculate on why his eyes were like that. Some thought it was a genetic mutation while others believed they were the result of surgery. They speculated he had enhancements which allowed him to see more than anyone else could.

Still others were certain his eyes were evidence of alien blood circulating inside him.

Inquisitor Cer also wondered, yet never asked him about it.

Those black eyes stared past the tinsel glass separating the observation deck from outer space. The *Titus* station was already visible in the far distance, the largest of the stars beyond the last of the asteroids.

Inquisitor Cer approached the Independent's side. She felt the strange emotions bubble up inside her and was frustrated by them. Inquisitors could not afford to lose their edge. And yet, these emotions were so...

You are happy.

The Independent hadn't noticed her.

Perhaps.

Inquisitor Cer silently stared at B'taav for a few more seconds before saying:

"I'll be leaving as soon as the *Dakota* docks."

B'taav faced Inquisitor Cer. If her presence surprised him, his face didn't reflect this. His eyes, at first so devoid of emotion, were like pools of warm water. His normally stern expression, to her, revealed a kindness beneath.

"They've finished with your ship?" B'taav asked.

Just as the Epsillon military would not allow a Phaecian officer free access to all areas of their battleship, neither would they allow a Phaecian ship on board the *Dakota* without giving it a thorough search.

"Days ago," Cer said. "But they had to re-check the *Xendos* a few more times. Just in case."

At that, the Independent smiled and melted yet another sliver of ice within the Inquisitor. She soaked up his smile, knowing it might well be the last one she saw from him.

"You'll have to pardon our suspicious nature," B'taav said. The smile faded. "It's been a pleasure working with you."

For a few moments the two watched the approaching space station. *Titus* was very old and battered. Until recently, she was the only known survivor of the mighty Erebus explosion. With the *Argus* gone, that title was hers once more.

"I hope we see each other in the future," Inquisitor Cer said. "I hope that the... the circumstances for such a meeting don't prove quite *this* interesting."

"Agreed," B'taav said. "Have a good flight back."

Inquisitor Cer could no longer hold back. She reached up and gently laid her hand on B'taav's cheek. Despite his granite exterior, his skin was surprisingly warm. Surprisingly human.

Inquisitor Cer's stony brown eyes lost their harshness in the *Dakota's* artificial lights. She held her hand in place and B'taav didn't move. His eyes stared into hers and she realized he shared her feelings. After a while, she reluctantly retracted her hand.

"You too," she said.

She walked away, leaving B'taav alone on the forward deck.

By the time Inquisitor Cer reached the elevator, her mind was drowning in thoughts.

You love him? she wondered.

I can't, she countered. *I shouldn't.*

Perhaps you feel lust.

Vile, whispered rumors proclaimed that even the Overlords were not immune to the temptations of flesh.

Inquisitor Cer steadied herself.

No. It isn't lust.

Before taking on this mission, she read through the Independent's files, meager though they were. She had to know everything she could about him. He had a reputation for cold efficiency and was one of the most effective Independents out there. But the files said little else about the man himself.

Now she knew. She had a deep gap in her soul, a yearning she feared would never be filled. She dared not look back, instead wiping the single tear from her eye while stepping into the elevator.

The doors closed behind her.

She sensed the elevator's other passenger before seeing him. He was a giant of a man, easily six feet five inches tall and covered in muscle. He stood at the elevator's rear corner. He was young, no older than thirty, yet his eyes hinted at ages-old wisdom. He was dressed in the dark, formfitting jump suit of the Epsillon Military Guard and had a large, multi-pouch belt around his waist. One of the many pouches on this belt had the shape of a fusion handgun.

The man offered Cer a nod. He reached down, to the pouches, and for a moment Inquisitor Cer feared he was going for his weapon. Instead, he opened one of the smaller pouches and produced a black remote unit. The man pressed a button on it and the elevator slowed and stopped. The electricity within was completely shut off, leaving the dull red glow of emergency lights.

"We don't have much time to talk, Inquisitor Cer. I'll have to restart the cameras and recorders in exactly twenty seconds."

"Who are you?"

The man ignored her question and said:

"I have something for you."

He reached into another of his belt pouches and produced a microchip.

"You'll want to see the information on this," he said. "In private."

Inquisitor Cer took the chip.

"Whatever I see is also seen by my Overlord."

"Share it with whoever you want, but I strongly recommend you see it on your own first."

"What am I to do with this information?"

"You'll know," the man said.

He stepped back, returning to the exact position he had at the corner of the elevator. He again pressed the button on his remote device and the elevator returned to life. The man quickly pocketed his device. When the elevator reached its first destination, the door opened. The man stepped past Inquisitor Cer and out.

"Who are you?" Inquisitor Cer said.

"If you must know, my name is Delmont. Lionel."

"Are you military?"

"I was, once."

"Lieutenant?"

"No. Sergeant," Delmont said. "That was a very long time ago."

15

Inquisitor Cer returned to her room.

Outside her door, she keyed in her lock code.

There was still time left before the *Dakota* docked at *Titus* and Inquisitor Cer expected a few minutes of silent meditation. She looked down. The microchip was still in her hand.

Maybe I can spend a few minutes looking at that, too.

To her surprise, Overlord Octo and his personal security staff of Inquisitors Deveri and Loalla were inside her room. Overlord Octo was an elderly, thin man. He sat in the chair opposite her bed and watched the rapidly approaching *Titus* space station through her window. His Inquisitors stood beside him. They were younger than Cer and familiar to her. She had a hand in their training.

"Ah, you're back," Overlord Octo said. He rose, allowing his robe to flutter out.

"Your eminence," Inquisitor Cer said and bowed. "Was there something...?"

"I've come to pick you up," Overlord Octo said. "It is time to board the *Xendos* and prepare for our return home. I see no need to linger in this Empire a second more than is necessary."

Inquisitor Deveri picked up Inquisitor Cer's backpack.

"Do you have any other possessions?" Overlord Octo asked.

Inquisitor Cer looked the room over.

"No sir," Inquisitor Cer said.

She grabbed her backpack from Inquisitor Deveri and, while they weren't looking, slid the microchip Sergeant Delmot gave her into one of its outer pockets.

"Then let's be off."

They walked through the corridors of the *Dakota* and used the elevators to reach the flight deck.

There, parked in her berth, the members of the Phaecian delegation found the two hundred year old transport craft *Xendos*. During the very brief Galactic War, it was used as a spy craft by the Phaecian Empire and lay abandoned all the years since in a hidden asteroid base.

Standing before the *Xendos* was a small contingent of Epsillon military men. At the front of the group were General Jurgens and Lieutenant Daniels, the senior most officials within the *Dakota*.

"Here to see us off?" Overlord Octo said even as he extended his hand.

General Jurgens bowed before the Overlord. He then grasped the Overlord's hand and shook it.

"It's the least we could do," Jurgens said. "Speaking for myself and the crew of the *Dakota* and the Epsillon Empire, we wish you and your group a pleasant flight back home. Perhaps this one, small partnership might lead to better, more fulfilling partnerships in the future."

"One can only hope, General," Overlord Octo said.

Overlord Octo released General Jurgens' hand. Without saying another word he walked up the small ramp and into the *Xendos*, followed closely by Inquisitor Cer and the two person Inquisitor security staff.

Standing at the far end of the *Dakota* landing pad and on an upper level balcony watching the proceedings was a brown haired woman with pale green eyes. A large man, Sergeant Delmont, entered the balcony area from a door near her and walked to her side.

"Did you give her the chip?" the woman, Latitia, asked.

"Yes."

"Good."

The two watched as General Jurgens and Lieutenant Daniels walked away from the *Xendos* and disappeared into an elevator. The Epsillon Security staff around the ship also dispersed as the ship's engines came to life. From Latitia's vantage, she spotted the small metallic box that blended seamlessly in with all the other indentations and equipment on the roof of the *Xendos*.

It wasn't easy attaching that piece of equipment on the Phaecian ship.

The two watched as the *Xendos* prepared to lift off.

After putting away their luggage, Inquisitor Cer sat in her chair before the *Xendos'* controls. She was as familiar with these ancient controls and the ship itself, but found a new piece of tech lying on the control panel. It was a gift from the Epsillon Empire, a remote control pad interface linked to the *Xendos'* computers. Inquisitor Cer tested the equipment a couple of times while the *Dakota* was on its way to *Titus*. She snapped the device over her left forearm and pressed a button. A small holographic display appeared just over the remote panel. It immediately linked up to the *Xendos* and was ready for use.

Overlord Octo appeared on the bridge. Next to him were Inquisitors Deveri and Loalla. They remained by the door while Overlord Octo approached the cockpit controls. Inquisitor Cer stood up and bowed.

"Please, continue with what you're doing," he said.

Inquisitor Cer motioned for the Overlord to sit in the chair beside hers. As he did, Inquisitor Cer couldn't help but think of the man who sat in that same chair for the past few weeks.

"What are you doing?" Overlord Octo asked when he noticed the remote unit on her arm.

"Linking this remote CPU to the *Xendos'* computer banks," Inquisitor Cer said.

"Oh? I wasn't aware these ancient ships carried such units."

"They didn't," Inquisitor Cer said. "The *Dakota* offered her to us as a gift."

Overlord Octo eyed the device.

"Is it clean?"

"Yes sir," Cer said. "I checked it myself."

"Is it a standard remote unit?"

"It's a little more state of the art than what we're used to. This device allows me to control the ship from as far as five hundred miles away. Too bad we didn't have it when we were inside the *Argus*. It would have helped considerably."

She looked over the data displayed on her remote unit and read the monitor displays. She found Overlord Octo staring at her.

"Sir?" she asked.

"I'm impatient, Inquisitor. Let's go."

There was an edge in the Overlord's voice. Despite what he said, his voice betrayed something beyond simple impatience.

"My apologies," Inquisitor Cer said. She reached for the radio. "*Dakota*, this is the *Xendos*. Request permission to depart."

There was a burst of static followed by:

"We read you *Xendos*. Systems check?"

"All systems optimal."

"Understood," the control tower said. "We're pressurizing your section now."

A bright blue light, a compression energy field, surrounded the ship. The energy field shut the *Xendos* from the rest of the landing deck while air was sucked from her birth. A row of lights extended behind the *Xendos* and to a bay door.

"All depressurization is complete," the control tower said. "Opening the bay doors now."

On the right side cockpit monitor was a display of the *Xendos'* rear camera. The bay door slid open, revealing the darkness of outer space.

"Bay doors are open," the control tower said. "You are free to depart."

"Thank you, *Dakota*."

"Gods' speed, *Xendos*."

Inquisitor Cer shut the radio off. She added thrust to the directional rockets and the *Xendos* gently lifted off the *Dakota's* flight deck before initiating a turn. Once the ship was properly aligned, Cer gave her forward thrust. A string of red lights pointed the way out of the bay.

Inquisitor Cer followed them while hovering a few feet above the *Dakota's* flight deck. It took only moments for the ship to leave the *Dakota* and enter outer space. Once out, Inquisitor Cer made another turn and the *Xendos* was lined up with the center of the Erebus Displacer. She began her approach.

As the ship moved, she stared out the window and to her left, at the *Dakota*. She spotted the silhouette of a single person on its forward deck. Even from this distance she recognized B'taav.

"Let's not linger, Inquisitor," Overlord Octo said.

There remained a strange edge in Overlord Octo's voice. To Cer, it bordered on dangerous.

Tread carefully.

"Yes sir," Inquisitor Cer said.

She applied thrust and in minutes the *Xendos* was parked outside the Erebus Displacer's hollow core. Inquisitor Cer requested clearance for departure and offered her destination code. The monitors before her displayed a full view of all angles of the ship. One of them displayed the front of the *Dakota*. The silhouette of B'taav remained in place. He still watched as the *Xendos'* departed.

For a moment, Inquisitor Cer thought of turning the ship around.

And then the Displacer gate came alive with energy. The *Xendos'* thrusters ignited and the ancient ship moved forward and entered the Displacer's energy core.

There was a burst of light and the *Dakota*, Erebus, and B'taav were gone.

The bright energy field surrounding the *Xendos* faded.

After almost a minute of inter-dimensional travel, the ship

was back in regular space. The star field surrounding her, however, changed dramatically. In that short amount of time, the *Xendos* traversed hundreds of light years. Behind them was the familiar *Vera Epsillon* Displacer, the Phaecian Displacer closest to Epsillon Empire space.

"Set course for the Remolla System," Overlord Octo ordered. He rose from his chair and exited the cockpit.

"Yes, your eminence," Inquisitor Cer said.

The *Xendos* moved through the rarely used Gobi sector.

They were the only ship within this section but that would soon change when they merged with the Longshore Space Lanes.

As with all flights involving Overlords, their exact route was a secret known only to other Overlords. Their destination following arrival at the Longshore Space Lanes was a small, unnamed solar system. Within that system was one of the Overlords' best kept secrets: a Displacer used only by them which provided a link to Helios, the forbidden fortress world of the Overlords and the center of the Phaecian Empire. Few were privileged to know the location, much less the existence, of this well-defended planet.

Inquisitor Cer remained at the controls of the ship, checking her sensors and equipment to make sure all functioned properly. Though Overlord Octo retired from the bridge, Inquisitors Deveri and Loalla remained at their post by the cockpit door.

Inquisitor Cer couldn't help but wonder why. An odd feeling enveloped her, a premonition of something bad about to occur.

You served Overlord Octo faithfully your entire adult life. You would gladly die for him and he knows this. Why do you feel so uncomfortable now?

She double checked the instrument panel and found no problems with the ship. She stole a glance at the door leading out of the cockpit and the Overlord's Inquisitors. Were they ensuring her safety or were they keeping her here?

Am I their prisoner?

At the fifth hour of flight Inquisitor Deveri, the younger of the two Overlord security staff members, left his post and returned a few minutes later carrying a tray of food. He offered it to Inquisitor Cer.

"Thank you," she said.

"How's it going?" Deveri asked.

"We'll reach Longshore in three hours," Inquisitor Cer said.

She grabbed the food stuff, nothing more than nutrition cubes, and popped them into her mouth.

"I'll inform Overlord Octo," Deveri said.

After Inquisitor Cer finished her meal, he took the empty tray and departed.

Forty minutes later Overlord Octo returned to the cockpit. Inquisitor Cer rose but he motioned her to remain seated.

"Inquisitor Deveri told me we are nearing the Space Lanes," he said.

"We are, your eminence," Inquisitor Cer replied.

"Is our route clear?"

Inquisitor Cer re-checked her sensors. There were no ships within range. At least none visible.

"It is."

Overlord Octo folded his arms over his chest.

"It will be nice to return home," Overlord Octo said. "Are you looking forward to resuming your duties?"

"I am," Inquisitor Cer admitted.

"Are you ready for the debriefings? They will be intense."

"It is to be expected."

"They may take days, perhaps months."

"I know, Over... Overlord," Inquisitor Cer said.

She shook her head. Her last words came out slurred.

"Wh... what...?"

The stars beyond the front view screen blazed white hot. They blurred. Inquisitor Cer rubbed her eyes.

"I'm sorry, sir," Inquisitor Cer said. "I must... must be more tired than I thought. Is there something else—?"

Inquisitor Cer could not finish her thought. She tried to move. She couldn't. Her body felt as if it were asleep. The stars blurred even more. Her vision dimmed.

"What...?" she muttered.

"Heridian," Overlord Octo said. "It was in your food."

"...Heridian...?" she repeated.

"This particular batch was cultivated in the Damanos system," Overlord Octo said. "If taken in even small doses, it is quite lethal."

Abruptly, Inquisitor Cer's seat moved. Overlord Octo spun her around until she faced him.

"Don't worry my child," Overlord Octo said. "You have only a few moments of suffering before it will all be over."

16

Inquisitors Deveri and Loalla remained at their post beside the cockpit door. Neither showed concern for the fate of Inquisitor Cer.

"It pains me to do this," Overlord Octo said. "There are so many good things we've done these past years."

Inquisitor Cer tried to fight the poison's effects. She knew there was still a chance to flush the venom out. Overlord Octo removed the remote control from Inquisitor Cer's arm and set it aside. He then reached into his pocket. When his hand emerged, it held the microchip Sergeant Delmont gave her back in the *Dakota*.

"I found this in your backpack," he said.

"What... what..."

"Shh," Overlord Octo said. "You didn't have time to look the information on this chip over, did you?"

"Pl...please," Inquisitor Cer managed.

Overlord Octo motioned to Inquisitors Deveri and Loalla.

"Leave us," he said.

The Inquisitors bowed and did as told. The cockpit door slid shut.

Overlord Octo inserted the chip into a slot on the control panel. A monitor above the slot lit up, revealing hundreds of lines of information.

"This chip is quite full," he said. "It would take weeks to process the information on it and, well, you don't have the time."

Overlord Octo scrolled down the list of files. One of them was highlighted.

"The person who gave this to you wanted you to see this file first," Overlord Octo said.

He accessed the file and video footage appeared on the monitor. It featured a split screen video communique between two parties. On the left side of the screen was a grizzled, elderly man. He spoke in a Far Western Epsillon dialect. On the right of the screen was the man he was in communication with. Inquisitor Cer recognized him. It was Cardinal Duval, second in line to Overlord Sept's position. He was considered one of the Holiest of the Secondary File.

"I must inspect the cargo, Captain," Cardinal Duval told the elderly man.

"Of course," he replied.

The elderly man pressed a button and his image was replaced with what looked like security footage of a freighter's cargo hold. The camera panned around, revealing small, filthy cages that housed over seventy people. They ranged in age from very young to roughly in their mid-thirties. They were male and female and barely clothed. The youngest ones cried while the adults looked drugged or in shock. Guards stood at the far end of the cages, the expression on their faces one of routine boredom.

"By the Gods…" Inquisitor Cer said.

The Captain of this cargo ship, the man Cardinal Duval was speaking to, was a sex-slaver. Not just any slaver, but the very worst kind: The type that trafficked in children as well as adults. The camera lingered on each of his captives while descriptive lines of information appeared at their sides. Most of the children were orphans. Several others were listed as runaways. Other than their overall health, far less information was offered regarding the adults.

"The cargo is acceptable," Cardinal Duval said after completing his examination.

"The best for the best," the Captain said. He flashed the Cardinal a frosty grin.

"The Golden Jubilee is in three weeks' time," Cardinal Duval said. "We will not pay if this cargo is not delivered on time."

"Your schedule is tight. Skirting borders and avoiding checkpoints can be dangerous."

"Your only worry is getting past Epsillon security," Cardinal Duval said. "Once you reach Phaecian territory, you'll have a clear path to Cumea. I trust you can handle your own people?"

Cumea was a small planet in the Alaneto System. It was home to Cardinal Duval and housed his private villas. The Golden Jubilee and the meditations had taken place six months ago.

Meditations, Inquisitor Cer thought, the horror of realization dawning on her.

"I'll have them in time," the Captain said.

The rest of their conversation was focused on payments. The two talked as if they were arranging the sale of used vehicles. Overlord Octo cut the video feed and removed the chip from the player. He sighed.

"So much trouble in such a small package."

He dropped the chip on the floor and, with the heel of his boot, crushed it. Left behind were tiny pieces.

"Vacuum floor," Overlord Octo said.

The *Xendos'* cleaning system came to life and the microchip pieces were whisked away.

"Purge cleaning system," Overlord Octo then said.

The distant sound of trash ejected from the *Xendos* was heard. Overlord Octo contemplated the darkness before them. He then looked at the clock on the cockpit dashboard.

"It's been fifty minutes since you ate," Overlord Octo said.

Sweat dripped down Inquisitor Cer's face.

"The time to flush the poison from your system is past. By now your organs are shutting down."

Overlord Octo rubbed his hands.

"You still have a few moments," he said. "Speak."

Inquisitor Cer coughed.

"What... what would you have me... say?"

"Who was the man that gave you this chip? Why did he do this?"

Despite it all, Inquisitor Cer could barely contain her surprise.

"You know... it was a... a man?"

Overlord Octo pressed a series of buttons and one of the monitors before them displayed security footage from the *Dakota's* elevators. The meeting between Inquisitor Cer and Sergeant Delmont, at least the parts he didn't black out, played before her.

"You have... contacts... aboard the *Dakota*?"

That knowledge frightened Inquisitor Cer. It meant the Overlords were far closer to the Epsillon Empire's heads of power than either party let on.

"Who was he?" Overlord Octo said.

"I... don't... don't..."

"You're lying," Overlord Octo said. "Even as you pass, you sin."

Overlord Octo pressed another button and the monitor once again displayed elevator footage. This time, Inquisitor Cer was on the elevator with the mysterious brown haired woman.

"Two rides in the elevator and two different companions," Overlord Octo said. He pressed the button again and the image changed, this time revealing security footage of a balcony within the *Dakota* overlooking the ship's docking bay. On a landing pad below the balcony was the *Xendos*. In the foreground were Sergeant Delmont and the mysterious woman. They were watching the ship depart.

"We can't identify the man but we know the woman. Her name is Latitia. She is an Independent most recently in the employ of Jonah Merrick, my partner in crime, as it were, in finding and destroying the *Argus*. She's on the *Dakota* in spite of the fact that she left Merrick's employ well before you were stationed on *Titus*. She, along with her partner, were not listed as passengers aboard that ship. Imagine, two stowaways in plain sight in one of the best guarded military vessels of the Epsillon Empire."

Inquisitor Cer gritted her teeth. A burning sensation rolled throughout her body. It was hard to keep from screaming.

"Since... since when do Overlords and C-Cardinals deal... deal with sex slaves?"

"Everyone has needs," Octo said. "It's a pity. In time, you would have become one of our top Inquisitors. You might even have risen to the rank of Inquisitor Prime. Instead, here you are, another member of the Blessed family tragically lost in the performance of her duty."

Inquisitor Cer tried to reply, but the Heridian's effects overwhelmed her. She closed her eyes tight and could no longer breathe.

"Goodbye, Inquisitor," she heard Overlord Octo say.

Her world went completely black.

17

Inquisitor Cer's eyes fluttered open.

For a moment, she was disoriented and more than a little confused. Flashes of recent memory filled her mind, images of Overlord Octo and microchips and poison...

Poison.

She heard a noise and quickly closed her eyes. She remained still.

Where am I?

The fingertips felt around.

You're lying on a metal floor. You're no longer in the cockpit. Where?

The noises continued. It was a conversation between Inquisitors Deveri and Loalla.

Inquisitor Cer carefully opened her eyes.

At first she saw vague, blurry shapes. Her vision cleared. She was lying on the floor just outside the *Xendos'* decompression chamber. Inquisitors Deveri and Loalla stood a short distance away, working the chamber's controls. A chill passed through her.

You're going to dump me.

Lights before the decompression chamber's computer panels lit up. The chamber was almost ready for its one way passenger.

The Inquisitors approached Inquisitor Cer. She remained perfectly still.

"What a shame," Inquisitor Deveri said. He grabbed Inquisitor Cer under her arms as Loalla grabbed her by the ankles. They lifted her up.

"What do you mean?" Loalla said.

"Haven't you looked at her? I mean, really looked at her?"

"She's beautiful," Loalla admitted. "But we have our vows."

"Give me a woman like Cer and I can..." Deveri began.

"What?"

"Never mind," Deveri said.

They moved to the chamber's entrance and stumbled walking in. Deveri almost lost his grip.

"Easy," Loalla said.

"What does it matter?"

"She is one of ours, even if Overlord Octo says she was corrupted."

"Is that why he had you poison her?"

"He regretted the need to do so."

"Not nearly enough."

"He said her mission in Epsillon forced her to renounce her vows. There can be no forgiveness for that."

"Are you suggesting poisoning was a kindness?"

"If she were brought before the courts, she would have faced the Machines."

Inquisitor Deveri involuntarily shook. Few citizens could withstand the pain inflicted by the Machines. Inquisitors were different, of course. They could take the pain for weeks before admitting any wrongdoing. Weeks of savage, cruel pain...

"This way she didn't suffer."

"Much."

The haziness within Inquisitor Cer's mind was almost gone. Incredibly, her strength was rapidly returning.

They think I'm dead. By all rights I should be. How am I still alive?

Had Overlord Octo mistakenly given her a different drug? That was unlikely. The Overlord was a careful man. For him to accidentally give Inquisitor Cer an incorrect drug was beyond incompetent, and the Overlord was anything but incompetent.

So why hasn't the Heridian killed me?

That mystery would have to wait. For now, Inquisitor Cer had to deal with Inquisitors Deveri and Loalla. There was no time to convince them of Overlord Octo's corruption.

Inquisitor Cer's mind was suddenly razor sharp.

Choose your next move wisely.

She waited for the Inquisitors to carry her to the back of the decompression chamber. When they bent down to lay her on the chamber's floor, she acted.

Her left leg kicked out, smashing Inquisitor Loalla in the jaw. The Inquisitor fell backwards, blood splashing from his cut lips while the back of his head slammed against the chamber's metal wall.

Inquisitor Deveri could barely react before Inquisitor Cer grabbed him by the neck. She flipped him over and slammed him on his back. The Inquisitor tried to fight but the force of the impact took both his strength and breath away. Inquisitor Cer was on him, her hands tight against his throat.

"Don't worry, Brother Inquisitor," Cer told him. "Like me, your days in this world are not yet over."

It was a promise she could not keep.

Moments later Inquisitor Cer had Overlord Octo's security staff tied and immobile. She took their weapons and locked all but one fusion handgun away. She left the Inquisitors just outside the entrance to the decompression chamber and began the search for Overlord Octo.

Inquisitor Cer moved carefully. Though Overlord Octo was an elderly man, he was obviously far from helpless.

He was crafty enough to have almost killed me, Inquisitor Cer thought.

She found him in the lower forward deck of the *Xendos*.

At one time the area served as a small lounge for the craft's personnel. A window within looked out at the universe while a secured table and set of chairs were there for star gazers. Overlord Octo sat in one of the chairs. Before him, the table housed three monitors. On one of them was a feed of the ship's internal security camera footage. It displayed Inquisitor Cer in the lounge's doorway.

"Hello, Inquisitor," Overlord Octo said. "I see you're back from the dead."

Inquisitor Cer gripped the handle of her fusion handgun tight. She aimed it at Overlord Octo.

"Please, join me," he said.

Inquisitor Cer approached the Overlord's side. His face was very pale and his breathing shallow. There was an empty glass before him. Grainy white particles littered its sides.

"How long?" Inquisitor Cer asked.

"If you're wondering whether there is time to save me, the answer is no," Overlord Octo said. His voice grew weaker. "I took considerably... considerably more Heridian than you. Which one of the Inquisitors betrayed me?"

"Betrayed?"

"Which one gave you the antidote?"

"Neither."

"Then how... how are you still alive?"

"I don't know."

Overlord Octo thought about that.

"Oh," he said, as if discovering the answer to his own question.

He coughed. A drop of blood rolled down the side of his mouth.

"Why poison me?" Inquisitor Cer said. "Why not expose this corruption and clean the Council ranks?"

"There are two sets of rules, Inquisitor Cer. Those that govern the masses and those that cover the Overlords."

"Corruption is corruption. With this information—"

"Don't be naïve, Inquisitor," Overlord Octo spat. "The Overlords are above rules. It has been that way ever since... since the time immediately after the Arks. They will... will continue to do... what they want until the Universe is cold and lifeless and..."

Again he coughed.

"Why bury the information?"

"My dear I should think... think it obvious. I'm saving the Empire."

"By hiding some council members' crimes?"

"Some?" Overlord Octo said and laughed.

Inquisitor Cer finally understood.

"They know," Cer said. "All of them."

"Everyone has urges. Chasity, purity... it doesn't exist. Never has."

The statement shocked Inquisitor Cer.

"I don't believe it," she said. "I'll get the information together again and I'll—"

"You've already done your worst," Overlord Octo said.

"What do you mean?"

"The automated transmissions," Overlord Octo said. "Very clever to have the ship broadcast the video feeds as I was showing them to you. Was that some kind of failsafe?"

"I didn't do that."

Though Overlord Octo's face was deathly pale, his eyes remained sharp. They scanned Inquisitor Cer, testing her truthfulness. Finally, he chuckled.

"I never thought... never thought I'd bear witness..." he said and stopped. "As soon as I realized the information was transmitted, I was forced to issue my own statement to the Overlord Council. I've taken full responsibility for the sex trade crimes. My office, my legacy... will be expunged from the official transcripts along with... with Cardinal Duval and at least twenty others. It will take a while to sort the mess but the Empire... the Empire still stands."

"The slave trade?"

"It'll stop... for now," Overlord Octo said.

"What about me? What about Inquisitors Deveri and Loalla?"

"What do you think, Inquisitor? As a senior member of my staff, how do you think the Council will feel about you three? You'll be found complicit in my crimes. If they were to get their hands on you, they'd give you a nice... nice show trial before handing out the maximum sentence. Death."

Inquisitor Cer lowered her weapon.

"You see what's coming, don't you?" Overlord Octo said. He was fading. Drool and blood dripped from the side of his mouth.

"If the Inquisitors didn't give me an antidote, who did?" Inquisitor Cer asked. "How am I still alive?"

"It... it doesn't matter."

"You know."

"What I know is that there are angels... angels and devils. They're real. They fight in the shadows of Empires, pushing Phaecia and Epsillon this way and that... playing their games. Someone... some*thing*... is out there..."

Overlord Octo paused and caught his breath. He wiped the blood from his lips.

"We're not as independent as we'd like... as we'd like to think. The shadow people move... subtly toward their goals..."

Overlord Octo let out a breath. His body relaxed.

"For us... the game is over," he said. He noted the cup still at his side. "A pity you couldn't join me. I hope you feel no pain..."

The Overlord took one last breath before closing his eyes. Inquisitor Cer heard a faint beep emanating from somewhere within his dark robes.

At the sound, Inquisitor Cer jumped to her feet. Without hesitation, she ran as quickly as she could toward the *Xendos'* decompression chamber. All the while, the beeps behind her grew louder and louder.

When she reached the decompression chamber's entrance, she grabbed three space suits from the Charging Rack and threw them inside.

She then grabbed Inquisitors Loalla and Deveri. The gagged Inquisitors looked at Inquisitor Cer with a mixture of anger and confusion. Inquisitor Cer pulled the two into the decompression chamber before facing the door's computer panel and initiated it.

The decompression chamber's door slowly -*too* slowly- closed.

Inquisitor Cer grabbed the door's handles and pulled with all her strength, trying to get it to shut and seal. The ancient machinery, however, took its time and would not be hurried.

The beeping stopped.

Inquisitor Cer felt a heavy rumble and was nearly knocked off her feet.

In his final act, Overlord Octo set off explosives in the ship!

Inquisitor Cer held on. When the initial shock was over, she continued to desperately pull at the door. Abruptly, the air around her was sucked away in a hurricane-like gale. The winds slammed Inquisitor Cer against the closing door.

She tried to lift herself up but couldn't.

Inquisitors Loalla and Deveri, their faces masks of terror, tried to wedge their feet and legs into the machinery around them. But their bodies along with the space suits were sucked to the closing door.

Inquisitor Cer reached out and grabbed them just before they rolled out of the chamber. For a second Cer had Deveri by the collar. The young Inquisitors' looked up at Cer and fought to keep from moving. One of the space suits was sucked from the chamber and disappeared down the corridor, leaving two behind. Still the air roared out, pulling the Inquisitors away. Inquisitor Cer's grip on Deveri's collar weakened. The duo was simply too heavy to—

The fabric on Inquisitor Deveri's shirt ripped and the Inquisitors were sucked out of the Decompression chamber along with the second spacesuit.

"*NO!*" Inquisitor Cer yelled.

Despite her horror, she grabbed the last space suit before it too was pulled out.

It was all she'd need now.

Inquisitor Cer remained in place, trying her best to remain inside the Decompression chamber. She felt the cold of space and the lack of atmosphere. The rushing air slowed, but only because it was almost all gone. Cer's grip on the Decompression door loosened. She could barely move her joints. The cold was overwhelming.

Finally, the Decompression door closed and sealed.

The violent suction was over and Inquisitor Cer fell to the icy floor. In mid fall, the *Xendos'* artificial gravity gave out along with the rest of the ship's primary systems. Inquisitor Cer hit the floor and bounced up. She hovered in mid-air while red emergency lights came on.

Inquisitor Cer shook her head and focused her thoughts. She reached for the space suit and struggled to put it on. She moved as fast as she could, yet far too slow for comfort.

Once dressed, she activated the suit's life support system.

Warm air flowed through her suit and Cer greedily took it in. Her strength slowly returned.

Inquisitor Cer activated her magnetic boots and set them on the metal floor. She walked to the decompression chamber's door and looked out the window and at the corridor beyond.

Floating outside the chamber were the bodies of Inquisitors Loalla and Deveri.

Overlord Octo didn't intend for anyone to survive the trip back home.

He almost succeeded.

18

PLANET ONIA, Border of the Epsillon Empire

The burial was a solemn affair.

There were only three witnesses and when it was done, they returned to their automated desert vehicle, loaded up, and departed.

The vehicle's thick tires skimmed the bright white sands of the Onian desert and left a cloud of dust in their wake. Night was falling fast, and the stars grew bright in the sky. Directly before them and another thirty miles away were the even brighter lights of the once mighty Onian Capital. At one time it was the largest and most modern of the Ports within the Epsillon Empire, a stepping stone for trade between the Epsillon and Phaecian Empires. But the buildup to and eventual Galactic War between the Empires and the cold peace that followed wrecked the planet's fortunes.

A souring economy and environmental disasters turned this once fertile, green planet into a harsh, superheated desert housing crumbling buildings, dead end tech, and scavengers. Few visited Onia and those who did kept their visits brief.

For the occupants of the desert vehicle, the Space Port at the center of the city was their destination, but to get to it they would have to first pass through the city's decaying outer edges. The bumpy sands receded, replaced by bumpy roads. This outer section of the city was filled with dark streets and boarded up buildings.

After a few minutes, they passed the decay and found lighted streets and sparsely inhabited buildings. They were fewer of either each year. They eventually reached the Star Port and the desert vehicle parked in its designated space. Her side door opened.

Closest to the door sat a young boy. His name was Nathaniel and by the bewildered look in his eyes, he was greatly confused by his surroundings. He had short black hair and a white medi-cast over his right arm. Though he recently lost a finger, he did not appear to be in any obvious pain. The memories implanted in his brain were those of Nathaniel Torin, Captain of the once long lost ERF Super Juggernaut *Argus*. Those memories were decaying and it wouldn't be too long before the boy carried no memories at all.

Dave Maddox sat beside the young man and held his left hand. Maddox was a short, slightly built man in his late thirties. He had slick, jet black hair and walked with the aid of crutches for he too suffered a recent injury. In his case, an errant fusion blast dissolved his lower left leg. Each move he made was followed by a wince or grunt. The pain from his lost limb and the treatment to regrow it caused considerable discomfort, all of which he bore with each facial tick.

The two exited the vehicle and were followed by the last of the trio, the Independent known as B'taav.

A sonic boom was heard and they looked up into the night sky. They spotted the lights from the shuttle craft *Solaris* high above. It was coming in for a landing.

"There's our ride," Maddox told the boy. "Right on time."

The boy did not react.

They made their way past empty counters and sparsely populated subsections within the Port and were soon in the *Solaris'* waiting area. They watched from behind thick tinsel glass windows as waves of sand whirled around, blasted by the shuttle's thrusters as she came in for a landing. Once on firm ground, the thrusters shut down and the sands settled. There were only a handful of passengers waiting to board the ship. They grabbed their luggage and made a line to the door leading out.

"I guess this is goodbye," Maddox told B'taav.

For most of their just completed mission, Maddox didn't trust the Independent and held him in great contempt. It wasn't until the mission neared its end that Maddox realized B'taav and he shared the same goal: the destruction of the *Argus*. With the super juggernaut gone, Maddox's life mission was realized. He chose to spend the rest of his time taking care of the boy with the decaying memories.

Young Nathaniel laughed. He watched in wonder as the last of the sands swirled on the landing pad. He pointed at the *Solaris* and tried to speak. Whatever thought he had proved too difficult to put into words.

"I... I will miss..." the boy managed. The smile on his face disappeared, replaced with a look of confusion and frustration.

"I'll miss you too," B'taav said. He laid his hand on the boy's shoulder and addressed Maddox. "You know where you're going?"

"I have some ideas," Maddox said.

"Good," B'taav said. "Keep them to yourself."

The *Solaris's* loading ramp slid into place on the landing deck. Over the departure gate, a green light came on.

"What about you?" Maddox asked.

"I'm not sure."

"C...Cer?" Nathaniel said. "You... you want to see her again."

"She's an Inquisitor, Nathaniel," Maddox said. "She's in Phaecia. She won't come back—"

"You go... go to her."

B'taav released the boy and nodded.

"I'll try," he said.

Maddox leaned in closer to the Independent.

"Is the boy right? Are you planning to...?"

He didn't finish his sentence. Instead, he slapped himself on his forehead.

"Of course you are," he said. "It takes a child to show me how blind I am."

B'taav said nothing.

"You'll have to smuggle yourself into the Phaecian Empire," Maddox said. "No way they'll let an Independent in legally. I know some trade vessels that skirt the borders. They have contacts within the Empire and may be able to help you find her. If you want I can give you a list."

"That won't be necessary."

"I don't have to tell you what you're planning is dangerous."

"I know."

"Then... take care of yourself, B'taav."

"I will."

Maddox offered B'taav his free hand and the two shook.

"I'll see you around," Maddox said. "Maybe."

There was no more fanfare. Maddox and Nathaniel walked to the departure door and joined the short line of passengers. The group made their way into the shuttle, with Maddox and Nathaniel the last to climb aboard. Shortly thereafter, the *Solaris's* outer door closed. Soon after, the ship's thrusters came to life and again sent desert sands swirling. The ship took flight and it wasn't long before the star port was well below her.

The shuttle craft shrunk until she was a tiny speck in the sky and then nothing at all.

Five full days passed since Inquisitor Cer left the *Dakota*.

During that time B'taav endured a series of grueling debriefings regarding the events leading to the destruction of the *Argus*. Epsillon Military Intelligence needed to satisfy themselves that the super juggernaut and all Intel within her were indeed gone. After the debriefings, Maddox, Nathaniel, and he were released. Along with Inquisitor Cer, they were the entire group that ensured the super-juggernaut's destruction.

Inquisitor Cer.

Images of her flooded the Independent's mind. Of his time with her. Of their last meeting. Of her gentle touch...

She laid her hand on his cheek. Her touch lasted only seconds yet the warmth remained. In Inquisitor Cer, B'taav found an unexpected kindred.

Young Nathaniel was right. He had to see her again. And to do so, he had to somehow get into the Phaecian Empire.

I will find a way.

B'taav walked from the star port's central building outside. He stood on the faded gray sidewalk. Around him were only a few transport vehicles and even fewer people. With the *Solaris* gone, there was no reason for anyone to be here as there were no other shuttles scheduled to come in until the following day.

B'taav had no specific plans as to where he would go from Onia. He had a room in a dreary hotel on the west side of the Capital and intended to stay another day or two. He would develop his plans during that time.

He motioned for a Hover Cab. It picked him up and he was off.

The cab driver was flesh and blood, a throwback to ancient times.

"You looking for tours?" the cabbie asked B'taav. "Girls? Boys?"

"Peace and quiet."

"Huh?"

"You heard me."

The cabbie shut his mouth and drove on.

B'taav's dark eyes were on his surroundings as the cab moved through the city. An Independent is always aware of what goes on around him. Just in case.

As it turned out, such attention often proved necessary.

The tail wasn't hard to notice as there were so few other vehicles on the street. There were two people in the cruiser following the cab. Both were male and both had intense looks on their faces.

B'taav wondered who would send someone after him and, in that same moment, whether they were babysitters or if he was in any kind of danger.

What of Maddox and Nathaniel?

It seemed unlikely anyone would follow them. B'taav and Maddox kept the Epsillon military staff in the dark about Nathaniel's memory implants. For all anyone knew, Maddox was an ornery bartender and the boy a damaged orphan, neither of which were worth bothering over.

They're after you.

B'taav's many years as an Independent made him a host of allies and enemies. Either could be following him.

"Take a left here," B'taav said.

"Didn't you want to go to—"

"Now."

The driver shrugged and made the left. The cruiser behind them did the same.

"Turn right," B'taav said.

"Sure," the driver replied.

The car turned into a dark alley and B'taav reached for the fusion gun within his jacket. He gripped the handle of the weapon and looked back.

The cruiser following them continued straight.

B'taav released the gun's handle and faced the driver.

"Thanks," he said. "It's been a few years since I was here. Just wanted to see the old neighborhood."

The driver looked around and frowned. Surrounding them were dreary, decaying buildings. It didn't look like anyone had lived here in many decades.

"It's your money. Anywhere else you want to go?"

"No," B'taav said. "Head to the Hotel."

The Cab arrived at the Berkeley Hotel a few minutes later.

B'taav paid the fare, exited the vehicle, and took a few moments to check if his tail was already there, waiting. He spotted neither the cruiser nor the individuals in it. B'taav walked into the Hotel's lobby. Video monitors along the lobby walls displayed newsfeeds from around the Empire. Though the Independent had no interest in catching up on the news, his attention was drawn to one of the six monitors on the lobby's east side. On it a reporter was talking and over his left shoulder was the image of Overlord Octo.

B'taav approached the monitor. Motion detectors sensed his presence and the monitor's volume automatically increased.

"...to locate any possible wreckage or survivors. We will bring you updates—"

"Replay story," B'taav said.

The screen image froze before repeating the news story from the beginning.

"Representatives of Phaecia are reporting the disappearance of Overlord Octo, one of the senior most members of the Council of Twelve," the reporter read. The image of Overlord Octo appeared once again over his left shoulder. "Though reports are incomplete as of this hour, Overlord Octo is reported to have been returning to the Council Homeworld when his transport craft disappeared from traffic sensors. Attempts to contact the ship, listed as the *Xendos*, have thus far yielded no results. Phaecian authorities are sending rescue vessels—"

"Stop."

B'taav's voice was a ghostly whisper.

Cer.

B'taav's recalled the first time he, Maddox, and Inquisitor Cer stood before the *Xendos*. The ship sat abandoned for over two hundred years in her landing pad on the lost Phaecian Asteroid base. They wondered if they could get her moving again...

"Our first step is to fix any leaks and replace batteries, liquids, and fuels."

"Let's hope none of that material has degraded, and there's enough to take us where we need to go."

As old as the *Xendos* was, she took them to the *Argus*. When their mission was done and the ship was safely parked on the flight deck of the *Dakota*, it was thoroughly checked by Epsilon military. Their job was to make sure no intelligence from the *Argus* remained aboard. Their secondary goal was to make sure the ship was ready for her trip back into Phaecia.

Had the *Dakota's* techs missed something?

That was unlikely. All defects were found and fixed. The last thing the Epsilon Empire needed was to be blamed for any harm to a Phaecian Overlord.

Unless...

Could someone on board the *Dakota* have deliberately sabotaged the *Xendos*?

It wouldn't be beneath some to take advantage of the situation...

The Newscorp screen darkened before returning to the initial news items.

B'taav didn't notice. He mind was back on Inquisitor Cer.

If the *Xendos* was lost, so too was she.

B'taav experienced much during his life. He saw many good – and bad– people die well before their time. He mourned for some and not at all for others. Death was an integral part of his profession.

Yet he found it hard to accept this.

How can you be gone?

B'taav struggled to focus.

It was difficult to put his sorrow into words. His stomach tightened. His eyes closed.

No.

He couldn't believe she was dead. The feelings within him were strong. Somehow, he *sensed* Inquisitor Cer was still alive.

Impossible.

And yet...

B'taav felt a growing anger.

You deal in facts, not feelings.

So many thoughts poured through the Independent all at once. Tentacles of conspiracy, worries about what would happen next. He thought about the people following him and wondered if the loss of the *Xendos* was the first step in the elimination of those associated with the *Argus* mission. If that was the case, Maddox and Nathaniel were also in danger. They were the only people to have actually been on the *Argus*...

If they were all being targeted, who would have the desire and, most importantly, the means to do so?

Merrick.

Jonah Merrick, B'taav's employer and the head of the powerful Merrick Enterprises, was the only person with the wealth, the connections, and the political muscle to pull something like that off. If he managed to destroy the *Xendos* in Phaecian space, then what could he do here, on his home turf?

B'taav's body tensed. He turned, suddenly aware there were eyes on him.

She sat in the table beside the entrance to the Berkeley Hotel's Café. Her outfit was black formfitting leather. Her pale green eyes were on him. He knew her, though not very well.

Latitia.

B'taav met her briefly on Merrick's personal shuttle craft shortly after completing his first mission for the Industrialist and just before being sent to find and destroy the *Argus*.

As during their first and only meeting, Latitia's eyes did not waver.

B'taav reached into his jacket and gripped the handle of his weapon. She did not react.

If she's here to kill you, why is she sitting there, fully exposed?

B'taav released the weapon. His hands returned to his side and he walked to her table.

"We need to talk," she said. Her voice was as cold as her stare. "We don't have much time."

19

B'taav and Latitia retreated to a table deep inside the empty Café.

B'taav placed an order on a touch screen monitor and entered payment information. Shortly afterwards, a waiter showed. She carried a small tray with a blue liquor. She offered B'taav and Latitia a well-rehearsed smile before placing the drink down.

"Onian Skyfall," she said. "Anything for you ma'am?"

"No thanks," Latitia said.

The waitress nodded.

"And what about you, sir?"

"Thank you, no," B'taav said.

The waitress lingered beside the table. After a few seconds Latitia reached into her pocket. Her action made B'taav stiffen. Latitia smiled and shook her head. Her hand came out of her pocket. She held a silver coin and gave it to the waitress.

"Thank you," the waitress said. She walked away.

"Don't you believe in tipping?" Latitia said.

B'taav took down his drink.

"You know, once upon a time... a hell of a long time ago, I worked at a dive not all that different from this one," Latitia said. "I had the pleasure of serving assholes like you on a daily basis."

"Did Merrick send you?" B'taav said. "Did he get to the *Xendos*?"

"No to your first question and I don't know the answer to your second, though I can understand your suspicion."

"The crew of the *Dakota* went over the *Xendos*. If the ship had any problems they would have found them. Unless they were more interested in planting them."

B'taav ordered another drink. Latitia pressed a button on the touch screen, cancelling the order.

"There isn't time for that."

"If you aren't here for Merrick, then why are you?"

"There are things we need to talk about."

"I don't have anything to talk to you about."

"If you're still bothered by what happened at Salvation—"

"There was no need for more deaths."

Latitia sat back.

"The man waiting for you at your apartment on Salvation was named Sullivan. He was wanted on multiple worlds for everything from pedophilia to smuggling to drug abuse. His last job before Salvation was to get rid of the head of the Worker's Union in Sentai. Sullivan found his target regularly dropped his daughter off at a primary school each morning. So he bought some explosives, set them up, and waited for his target to show. Sullivan got his man... along with twenty children. After that, even the few friends he had didn't want anything to do with him. Merrick was after Sullivan's employers. Even with Merrick cleaning house, you think he would let the papers know his employees and a piece of shit like Sullivan were in bed together? If I didn't kill them, someone else surely would have."

B'taav considered this.

"You used to work for Octi, didn't you?" Latitia asked.

"You know I did."

"You left them because they hired people like Sullivan," Latitia said. "Merrick is no better than any other industrialist."

Latitia smiled.

"So here you are, trapped and restless. You want to do what's right but the people hiring you always have other ideas."

"Why are you here?"

"You've been looking for a way out and I'm offering it. Only things won't be easy and you'll face danger. But you'll be under no obligation and you will do what's right. Best of all, you'll do this under your own free will."

"I must be really desperate," B'taav said. "Because I'm still listening to this fairy tale. What do you want me to do?"

"I thought you'd never ask."

They left the Café and walked into the Hotel's lobby. At the courtesy desk they requested a private desert transport.

"We're going to the desert?" B'taav asked.

"Yeah."

"What's there?"

"You'll see."

Moments later, the vehicle arrived at the Hotel's entrance. B'taav entered the transporter's passenger compartment while Latitia took the driver's seat. She disengaged the automatic driver.

They sat for a few seconds.

"What are you—?" B'taav began and stopped.

B'taav followed Latitia's gaze. She was looking at a familiar cruiser parked across the street.

"Who are they?" B'taav asked.

Latitia drew a slow, deep breath and said:

"After finishing the job for Merrick on Salvation, I realized I was being followed. I froze out a couple of fixers that tried to get too close to me while on my way to Onia. I thought I was free. Guess not."

"They're Merrick's?"

"I'm not sure, though it's certainly possible," Latitia said.

"They followed me from the Port here," B'taav said. "Looks like they're after both of us."

"You still want to come?"

"At this point, it doesn't look like I have much choice."

The men across the street turned their cruiser on. Headlights shined on the road. The cruiser's passenger then pulled a large fusion rifle from the back seat. He loaded it, not caring if Latitia and B'taav saw him do so.

"Then we better get moving."

20

Latitia drove out of the Hotel's parking lot and into the dimly lit streets. The cruiser behind them did the same. The two vehicles moved along slowly.

"They'll make their move as soon as we reach the decay," Latitia said.

To get to the desert, they would have to pass the decay. B'taav reached for his fusion gun.

"Whenever you're ready," he said.

The tires of the rented desert transport abruptly squealed while creating a cloud of smoke. Despite her bulk, she roared down the darkening street, gaining speed.

Their pursuers sped up as well. Their cruiser was made for city driving and would be difficult to lose.

"Two against two," B'taav said. "Even odds."

The lumbering transport was on a straightaway and building speed. The few other vehicles around them fell back until there were none. The streets grew very dark.

"We're in the decay," Latitia said.

The cruiser gained on them. The man in her passenger seat lifted his fusion rifle. He aimed.

Latitia spun the wheel violently to the left and the desert transport entered a narrow road. The oversized tires bounced as they passed a series of abandoned buildings. No lights came from any of them.

B'taav looked back at the cruiser. The rough road forced them to slow.

"We get to the desert and they can't follow us," B'taav said.

A fusion blast slammed into the rear of the Independents' transport, scorching the trunk and sending a shower of sparks. A chunk of metal ripped and clanged away while smoke filled her interior.

"We're too far away," Latitia said. "We have to take care of them now."

B'taav leaned out of the transport's side window and aimed his gun at the cruiser. His weapon roared and delivered a strong kick. Projectiles hit the cruiser's windshield and left large round cracks. The man in the passenger seat twitched wildly and fell back.

B'taav's aim was true. At least two of his shots hit the man.

"One down," B'taav said.

B'taav aimed at the driver. Before he could fire, the pursuing cruiser sped up and rammed them. The force sent B'taav back into his chair.

"They're getting desperate," B'taav said.

The Independent again leaned out the window and aimed. The pursing cruiser shifted to their left, making it hard for B'taav to see his target.

B'taav swore and slipped back into the desert transport. He moved to the back seat and had a clearer view of the driver. He aimed his weapon and was about to fire when he stopped.

"What in Hades?"

The man in the passenger seat, the man B'taav knew he hit twice, was up. He lifted his fusion rifle.

"Turn!" B'taav yelled.

Latitia did, sending B'taav flying against the side door. The fusion blast barely missed them, its heat scorching the side of the desert transport before incinerating a rusted light post.

"The shooter's back up!" B'taav said. He shook his head. "Even with a force shield, the impact and heat should have taken him out!"

Latitia swerved back and forth along the road but the Independents knew it was a matter of time before their luck ran out.

"What's happening?" Latitia yelled.

B'taav looked up and over the edge of the rear seat. The cruiser's passenger –the man that should have been dead– was taking his time aiming his rifle. His fingers tightened on the trigger.

"Hang on!"

Another blast slammed the desert transporter's rear, completely shattering the back window and ripping the tailgate. B'taav felt the intense heat and was bathed in glass and sparks.

"Shit!" Latitia yelled.

She slammed down hard on the brakes, surprising her pursuers. Their cruiser smashed into what was left of the rear of the desert transport.

Latitia pressed hard on the accelerator and pulled ahead. The cruiser's engine belched white smoke but remained mobile. It gained speed.

"They're still with us," B'taav said. The interior of the desert transport was exposed. "Another fusion blast and we're done."

"Hang on," Latitia said.

Latitia took another turn. She spotted an old building and took another, even sharper turn. The desert transport jumped onto a cracked sidewalk and bounced against brick stairs. It was momentarily in the air before her wheels dug in and she climbed up and up. The desert transport crashed through a wooden double door, sending splinters in all directions as it burst into an abandoned building. The brakes locked and the transport made a half turn before skidding to a stop. The driver's side door faced the building's destroyed entrance.

"You ok?" Latitia asked.

"Yes."

"Get out."

B'taav pushed his door open and Latitia followed him out.

The interior of the building was bathed in darkness. B'taav heard the flutter of bird's wings somewhere high above and looked up. Despite the heavy shadows, he noticed the building's high arched ceiling. To his side and around him were rows of wooden benches. They faced the building's rear. That area was made up of an elevated platform and a dusty dais.

"We're in a church," B'taav said.

"Beggars can't be choosers," Latitia said.

The sound of tires squealing was heard coming from outside. The pursuing cruiser came to a stop at the foot of the stairs and her passengers emerged. Each carried a fusion handgun and hurried to the church's entrance. Their movements were very, *very* fast and eerily quiet.

"Either they have augmented limbs or are using some kind of adrenal enhancer," B'taav said.

"Get to the other end of the dais," Latitia said.

She bent down behind one of the wooden benches and waited.

B'taav made it to the dais and hid behind a large wooden chair. At one time, the church's High Priest offered sermons from this lofty perch. Sturdy though it was, it could withstand at best a couple of fusion blasts before being vaporized.

The interior of the church grew very quiet. The destroyed front door looked out at the dark street and the emptiness beyond. There were no people around and no help to come.

B'taav's attention turned to Latitia. He looked through the benches and pews and tried to find her. She was nowhere to be seen.

B'taav frowned.

The silence was thick and hinted at the violence to come.

B'taav checked his fusion handgun. He thought of the cruiser's passenger and wondered if his weapon would be effective against them.

How the hell are you still alive?

There was a commotion on the far end of the church. Besides its shattered entrance, B'taav saw someone move from one shadow to the next. It was Latitia. She moved quickly, but not quickly enough. A fusion blast roared from the darkness and clipped her left leg.

"Latitia!" B'taav yelled.

He raised his weapon to fire but a powerful hand clamped down on it. B'taav tried to fight the grip yet, incredibly, was unable to move. Whoever held him spun B'taav's body around like a marionette before slamming his chest. The blow knocked B'taav off the dais and sent him sliding between the pews.

For a moment, B'taav blacked out. The padding in his clothing took much of the force of the blow yet the wind was knocked from him. Had he not worn protective gear, his insides would be liquid.

B'taav shook his head and looked back at his attacker. He gasped.

The man had two large fusion blast wounds in his head. One ripped apart his right cheek and revealed broken and charred teeth. The other blast hit him above his left eye and exposed dark matter. Blood and ooze filled the gory wounds, yet the wounds... moved.

It was as if they were slowly closing.

"What the hell are you?" B'taav said.

The being was instantly at his side, its speed beyond astonishing. B'taav tried to pull back but could not. The man grabbed B'taav by his neck and for a second the Independent felt a flash of heat –an electric shock– in his attacker's touch. That heat spread through his body.

"What...?" he managed.

The being stared at him through a single dead eye. His grip on B'taav's throat tightened until the Independent could no longer breathe. The man's terrific wounds continued moving, closing.

With what was left of his strength B'taav raised his gun and jammed it against his attacker's jaw. He fired once. Twice. Three times. Blood splatted from the man's face and flesh was torn away but the man remained still. The heat B'taav felt turned into a dark, bitter cold and he was no longer in control if his body. His hand dropped to his side. His gun fell to the floor.

B'taav could barely keep his eyes open. He knew this was the end...

A blinding burst of light flashed from somewhere behind them.

The thing holding B'taav turned its head ever so slightly. Its grip relaxed and B'taav dropped to the floor.

The man stood still, his remaining eye alive now, taking in the darkness and searching for the source of that light.

B'taav coughed and gasped for air. He regained control of his body and reached for his gun. He again fired at his attacker, this time aiming for his heart. The fusion blasts sent the man stumbling backwards.

For the first time the shots appeared to have an effect on him.

It, not him.

The creature fought to regain its balance. Its movements were jerky. Mechanical.

You're a machine.

The creature's eye was on B'taav.

The flesh that made up its face was almost entirely ripped away, revealing a dark underside. That matter was like heavy, gelatinous water. The creature reached out, intent on grabbing B'taav.

The Independent rolled away. As he did, he felt more chills. The creature's touch had done something to him. Strangely, B'taav knew *he* had done something to the creature.

B'taav was back on his feet. He ran to the desert transport and crouched behind it before moved around. His gun drawn, he searched for Latitia. She was at the front of the transport, sitting on the floor.

In her hand was a strange weapon, a handgun the likes of which B'taav had never seen before.

A few feet away from her was a dark form. At first B'taav thought it was a pile of refuse left behind years before. He then realized it had the shape of a human body. It was the other person from the cruiser. His body was completely incinerated.

"Are you OK?" B'taav asked. His voice was hoarse.

Latitia looked the Independent over. She noted the bruising and cuts on his neck.

"The other one grabbed you?" she asked.

B'taav felt his neck. The tips of his fingers were wet with blood.

"Yeah," he said. "Hurts like hell. It's not bleeding all that much."

B'taav examined Latitia's left leg. The fabric of her jumpsuit was charred from the fusion blast.

"You're injured," he said.

B'taav removed the fabric to get a better look at the wound. Instead of flesh, he found metal.

"What...?" he managed before Latitia violently pulled him to the ground.

As he fell, B'taav spotted their second pursuer. The creature was only feet away. The skin on its face was falling away in strips, bloody yet strangely bloodless. It roared as Latitia's gun came up.

She fired her weapon only once, sending a cascade of light and electrified heat. It enveloped the creature and stopped it in its tracks. What was left of its flesh caught fire. The dark matter below it released clouds of steam and energy spikes.

In a second it was over.

The creature remained upright yet its body was completely charred. It looked like a strange, black statue, its composition identical to the charred remains of its partner.

Latitia calmly put her gun away. She got to her feet and offered B'taav her hand. As she helped B'taav up, she noticed he was shaking.

"What's wrong?"

"I don't know," B'taav said. "I feel cold."

Latitia looked him over. She checked the cut that caused the bleeding on his neck.

"That thing cut you?"

"Yes," B'taav said. His teeth chattered.

"You might be infected," Latitia said.

21

Latitia helped B'taav back into the desert transport.

She drove it out of the abandoned church, down the brick stairs, and back on to the road before coming to a stop next to their pursuer's cruiser. She drew her strange weapon and aimed it.

"What are you...?" B'taav said.

Latitia opened fire, sending energy blasts at the empty vehicle. They hit the engine, tires, and trunk. She moved the desert transport in closer and aimed at the cruiser's interior before firing one last time.

That shot set off a series of sparks which enveloped the cruiser's console and seats and left behind the smell of burnt plastic. The sparks flamed out and all that was left were ashen shapes.

"It looks like... like those people," B'taav said.

"Not people," Latitia said.

She put her gun away.

"Are you like them?" B'taav asked and pointed to her metal leg.

"Just that part," Latitia said.

She drove down the street, leaving the decay and eventually entering the desert.

B'taav didn't know where Latitia was taking him and, at the moment, didn't feel like asking. His body temperature swung wildly, alternatively producing sweats and chills.

All the while, Latitia kept a steady course due west.

After a half hour of travel, B'taav felt a little better. By then it was pitch black and they were deep within the desert.

"Where are we going?" he asked.

"There."

In the distance and at the edge of the desert transport's lights were the remains of a weathered private star port. It consisted of three structures: A hanger, a landing pad, and a small, rusted out building. Latitia drew close, eventually entering the port's perimeter and parking their transport beside the hanger.

Latitia exited and walked to the passenger door. She opened it and offered B'taav her hand.

"I can do this," B'taav said.

He grasped the side of the door and tried to pull himself out but was too weak. He clenched his teeth and tried again. This time he exited, though his legs shook. He looked up. The door leading into the hanger was ten feet away.

"You should have parked closer," he said.

Latitia laughed. She again offered her hand.

B'taav took it.

Despite the building's wear, the door into the hanger had a state of the art security pad. Latitia pressed her right hand against it and, after confirming her identity, the heavy door slid open.

Within the hanger was a large private shuttle craft. There were markings on its body identifying it as belonging to Merrick Industries.

"Did... did Merrick let you borrow her?"

"He isn't the borrowing type."

Latitia reached into the pocket of her black jumpsuit and pulled out a remote control unit. She pressed a series of buttons and the craft's outer lights came on. After a few seconds, its entry door uncoupled and slid open. A walkway extended to the ground.

Latitia helped B'taav up and into the shuttle.

The ship's upper deck was spacious. A group of seats were arranged in a neat row on either side allowing for a total of twenty passengers. At the end of this deck was a door leading to the cockpit.

With Latitia's help, B'taav walked past the passenger compartment and into the cockpit. The shuttle contained the most modern of comforts and a small but effective defensive array.

"How fast is she?"

"She has a Pegasus IV motor," Latitia said. "You tell me."

"We're going to need that kind of power for where we're going?"

"Probably."

B'taav slid into the co-pilot's chair and Latitia sat next to him. She pressed a button on the main console and the walkway retracted while the outer doors closed and sealed. The distinct sound of compartment pressurization was heard as Latitia pressed another series of buttons and checked the shuttle's status.

Satisfied all was in order, she left her seat and reached for the Medi-Kit strapped to the side of the cockpit controls. She opened the small case and looked over the medication before pulling out a hypodermic shooter.

"What is that?" B'taav muttered.

"A tranquilizer. Should ease the pain."

She injected him.

"What... what was I infected with?"

"I'm not sure," Latitia said.

"You have some idea."

"That's about all I have," Latitia said. "Rest."

"Will I live?"

"You better."

Latitia strapped B'taav in and did the same for herself.

She then gripped the shuttle's controls and the craft rolled out of the hangar. It gained considerable speed before going airborne and sailing above the Onian sands. Moments later it was past the range of the Capital's scanners.

Latitia pulled at the controls and the ship made a sharp turn straight up. The night sky cleared with each passing second until they were in outer space.

By the time the shuttle approached the Onian Displacer, B'taav was sleeping.

Three ships waited just outside the Displacer for their turn to depart. The last of the three was the *Solaris*.

Latitia approached that craft but kept her distance. She opened her communication systems and allowed a pre-recorded message to play. The message had no words, only a burst of seemingly random static.

A dark craft suddenly appeared near the *Solaris's* bow. The ship was unlike any in either the Phaecian or Epsillon Empire. She had no lights or identification marks and did not show up on any of the Merrick shuttle's sensors.

The ship was lying in wait, as if to ambush the *Solaris*. It approached that craft until it was directly below her. By then the *Solaris* was next in line to enter the Displacer. As she moved forward, the dark craft mimicked her movements. The Onian Displacer came on. Its hollow center turned into a field of high intensity energy. Thousands upon thousands of white hot arcs flared within and ran back and forth along the Displacer's rectangular frame.

The *Solaris* and her unseen shadow gained speed as they moved directly into the Displacer's center. One moment they were there and the electrical arcs blasted with unimaginable energy.

The next, the *Solaris* and her companion were gone and the electrical blast in the hollow center of the Displacer disappeared.

"What was that craft? Who is following... following..."

Latitia was surprised to find B'taav awake. Despite his drowsiness, he tried to reach for the radio controls.

"They're with us," Latitia said as she gently grabbed his hand. "They'll make sure Maddox and Nathaniel have no difficulties."

"I've never seen... never seen a ship like that."

"Sit back and relax."

B'taav did as told while Latitia activated the communication controls.

"Onia Displacer, this is Merrick Shuttle Three One Five. Request transport."

"Acknowledged," the Onian Displacer replied. "Standing by for coordinates."

Latitia pressed a series of keys and leaned back in her chair. Soon, the Displacer would re-activate for them.

"Where are we going?" B'taav asked.

"Our eventual destination is Pomos."

"Pomos?" B'taav repeated, bewildered. "Isn't that planet off limits? It's a... a lifeless husk."

"The planet is off limits," Latitia said. "But it's hardly lifeless."

22

The derelict craft was little more than a speck of dust lost in the infinite cosmos.

Inquisitor Cer spent the first day after the explosion in the decompression chamber. She had limited access to the ship's computers, but what she could glean from the readouts available to her was unmistakable: The *Xendos* was dead. There was no atmosphere beyond the decompression chamber's doors. Neither was there artificial gravity or heat. The only section of the ship that was still habitable was the decompression chamber itself.

Yet bitter cold seeped into the chamber by the second and Inquisitor Cer was forced to increase the heat. For a while the heaters worked but it didn't take long before the decompression chamber's systems started failing. By the end of that day, Inquisitor Cer was back in her space suit. She had the suit's storage tanks suck in what atmosphere remained in the chamber. The process would take several hours.

She slept.

The next day, when all traces of atmosphere were safely removed and stored in her suit's tanks, Inquisitor Cer opened the decompression chamber doors. Beyond them was darkness. Inquisitor Cer turned on her helmet's lights and shined them down the corridor. She found Deveri and Loalla's still tied corpses floating at the rear of the passageway. She removed their ropes and took their bodies back to the decompression chamber where she pulled out a pair of body bags from a storage compartment. She sealed their bodies within the bags and offered a prayer for their lost souls.

Inquisitor Cer then made her way to the cockpit.

The cockpit and its complement of instrument panels were in pristine shape. She tried starting the central computers from there but couldn't. A few internal sensors were active and displayed minimal to negligible energy readings. It was impossible to start the ship. Inquisitor Cer turned her attention to the Comm systems. They, like the central computers, were offline. There wasn't enough energy to power them.

Inquisitor Cer left the cockpit and made her way to the forward lounge. She found Overlord Octo's frozen corpse where she last saw him and still seated at his moment of death. His head was bent down as if taking a short nap. Inquisitor Cer searched him, looking for the homing beacon she knew all Overlords carried. Because their travel routes were kept secret, these beacons were used in case of emergencies. They emitted a signal powerful enough to show on any approaching Phaecian vessel Comm systems.

Inquisitor Cer did not find the beacon on him.

She stepped back and thought of offering a prayer for the Overlord's soul.

She didn't.

Inquisitor Cer left the forward deck and moved to the back of the ship and down the stairs to the cabin corridor. There, she found the floors and walls were warped. Debris, some as small as a speck of sand, floated throughout. Inquisitor Cer moved forward to Overlord Octo's room. The warping in the corridor became more pronounced as she approached.

She stopped before what remained of the door leading into the Overlord's room.

More than half of it was gone, ripped apart by the force of the explosion and sucked back into the room. Inquisitor Cer pushed at the door's remains, trying to get it fully open but was unable to. She gave up and leaned down to look through the cracks.

The room was a mess.

This was ground zero, the place where Overlord Octo planted the device meant to destroy the *Xendos* and kill everyone on board.

On the opposite side of the room was a gaping hole and beyond it the darkness of outer space. Given the hole's size, it was a miracle the explosion hadn't destroyed the entire vessel. Other than a half-blasted cot and a desk, both of which were bolted to the floor, almost everything else that was once within the room was sucked out.

The engine room lay below Overlord Octo's cabin and between breaks in the floor Inquisitor Cer spotted sheared coolant and fuel lines.

"You picked a good spot," Inquisitor Cer said before heading downstairs.

The damage to the engine room was as bad as she feared.

Along with the destroyed coolant and fuel lines there was considerable damage to several crucial computer components. Without them, there was no way to get the engine running.

And yet, the ship was still in one piece.

"They don't make 'em like they used to," Inquisitor Cer muttered before heading back upstairs.

Inquisitor Cer respectfully stored the last of the three corpses in the decompression chamber's storage locker.

She made a quick inventory of her spare oxygen tanks and food rations. There was enough food for three weeks but only a week's worth of air.

Inquisitor Cer grabbed the two space suits she took from the charging rack and hung them back up. There were five suits hanging on the rack and, with the ship dead, they would no longer charge. Inquisitor Cer took a replacement battery from a storage drawer and hooked it to the rack's system. She then discharged all the spare space suits' remaining energy and transferred it to the replacement battery.

While the rack transferred the energy, Cer checked the remaining charge in her suit. She had a little less than twelve hours' worth. She then removed and checked the replacement battery's charge.

The total charge amounted to three more days' worth of energy.

On the plus side, you don't have to worry about starving or suffocating, Inquisitor Cer grimly thought.

She took the replacement battery with her and left the Decompression chamber. There was little to do but make a second, more detailed examination of the damage to the craft.

Maybe there's something I missed.

For over an hour Inquisitor Cer examined the ruptured coolant and fuel lines before retreating to the storage rooms next to the engine room. She searched for any spare pieces of equipment she could use to fix at least a portion of the damage.

She searched through the boxes and equipment in increasing desperation and found a few tubes and tinsel patches. Not nearly enough.

Inquisitor Cer eventually left the storage room and returned to the cockpit. She more thoroughly examined the communication equipment while eying her replacement battery. It was possible to wire the battery directly to the communication system and bring it back to life. She could then send an emergency signal.

The problem was that these older panels were notoriously inefficient. They would drain the battery's charge very quickly. Too quickly for her to use the battery on her suit.

Cer faced two equally grim options.

She could use the replacement battery on herself and survive three days with the hope that a vessel would find and rescue her or she could use the battery to send out a distress signal and hope it was answered before the twelve hours of energy remaining in her suit was gone.

"Damned if you do," she muttered.

In the end, there was only one option.

Let's get this over with.

It took Inquisitor Cer an hour of her increasingly precious time to connect the replacement battery to the *Xendos'* control panel. Once done, Inquisitor Cer checked the connections. All appeared good.

Inquisitor Cer reached down and flipped a switch.

At first, nothing happened.

A few seconds passed.

A sliver of fear passed through Cer's body. Was the equipment too damaged for even—

Abruptly, the lights came on and the *Xendos'* Comm center was alive. Inquisitor Cer accessed the communication system and tried to send out a distress signal.

The controls were frozen.

She continued working, her despair growing with each wasted second. Again and again she tried to send off a distress signal yet couldn't.

Did Overlord Octo sabotage this as well?

The emergency communication system was designed to be both simple and foolproof yet she couldn't get it to work. Inquisitor Cer pulled the Comm panel up and checked the circuitry below. All seemed to be in order. She laid the panel back down and pressed more buttons.

Something to her right sparked. She turned her head just as the replacement battery's connections melted.

"NO!" she yelled.

She pulled at what was left of the connections but by then the damage was done.

The replacement battery had suffered a crippling overload.

Inquisitor Cer checked its readout to see if there was any charge left in the unit.

The readout indicated there was none.

"Dammit!" Inquisitor Cer yelled.

She threw the battery at the back of the cockpit. It slammed against the wall and fell apart. Its internal mechanisms were charred to dust.

She looked to the side, at the empty seat beside hers.

She felt very much alone.

Hours passed.

Inquisitor Cer sat in her seat, motionless.

After a while, she checked the charge left in her suit's battery. *Six hours.*

Inquisitor Cer leaned back and stared out the front window of the *Xendos*.

The view before her remained frustratingly stagnant. The Medusa Constellation, ten stars arranged in a roughly spherical pattern, stared back at her. A few asteroids drifted by, their motion elegantly silent.

Inquisitor Cer thought about her life to this moment, of her successes and failures.

She prayed.

Not for a miracle but for forgiveness for any sins committed, whether purposely or not. She prayed for the Gods to grant her peace in her passage from the world of flesh and blood. She took stock of her life. There were blemishes but that was to be expected.

None can walk perfectly in the footsteps of the Gods.

She also had one major regret. One—

She felt the first nibble of cold intrude in her suit. She felt it in her toes and at the tips of her fingers.

It was a small variation in temperature and almost welcome given the stagnant, warm air flowing in her suit. It was a sign of the bad things to come.

Soon, that cold would turn into a life threatening freeze.

Dying slowly is the very worst way to die.

She shook her head.

No, not the worst.

Inquisitor Cer looked to her side, at the Navigator's chair.

She thought of the times B'taav sat beside her. She didn't feel like praying anymore.

More hours passed.
After a while, it was difficult to move.

The air within her suit grew increasingly foul. The purification systems were dying and the cold of outer space was becoming more and more pronounced.

Inquisitor Cer's breath fogged up the glass in her helmet until she could barely make out anything in front of her. She felt so very tired and it was hard to keep her eyes open.

She looked down and at the readout within the helmet. Her battery was at five percent. Four.

She thought of her training and her service to the Phaecian Empire. She thought of her mother and her very few friends...

She thought of B'taav.

She felt the electricity of her touch upon his cheek.

She would never see him again.

Never.

Her one regret.

Inquisitor Cer could no longer focus on her surroundings. The spacesuit's power supply was all but exhausted and her limbs were numb. At least she felt no pain.

She had a vision of childhood and her long lost father.

She forced her eyes open and saw a blinding light coming from somewhere outside.

Dying slowly is the very worst way to die.

No.

Dying alone was the worst way to die.

"I'm sorry father," she said.

Take me. I'm ready to go.

23

Inquisitor Cer slowly, painfully, opened her eyes.

She was still in her seat before the *Xendos'* cockpit. Everything around her was the same.

Only... different.

Instead of gasping at stagnant air, she breathed easy. She no longer felt the awful ache of cold. She was *warm*.

I'm dreaming.

She looked down at the information display within her suit's helmet. It indicated her battery charge was ten percent.

Ten? It was down to—

Eleven.

Moments later, it was at twelve.

Somehow, her suit's battery was charging.

Impossible.

Thirteen percent.

Fifteen.

She closed her eyes.

You're hallucinating.

She opened her eyes and gazed at the *Xendos'* controls and monitors. They showed fragile signs of life. A light flickered here, another there. The central computer's monitor abruptly turned on, its light blinding in the darkness.

Inquisitor Cer forced herself up. She looked around the cockpit, almost expecting to see someone –her saviors– standing there.

She was alone.

What's happened? What's changed?

The door leading out of the cockpit was closed. A light next to it indicated it was sealed. Inquisitor Cer again checked the suit's readout. There was a very low level of atmosphere in the cockpit. Like the charge in her battery, it grew. Another impossibility.

She stared out the front window, to see if there were any vessels alongside the *Xendos*. All she saw was darkness.

Inquisitor Cer fell back in her chair.

The harder she tried to think, the foggier her mind.

"You're tired. Rest."

Inquisitor Cer's eyes shot open. The words were whispered into her ear.

"Sergeant Delmont?" she said. "Whe... where are you?"

She waited for an answer. None came.

Though she tried, she could no longer stay awake.

"Thank you," she managed before closing her eyes and falling back to sleep.

When she awoke, Inquisitor Cer was still in her space suit sitting before the *Xendos'* cockpit.

Only now, almost every one of the ship's controls were illuminated. All the monitors were alive and glowed with information. The digital readout within her helmet indicated her battery was at 100 percent. The cockpit temperature was a cool but bearable 44 degrees Fahrenheit. It had a breathable atmosphere.

Inquisitor Cer was saved.

How?

The cockpit door was still closed and sealed from the rest of the vessel. Inquisitor Cer leaned to her right, to the computer system that regulated the ship's life support. She pressed several buttons. The readings within the cockpit were nominal.

She pressed several more buttons and the atmospheric and life support readouts from the rest of the ship appeared. While the cockpit was relatively warm and habitable, the rest of the *Xendos*, beginning with the corridor beyond the cockpit door, remained an icy vacuum.

Inquisitor Cer shifted to her left and accessed the ship's energy levels. They were a marked improvement from before but remained very low.

Going from non-existent to very low is a hell of a difference, but these things don't just fix themselves.

Inquisitor Cer clicked on her communicator. Someone *had* to be doing this. She was about to speak but stopped.

From somewhere deep within, she knew sending a radio communique would be a mistake.

Inquisitor Cer shut the radio off.

She took another step to her left and accessed the navigation station while running a check of the *Xendos'* engines. They were online but seriously underperforming. In combination with the very low levels of energy, the *Xendos* could do little more than crawl. It was doing so and headed in the general direction of the Longshore Shipping Lanes. She would reach the space lanes after passing the Norman Asteroid field. Though not as dense as the Erebus field, it offered cover.

Will I need it?

She had no answer to that question.

Inquisitor Cer activated the security monitors and did a sweep of the compartments and rooms within the ship. She stopped at Overlord Octo's suite. The damage from the explosive remained, but the shattered door leading into his room was almost fully sealed.

Inquisitor Cer stared at the footage. Incredibly, she spotted movement.

Millimeter by millimeter, broken pieces of the door welded themselves together, as if guided by invisible repair techs. At the rate the door repaired itself, it would take no more than another hour or two before it was completely sealed. Once it was, the rest of the *Xendos* would again be able to sustain atmosphere.

Inquisitor Cer switched the monitor's image to that of the engine room and made a quick check of the energy lines. Those that were severed in the explosion for the most part remained that way. Yet a few primary energy feeds were rerouted. Enough mass energy was present to allow the *Xendos* its very slow movement. She found the same mysterious –and invisible– patchwork was being done there as well. A pair of fractured wires slowly converged, as if magnets drawn together. Once the wires touched, they merged.

Inquisitor Cer cycled through each of the security cameras in every one of the compartments. There had to be someone on board doing this. Yet she could find no other living person aboard. Finally, she switched to the external monitors, going through them one at a time, looking for any ship parked near the *Xendos*. There were none.

It's as if the ship were a living being and in the process of healing its wounds.

"Living being?" she muttered.

Years before she heard whispers of research into biological augmentations to machinery. In theory, the biological elements acted as if part of a living system, one that would eventually possess the capacity of self-repair. The research was far from yielding any positive results but even if it had, how would such high tech, state of the art equipment make its way onto a two hundred plus year old vessel?

"Fortune favors fools," Cer muttered. "I'm beyond favor and much more than a fool."

A low electronic beep drew her attention back to the pilot's chair.

Inquisitor Cer sat down.

The navigational system was operational. She could pilot the craft.

Did you make a deal with the devil? She thought before chiding herself for such blasphemy.

No. You did nothing of the kind. Time to assess this situation fully.

Inquisitor Cer bit her upper lip and reached for the security clasps on her helmet. She pushed them down, springing the locks that held the device in place. She twisted the helmet until it was freed.

She then paused, unsure if this was a wise thing to do.

Get it over with.

She braced and, with a quick pull, removed her helmet. The cool air from the cockpit surrounded her. She took a deep breath and was pleasantly surprised –and more than a little relieved– that the atmosphere was exactly as the instruments said it was: breathable.

Inquisitor Cer laid her helmet aside. She removed the rest of her suit and examined her fingers and toes. They were small patches of ugly black bruises on her left hand and foot, the very early stages of frostbite.

Inquisitor Cer grabbed a Medi-Kit and, from within, pulled out several containers of crème and wraps. She applied them to her fingers and toes. The bruises would last several days but the medication would cure her.

Once done, Inquisitor Cer took out the medi-sensor and checked her status. Her body temperature and blood pressure were both elevated. A recommendation to apply medi-patches was offered. Cer did so, placing patches on the side of her neck.

You'll be good as new. Eventually.

Inquisitor Cer put the Medi-Kit away and put her space suit back on. She left the helmet where it lay, using the warmth from the suit to keep her comfortable. As she did, the *Xendos* drew still closer to the Norman Asteroid field. It would arrive at her outer fringes in only a few minutes.

Inquisitor Cer reached for the communicator.

I have to send out a distress signal.

Her deep unease returned. Sending a distress signal was the logical thing to do.

So why do you feel you shouldn't?

Inquisitor Cer's fingers hovered over the communicator buttons. All she had to do was press a couple of buttons and the emergency signal would be sent out. She could then sit back, relax, and wait for her saviors...

She withdrew her hand.

An electronic beep come from the far side of the navigation controls. It indicated there were files loaded and waiting for her attention.

She pulled them up on her central monitor.

She was familiar with these files. At least some of them.

They were from the microchip given to her by Sergeant Delmont on the *Dakota*.

Inquisitor Cer reluctantly pressed another button and the list was refreshed. There were thousands of files and videos, some dating back hundreds, even thousands, of years. She found the one file that was flagged for her to read first. It was the information Overlord Octo was willing to murder –and commit suicide– for.

Inquisitor Cer hesitated a moment before pressing another button.

Once she read that first file, there was no turning back.

Several hours later she stopped.

There were still so many more files to go through but, for now, she was overwhelmed and exhausted.

The files presented a familiar yet very different history of the Phaecian and Epsillon Empires. It was a dark picture of the heroes of the Church and the leaders of Empire. Of corruption, vanity and struggle. Of sins and filth and...

Inquisitor Cer felt her stomach twist.

...decadence and power struggles never revealed...

Power.

Of shadowy and not so shadowy individuals who used the Holy Words for political gain... and worse.

She was familiar with many of the stories, but if this information was to be believed, her knowledge was incomplete or, worse, cleaned up for the purpose of offering moral lessons and teachable moments.

Not all the heroes of the Holy Texts were exposed as villains but almost none proved immune to at least some form of sin. All faced temptations. More than a few succumbed. Some sank into the depths of despair only to rebound and reaffirm their faith. Too many preached the Holy Word by day and gave in to cravings by night.

There was a history of the early days of settlement following the Exodus and how the Church turned a blind eye to their own corruption, a practice that continued to this day. In the Holy Texts the early days were presented as a struggle between good versus evil when in reality the borders between the two were –are– blurry. The Church and the religion Inquisitor Cer had devoted her life to was a shining, impossibly beautiful coin on one side and marred, scratched, and weathered one on the other.

Tears fell down her cheeks and Cer prayed for guidance. But her prayer, so helpful in times of need, rang hollow.

How do you ignore this? How do you keep your direction... your faith?

"The Gods help me."

In her mind she stood before a precipice and stared into a great darkness. Years of devotion to the Holy Texts... were they a lie? Had she and so many others like her wasted time on a system that was just as corrupt as the one in Epsillon?

Though these people are not divine, are they not human?

"Human."

Like your father.

How she hated him for so many years for abandoning her mother. Her mother died alone and unloved while Cer was in the academy. Once an Inquisitor, Cer searched for information on her father, determined to prove he was just as bad as she suspected.

Instead, she found a man who was devoted to science and whose worst sin was his strict allegiance to the church. When she tracked down and heard his final transmissions from his last, doomed expedition, she cried.

It was the first time in her adult life she did so.

He was no saint and, yes, he abandoned Cer and her mother. Yet he was also a caring man who thought of her even as he knew his end was near.

Inquisitor Cer recalled Maddox and the crew of the *Dakota* and, especially, B'taav. All were citizens of the Epsillon Empire and none devoted to the Church. Yet they fought to make this vast yet small universe a place where people can live in peace.

B'taav.

"I'll see you again," she swore.

Her right hand moved to the communication systems. Instead of sending a distress signal, she checked the Phaecian news traffic.

By then, the *Xendos* was inside the Norman Asteroid Field and close enough to the Longshore Space Lanes to get real time news. Hundreds of official news sites and several hundred more pirate stations fueled with paranoia and fringe beliefs were available to see and hear.

Yet Inquisitor Cer was surprised when it took several minutes for the *Xendos* to receive only a handful of very weak transmissions. On these sites, news of Overlord Octo's disgrace was the central topic. One channel was devoted to an endless video loop of his startling confessions. Overlord Octo, more solemn than Inquisitor Cer had ever seen him, sent out a testimonial taking sole blame for the sex slave trade. He concluded this devastating admission with the announcement that he would do the honorable thing and rid the Universe of his presence.

"My sins are unforgiveable," Overlord Octo said. "The Empire remains strong. The Empire breathes and lives. It will survive without us."

Us.

It was assumed by the news stations Overlord Octo sacrificed himself and the crew of the *Xendos* to atone for his sins. The stations minimized the involvement of the other Overlords, and many others in the Phaecian Empire's power structure, in the sex slave trade.

Inquisitor searched the feeds for information on the ships sent to her area. One of the news stations reported a fleet of battleships, hardly the standard search and rescue crafts, were on their way to find the *Xendos'* remains.

They're not here to find survivors, Inquisitor Cer realized. *They're here to retrieve corpses.*

With Overlord Octo and the files given to Inquisitor Cer gone, the remaining Overlords could quietly bury, along with the remains of the *Xendos,* this entire sordid affair.

But Sergeant Delmont's information screamed for action.

For a moment Inquisitor Cer considered broadcasting it and informing everyone within earshot of the realities of the sex trade along with the real history of the Church and her Empire.

She couldn't.

The reason only a few newscasts were available to her was because those same "rescue" ships were jamming the Comm signals. The signals the *Xendos* received, weak though they were, came from the largest, most powerful broadcasters. The *Xendos'*

Comm system stood no chance of breaking through the jam. Worse, any signal sent out would immediately alert the fleet of her location.

They think you're dead. Keep it that way and get out of here.

But where could she go?

Inquisitor Cer was a part of Overlord Octo's guard and, as he correctly stated, complicit in his sins. Even if she had no knowledge of them until now and she made it to another world in the Phaecian Empire, any evidence she brought against the church would be labeled a lie… or worse.

You have to go very far away and bide your time. Even if it's a lifetime's worth, you cannot come back until you're ready to take on the Council. In the meantime…

Inquisitor Cer returned to the information from the microchip.

She noticed the flashing file, the one that Sgt. Delmont wanted her to read first.

Why is this so important?

Inquisitor Cer opened the file.

For a second time she read about the sex slave and watched the vids. Curiosity got the better of her. She traced the paths of the many vessels that carried their profane cargo from the Epsillon Empire to Phaecia. Their paths were, for the most part, seemingly random. However, as she moved back in time, to the origins of the sex slave, she found a commonality, a planet where every one of these early ships passed at one point or another.

A planet deep within the Epsillon Empire.

That's where she would go.

Provided she made it out of the Longshore Space Lanes alive.

24

The journey to Pomos was a circuitous one.

Latitia jumped from Displacer to Displacer, traveling further and further from one end of the Epsillon Empire to the other. Despite fighting off waves of nausea, B'taav realized her multiple Displacer jumps were designed to spot anyone following her while keeping their destination as much of a mystery as possible.

"The medicine is working," B'taav said after a while.

The Independent leaned closer to the computer console and requested information about their destination.

B'taav knew at one time Pomos was the hub of scientific research for the entire Epsillon Empire and that the once beloved Saint Vulcan made her headquarters there. He had access to mountains of information on the planet's history but skipped it. His focus was on her destruction.

To this day, the details of Pomos' outbreak were shrouded in mystery. Though no one was certain, it was theorized some kind of biological weapon escaped one of Saint Vulcan's laboratories and infected the population. The infected displayed aggressive tendencies that grew with each passing minute. The end result was the stuff of nightmares.

Cities fell and millions perished. Saint Vulcan quarantined her planet, calling in her fleet of ships and tricking the Captains of the vessels into thinking they were there to evacuate personnel and offer comfort and aid. Instead, Saint Vulcan took control of the ships and used their weapons to torch her planet and wipe out every citizen, including herself.

Outrage over her actions was immediate. Though there were those who recognized the cold logic of destroying the planet to save the Empire, Saint Vulcan was nonetheless reviled. To this day, she was considered a monster.

Latitia looked over B'taav's shoulder.

"The first missile fired on Pomos was a two hundred kilo-ton Proto-fusion bomb," she said. "It detonated on the planet's southern hemisphere instantly killing fifty million citizens. Whoever survived the first round of blasts most certainly didn't survive the next sixty."

B'taav clicked a button and the monitor displayed Solyanna, Pomos' moon. Its northern hemisphere was cracked. Splinters as large as cities broke off her surface and floated in orbit around her.

"Saint Vulcan had a base there, too," Latitia said. "As you can see, she fired upon it as well. To this day, over two hundred years later, debris from the moon still rains on Pomos."

"Nothing was left."

"The Epsilon Empire's business consortium begged to differ," Latitia said. "Even as they vilified Saint Vulcan and declared the planet a lost cause they funded a wave of automated drones to check the planet's surface."

"Why?"

"To get their hands on any research that might have survived."

"Did they find anything?"

Latitia shook her head.

"After a couple dozen years, there were only a handful of companies still sniffing around. Those that were left pulled out when the Epsilon and Phaecian Empires went to war. Pomos, for all intents and purposes, was forgotten. Today more people remember Saint Vulcan, the woman who sold out her world, than Pomos, the world she sold out."

"Why exactly are we going there?" B'taav asked.

Latitia pressed a button before her and the image on B'taav's monitor changed. A Pomos sensor scan appeared.

"That's from last year," Latitia said. "See the energy blip on the northern quadrant, 24 by 43?"

B'taav clicked on the image, blowing it up until he had a clearer view. The energy blip was small, indicative of nothing more than a small vessel.

"Could be a ghost trace," B'taav said. "Some old equipment?"

Latitia pressed another button. A different sensor scan appeared.

"This is from one month later."

The energy blip was present. It was slightly larger.

"Someone's down there?"

"Yeah," Latitia said. "For the first couple of months the energy blips were inconsistent, appearing for a few hours or days before disappearing for about the same amount of time. Then things changed. This image is from three months ago."

Latitia pressed a third button. Revealed in almost the same spot as before was another energy blip. This one was much larger.

"It's grown."

"Quite a bit," Latitia said. "By our calculations, it's ten times its original size."

"What could anyone want down there?"

"Maybe something was left behind after all," Latitia said. She smiled. "The past is never entirely gone. You, more than anyone else, should know."

B'taav was silent. Was Latitia referring to the *Argus*? If so, how could she know?

"Does this have something to do with Merrick?"

"It's possible."

"Why involve me?"

Latitia didn't reply. B'taav shook his head.

"What aren't you telling me?"

"Plenty."

"Do you have some idea of what we're going to find?"

"No."

"Why just us? Shouldn't we go with a larger force?"

"Who says there isn't one?"

B'taav sat back. He stared at the Pomos energy blip. He stared hard.

"How about it, B'taav?" Latitia asked. "You up for solving a mystery?"

25

The *Xendos* limped along as Inquisitor Cer paced the cockpit.

In the previous hours, the ship's performance improved considerably. The engines now provided a fifth of the ship's original capacity. Given the rate of repair, in another day or two the *Xendos* might actually reach near peak performance level.

And I still have no idea how this is happening.

Inquisitor Cer longed to leave the cockpit and examine the engine room but the corridors and rooms beyond this one remained uninhabitable. Even so, conditions kept improving. Atmospheric levels, which were nonexistent before, were registering, though the amount of breathable air remained far too low for human survival. Life support systems were also coming back online. If enough of them became operational, Inquisitor Cer could set livable temperatures throughout the rest of the ship.

Still, Inquisitor Cer kept the cockpit's temperature a chilly forty degrees Fahrenheit and heated her body through her space suit. With the rescue fleet somewhere nearby searching for her, she dare not elevate internal temperatures too much and provide them something their sensors could detect.

Inquisitor Cer skirted the ship along the edges of the Norman Asteroid Field and just outside the Longshore Shipping Lanes. She used the *Xendos'* cameras to monitor for movement.

It was normal for hundreds of merchant ships to pass through the Longshore Lanes at any given time yet at this moment it was devoid of all traffic. Inquisitor Cer was tempted to activate the *Xendos'* sensor array to see if any ships were hiding in her proximity but, like sending out a radio signal, doing so would give away her position.

With no ships in sight, Cer spent more and more time on the communication system checking for transmissions. Now and again, she heard stray chatter from distant frigates.

One of the last such transmissions involved a frigate commander's anger at being re-routed from the Longshore Lanes.

"They're closing it all down," the Commander complained.

After speaking those words, his transmissions went silent. Less than an hour later the remaining news feeds were gone. An eerie silence filled the airwaves.

Inquisitor Cer had never witnessed such a complete wall of silence erected in one location.

She parked the *Xendos* behind a large asteroid and concentrated on the magnified real time visuals streaming on her monitors. She searched the darkness for signs of any movement. She examined every flash of light and honed in on any blur in an attempt to locate the ships searching for her.

"There you are," she said after a while.

She spotted three distant lights and zoomed her cameras on them.

Several ships, twenty in total, broke off and spread out. They were approaching fast.

Inquisitor Cer locked the *Xendos'* aft cameras on them. She moved to another monitor and activated the side and forward cameras. She detected more lights.

There were at least three more sets of battleships coming from opposite directions. One, the largest of the group, was closest to her. She recognized her lines.

It was the *Cygnusa*.

"By all that's Holy," she muttered.

She knew the commander of that vessel only too well.

"Of course they would send you to get me, Inquisitor Raven."

A group of twenty officers manned their stations on the bridge of the *Cygnusa*.

They sorted data and watched for any sign of their prey. In the center of the bridge stood a very tall, wiry man. His gray hair reached his shoulders and a black cloak covered much of his body. The few crewmembers walking about actively avoided coming too near him.

"Inquisitor Raven," one of the officers said.

"Yes, Lieutenant Sanders?"

"Fighter craft Group Theta ready for launch."

"Tell them to go."

On the central view screen a squad of fighter craft emerged from the port side of the *Cygnusa* and spread out in all directions.

The *Cygnusa* and her complement of fighter craft swept this section of the Longshore Shipping Lanes and approached the lee side of the Norman Asteroid field. They neared a cluster of rocks.

"Captain Antoni, examine the cluster before you," Raven said.

The view screen split into parts, each showing camera feeds from individual members of his squad.

"Give them light," Inquisitor Raven ordered.

Lights flared from the *Cygnusa's* side and illuminated the rocky mass.

"Plenty of places to hide," Inquisitor Raven said.

Minutes passed as the fighter craft searched.

"There's too much area to cover," Inquisitor Raven said after a while. "Send a signal. They are to clear the area in exactly five minutes."

"Yes sir," the Comm officer said.

The fighter craft withdrew. Another light blinked on and off the side of the *Cygnusa*. It was blood red and warned of danger.

"Charge the fusion cannons," Inquisitor Raven said. "Aim at the cluster."

The last of the fighter craft left the area. More seconds passed. The five minutes were up.

"Fire," Inquisitor Raven said.

A concentrated energy beam roared from the battleship's fusion canons and blasted the clump of asteroids. The ancient rocks were ripped apart.

"Captain Antoni, give it another look," Inquisitor Raven said.

The fighter craft flew back into the remains of the asteroids. Detecting nothing, they withdrew. The *Cygnusa* followed. Flickers of light sizzled along her lee side. Her cannons were recharged and ready.

The ghost of a smile appeared on Inquisitor Raven's face.

"Target the next cluster of asteroids," he said.

He knew it was only a matter of time before the *Xendos* was found.

With each passing hour, Inquisitor Cer's desperation grew.

The communication system remained dead silent. The ships searching for the *Xendos* were coordinated their search by using low level radio waves. There was no way for Inquisitor Cer to anticipate their movements.

She drew deeper into the Norman Asteroid field while keeping a close eye on the *Cygnusa*. The ship continued firing on the larger asteroid clumps, working her way closer and closer to the *Xendos*.

Inquisitor Cer hoped for the opportunity to slip past the patrols and make it to the Genna Displacer at the end of the Longshore Shipping Lanes.

Though the Displacer would surely be well guarded, there had to be heavy merchant traffic around it, certainly enough for the *Xendos* to lose herself in.

But the fleet around her were taking their time and systematically flushing out every possible hiding place. The *Cygnusa* fusion cannons came to life and destroyed yet another cluster of asteroids.

Inquisitor Cer swore.

She was boxed in. It would take less than a day for the *Cygnusa* and her group of ships to reach her position.

Inquisitor Cer considered alternatives.

How about talking to them directly?

Inquisitor Cer loathed the idea. Her brief history with Inquisitor Raven when she was in the Royal Academy was still a very raw wound.

In spite of this, perhaps she could reason with him and convince him the deaths of Overlord Octo and his two guards were not her doing. She could present Raven the information given to her on the *Dakota*.

If you're an honorable man, you will take this information and join me. Together and with the power of this fleet, we can overthrow those who disgraced the Holy Word and restore honor to the Empire.

Inquisitor Cer shook her head.

As much as she despised him, Inquisitor Raven was as straight as they came. He, like the Captains and Commanders of the other ships searching for her, were brought in to clean up this mess because they followed their orders. Implicitly.

Inquisitor Cer pulled the *Xendos* closer to a small asteroid. It floated away from all other clusters, a pebble in the darkness.

It wouldn't be long before they were in her area. It wouldn't be long at all.

26

Sweat poured down B'taav's forehead. His teeth chattered. Latitia gave him another injection.

"I've...I've never felt like this before," B'taav said.

Latitia returned to the ship's controls.

"I'm no good to you like this," B'taav said. "Take me to a Doctor. I have contacts..."

"I've done everything a doctor could to help you," Latitia said.

"What do I have?"

"Rest," Latitia replied.

B'taav didn't argue. He didn't have the strength to.

For the next hour, he made himself as comfortable as he could. Latitia looked in on him now and again, offering warm drinks and protein pellets while focusing on their flight. The shuttle leaped from Displacer to Displacer, at least five during that hour, all in locations B'taav knew little about. Traffic along these Displacer lines was at times heavy and Latitia used that to full advantage, hiding their vessel between merchant haulers and on a couple of occasions, even piggybacking with cargo caravans.

She grew more and more confident there were no tails.

Latitia hid the shuttle within the mile wide folds of a merchant trawler's starboard side and set the controls to automatic pilot. She got out of her chair, stretched, and approached B'taav. His eyes were closed and he appeared to be sleeping. Latitia reached up to touch the Independent's forehead. B'taav's hand shot up. He grabbed her wrist.

"That's not the way you acted with the last person who touched you," Latitia said.

It took B'taav a moment to realize what she was talking about.

"How long have you been watching me?"

"Quite a while," Latitia said. She pulled her hand away.

"How long?"

Latitia smiled. As with most of B'taav's questions, it was clear she wasn't willing to give him answers. She eyed the medi-scanner's readings.

B'taav sighed.

"How are you getting us to Pomos undetected? If we use their Displacer, whoever is on the planet will know of our arrival and be ready for us. All this running around will be for nothing."

"We're not using Pomos' main Displacer," Latitia said.

"You're not planning to take the long flight, are you? The closest Displacer to Pomos is on Signat III. It'll take six months to get to Pomos by impulse."

"Seven, actually."

"We won't be able to take each other's company for that long."

"There is another way," Latitia said. "Pomos has a second Displacer."

"What?"

"It's a Type 2," Latitia said. "Old school stuff. It was sent there at the dawn of Empire and helped settle the planet. After Pomos became an economic powerhouse, Saint Vulcan had enough funds available to replace it with a Type 6 Displacer. The Type 2 was retired."

"It's still in operation?" B'taav asked. "Those older units were usually scrapped."

"The people of Pomos abandoned her. Her last reported location was around Solyanna."

"The moon was destroyed. Wouldn't the Displacer—"

"Solyanna's northern hemisphere took the brunt of the damage," Latitia said. "The Type 2 was in geosynchronous orbit along the Moon's equator, far enough away from the area to avoid catastrophic damage."

"You hope."

"I know."

"You've contacted her?"

"Before meeting up with you, I logged into the Onian Displacer and conducted a couple of thousand signal tests. They disguised the fact that I was communicating with the Type 2. When I sent her a pulse, I got an answer. She's alive all right."

"She may be alive, but will she work?"

"We'll see," Latitia said. "Because of her age and the time since she was last used, it's best not to push her too far. That's why I'm getting us as close to Pomos as possible. That way, we use less energy to make the jump."

"What if she can't handle even a near jump?"

"Then we'll have no choice but to use the Type 6. One way or another, we're going to Pomos."

"And if I'm still... still like this?" B'taav asked.

"You'll get better," Latitia said. Her eyes returned to the Medi-Scanner. The readings were dipping.

"What's happening?"

"Relax."

"I don't... I don't feel..."
Latitia rushed to B'taav's side.
He was no longer breathing.

27

B'taav dreamed of darkness and of dread.

He dreamed of creatures hidden in the night...

The darkness drifted away, replaced by light.

B'taav walked the shores of a red beach and gazed at a mighty alien city. Above it and in low orbit around the planet was a nightmarish machine. Metallic tentacles spread out from it and crisscrossed the skyline.

The creatures, he knew, were up there.

His gaze returned to the city. It was in flames. Untold billions died before B'taav's eyes, the victims of these creatures' planetary destruction.

The annihilation complete, the darkness returned.

B'taav felt the creatures move around him. He felt their insatiable hunger.

Shiny silver eyes pierced through the darkness. They stared at the Independent.

Why are you still alive? they asked, their voices guttural roars.

B'taav spun around. He tried to see them. See them as they were. All he saw were shadows.

You fight.

The creatures' corrosive breath enveloped the area, poisoning him.

You die now.

"No," B'taav said.

He sensed their surprise. The metallic eyes turned red.

Why do you still fight?

B'taav remained still while the creatures roared. A bloody claw reached out from the darkness. It stopped inches from B'taav's face.

"You can't touch me," B'taav said.

The creatures roared one last time.

We will meet again.

The darkness lifted.

B'taav opened his eyes. All was light.

He was standing at the entrance to the cockpit of Merrick's shuttlecraft.

"Latitia?" he said.

She was in the cockpit chair. She spun around, surprised to find the Independent on his feet.

"What are you doing?" she said.

A dull haze clouded the Independent's vision.

He was gone.

When B'taav awoke, he was in the cockpit and sitting in his chair. On the view screen before them were a variety of ships, from slick military craft to cargo vessels. They were in a heavy clump, awaiting their turn into an ancient Displacer.

"How are you feeling?" Latitia asked.

B'taav moved his hands, flexing his fingers into fists and then releasing.

"Better," he said. "Where are we?"

"The Mellore Displacer," Latitia said.

It was one of the busiest Displacer Units and located just outside the heart of the Epsillon Empire.

Latitia piloted the shuttle closer to one of the enormous merchant barges waiting in line to use the Displacer. She matched its speed and swung her ship under its body. Their Merrick shuttle was dwarfed by the barge and easily lost among its spires and underside. Latitia drew the shuttle closer and closer, finally engaging the ship's magnetic locks. The Merrick craft pressed against the barge's body and was still. Latitia powered the ship down.

Sensors within the merchant barge no doubt alerted the craft's crew of this stowaway yet no attempts were made to get rid of her.

"They're with us?"

"Yeah," Latitia said.

Given the barge's size and the amount of traffic in the area, unless someone was looking really hard, there was no way anyone outside the barge's crew would noticed this insignificantly small shuttle craft attached to her side.

"Hang on," Latitia said.

The merchant barge was on the move. Slowly at first but with greater and greater speed it approached the Mellore Displacer. When they were within a few miles, the Displacer's center lit up in a cascade of brilliant energy.

Over the Comm system B'taav heard the merchant ship's Captain interact with the Displacer crew.

"Mellore Displacer, this is the *Nelly-Anne*," she said. "Approaching transfer."

"Acknowledged, *Nelly-Anne*," Mellore's dispatcher replied. "All systems are green and your coordinates are locked in."

"Thank you, Mellore," the Captain said. "See you in a couple of weeks."

"Good hunting."

The tip of the merchant craft touched the Displacer's energy field and the electrical sparks grabbed hold of her. They moved across her body and enveloped the stowaway shuttle.

Latitia and B'taav covered their eyes as the Displacer's light became a supernova.

Then, in the blink of an eye, the lights were gone.

They were in inter-dimensional space, the territory between Displacer travel points. Around them was a reddish tinged darkness and warped clouds. The radiation counter on the shuttle ticked high as they proceeded. Seconds passed and the radiation spiked. Then, it dropped. Lower and lower until, abruptly, the red hue surrounding them was gone. There was a blast of bright lights. They were gone almost as quickly as they came. The radiation levels dropped to near normal.

They emerged into a dead solar system.

The faraway sun at the center of the system emitted a sickly blue light. A rocky band of debris, what at first looked like a ring of asteroids, orbited near the barge. It extended out for as far as the eye could see.

Latitia deactivated the shuttle's magnetic locks and was freed from the barge's underside. The shuttle floated away, giving B'taav his first clear look at their carrier. It was an ancient craft, dark and ominous and roughly rectangular in shape. Its surface was scarred and worn. Once magnificent spires were beaten down and warped.

"We're in the fields," B'taav said.

What appeared to be asteroids were in fact a vast and very dense field of garbage.

"The dead end of the Empire," Latitia said. "Where all the waste of the Industrial Worlds ends up."

Not many ventured into these parts as much of the detritus was either radioactive or biologically unstable. Nonetheless, several thousand ships of all sizes swarmed the area. They were relics from the old days of Empire.

"Who are they?" B'taav asked.

"Scavengers," Latitia said.

The radioactive readings on the cockpit's dash spiked.

"Their ships aren't made to withstand this."

"No, they aren't," Latitia agreed. "But that's about all the scavengers can afford. Thin shields, misfiring propulsion systems. The Gods alone know how many of them never return home."

Several of these smaller ships drew close to the newly arrived barge. They followed it to the edge of the dumping grounds and waited while the barge's sides opened. They then moved in like hungry rats when its cargo was jettisoned. They began their search from something *–anything–* of value.

"You've been here before?" B'taav asked.

"More times than I care to remember," Latitia replied.

The radiation gauges dropped as the shuttle moved away. In the view screen B'taav spotted a stationary object. It was an ancient Displacer.

"Incredible," B'taav said.

The unit was an automated Type 1. It was among the very first put into service within the Epsillon Empire at the dawn of the era of exploration.

"She still works?" B'taav asked.

"Of course," Latitia said.

"What's her model number?"

"Twenty two."

"Then this is one of the first systems ever explored?"

"She was a real gem a couple thousand years ago," Latitia said. "She had a planet in her system filled with the most beautiful plants and wildlife. Then we came. We chewed her up and made her a dumping ground. Humans are alchemists. We turn gold into shit."

"Alchemists?"

Latitia smiled.

"It's an ancient term."

"Never heard of it."

"You should read more."

Latitia hit several keys on the communication system.

"I'm linking to the Displacer," she said. "The Type 1 has a simple processing core. The destination I'm sending contains a small virus. All evidence of our journey will be deleted right after we're gone."

She finished her work and turned to the defensive systems. She typed in a series of commands.

"Now what are you doing?"

"Preparing for our arrival outside Pomos," Latitia said. "When we clear Pomos' Type 2, our ship will send an electric pulse. Any defensive systems within three hundred miles will be temporarily shut off, including the Displacer itself."

"For how long?"

"Five hours."

"That's a long time."

"Long enough for us to get to Pomos and back."

"What's the plan?" B'taav said.

"We get our bearings, see what kind of defensive systems, if any, are spread around Pomos before making a run for her surface. We touch down a couple hundred miles from that energy source and drive the Rover stored in the cargo bay the rest of the way."

"If it breaks down?"

"We walk."

Latitia leaned back in her chair, her hands on the shuttle's control. The Type 1 Displacer's hallow center slowly came to life and filled with a sea of energy arcs.

"Here we go," Latitia said.

She applied thrust. The Merrick shuttle entered the Displacer's energized center.

28

From a distance, all was eerily still.

A large, blasted rock, the moon Solyanna, floated in the heavens, her body a violated corpse. Her northern hemisphere was pitted and gashed with wounds caused by massive explosions. The rocky debris from a crater, the after effects of the grisly wounds, floated around her.

In the still darkness a tiny, almost insignificant pinprick of light appeared.

Somewhere deep within the rocky debris, a bruised Type 2 Displacer floated. Lights around its surface came on and, moments later, her hollow core was alive with energy. The energy arcs built until their light was blinding. A shuttle craft emerged.

Within the shuttle, Latitia barely had time to examine her surroundings. Her fingers worked over the ship's controls while the remains of the obliterated northern hemisphere of the moon floated before them.

Smaller rocks hit the shuttle. The noise was eerie, as if ancient ghosts demanding entry.

"Cover your eyes," Latitia said.

A sudden blinding flash filled the view screen. The surge flooded the interior of the craft but was gone almost as quickly as it began.

Latitia spun the shuttle around. The Displacer was dark, knocked out by the power surge.

"So far so good," Latitia said.

At the moment the Type 2 was hidden from Pomos by Solyanna itself. After another few hours, it would emerge.

Latitia drew the shuttle close to the Displacer. Its body was covered with a thick layer of dust and several of her protective panels were missing. Latitia used the ship's floodlights to look into the ancient Displacer's Control Room. Chairs, paperwork, and computer gear lined the tight quarters. Several items floated chaotically about. B'taav pointed to a large crack in one of the outer windows.

"Interior's been compromised," he said. He noted the dusty stains along the inner walls. "Quite a while ago, from the look of things."

Latitia allowed the spacecraft to drift beside the Displacer while she monitored every blip, sign of movement or, specifically, incoming sensor signals. Minutes passed and the shuttle and Displacer rotated closer to the edge of Solyanna.

"I'm not detecting any activity," Latitia said.

Far in the distance a cluster of rocks pulled away from the stricken moon. They moved faster and faster away from their source of origin, drawn by gravity toward the planet that lay beyond the moon's horizon. Even after all these years, tons of debris from Solyanna rained down on the planet each day.

"Still nothing," Latitia said. "Time to move."

Latitia activated the shuttle's gravity hook and drew the Type 2 Displacer out of her centuries' old orbit. She began the motion with a light thrust before increasing it. The engines were strained, but the ship managed to counter the Displacer's orbit, pulling her back.

"A little more," Latitia said.

Warning lights flashed. The Displacer was very old and very large, capable of fitting battleships through her energy door. As sophisticated and state of the art as the Merrick shuttle's engines were, she could barely move her.

"Come on."

Warning lights flashed. B'taav felt the floor vibrate.

"A little more," Latitia said.

"Latitia," B'taav said.

Latitia didn't respond. She kept the engines going.

"Latitia!" B'taav repeated.

The Independent reached out. Latitia grabbed his arm. She held it very tight.

"I know what I'm doing," she muttered.

She pressed several buttons. The ship powered down.

They looked through the front view screen. The Displacer was parked beside a large chunk of rock. It was effectively hidden from sight.

Latitia read the engine displays and nodded.

"We're good," she said.

B'taav rubbed his hand.

"You've got quite a grip," he said.

"Pays to exercise."

"Why move the Type 2?"

"A precaution," Latitia said. "If we're discovered, the people who set up shop on Pomos will know we didn't use the Type 6 Displacer to get here. It won't take them long to realize we used the Type 2 and go after it. If they get to it before we do, we're trapped."

"What if someone notices it isn't in its regular orbit?"

"Even in Pomos' golden age the Type 2 was a forgotten relic. I'm betting she remains just as forgotten today."

Latitia entered a series of commands. A small device, no larger than a shoe box, emerged from the front of the spacecraft. It floated toward the Displacer and attached to its side.

"When we're ready to go, that box will activate the Displacer," she said.

Latitia shut off the gravity hook and pulled the shuttle away. The Merrick craft dodged debris while circling Solyanna. Over the horizon came a cascade of light. Pomos emerged over the moon's horizon.

The planet lay before them and so very far away. Light from the sun gave her a radiant glow and revealed a dark, ravaged world.

"By the Gods," B'taav said.

Even from this distance it was obvious the planet was an ecological disaster. Heavy black clouds hovered over her inky black surface. Despite the nuclear winter resulting from the bombings, there was little evidence of snow. Pockets of what appeared to be volcanic activity were visible. They were more likely toxic radioactive pools.

Latitia shut the shuttle's engines and allowed the craft to float among a group of asteroids. Together they fell toward the planet.

A low buzz startled them. Latitia immediately checked the monitor's readout.

"I'm detecting sensor signals."

The sensor readings grew stronger and stronger before abruptly fading.

"They're running a loop," Latitia said. "Five minutes in, five out."

Latitia powered up the gravity hooks and grabbed several asteroids around the ship. She drew them in closer to their ship.

"Next downtime, we're going in."

Latitia angled the shuttle's nose until it faced the planet.

"Coming up on five minutes," B'taav said. "Three, two..."

Latitia activated the shuttle's thrusters the moment the sensor signals were gone. She moved the shuttle and her asteroid cover directly at Pomos.

"Damn!" Latitia muttered.

"What?"

"These sensor scans are military grade," she said. "They don't just detect movement, they see electronic signatures."

Latitia shut down the shuttle's thrust and almost every computer before her.

"Get into your spacesuit," she said. "Quickly!"

B'taav and Latitia unbuckled their seatbelts. Latitia opened a cabinet at the rear of the cockpit. Within were a pair of spacesuits. Latitia had hers on before B'taav. She helped him into his and locked his helmet down.

"Sensors coming on!"

Latitia ran back to her seat. She shut the ship's remaining electronics off, including life support. In seconds they felt the frigid bite of outer space.

"Keep the suit's power low," Latitia said.

B'taav adjusted the settings and returned to his chair.

Because the ship's electronics were shut off, they had no way of knowing if they were spotted.

"Hopefully, the electronic signatures from these suits aren't enough to trip their sensors," Latitia said.

"What if the sensors extend all the way to the ground?" B'taav said. "You can't glide the shuttle to a landing. We'll have to power up at some point."

Latitia nodded.

"Better put on your seatbelts."

They spent the next half hour in the void between Solyanna and Pomos, slowly dropping toward the larger object. Without electronics, they could do little but look out their front window.

"We'll be entering Pomos in the next few minutes," Latitia said.

Before them another large group of rocks hit the planet's atmosphere. They glowed red and let off dust and smoke. Latitia looked away from them and at her helmet's internal readout.

"The sensor signals are fading," she said. "With so many rocks dropping into Pomos, there's no way to track them all. I'm guessing whoever's down there focuses on the rocks that may pose a risk to whatever they're doing."

The meteor shower they were a part of dropped down and down, closer and closer to Pomos' toxic atmosphere.

"Here we go," Latitia said.

They entered the atmosphere in silence, the only realization of this fact being a low rumble. Several of the asteroids around them tore away. Reddish flames streaked across their bodies as well as the shuttle's heat shields.

Latitia gripped the ship's controls.

"I was serious about not gliding all the way down," B'taav said.

The ship's power remained off and, without thrusters, Latitia fought to keep the ship stable. It turned, threatening to spin around.

"I'm reactivating," she said.

She pressed a series of buttons and many of the cockpit's panels came to life.

"Anything?"

Latitia held her breath. Her eyes were on the readouts.

"No sensors," she said.

Flames formed a bloody arc across the shuttle's body. The freshly activated instruments indicated heavy levels of radiation. The ship shook as thrusters leveled her entry. Flames licked the heat shields, for a while blinding their view of what lay before them.

Once the flames cleared, they made out mountains and streams. Pomos' surface on the southern hemisphere was hideously charred and looked barren of any life. The already high level radiation readings spiked. The shuttle passed over a heavily bombarded area. Craters as large as continents rolled by.

Still they dropped, closer and closer to the planet's surface.

"Looks like we made—"

A siren howled over their spacesuit speakers. One of the monitors turned red.

"Something's over us," Latitia muttered. "She's too small to be a shuttle."

"She has to be a missile or a drone," B'taav said. "She's just below the edge of Pomos' atmosphere."

The drone cruised above the rocky meteor shower and released sensor scans.

"Motion detectors only," Latitia said, relieved.

The ground was rushing towards them. They were fifty miles above the surface. Forty five.

"Does it see us?"

"Hard to tell," B'taav said. "It's maintaining course."

Thirty five.

B'taav could make out hills and small valleys and the gleam of metal. They were over a melted city.

"We need to use our thrusters," B'taav said. "We need to slow down!"

"We use them and that drone's sensors will detect our movement."

Thirty.

They saw the remains of a large river. Fetid water gleamed in the sunshine.

Twenty.

B'taav held his breath. The surveillance drone moved away from them and followed another mass of Solyanna rock.

Ten.

The remains of petrified tree trunks stood up like burnt toothpicks. A highway lay in pieces. The drone continued its steady movement.

Five.

The drone moved farther still. It was nearly out of range. Nearly...

One.

"Shit," Latitia yelled. "Hang on!"

There was no more margin for error. Latitia activated the ship's thrusters and grasped the yoke. The shuttle screamed against the pull of gravity and fought the speed of their drop. Latitia leveled the ship just feet from destruction while clipping the petrified trees.

The danger was far from over.

The asteroids they traveled with slammed against the surface of Pomos and sent thick clouds of dust into the air. It proved a mixed blessing. Whatever was above them couldn't see them through that dust. Latitia, however, couldn't see where she was flying.

Sparks flew from the ship's instrument panel as the shock waves from the asteroids' collisions buffeted her. The passengers were rocked back and forth.

They flew in this heavy dust for several agonizing seconds, not knowing if they were about to fly into a rocky outcrop or jagged city remains.

Latitia applied the air brakes. Their forward momentum was great, and it would take a good distance to slow.

The dust clouds abruptly cleared and before them were the remains of a city. Towers still hung in the air, their frames bent away and melted like ice cream on a summer day. Another cloud from another fallen asteroid enveloped them.

Latitia activated the shuttle's secondary brakes and the howls of deceleration reverberated throughout the craft. The view screen was covered in dust and filth. More asteroids fell around them, a second wave of deadly projectiles easily capable of destroying their ship. They heard the groans of the brakes and the smash of debris large and small slamming against their craft's outer hull.

B'taav grasped the sides of his chair even as the seatbelt pressed back.

The shuttle slowed but the city's remains grew larger and larger.

"We're not going to make it," Latitia said.

The chaos around them was too much for the small craft to bear.

Latitia pulled at the yoke and the shuttle banked to the right, barely avoiding the remains of a building. The right wing clipped it as it passed.

Latitia let out a hopeless grunt as the shuttle flopped down. Its belly hit the ground hard.

Latitia pressed several buttons in vain, trying to regain control over the stricken craft. It was too late. The ship continued its skid, smashing through thick brick walls and metal. Within the ship things fell apart. One of the monitors burst while a second went dark. Electric crackles and pops erupted and steam hissed from ruptured hoses.

Slowly, ever so slowly, the ship slowed until it stopped. All was quiet.

B'taav's eye's fluttered open. Blood dripped from his nose and his breathing was ragged. His entire body ached. Beside him Latitia stirred.

"That... that went well," she muttered. She looked at B'taav. "You look like I feel."

Latitia struggled with the seatbelt before releasing herself. She examined the remaining monitors.

B'taav also freed himself from his seat. He looked outside. In the far distance more asteroids rained down on the planet and sent plumes of dust into the air. The rock swarm was spent and the drone far up in the sky continued her journey. Sensor bursts reappeared now and again, their signal weaker and weaker with each passing second. There was no sign of other crafts coming to take its place.

"We avoided detection," Latitia said. "Let's see at what cost."

Latitia checked the ship's readouts. She shook her head.

"Ship's badly damaged," Latitia said. "Hard to believe we're still in one piece."

Latitia fiddled with the controls but her attention was quickly drawn away by a flicker of light coming from outside.

"B'taav?" she whispered. "Do you see this?"

B'taav followed her stare. In the very far distance, he saw an enormous structure. It was like a square tank, dull gray metal and rusted and self-contained and far, *far* larger than most cities. Through its center rose two thick, clear tubes, likely constructed with a heavy duty tinsel glass. The tubes extended from the center of the object and stretched up into the sky, disappearing beyond the thick black clouds.

"Is that what I think it is?" B'taav said.

"Yeah," Latitia said. "A Space Elevator. That's where the energy readings are coming from. They –whoever they are– built a Godsdamned Space Elevator!"

29

The Xendos' cameras followed the progress of the *Cygnusa* and her fighter craft as they approached. Inquisitor Cer carefully moved the ship back, drawing deeper into the asteroid field. On at least three occasions her cover was very small and she felt lucky she wasn't discovered.

If this was a fleet exercise, I'd have a few of their heads.

It was only a matter of time before the *Xendos* was found and Inquisitor Cer had to do something. Quickly.

The hour before she put on her helmet and depressurized the cockpit. She exited the area and for the first time in a long while walked the stricken ship's corridors. She grabbed whatever loose debris she could carry and loaded it, along with the corpses of the Overlord and his two personal Inquisitors, into the decompression chamber.

It'll have to do.

It was a very old trick, jettisoning debris in the hopes that your pursuers would think your craft was destroyed. Cer prayed the three corpses would sell the deception, if only to allow her enough time to escape.

Inquisitor Cer then took all but one of the ship's fusion guns and broke them apart. She used rope and tape to tie the weapons' energy packets, spare oxygen canisters, corpses, and debris together. When she was satisfied with her work, she closed the inner decompression chamber door and opened the outer one.

In the weightless conditions she easily shoved the tied up mass out of the *Xendos* and used her suit's thrusters to move it closer to the asteroid the *Xendos* was hiding behind.

She placed the corpses and debris in position and examined the fusion energy cores. They were wrapped tight against the oxygen canisters. Inquisitor Cer produced a simple timer and connected it to one of those energy cores. The timer was set for an hour. It would allow Cer enough time to get the *Xendos* away before the core slid open and ruptured the other energy cores and oxygen canisters.

The result would be more light than explosion, with debris and corpses flying in all directions and providing the *Cygnusa* and her fighter craft plenty of moving parts to engage their attention.

"Hurry."

Inquisitor Cer froze. A man had whispered the word in her ear. She turned around, bewildered.

There was no one near her.

She checked her radio system. It was the same primitive, limited range equipment used on the *Argus*. If someone spoke through it, he had to be close. Close enough to see.

Am I dreaming this? she wondered.

Inquisitor Cer shook her head. She spotted a flash of light several hundred miles away.

"Whoever you are, you're right," she said.

Inquisitor Cer returned to the *Xendos* and ran to the cockpit. She slowly moved the ship away from the asteroid, corpses, and debris.

She knew the other crafts in the area had their sensors on full and, should the *Xendos* stray even a little from the cover of the asteroids, it would be found.

Using her ship's cameras as guides, Inquisitor Cer retreated further and further into the sparsely filled asteroid field. She cleared several miles, inching her way and retreating deeper into the field. Even at its relatively slow speed, the *Xendos* was certain to make good distance before the energy cores detonated.

Inquisitor Cer eased the ship's thrust and parked the ancient craft beside the largest rock she could find. She looked at the timer on the central monitor before her.

Three minutes.

She eased back in her seat.

Her very survival depended on what happened next.

30

Latitia spent nearly an hour going over the shuttle. She walked in and out of the cockpit several times, her movements slowed by her space suit.

B'taav was eager to help but was limited by his waning strength. He used the shuttle's outward cameras to get as close a look at the Space Elevator as possible.

Even from this distance, it proved an impressive sight.

He witnessed long, train-like machines rise from the Space Elevator's concrete base and shoot up through the tinsel glass tube before disappearing into the clouds. Moments later, another near identical machine dropped from above, its destination the concrete base.

As sophisticated as it was, the Space Elevator appeared to operate as a simple counterweight elevator. One side rose while the other dropped. B'taav showed this to Latitia.

"There has to be a space station in geosynchronous orbit above the base," Latitia said. "It's where the trains go."

"Given their size, they were designed to move tons of material from the surface up."

"The planet is –*was*– rich in minerals," Latitia said. "But it's been irradiated. It's worthless."

B'taav thought about that.

"Doesn't make sense to create a structure like this and haul contaminated product," B'taav said. "But what else could the train take?"

"Nothing," Latitia said.

B'taav thought some more.

"You think the people behind the elevator discovered a way of cleaning the radioactivity out of the ore?"

Latitia leaned in close to the monitor and stared hard at the camera's images.

"That'd be quite a breakthrough," she said. She was silent for a while before nodding. "Very clever."

There was a noticeable trace of fear in her voice.

"That means something to you?" B'taav asked.

"No, nothing," Latitia said, unconvincingly. She pressed a series of buttons and the shuttle's engine revved. "This will take a moment."

Outside, plumes of dust rose from beneath their vehicle. Despite this, the ship's turbines emitted a sickly sound. Latitia kept revving them. In between bursts, she pulled a memory chip from the paneling before her.

"Take this," she said while handing the chip to B'taav. "In case we separate and you need to get the hell out of here, this will activate the Type 2."

"I'm not leaving alone," B'taav said.

Latitia smiled.

"I don't expect you to."

B'taav took the chip and placed it in his space suit's side pouch while Latitia's attention returned to the engines.

"All right," she said. "Let's give this a try."

Latitia pressed a series of buttons. The shuttle rocked to the side and rose in the air. Several lights screamed bloody warnings. Latitia tried to keep the shuttle in the air.

"Come on!" she yelled.

The ship lifted only a few feet into the air. The engines rattled and coughed. They were dying. Latitia swore and set the shuttle back down.

"That's that," she said.

She shut the engines off.

Dusk settled on Pomos and the light of her faint sun disappeared in the northeast just as Solyanna appeared in the south. From the surface of Pomos, the moon looked like a rotted apple.

B'taav and Latitia exited the cockpit and walked to the shuttle's lower deck, passing the engine room and reaching the end of the lower corridor. There, they opened the door to the rear compartment. Parked within was an all-terrain four-seat Rover. Latitia examined the vehicle to make sure it suffered no damage during the hard landing. She inspected its oversized tires and spongy shocks before moving to its engine.

"We've got approximately one hundred and fifty miles of terrain to cross," Latitia said. "This is going to be a long, slow, and very uncomfortable trip. Hope you're up to it."

"What about the drones?"

"The Rover has electronic dampeners. It'll be hard for sensors to detect her from orbit."

"What if a drone goes suborbital? What if the space elevator's base is surrounded with security measures? There could be mine fields or fusion cannons or—"

"We're going to have to bet on those things not being there," Latitia said.

"Quite the bet," B'taav said. "I'm afraid my credit's limited."

"So's mine," Latitia replied. "Well, you know what they say, spend what you've got. There might not be another day."

B'taav helped Latitia free the vehicle from its magnetic moorings before loading up on supplies. Once done, they sealed and decompressed the interior of the chamber.

"Ready?" Latitia asked.

"Whenever you are."

Latitia climbed into the driver's seat and B'taav sat beside her. Once their seatbelts were on, she started the Rover. The sound of her engine was low, bordering on imperceptible.

B'taav examined the screen on the panel before him.

"Winds are fifteen knots," B'taav said. "Not too bad. At least compared to the radiation."

"Provided all goes reasonably well, it'll take us maybe three hours to reach the elevator's base," Latitia said.

She pressed a button before her and the shuttle's rear compartment door lowered. Dusty winds whipped up from outside.

Latitia put the Rover in drive and pressed the accelerator. They drove onto the surface of Pomos.

The first half-hour of the ride was made in silence.

Latitia kept the Rover's forward lights low and avoided the most hostile terrain. Plasma blasts from years before left much of the surface before them remarkably smooth. The limited sensors on the Rover gave them an idea of their route and allowed them to avoid the largest obstacles.

While Latitia drove B'taav tried to rest. He couldn't. A sudden, troubling thought occurred to him.

"Is the infection I have similar to what ravaged Pomos?"

"You're showing no signs of aggression."

B'taav's eyes were on Latitia.

"You didn't answer the question."

Latitia drew a breath.

"It's possible."

"A different strain?"

"As I said, it's possible."

"What exactly happened here? Saint Vulcan had a state of the art security system. How did the virus get loose?"

"It didn't get loose. It was brought in."

"On purpose?" B'taav said, incredulous.

"Ships and personnel coming into Pomos were screened with passive and active scanners. Anyone that had so much as a simple cold was flagged."

"Then how exactly was it brought in?"

"Piece by piece," Latitia said. "The virus wasn't biological. It was mechanical... and microscopic."

"Nano-technology?" B'taav said.

"Yeah," Latitia said. "Nano-probes have a variety of uses, from exploration to construction to medicine to... you name it. Every large corporation in Epsillon has money invested in their research and development. Some have made more progress than others but none made as much progress, even in the two hundred and fifty years since Pomos' destruction, than Saint Vulcan. That was her big secret. All her factories and research were built on a nano-tech foundation. Turned out she wasn't the only one researching it."

Latitia paused before continuing.

"Our best guess is the virus was broken down into as many as a thousand individual pieces and smuggled into Pomos by merchant crafts over a period of years. Saint Vulcan's scanners, as good as they were, didn't see the danger in those components. When the pieces were here and assembled, the resulting single, very potent nano-probe was released. It multiplied. Quickly. In a single day it infected most of the planet's Southern Hemisphere."

B'taav pointed to the Space Elevator.

"You think the people behind the virus are also behind this?"

Latitia shrugged.

"Whoever built that is not some low level squatter. This kind of tech requires intellect, almost limitless funds, and an incredible amount of personnel. It's the type of thing Saint Vulcan might do."

"Or her enemy."

B'taav stared up at the moon.

"The nano-probe infection was confined to Pomos," he said. "Why did Saint Vulcan have the fleet take out Solyanna?"

"I don't know," Latitia said.

"She had control over her ships and their weapons," B'taav said. "As far as I can tell, Solyanna wasn't exposed to the virus. Why open fire on her?"

A heavy silence hung in the cabin for several seconds. B'taav pulled up records of Pomos' destruction and skimmed through them. He found the information he was searching for. His face grew pale.

"What is it?" Latitia said.

"The last missiles targeted at Pomos fell thirty five seconds before the order came in to destroy Solyanna," B'taav said. "Either Saint Vulcan survived Pomos' bombing and *then* sent the order to bomb Solyanna or—"

"That's impossible," Latitia said.

She looked over B'taav's shoulder at the data displayed on his screen. She read it. It was all there.

"By the Gods," Latitia said.

"Saint Vulcan wasn't on Pomos," B'taav said. "She had Solyanna destroyed after the fact. Why?"

"Maybe..." Latitia began and stopped. "Maybe she was covering her tracks."

"Saint Vulcan survived the bombings," B'taav said. He stared directly into Latitia's eyes. "Didn't she?"

31

She lay at the top of the asteroid, her body pressed into the shadows of a narrow crevasse. She used the magnification in her space suit's helmet to find the *Cygnusa*.

The ship and a cloud of fighter craft were heading in her general direction.

Inquisitor Cer turned. The *Xendos* was below her and parked against the asteroid she lay on. It too was hidden in deep shadow.

Inquisitor Cer checked her watch. There were only a few seconds left. She looked up, in the opposite direction of the *Cygnusa*, and at another cluster of asteroids.

Ten seconds...

She couldn't see the debris she left behind it.

Five seconds...

She adjusted her magnification.

Three seconds...

She had a clear view of the rocks and the general area that—

Detonation.

The explosion was a momentary, noiseless burst of light. Debris spread out and flew in all directions.

Inquisitor Cer spun around and gazed at the *Cygnusa*. At first the large craft and her fighters didn't appear to notice the detonation. Then, one of the fighter craft broke formation. It was followed by another. And another.

Inquisitor Cer got to her feet and, using her suit's thrusters, floated to the *Xendos'* decompression chamber door. She entered the craft and closed the outer door before quickly making her way to the cockpit. She checked her monitors.

The *Cygnusa* and most of her fighter craft altered their courses and were moving exactly where she wanted them to go: The source of the explosion.

A small group of fighters circled the area while others kept a wary distance. Magnetic hooks picked up stray pieces of debris. The *Cygnusa* was the last of the vessels to arrive. She parked beyond the outer wave of fighter craft.

Minutes passed. The intensity of the fighter crafts' search bordered on zeal.

"Come on," Inquisitor Cer muttered.

She hoped the smaller ships would congregate in a tighter area before beginning their outward search. The tighter their formation, the larger the window of opportunity to slip past them and to the Longshore Shipping Lanes.

"Come on," she repeated.

The proximity of the fighter crafts to each other allowed the *Xendos'* communication system to overcome the jamming devices and snatch garbled transmissions.

"We...ound bodies," an unidentified woman said.

"How ma...?"

"Two," the woman replied.

A long period of silence followed. The fighter craft slowed to a crawl.

"...ird body foun..."

"All units...in," a rough voice replied. Inquisitor Cer recognized it as Inquisitor Raven's. "...and by."

Inquisitor Raven's attention was on the central view screen. Beside the real time footage of his fighter craft exploring the area were fresh pictures of the recovered body fragments.

"Inquisitor Raven?"

Lieutenant Sanders stood at his side. She offered him a small computer tablet.

"I have the early DNA results," she said.

Inquisitor Raven took the computer tablet and looked over the information.

"Overlord Octo," he muttered. "Inquisitor Deveri."

The tablet let out a beep. Inquisitor Raven refreshed the data.

"Inquisitor Loalla."

Inquisitor Raven waited for the arrival of more information. It came.

"We have five hundred pounds of debris and three bodies," Inquisitor Raven read. "Amount of debris, considering the size of the *Xendos*, is minimal."

"Yes sir," the Lieutenant said.

"The only passenger unaccounted for is Inquisitor Cer."

"I'm sure we'll find her remains in—"

"I doubt it," Inquisitor Raven said and handed her the tablet. "Think, Lieutenant. We find an almost insignificant quantity of ship debris yet the remains of not one, not two, but three of her four passengers. You don't find that remarkable?"

"Sir?"

"The debris and bodies were left for our benefit," Inquisitor Raven said. "We were meant to assume, just as you did, that the last body was somewhere nearby. Based on that assumption, the *Xendos'* sole survivor hoped we would devote our resources to a detailed examination of this area. We were expected to form a tight little circle, tight enough to allow Inquisitor Cer space to escape."

The Lieutenant thought about that.

"Clever," she said.

"Inquisitor Cer was a student of mine for a few months at the end of her sophomore year of training. She was a handful and it took me some time to break her."

A frosty smile appeared on Inquisitor Raven's face.

"To this day, I don't know if I ever did break her all the way."

The smile disappeared.

"We're going to give our missing Inquisitor exactly what she wants. Have all Alpha through Pollox fighter craft converge on this area and continue their search for her remains."

"Sir? If she's waiting for us to—"

"While those fighter groups search, all Sigma craft are to circle around the port side of the *Cygnusa* and use her for cover while they make their way to the Longshore Shipping Lanes. They are to go dark and wait for any craft attempting to make its way out of the Norman Asteroid field. When Inquisitor Cer moves, and she will, they are to close in and intercept. Understood?"

"Yes sir."

Inquisitor Raven nodded.

"We'll have Inquisitor Cer in our hands before the day is over, Lieutenant."

Just like that, the window of opportunity Inquisitor Cer hoped for appeared.

The *Cygnusa* drew in closer to the source of the explosion while the majority of her fighter craft followed their mother ship.

Inquisitor Cer reached for the *Xendos'* controls. She made one last check of her surroundings. There were no ships between her and the Longshore Shipping Lanes. She plotted a course. When the last of the fighter crafts edged away, her path was clear.

She applied thrust and sat back, elated at the prospect of escape.

The *Xendos* didn't move.

Inquisitor Raven impatiently paced the bridge of the *Cygnusa*. He stopped.

"Update?"

"Our status remains unchanged," Lieutenant Sanders said.

"How long has it been?"

"Two hours."

"Has any more debris been found?"

"No sir. It appears we got it all."

Inquisitor Raven pursed his lips.

"Permission to speak, sir?" Lieutenant Sanders said.

"Granted."

"Sir, I agree with your initial assessment. Inquisitor Cer is alive and in hiding and it greatly shames me to admit that if I was commander of the *Cygnusa*, the *Xendos* would have slipped away just as Inquisitor Cer intended. However, given the amount of time now passed, if she is as near as we suspect she will surely have realized we've finished searching this area and are now waiting for her to move."

Inquisitor Raven nodded.

"Call back all fighter craft," he said.

Inquisitor Cer couldn't understand it.

The *Xendos'* engines were running better than before the explosion yet the craft would not move. She desperately tried all means of getting her to go and take advantage of the opportunity to escape, yet the craft remained in place in the shadow of the asteroid.

She wasted over an hour of precious time in the engine room before giving up and returning to the cockpit. There, she checked the cockpit controls, desperately searching for the reason they were locked up.

She soon realized the *Cygnusa* and her fighter craft also remained in place. They did so for far too long.

"Clever," she said.

She trained her ship's cameras on the Longshore Space Lanes. She couldn't see any fighter craft waiting in ambush, but she was certain they were there.

Both sides were frozen in place, waiting for the other to move.

Then, two hours after her window of opportunity first opened, the *Cygnusa* turned while her fighter craft spread out. Beyond them and in the distance, a series of lights came on. At least three dozen fighter craft hiding in darkness along the Longshore Shipping Lanes made their presence known.

"By the Gods," Inquisitor Cer muttered.

Had she tried to flee...

Inquisitor Cer cycled through the cameras. The *Cygnusa* completed her turn and Inquisitor Cer's blood ran cold. The ship was now heading at the *Xendos*.

Have they found me?

No. The asteroid she hid behind still covered her.

For now.

The fighter craft continued spreading out. Her communication equipment, silent for so very long, came to life and a crystal clear message was transmitted from the battleship.

"Inquisitor Cer, this is Inquisitor Raven on the *Cygnusa*. It is time to give yourself up."

A great loathing bubbled up from deep within Inquisitor Cer's soul and she had to force herself not to respond to the message.

"You won't get your hands on me again," she swore.

As she did, a deep chill passed through her body.

Even if she had to take her own life, she wouldn't let Raven near her ever –*ever*– again.

Inquisitor Raven shut the communications off.

He waited for a reply from Inquisitor Cer but didn't expect one.

You were quite the fighter, Inquisitor Raven thought.

After a few minutes, he walked to the center of the bridge and cleared his throat. All bridge personnel's eyes were on him.

"Inquisitor Cer chooses the cowardly path," he said. "As it is written in the Holy Texts, '*those who hide have something to hide from*'. Overlord Octo is dead and so too are his security personnel. Inquisitor Cer shows her guilt by her actions. It is past time she faces judgment."

Inquisitor Cer did not bother with the ship's engines. She did not bother with anything.

Even if she could get the *Xendos* moving, she was surrounded and there was no longer any possibility of escape.

She cradled her sole remaining fusion gun. Gently. Then tight.

On the monitors, the fighter craft circled her area and beyond. They were a mass of wasps. The *Xendos* floated closer to the asteroid. Its rear scrapped against hard granite.

How much longer?

She closed her eyes. The fusion gun felt so very heavy...

When she opened her eyes, she gasped.

An incredibly large shadow, the *Cygnusa's*, settled over the *Xendos*. Her ship's upper cameras captured the battleship as it flew directly over the asteroid she hid behind.

"The Gods have mercy on my soul," she muttered. The grip on the gun tightened even more.

The *Cygnusa* was directly over her. Hundreds of lighted windows, heavy fusion cannons, and torpedo bays sailed over her. She saw fighter craft launch from the ship's lower bay, thrusters firing in a kaleidoscope of colors and trailing off into the distance. Other fighters floated in, disappearing into the mighty vessel's many landing bays.

Then, bright flood lights stabbed through the darkness and swirled around her.

The lights from the *Cygnusa* settled on the asteroids. Every one of the shadowy crevasses were exposed. The lights moved from one asteroid to another.

Toward her.

Inquisitor Cer looked down at the handgun.

Just a little pull and it's over. A little—

Inquisitor Cer released the trigger. She angrily tossed the gun aside.

"No," she yelled.

I won't give that bastard the satisfaction.

Inquisitor Cer reached for the ship's controls.

"You want me, Inquisitor Raven?" she yelled. "You won't get me without a fight."

Inquisitor Cer's fingers pressed several buttons. Perhaps there was something she missed. Perhaps she could get the ship to respond. Perhaps…

It was a hopeless exercise.

Even if she could move, the many eyes surrounding her would easily spot her.

If she could move.

Defeated, Inquisitor Cer fell back into her chair.

She was a cornered animal with nowhere left to go.

Lights from the *Cygnusa* moved toward the asteroid she hid behind. In seconds, they would light her up and expose the *Xendos* to the entire fleet.

She whispered one last prayer.

As she finished, the lights of the *Cygnusa* blazed through the *Xendos'* cockpit.

32

"I don't know if she survived," Latitia said.

"But you have some idea."

"We do," Latitia admitted.

B'taav's eyes narrowed.

"Who do you work for? Which Corporation?"

"Our group is a little beyond that," Latitia said. There was a finality to her non-answer.

B'taav leaned back in his chair. He felt winded, helpless. Frustrated. Perhaps sensing this, Latitia said:

"It's complicated. Very complicated. We'll talk after the mission. I promise. In the meantime, let's focus on that structure and who's behind it."

"At least tell me why it's so damn important we do this."

Latitia nodded.

"Whoever is behind it might be a threat."

"Not to any Corporation?"

"No," Latitia said. "To humanity itself."

B'taav thought about it.

"Looks like I don't have much choice," B'taav said.

The Rover climbed a small hill and from there her passengers had their clearest view yet of the extended base of the Space Elevator. Beyond it and spread out for many miles were an army of enormous machines. They moved slowly, either breaking up, shoveling, or loading dirt and rocks. A group of machines close to them carried enormous drills that tore into the muddy, radioactive ground and dragged tons of material to the surface. This material was then deposited onto the backs of huge haulers that, once filled, drove back to the Space Elevator's base. Other stationary machines were set up in a grid around the many miles of excavation overlooking the site. B'taav recognized these machines as powerful surface to air defensive systems capable of taking down any threat coming in from above.

"This is… incredible," B'taav said.

The scale of the enterprise was beyond anything he had seen before. Latitia drove on, nearing a series of enormous, gaping holes in the planet's surface. The holes extended down for hundreds of meters. Wide circular tracks lined the edges. It was the means by which machinery entered and exited the abyss.

"There's no way to get to the Space Elevator's base without being seen," B'taav said.

"We have no choice," Latitia said.

She moved the Rover forward. After a few minutes, they were in the dig site. Latitia darted in an around the machines and avoided their gaping mauls while moving closer to the Space Elevator's base. At first the machines ignored the insignificantly small Rover.

All of a sudden and in unison, they stopped and strong lights coming from them lit up the Rover.

Latitia applied the brakes and stopped. The Independents held their breaths as several long, tense seconds passed.

Abruptly, several of the more distant machines reactivated and continued their work. A line of machines stretching out to the Space Elevator base, however, remained frozen. The lights mounted on them swiveled and formed an illuminated path from the Rover to the Space Elevator.

"They're inviting us in," B'taav said. "Maybe you had it all wrong. Maybe they're friendly."

"I wouldn't count on it," Latitia said.

The Rover made good time approaching the Space Elevator.

The well-lit terrain before them was smooth and allowed Latitia to keep up a steady speed, cutting down their journey by hours. Latitia and B'taav gazed at the area around them, amazed by the scope of industry.

What at first looked like standard digging and hauling machines were, on closer examination, a variety of models. The two largest machines hauled and broke up the terrain. A smaller machine surveyed land and took samples. A fourth variety, much smaller than any of the others, swirled around its bigger brothers and was dedicated to cleaning the larger vehicles' treads or welding and fixing damaged parts.

Through their journey, B'taav and Latitia didn't see a single person in or around any of the vehicles. For that matter, none of the machines had visible crew compartments or windows.

"They're automated," B'taav said. "Every one of them."

As they moved forward, every light they passed turned off, leaving inky darkness behind them.

"Take a look at this," Latitia said.

B'taav checked the Rover's external readout monitors.

"Radiation levels are dropping," Latitia said. "You were right. Whoever is behind this discovered a way to clean the radiation from the soil. At the rate its dropping, by the time we get to the Space Elevator's base there might not be any at all."

An hour later, they neared the end of the path and the Space Elevator's ground base.

"Incredible," Latitia said.

There was no other way to describe it. The base dwarfed the largest cities in the Epsillon Empire.

The light path they followed was down to a single spot. Latitia slowed and stopped.

"I'm detecting very minor levels of radiation," Latitia said. "Even on the Rover."

Latitia shut the engine off.

"Now what?" B'taav asked.

"Let's go outside."

"Do you have any weapons?"

"Only a couple of fusion handguns," Latitia said. "I doubt they'll be much help."

Latitia stepped to the Rover's rear entrance. B'taav and she put on their helmets. When their space suits pressurized, she opened the vehicle's rear hatch. A stiff breeze blew inside the vehicle. Other than that breeze, nothing else moved.

B'taav and Latitia walked onto the illuminated circle. Muddy dirt surrounded them.

"We're being checked out, I imagine," Latitia said.

Some two hundred feet away was the Space Elevator's base. Its gray walls rose up and up, disappearing into the sky.

The Independents remained in place for several minutes, unsure of what to do. No one came to greet them, nor was any attempt made to communicate.

B'taav noted a small protrusion in the muddy ground a dozen feet away. He walked to it.

"B'taav? It might not be wise..."

B'taav crouched next to the protrusion and wiped sludge from its top. The protrusion proved to be a heavy metal grill.

There were many more such grills in the ground and at regular distances. A sudden rush of air blew out from it, sending sludge in all directions.

"It's some kind of exhaust vent," B'taav said.

Latitia pulled an electronic screwdriver from her space suit belt. She detached the grill from the vent.

"Give me a hand," Latitia said.

Together, they lifted the grill and set it aside. They then illuminated the area below. The vent dropped some six feet before taking a ninety degree turn toward the Space Elevator's base.

"This may get us in," B'taav said.

Latitia noted the bones of a small rodent at the bottom of the shaft.

"If we go this way, let's hope we have better luck than the rat—"

Latitia stopped talking. A shape high in the air caught her attention. It was dark, barely visible, and moved toward the Independents at incredible speeds. It took two sharp, near impossible turns. A human pilot would have been squashed by the maneuvers.

"It's a drone!" Latitia said.

The object hurled at them and there was little the Independents could do. If the drone was a missile, they were finished.

Latitia grabbed B'taav's hand.

"Steady," she said.

The black object gained even more speed.

Latitia and B'taav took a step back. The object continued its drop, falling with greater and greater speed.

"Run!" Latitia yelled.

They did, moving away from the Rover. They fell to the ground as a burst of energy slammed into their vehicle. The Rover erupted into a ball of flame.

"Are you OK?" Latitia yelled.

"Yes," B'taav replied. He got to his feet and helped Latitia up. "You?"

"I've been better."

They looked up but could no longer see their attacker. Their Rover was in pieces.

A loud clang came from their right and the Independents spun around.

A large concrete panel slid away from the side of the Space Elevator's platform and revealed an equally large opening. A dozen figures stood just inside the granite-like walls. Their bodies were thin, muscular, and, from a distance, almost looked human. None of them had faces. Instead, they bore a dark, shining ceramic surface without eyes, ears, nose, or a mouth. The figures did not wear spacesuits. In the harsh light, their skin was equal parts grey and dark blue. Their hands had no fingers, instead merging into what appeared to be an equally amorphous rifle. The weapons were aimed at the Independents.

"Robots?" B'taav said.

The figures motioned B'taav and Latitia into the Space Elevator's platform.

There was little either of them could do but oblige.

33

The sliding doors separating Latitia and B'taav from Pomos' surface slid shut with a loud clang. They locked. The Independents were trapped inside the Space Elevator's platform.

According to the readings in the Independents' space suits, the structure's interior had traces of breathable air but the temperature was fifty degrees below freezing. It was also free of radiation.

The dozen metallic figures circled the Independents. Their formless faces turned on them. When they moved, they did so with remarkable precision. No motion was wasted and once stopped they were as still as statues.

As magnificent as the robots were, they projected a frightening power. B'taav sensed they could outrun or outmuscle any living being and snap them into pieces without much effort.

After a few seconds and, as if bored with their guests, most of the robots walked away. Three robots remained. Two stood behind B'taav and Latitia and the third faced them.

That robot stepped up to the Independents. A mouth appeared on its blank face. It spoke.

"Follow me."

The voice was pleasant, even polite. There was no mistaking it for anything other than a command.

B'taav and Latitia walked behind the figure while the other two robots followed. They moved through a dark corridor and up a flight of metal stairs.

They passed through chambers flooded with bursts of compressed air. The readings within their space suit confirmed that with each burst, whatever lingering radioactivity left on their space suits was scrubbed away.

After passing two such chambers, they walked through a set of increasingly larger rooms filled with lifts, pulleys, and trains.

"We're following their freight," B'taav said.

Cargo trains took the raw ore and dumped it into a series of processors. They moved from crushers to sorters. In time the ore was cleaned and separated. The purified product was then loaded onto smaller trains.

"I have yet to see a single person."

"I'm guessing we won't," Latitia said.

"You think this whole place is automated? There has to be some kind of human supervision, right?"

"Why?"

They walked some more, eventually arriving at a central station. The smaller trains dumped their refined loads into cargo boxes connected to a series of lifts. The cargo boxes were then moved into a container and parked, one after the other, in rows.

When each container was filled with the smaller cargo boxes, it moved up. Behind it was another empty container ready for more boxes.

"It's the Space Elevator's train," Latitia said. "Filled up one section at a time and preparing to depart."

B'taav considered the tons of ore.

"Whatever they're building, it's massive."

The robot before them came to a stop. The last couple of boxes of ore were loaded into the container and the robot moved once again.

Latitia and B'taav followed. They approached the side of that container. At the front of this last segment of the train was a small door. The robot stopped before it and pressed its hand against the metal side. There was a low hum and the door slid open. The robot motioned the Independents to enter and stepped aside.

"After you," Latitia told B'taav.

B'taav walked through the door. Beyond it was a small passenger compartment. It had twenty seats and faced a metal wall. The seats were simple yet designed to keep passengers secure and safe.

The robots remained outside the door. It slid shut.

As soon as it did, Latitia and B'taav felt the container move.

"Sit down," Latitia said. "Hurry!"

They strapped themselves in. Though doing so took seconds, they already felt the press of gravity. The Space Elevator quickly picked up speed. Their hosts didn't care if the human passengers were safely in place.

B'taav put on his seat belt just as the forces of gravity hit him the hardest.

The speed they were moving at was dizzying and his body felt like it was about to collapse. Then, just as the pain reached near intolerable levels, it was gone.

"B'taav?"

The voice came from the Independent's side.

"How are you doing?" Latitia asked.

The elevator slowed.

"Fine, I guess."

"We should be nearing the Orbital Platform," Latitia said.

B'taav took several deep breaths. He felt a series of chills and sweat dripped down his face.

Latitia removed B'taav's seatbelt and helped him to his feet. B'taav adjusted the magnetism of his boots and settled on the floor.

"You don't look so good," Latitia said.

"I feel... weak," he said. "Good timing."

They walked around the room, looking for a way out. Other than the sealed door they were brought through, there was none.

The Space Elevator slowed even more. It stopped.

Seconds passed and rumblings were felt. The vibrations grew until, abruptly, the Independents felt a violent pull. If it wasn't for the gravity boots, they would have crashed against the compartment's ceiling. There was a heavy groan and an even louder rumble. The walls of their section in the Space Elevator train opened and the cargo removed.

The Independents stepped closer to the compartment's exit. The vibrations stopped and they heard the sound of metallic groans. Once again the walls of this segment of the Space Elevator train slid shut with a loud clang.

As soon as the container walls were sealed, the door before them opened.

An intense beam of light flashed on the Independents.

Standing before them and just outside the Space Elevator compartment were another trio of robotic figures. They looked identical to the ones that accompanied them to the Space Elevator on Pomos. Their weapons were trained on Latitia and B'taav.

"Looks like this is our stop," Latitia said.

The Independents exited the compartment.

The area around them did not appear all that different from that in the Space Elevator's platform. They were again surrounded by very heavy machinery in a very large warehouse sized room. Smaller trains carried the refined ore away. They disappeared into a series of openings.

Latitia read the atmospheric display within her helmet.

"The atmosphere here is pure," Latitia said. "Temps remain well below freezing."

Two of the robots were at Latitia and B'taav's side while the third motioned to them and walked away. The Independents followed.

They walked through the warehouse and past a door to a large service elevator. They were silently whisked up. After rising an undetermined distance, they were bathed in complete darkness. The darkness lasted only seconds before their view radically changed.

"By the Gods," Latitia whispered.

This elevator, like the Space Elevator itself, ran inside a tinsel glass tube and this section of the ride allowed them a three hundred sixty degree view of their surroundings. They emerged from the lower base of a very large Space Station, one of the larger ones B'taav had ever seen, and zipped towards another smaller section above it. Far below them was the planet Pomos.

B'taav stepped up to the glass. He looked down at the lower section of the Space Station and tried to get some sense of its shape and design and, through that, an idea of who the manufacturer might be.

"She's so damn bland," B'taav said.

"The ultimate in functionality," Latitia said. "No windows, no lights. Unnecessary for this group."

Rockets and pulse cannons lined the walls of the Space Platform. They moved about silently, alert for any incoming threats.

The elevator continued its ascent while B'taav and Latitia's attention focused on their destination. They spotted a large sublevel of the Orbital Platform, a sphere on top of the sphere they emerged from.

They were again enveloped in darkness before the elevator came to a stop.

When the doors opened, they felt the pull of artificial gravity. Before them was a long hallway.

Latitia once again examined the atmospheric readings within her helmet's display. Temperatures were climbing while the atmosphere remained breathable.

"Move," one of the three robotic figures said.

B'taav and Latitia stepped into the hallway with their escorts following closely behind. The elevator doors shut. There was a rumble and the elevator descended.

B'taav and Latitia looked at the corridor before them. They spotted small apertures spread about the walls, floor, and ceiling.

B'taav paused before one of them. The apertures were little more than small black holes.

"Step to the middle of the corridor," a voice boomed.

B'taav and Latitia did so.

"Spread your arms out."

They did this as well.

A hissing sound filled the corridor and air was pumped in. It was followed by a heavy blue tinted liquid that gushed out of the holes and slammed into the Independents.

B'taav stumbled from the pressure of the liquid and Latitia grabbed him.

"You would have been better... better off without me," B'taav mumbled.

The liquid didn't stick to their suits and, abruptly, was shut off. More air whirled through the corridor, this time sucking what remained of the liquid in the corridor and on them out. The process done, Latitia once again examined the computer readout inside her helmet.

"We're clean," she said. "*Really* clean. No dust, no grit, no—"

"Follow us," the lead robot said.

The Independents did as told.

They were escorted past this small hallway and into a larger outer area.

There they found an ordinary, though immaculate, office room. The floor had a dark red carpet and the walls were pale white. There was a seating area and a computer console. Windows at the side walls looked out at Pomos.

The mechanical escorts moved past this room and into another small corridor.

"It's like a waiting room," B'taav said.

Rooms like these were usually outfitted with security devices ranging from infrared cameras to passive and active thermal scanners and metal detectors. Whoever waited beyond this room knew they were safe when their visitors stepped through... should the visitors be allow to do so.

The robots took B'taav and Latitia to the opposite side of the corridor and came to a stop. They waited for several seconds while the security equipment did its work. Then the first of the three robots pressed its hand against the wall. The wall slid away, revealing a large, elegant office.

The office was dimly lit and filled with dark shadows. A mahogany desk took up its inner half and a set of three very elegant chairs were arranged before it. Behind the desk was a large bookcase filled with what appeared to be very old and worn books. A brown globe on a dark wooden base stood beside the desk. The office was enclosed in an enormous tinsel glass bubble. In all directions except for the entry, the floor, and the ceiling were clear views of outer space. Pomos loomed large below. On the opposite side of the room the destroyed moon of Solyanna was visible.

As beautiful as it was, the office made B'taav's skin crawl.

"End of the line," he said.

The Independents and their robot escorts stepped inside. Latitia ignored the desk and walked to the side window. B'taav remained at the foot of the door. Their unease grew with each passing second. There was no one in the office to greet them, yet B'taav could *feel* a presence within. Something dark, evil. Worse, B'taav felt the infection was roaring back. He found it increasingly difficult to remain standing. He leaned against the wall.

Latitia was at his side.

"Sorry," B'taav said.

His vision grew cloudy.

"I'm surprised you lasted this long," a male voice said.

The Independents faced the source of the words. Sitting behind the mahogany desk was an elderly man. They did not know how he appeared when moments before the chair he sat on was empty. His hair was very thin and gray. His face was stern, his eyes charcoal. He was dressed in a business suit and, despite the deadly temperature within the office, didn't appear the least bit uncomfortable.

"Jonah... Jonah Merrick?" B'taav said.

The elderly man offered the Independents an equally cold smile.

"You've come a long way," he said.

"How can you... be there without a space suit?"

Merrick ignored the question.

"You have probes hidden in the rubble of Solyanna, don't you?" Merrick said. "They detected our energy signatures and that brought you here."

"Yes," Latitia said. "What are you up to?"

Merrick leaned back in his chair. His smile remained.

"You must have some ideas."

B'taav's body shuddered. Lines of sweat fell from his face.

"Let him be," Latitia said.

The grin on Merrick's face broadened. B'taav groaned. The pain within him grew until he was in agony. Merrick frowned.

"How strange," he said. "I told the nano-probes in his body to rip him apart. They most certainly are trying."

His frown remained.

"They may not succeed. In fact, the odds are your body will destroy them before they can do the same to you. How is it your system can fight them so efficiently?"

"Let him be!" Latitia repeated.

Merrick shrugged and, in that moment, B'taav let out a relieved breath. The agony was gone. His body relaxed.

"What... what is this?" B'taav muttered.

"As you said, the end of the line."

The robots around the Independents drew closer. They raised their hands and reached for the Independents' helmets.

"You don't think I'd come here alone," Latitia said.

The smile returned to Merrick's face.

"Your arrival intrigued us. We needed to figure out the hows and whys of your appearance. It was the only reason we allowed you to come this far. We found your –my– spacecraft planet side. You didn't use the Displacer to get here, so how did you make your trip to Pomos?"

"You won't find any answers in the shuttle," Latitia said.

"Won't we?" Merrick said. "We won't find a log? We won't find clues about your elusive masters?"

"No."

Latitia's denial carried more than a hint of panic in it.

"Good to know," Merrick said. "The ship is in our base. We're examining it as we speak."

Rather than displaying more panic at this revelation, B'taav caught the ghost of a smile on Latitia's face.

"You're not Merrick," she said. "What did you do to him?"

"What makes you think I did anything at all?"

The old man stood up. As he did, his face changed. Wrinkles disappeared and his pale skin gained color. His face became younger, feminine. Soon, and with the exception of the hair, he looked just like Latitia.

"Does it matter who I am?" the figure said.

"What... what is this?" B'taav said.

"A Chameleon," Latitia said.

"A what?"

The chameleon unit smiled.

"We're nano-tech robots made up of billions of individual nano-probes with the capacity of arranging into any shape."

The robots around them changed their looks as well. All three took on the form of B'taav. Unlike the figure of Latitia, their outer shell remained metallic.

"My counterpart has an organic layer over its machinery," Latitia said. "Helps to pull off the deception."

"You don't think we're only on Pomos, do you?" the machine that looked like Latitia said. "You must realize we're among you."

"How many?"

"That would be telling."

"Too bad," Latitia said.

"Too bad?" her duplicate repeated.

"Yeah," Latitia said. "I was hoping to find out a little more. Oh well."

Latitia looked at B'taav. Incredibly, she gave him a wink. Her attention returned to her duplicate.

"So, you hauled our shuttle into your base?" she said.

"Yes, we—"

Latitia's duplicate stopped talking. It looked away. Its hand came to its ear, as if receiving –or sending– a transmission.

"Too late," Latitia said.

Latitia released B'taav and pushed a button on the control panel of her space suit's sleeve.

In that instant, all hell broke loose.

One of the three robots guarding them abruptly grabbed its partner and hurled it at the other side of the room. That robot slammed against the tinsel glass wall, its flight so violent that it shattered into pieces. In a flash the renegade robot grabbed its remaining partner and the two were locked in a terrific struggle. They fell to the ground.

The dim lights in the room turned red and the Latitia chameleon froze. It looked up, then at the Independents.

"What's the matter?" the real Latitia said. "We got company after all?"

The chameleon Latitia scowled. It approached the Independents but before it could grab them, Latitia pressed another button on her suit. The remains of the robot flung against the tinsel glass wall erupted into white hot flame. The flame seared the tinsel glass, creating stress fractures along its surface.

There was the eerie sound of cracking and then, abruptly, the tinsel glass shattered. Latitia's magnetic boots locked onto the floor and she held B'taav tight as everything within the office that wasn't nailed down, including the two fighting robots, was sucked into space. The chameleon Latitia dropped to the floor. Its hands grabbed the carpeting and held tight.

"What did you...?" B'taav managed.

"Thing about machines is they can be hacked," Latitia said.

The chameleon Latitia coldly eyed Latitia and B'taav. It crawled along the carpet like a spider and approached the Independents. B'taav heard Latitia's voice through his helmet's speakers.

"Time for you to go," she said. "We'll see each other again. Soon."

To B'taav, the words barely registered. Latitia pressed a button on B'taav's space suit and released him. The suit's thrusters activated and he flew past the chameleon Latitia, the shattered tinsel glass, and into space.

B'taav looked back. He was soaring away from the platform at an incredible clip. In seconds he could no longer see Latitia or her duplicate.

He floated away and drifted deeper into outer space.

34

The suit's thrusters flamed out.

B'taav's body spun around and around without anything to slow his motion. He caught glimpses of Pomos and Solyanna. He saw an enormous explosion rip the Space Elevator's platform. Bright sparks rose from the base and traveled up, enveloping the Space Station. Debris and structural pieces ruptured in silence. A single large piece of metal flew by at tremendous speeds. He flipped around and saw darkness. When he finished his turn, he saw a mushroom cloud envelop the Space Station's planetary platform.

Why did it blow up? B'taav wondered. The answer came to him even as he asked the question. *That's why you wanted to know where the shuttle was.*

Latitia rigged it to blow. The people –*creatures*– of the Space Platform brought the shuttle right to its target.

"Latitia," B'taav called through his communicator. "Are you there?"

He received no reply. The Station crumbled even more, its structure tearing itself apart. B'taav desperately wanted to go back and help his partner. Even more, he wanted to figure out what the hell was going on...

He couldn't.

His body was unresponsive. His mind drifted into a haze.

What did you just witness? Why did she bring you here, only to release you?

It made no sense.

He floated on, up into the heavens, an insignificant body lost to the infinite.

He might have blacked out, he wasn't sure.

Another whirl and he faced the system's sun, so far in the distance.

I've got a long way to go.

Just like that whatever fear he had was gone, replaced by a strange sense of peace.

If this is to be my end...

B'taav closed his eyes.

No use waiting. With the flick of his wrist, he could shut off his life support and be dead in seconds. His body would float through space for an eternity, a loan guardian overlooking a dead world. It would be painless. It would be...

He felt something tug at his side and his body spun around clockwise.

B'taav opened his eyes. A star field lay before him. Below it was the lower edge of Pomos. He was far away from the planet but no longer spinning.

How did I stop spinning?

Stranger still, Pomos was moving away from him. Farther and farther. He was traveling faster than before. Faster still.

How can I be gaining speed? The thrusters in the suit are spent.

It took all the energy to turn his head.

And there she was, standing over him. Cradling him. Staring directly into his eyes.

She was in her own spacesuit and attached to a thick black security line. Her eyes were a stony brown and her hair a beautiful yellow.

She was dead. She had to be.

The angel gently spun B'taav around until he was before her. There was a sadness in her expression, something he hadn't seen before. Despite this, she offered the Independent a smile. He never thought he'd see it again.

"Hello, B'taav," she said.

B'taav could barely hear her voice through their touching helmets. Her voice was brittle. It held back tears.

If she was dead, then so too was he. He smiled back.

"Hello, Inquisitor Cer," he said.

35

B'taav fought hard to stay awake.

He had so much to ask of Cer yet it was difficult to think, much less talk. For her part, Inquisitor Cer said little.

While she carried B'taav's body, he looked around. He was unable to see where she was taking him. After floating a while, Inquisitor Cer's boots landed with a sharp, silent thump.

Inquisitor Cer spun the prone B'taav around. He expected to see the *Xendos* or whatever ship she appropriated below them. Instead, he saw darkness. Yet this darkness was blacker than what surrounded them. He could not see Solyanna through it, nor any stars.

"We're on the top of the *Xendos*," Inquisitor Cer said. "She's cloaked."

B'taav wasn't sure he heard her correctly.

"C...cloaked?"

"Shhh," Inquisitor Cer said. "There will be plenty of time to talk."

She moved along the near invisible surface of the ship and, abruptly, the two were bathed in a strong light. It came from an open hatch and what lay beyond it was familiar: The decompression chamber of the *Xendos*.

Inquisitor Cer carried B'taav into the chamber and closed the door behind her. She then laid the Independent on a chair and walked to the controls on its other side. A rush of air filled the area. Along with it came the pull of artificial gravity.

Cer was back at B'taav's side, her helmet off. She removed the rest of her space suit and did the same for B'taav. She checked his pulse and temperature.

"What happened to you?"

"D...don't... know," B'taav managed. "What...?"

"Easy," Inquisitor Cer said.

Lines of worry filled her face. She pulled a thin medi-cart from the wall and lowered the chamber's artificial gravity. She picked B'taav up and laid him on the bed before applying sensors to his chest, sides, and forehead.

Inquisitor Cer read B'taav's readout and frowned.

"I'm doing that good?" B'taav muttered.

Inquisitor Cer reached for the ship's remote control panel and snapped it onto her left arm. She sent a series of commands to the cockpit.

"Wish... wish we had one of those back in... in Erebus," B'taav said.

"I know," Inquisitor Cer replied. She pressed more buttons and B'taav felt the ship's engines come to life. Their sound was different from what he remembered.

"I thought you were dead. What... what happened?"

Inquisitor Cer drew a breath before explaining everything that happened to her since just before leaving the *Dakota*. She spoke of meeting the soldier who gave her a microchip and how Overlord Octo found it. Of how he poisoned her and, as she was dying, showed her what was on that chip. She explained her miraculous revival and her confrontation with the dying Overlord. Of how he sabotaged the *Xendos* and nearly destroyed it.

Inquisitor Cer led B'taav out of the Decompression chamber and through the living deck and paused before the door to Overlord Octo's room. The door was well sealed but, along with much of the wall around the door, bore the heavy scars of an explosion.

"When I first saw this door after the explosion, it was torn apart," Cer said. "This corridor was heavily warped and Overlord Octo's room was destroyed. Over the next hours and days, the hallway, the door leading into Overlord Octo's room, and the *Xendos'* engines repaired themselves. It's not a perfect fix, but it's a lot better than it was. I didn't know what to make of this. The Holy Texts talk of miracles, and I'm tempted to believe that's the only reason I'm still alive. Yet even faith has its limits."

Inquisitor Cer spun B'taav around. She moved down the corridor, up the stairs, and to the cockpit entrance. The door slid open and, despite his grogginess, B'taav was shocked by what he saw. The cockpit of the *Xendos* sported several new panels and sophisticated –and alien– equipment tied in to the more familiar controls. In the corner of the room one of the new panels was in the process of being created whole.

Inquisitor Cer pushed the medi cart closer to that panel. Small pieces seemed to appear out of thin air. It was like watching a candle burn in reverse.

"What is... this...?" B'taav managed.

"Nano-probes," Inquisitor Cer said. "They're all over the *Xendos*. I have no idea when they were put here or by whom, but they're the reason the ship was not destroyed in the blast. Perhaps they're the reason the poison given to me wasn't as potent as it should have been. And when I was surrounded by the fleet and thought there was no escape…"

"The cloak?"

Inquisitor Cer nodded.

"Nano-probes cover the *Xendos*' body like a layer of paint. When the *Cygnusa*, our most powerful battleship, shone its lights on me, the nano-probes emulated the colors and texture of the asteroid I was hiding behind. The battleship passed within three miles of where I was and didn't see me. Not only had this ship taken on the look of that asteroid, the nano-probes absorbed the *Xendos*' elevated temperatures and electronic signature. For all intents and purposes, I was invisible."

Inquisitor Cer moved B'taav closer to the front view screen.

"I remained in place, hiding, until the *Cygnusa* and her fighter craft passed me by. I then traveled to the shipping lanes and hid among cargo vessels while waiting to use a Displacer."

"Why… why did you come here?"

"The chip's information was still in the *Xendos*' memory banks. There was a detailed list of all the flights made by slave traders from their very early days. I was determined to find the people and institutions behind this savage practice so I searched for a pattern, something that would lead me to them. After a while, I found one: A port *all* those ships used… at least until a little over two hundred years ago."

"Pomos."

"The very last of the sex slave vessels arrived and left here only hours before the planet was quarantined and destroyed. Even though it happened so long ago, I knew this was where I needed to start my search."

She paused and sat in the pilot's chair.

"Last thing I expected was to find you," Inquisitor Cer said.

"How did you get past all the Displacer security?"

"The nano-probes gave out different ship registrations as I moved from jump to jump before arriving at Onia. Once there, I was forced to wait. The ship's energy reserves were low. Helpful as the nano-probes are, they use up a great amount of energy and need time to recharge."

"You used the… the type 6 Displacer?"

"Yes," Inquisitor Cer said. "When I exited it, I was hit with a burst of sensor scans. The nano-probes on the *Xendos* anticipated them. They blacked the ship out just as an army of defensive drones appeared. I passed them by, though not without difficulty. When I approached Pomos I spotted the Orbital Platform and Space Elevator. Just then, you popped out."

"We have to... have to go back there. I left someone behind."

"Who?"

"Another Independent," B'taav said. "Her name is Latitia."

Inquisitor Cer was dumbfounded.

"Latitia?"

Remember the name.

"You know her?" B'taav asked.

"I do."

"She's stuck... stuck..."

A burst of light filled the *Xendos'* cockpit. Something deep within the Orbital Platform erupted. The incredible structure blew into tiny pieces.

"By the Gods," Inquisitor Cer said.

She used the ship's cameras to search the Platform's wreckage. She spotted hundreds of defensive probes circling her remains like an angry swarm around a destroyed nest.

"It's gone," Inquisitor Cer said. "No one could have survived that."

B'taav forced himself up. The Platform, what remained of it, slowly, inevitably, was drawn down into Pomos.

"I... I barely knew her," B'taav said. "She brought... brought me here."

"Why?"

"To see all this," B'taav said. Though he felt weak from the effort, he recalled an earlier conversation between them.

I'm not leaving here alone.

I don't expect you to.

"She... she knew you were coming. She timed this..."

"Timed my arrival?" Inquisitor Cer said. Recognition dawned on her. Latitia and Sergeant Delmont were working together. One gave her the memory chip that began this series of events. The other probably placed the nano-probes on the *Xendos*.

The nano-probes timed your trip to Pomos. They made sure your arrival was at precisely the moment you needed to be here!

"We... we have to leave."

Inquisitor Cer switched to the *Xendos'* rear cameras. She focused the images on the Type 6 Displacer. Waves of drones circled her.

"We can't use the Displacer," Inquisitor Cer said.

"There's another one," B'taav said.

36

The cloaked *Xendos* moved through the rocky debris of Solyanna while the defensive probes around the Platform spread out and aggressively searched for those responsible for its destruction. Some drew very close to the fleeing ship.

B'taav watched their movements on the monitors. As much as he wanted to go back and search for Latitia, he didn't think there was any way she could survive.

We'll see each other again. Soon.

Her last words to B'taav were a promise, spoken as if she knew what was coming.

Inquisitor Cer kept her focus on the *Xendos'* controls. The ship flew around chunks of moon rock while approaching the hidden Type 2 Displacer. After they made enough distance between their ship and the Platform's remains, Cer said:

"Why are you here?"

B'taav's told Inquisitor Cer about his trip with Latitia from Onia to Pomos and what they found there.

"Was it Merrick on the Orbital Platform?" Cer asked.

"I don't know." B'taav said.

The Independent gave Inquisitor Cer Latitia's memory chip. She loaded it into the *Xendos'* computer. Now, as they approached the Type 2 Displacer, the ship made contact with their means of escape.

"Incredible," Inquisitor Cer said.

Floating before them and hidden between several large Solyanna rocks was the Type 2 Displacer. Cer positioned the *Xendos* before her mouth and prepared to send out the initiation signal.

She eyed the monitors and noted the proximity of a group of defensive probes.

"They know about the Type 2," Cer said. "The moment we activate the Displacer, they'll know exactly where we are and it'll take a few seconds for her core to fully charge. We may not have enough time to enter her slipstream."

"We have no choice."

Inquisitor Cer nodded.

"Hold tight."

Inquisitor Cer pressed several buttons. She waited with a mix of impatience and anxiety for the reply. It came.

"The Displacer accepted the codes," Inquisitor Cer said. "Where to?"

"Onia," B'taav said.

It was the most logical place to go. Lying between the Phaecian and Epsillon Empires, it allowed them the most options to disappear and re-group.

Inquisitor Cer relayed the information. She frowned.

"...what...?" B'taav asked.

Inquisitor Cer shook her head.

"The program on that memory chip lets me activate the Displacer but it won't let me set a destination. It already has one cho—"

Suddenly, the center of the Displacer lit up. Red alert signals blared.

"They've spotted us!" Inquisitor Cer yelled.

A monitor displayed at least a dozen defensive probes headed their way. Even more altered their course.

"Latitia did this," Inquisitor Cer said. "She got us together, and now she's set us up to go... to go where?"

The *Xendos* moved toward the Displacer's hollow center. It shimmered with powerful electric arcs. Unlike past Displacer jumps, the energy arcs were crimson red.

"What is this?" Inquisitor Cer said. "It looks like its overloading!"

"We have to... use it."

Inquisitor Cer clenched her teeth. Even as they closed in on the Displacer's energized center, Inquisitor Cer's kept a watch on the converging defensive probes. They were coming in so very fast...

There was another alarm.

A defensive probe appeared from behind a rocky mass opposite the Displacer. It ignored the *Xendos* and moved at high speed toward the Displacer's control room.

"If they take out the controls, we're trapped."

"Not if I can help it," Inquisitor Cer said.

She pushed the *Xendos'* engines.

"Going into the... the Displacer at full speed is dangerous," B'taav said.

"Not as dangerous as getting stuck here."

Inquisitor Cer adjusted the *Xendos'* path. The energy reading from within the Displacer fluctuated.

"Now what?"

The readings changed. The crimson arcs turned blood red.

"Readings are way past normal," Cer said. "Energy spiking."

The defensive probe sped up.

"The probe's over... overloading," B'taav said. "She's going to detonate!"

"Hades," Inquisitor Cer said.

The readings on the Displacer also spiked. Wherever it was Latitia was sending them, it was very, *very* far away.

"Damn it all," Cer muttered.

The *Xendos* moved into the center of the Displacer. The energy arcs were no longer confined to that center. They jumped across the transporter's body and threatened to tear the structure apart before the defensive probe did the same.

"Your girlfriend did a hell of a job," Inquisitor Cer said.

"Latitia's n... not... girlfriend," B'taav muttered.

Inquisitor Cer barely heard him.

An energy arc flew out of the Displacer's core and singed the defensive probe, knocking it off course. It corrected its flight path.

"Hang on," Inquisitor Cer said.

The *Xendos* closed in. The navigational computer erupted and the view screen went black.

The cockpit of the *Xendos* filled with smoke just as the ship lost all power.

37

Inquisitor Cer fought desperately to reactivate the ship's controls.

"Are... are we in...?"

"I can't tell," Inquisitor Cer said.

The smoke inside the cockpit was thick.

"Come on," she said.

One of the monitors came to life. Inquisitor Cer slid before it. She let out a relieved breath.

"Outer radiation climbing," she said. "We're in the slipstream."

She pressed more buttons. The radiation ticker continued its climb, a normal indication of their progression through the Displacer's slipstream.

"That's the good news," Inquisitor Cer continued. "Three of our four engines and most other systems are offline. I've got ruptures on our port side. We were caught in the drone's explosion."

The ship rocked as more smoke poured from the corridor beyond.

"I can't leave the controls," Cer said. "Can you do something about that smoke?"

B'taav used all the strength he had to get to his feet. He stumbled to the door. One of the central panel boxes outside the cockpit was on fire. B'taav pulled at the door, inching it closed.

"By... bypass external panels," B'taav said. "They're... they're sparking."

Inquisitor Cer pressed a couple of buttons. She heard a thump and turned. B'taav was on the floor. He coughed.

"Shut... shut it..."

Inquisitor Cer's attention returned to the controls. She pressed still more buttons.

The fiery panel beyond the cockpit door let out one last wave of sparks. The fire was out. Almost instantly, other lights came on.

"That did it!" Inquisitor Cer said.

The *Xendos* rocked some more. The central view screen came to life. Inquisitor Cer tightened her grip of the ship's controls and aligned the craft with the Displacer's event horizon.

"Radiation readings reaching their peak," Cer said.

The ride remained chaotic and Inquisitor Cer fought against veering too far off their path and straying from the Displacer's slipstream.

Inquisitor Cer took a second to display the ship's rear cameras, to see if any of the defensive drones made it into the Displacer and might be following them. None had.

B'taav lifted himself up and, despite the ship's heavy vibrations, made his way back to his seat. That short walk was agony. When he reached his seat, his face was pale and he was out of breath.

"Just like... just like old times," he said.

If Inquisitor Cer heard him, she didn't react. More time passed. Too much.

"Why haven't... haven't we reached the end?" B'taav asked.

Trips through a Displacer took between a few seconds to no more than two minutes of real time. In the early days of Displacer research, scientists theorized a ship could travel the entire length of the galaxy through a pair of Displacers. Those estimates proved wildly optimistic.

The maximum one could travel through a Displacer was approximately five hundred light years, but the tremendous energies expended for these journeys and intense radiation vessels were exposed to meant there were limits. Traveling beyond those limits increased the danger of a ship being torn apart and lost in the slipstream.

Once lost, there was no coming back.

After recognizing the Displacer's limits, there were few brave –or stupid– enough to push them. It was the reason distant trips involved the use of several Displacers.

"How... how long have we been...?" B'taav asked.

"Three and a half minutes," Inquisitor Cer said.

Chills passed through B'taav's body. He leaned forward and examined the *Xendos'* control panel.

"Rest," Inquisitor Cer said.

Despite the agonizing pain, B'taav focused on the readouts. Something wet fell over his lips. His nose was bleeding.

The *Xendos* shook, almost sending the Independent back to the floor.

"Buckle up," Cer barked.

B'taav ignored the nose bleed and reached for the seat belt. He put it on.

"How long?" he asked.

"Coming on five minutes."

The energy field around them, red and so very bright, turned blue. Mysterious arcs neither had witnessed before lashed at the ship.

"We might be lost," Inquisitor Cer said.

Her thought was interrupted by another circuit failure. Sparks flew across the cockpit's controls and one of the monitors cracked. Smoke bellowed from the destroyed screen and Inquisitor Cer initiated fire controls. The smell of burnt circuits filled the cabin and was quickly sucked out by the craft's emergency fans.

The outside radiation gauge reading remained dangerously high.

"There's no ship in the fleet that can take this much radiation," Inquisitor Cer said. "We should be—"

B'taav grabbed Inquisitor Cer's arm.

"We'll make it," he said.

Inquisitor Cer looked away.

"Seven minutes," she said.

The energy arcs abruptly disappeared, buried under a blinding white light.

"Radiation is dropping!" B'taav said.

Inquisitor Cer checked the gauge. Just as B'taav said, the outer readings were falling.

"We're exiting!"

Then, just as soon as it began, the white light was gone.

The energy field around the *Xendos* grew dull. The outer radiation gauge's readings dropped some more.

"Nearly there!"

The ship shook as if it was about to be torn apart. Bolts of energy arced through the cockpit panels, sending fresh waves of sparks. All at once the panels died and the monitors went black.

The emergency systems activated and the cockpit was bathed in a red glow. Inquisitor Cer was back at the controls. Three of the monitors came to life.

"Radiation is nominal," Cer said. She activated the ship's starboard camera. On the monitor was a view of darkness and stars. "We're... we're out."

"W... where exactly are we?"

Inquisitor Cer had the computer create a map of the stars around them and analyze their position based on it.

"We'll know soon enough," she said.

While the computers did their work, Inquisitor Cer checked the controls and accessed the *Xendos'* status. The results surprised her.

"Plenty of fried circuits, but they're repairable," Inquisitor Cer said. "I should be able to get things operational in—"

"Inquisitor...?"

She looked at B'taav and then followed his gaze. He was staring out the ship's front window.

At first she couldn't tell what it was that had his attention. There was darkness and a field of stars before them. Then she noticed. The star field abruptly ended three quarters of the way to the ship's port side, as if the stars on that side were sliced out of the galaxy.

"Impossible," Inquisitor Cer said.

She turned the ship until it faced that darkness. There were absolutely no stars to be seen. All was pitch black.

"Something is blocking the view," B'taav said.

"How is that possible?" Inquisitor Cer muttered. "It has to be *enormous.*"

It was as if the *Xendos* were parked in front of a black wall. From behind it came a dull, red light.

"Whatever it is, it's orbiting a planet," Inquisitor Cer said. She ran a sensor scan. "A giant. Equatorial diameter is 143,000 kilometers. Composition is hydrogen and helium. The structure between us and that planet is blocking any other scans. Behind us... I'm not detecting much. Plasma rays... we're... we're in a solar system."

"Where?"

Inquisitor Cer returned to the star map. An error message appeared. The computer could not find their location.

"That's impossible," Inquisitor Cer said.

"Either that or we're in unexplored territory," B'taav said. "Way... way out."

"Let's get a better look at this thing we're parked beside."

Inquisitor Cer focused the ship's cameras on the object. She used enhanced image and light filters to peer through the darkness. At the same time, mapping software developed a three dimensional picture of the vessel. After the computer finished its work, Cer fell back in her chair. Her face was pale.

"It can't be. It just can't—"

The object's shape was familiar to both B'taav and Inquisitor Cer. It was a starship, one whose likes they recently encountered and thought they would never –*ever*– see again.

"It can't be," Inquisitor Cer repeated.

Yet its shape was the same.

"It's the *Argus*," Inquisitor Cer said.

38

A stunned silence filled the *Xendos'* cockpit.

Inquisitor Cer pressed more buttons and the computer produced an even higher resolution map of the vessel before them.

She let out a relieved breath.

"We're not going crazy after all," she said. "The ship's shape and dimensions are almost identical to the *Argus*, but there are differences."

"Like?"

"For one thing, this ship is in pristine shape. She has roughly a half of the *Argus'* defensive and offensive weaponry systems."

"She's a... a stripped down model?" B'taav said.

"Yeah," Inquisitor Cer said. "Could be a prototype. But if what she's got inside her is anything like the *Argus*, then she's also a solar system killer. One we're parked right next to."

"We need to leave."

"As quickly as possible," Inquisitor Cer said.

She worked the controls of the *Xendos* and brought power to the engines. The ship remained in place.

"What's wrong?" B'taav asked.

"We've got power, but the damn thing won't move."

"The nano-probes?"

Inquisitor Cer slammed her fist against the panel.

"They won't let us go."

Inquisitor Cer grabbed the yoke and tried to spin the *Xendos* away from the *Argus* prototype and back to the Displacer they emerged from.

"Come on," she muttered. "Let me—"

Abruptly, the ship turned.

"Ok," Inquisitor Cer said.

She continued the ship's turn until the *Xendos* faced a very small Displacer. It was similar to Pomos' Type 2 but less than a third its size. It was designed to transport ships not much larger than shuttle crafts.

Inquisitor Cer's fingers glided along the instrument panel.

"Let's see if we can contact her."

She sent commands to the Displacer. After a while, she shook her head.

"The Displacer's onboard computer is locked. I can't get in."

"So... now what?" B'taav wondered.

As if to answer her question, a small, distant light appeared on the far side of enormous vessel. Inquisitor Cer and B'taav recognized the location. It came from one of the ship's many Docking Ports, in this case the same one they used to enter the *Argus*.

"Looks like they want... they want us aboard," B'taav said.

The *Xendos* approached the docking port's doors and slowed.

The ship was on autopilot and Inquisitor Cer's focus was on B'taav. She used the Medi-Cart's gear to draw his blood and analyze it. While she waited for the results, she offered B'taav three liquid packs. They were heavy in protein, nutrients, and medication.

"Filet mignon," B'taav said. The orange liquid splashed in its packet. "My favorite."

B'taav took down his meal. It was bland yet sated his appetite. He grabbed the second tube, this one a near fluorescent green, and took a smaller sip. It vaguely tasted of mangos.

"Complements... to the chef," B'taav said.

Inquisitor Cer's attention was on the medi-scanners yet her expression remained distant, troubled.

"You've been... been through a lot," B'taav said.

"Rest," Inquisitor Cer said.

Her eyes drifted to the monitor on the side of the Medi-Cart. The Independent's vitals were dangerously low. B'taav felt it. Ever since confronting Jonah Merrick on the Orbital Platform, he felt his body was shutting down. At this point, he was burning with fever and could barely move.

"How... how am I doing?"

"Not well," Inquisitor Cer said. "I have no medication that works against the machines inside you. The only reason you're still alive is because your immune system is somehow sapping the nano-probes' energy cores. It's like your body, your genetic makeup, was *made* to fight them."

"How... how is that possible?"

"I don't know," Inquisitor Cer said. "I just..."

She stopped talking.

"What?" B'taav said.

Inquisitor Cer folded her hands.

"A long time ago I had a prisoner in my charge. He was a brute of a man who and was wanted for all manner of crimes. He was captured on some distant rock and imprisoned. I was tasked to bring him before the Council for judgment. When I got to him, he was a ghost of his former self, skeletal, sickly. Any food or liquid he took was vomited out within seconds. He was... he was wasting away. He claimed he was infected with nano-probes that somehow developed self-awareness. He said they were getting revenge against him for a crime he committed years before. I couldn't tell if he lost his mind or was actually suffering from their presence."

"What... what happened... to him?"

"He died," Inquisitor Cer said. "We never found any nano-probes in his body."

Inquisitor Cer shook her head.

"Unlike him, I see the nano-probes in your body. I see their movement. They're aggressive. Really aggressive. Given the time we've been close together since Pomos, I was surely exposed to them as well. I checked and they're in my system too. At least a small amount of them."

B'taav's eyes opened wide. He tried to sit up.

"Easy," Inquisitor Cer said. "The nano-probes in me are weak and barely moving. They're half dead from fighting your system. Still, if I was like anyone else, even these weaker nano-probes could have done some damage. They haven't. I don't feel anything. Not even a mild headache."

Inquisitor Cer drew a sharp breath.

"My body is fighting them as well as yours, B'taav," she said. "It's almost as if we share this genetic trait."

"We're... we're related?"

"Only by this anomaly," Inquisitor Cer said. "The odds of us both having this identical anomaly defies all odds."

"What does it mean?"

"I wish I knew," Inquisitor Cer said. "We've got nano-probes covering, modifying, and repairing the *Xendos*. They're similar, yet very different from the ones attacking your system."

Inquisitor Cer gripped B'taav's hand.

"Some nano-probes help us while others try to kill us," Inquisitor Cer said. "It's like we're in the middle of a... a war. A war fought with machines the size of cities and capable of destroying entire solar systems... and machines so small they can only be seen through a microscope."

B'taav coughed. There was blood in his mouth.

"I've... I've thought about you a lot since... since Erebus," B'taav said. "I didn't think I'd see you again. If this is my last... last chance I'll... I'll..."

Inquisitor Cer gently laid a finger over B'taav's mouth. His dark eyes stared deep into Cer's. The Inquisitor moved her hand until it touched his cheek.

"I missed you too," she said.

She kept her hand there. B'taav tried to speak some more. He wanted to so very badly. But he was so very exhausted.

In the moment before he drifted into darkness, he thought he felt Inquisitor Cer's lips upon his.

He didn't know if it was real or a very pleasant dream.

39

Tears fell down her face and her breath came in short, sharp bursts.

B'taav's black eyes stared up at the ceiling, past her, his mouth open. She desperately pressed buttons on the medi-cart.

The machinery screamed warnings.

Its patient was dying.

The seemingly small opening grew larger as the *Xendos* approached. The vessel's docking bay door could easily allow simultaneous entry for fifty ships the size of the *Xendos*.

Inquisitor Cer didn't notice.

"Come on, B'taav!" she yelled. "Wake up!"

For a moment his eyes looked at her, then away. His mouth moved.

"This looks... looks familiar," he whispered.

Inquisitor Cer followed B'taav's stare.

A light came on at the docking bay opening and formed a path that stretched deep inside. It stopped before a berth. Next to it was an ancient shuttle.

B'taav's eyes lost their focus.

"We go in, we may never come out," Inquisitor Cer said.

"It's your... choice," he said. "I... I have faith in you."

"Leave it to an atheist to have faith in an Inquisitor," Cer said.

Another burst of thrust and the ancient Phaecian craft glided past the outer doors and into the *Argus* prototype.

Inquisitor Cer moved away from the autopilot and back to B'taav's side.

Once inside the docking bay, the outer doors closed. They were trapped.

B'taav coughed. Droplets of blood were at the corners of his mouth.

"Easy," Cer said.

"What's... what's it like...?" B'taav asked.

"Empty."

The berth was free of repair trucks, cranes, refueling stations, and shuttles. Where hundreds, perhaps thousands of officers in space suits would normally be busily attending to all these missing items, there were none. Stranger still, the hanger was remarkably clean. There were no nicks, oil stains, or skid marks along the floor or walls.

The *Xendos* approached the rear of the hanger and the end of the light trail. A tinsel glass sphere surrounding that docking bay retracted as the *Xendos* approached. The ship initiated its landing protocol.

Inquisitor Cer barely paid attention. She pressed her fingers against B'taav's neck to feel for his pulse.

B'taav could barely make out the look on her face.

"Radio on," Inquisitor Cer said. Her voice was cold steel. "Unknown vessel, this is the *Xendos*. We are landing in your docking bay with all weaponry disabled. We come in peace."

Inquisitor Cer paused, hoping for a quick response.

None came. She looked to her right, at the shuttle craft the *Xendos* parked beside. It was a Class II Shuttle easily twice the size of the *Xendos*. She was an antique, used by the Phaecian Empire at least a hundred years before the Galactic War.

"Unknown vessel, we have a medical emergency," she continued. "If you have any emergency personnel or facilities, we are in urgent need of care."

"...Cer..." B'taav muttered.

"Don't talk," Inquisitor Cer said.

The *Xendos* touched down on the landing pad. Gravity hooks locked her down.

"Please respond," Inquisitor Cer begged.

The tinsel glass slid back into place. Dust particles flew up and around the *Xendos*, whipping past the view screen as the ship was sealed in its landing pad. Atmosphere was pumped into the area.

"I repeat, we have a medical emergency," Inquisitor Cer said. "We are in urgent need of assistance."

The cockpit's monitor indicated the temperature outside the *Xendos* was rising to a comfortable level while the air was breathable.

"Please respond!" Inquisitor Cer yelled.

The Medi-Cart's computer panel displayed a new series of warnings. The device beeped loudly.

B'taav's black eyes were on Inquisitor Cer. He tried to reach up, to comfort her, but his energy was spent. He saw the worry on her face and tried to tell her not to. Her hands were on his chest, pushing down, forcefully.

He was no longer breathing on his own. Inquisitor Cer's face was over his. He felt her warm breath enter his lungs.

Then she was up again, pressing hard against his chest.

He wanted to say something.

The world around her darkened. After a few seconds, all B'taav could see was Inquisitor Cer.

Please don't worry.

He took in her features and felt a warmth he hadn't in the company of anyone before. He tried so very hard to reach up and touch her.

He could not move.

The machines B'taav was plugged into let out warning wails. The heart monitor flat-lined. Brain activity slowed until it was almost imperceptible.

"No," Inquisitor Cer whispered. "Please..."

She worked on B'taav while computer voices coldly, mechanically announced the cessation of bodily functions.

Inquisitor Cer slammed her fist against B'taav's chest.

"I haven't come this far to lose you," she said.

Inquisitor Cer yelled to the Gods for help while continuing her desperate work. She massaged his chest. She breathed into his mouth, she...

There.

The alarms blaring from the Medi-Cart control panel quieted.

A heartbeat!

Inquisitor Cer froze, the next second passing as if it were a year. Tears rolled down her face.

Another heartbeat.

Another.

Inquisitor Cer's hand came to her mouth. She let out a relieved laugh.

B'taav was alive.

Barely.

The Medi-Cart issued a revised reading. B'taav's body was stabilizing.

She detected another sound intruding on the others.

It was coming from the *Xendos'* central controls.

Reluctantly, Inquisitor Cer approached the controls. A single light indicated an incoming message.

Inquisitor Cer wiped the tears from her face and pressed the button below the light.

"This is the *Xendos*," she said.

She looked up and past the ship's front window. A large door at the end of the landing pad led into the vessel itself. A shadowy figure stood there. In his hand was a communicator.

"Welcome to my ship," he said.

The shadowy figure lowered his communicator and raised his arm.

He waved.

40

There were flashes of light and nightmarish visions.

B'taav saw alien worlds surrounded by equally alien starships. The scene shifted and he witnessed fearsome machines with jagged serrated edges stripping and transporting the entire surface of a planet into the sky. He saw a moon devastated by fusion torpedoes. He marveled and feared the visions of geniuses... and madmen.

The visions were abruptly gone and he felt peace.

There will be sacrifice.

He knew it. He accepted it.

Lights flashed in a pinwheel and colors merged.

His eyes flickered open.

He didn't know where he was nor what happened before his arrival.

My arrival... where?

His memories were like those lights. Mysterious, dizzying.

Slowly, too slowly, he remembered. Onia and the burial of Captain Nathaniel Torin. His return to Onia's capital. Latitia and those who tried to do them harm. The trip to Pomos and the mysterious wonders found there. He remembered...

His breath caught in his throat.

Cer.

B'taav closed his eyes tight. The muscles in his body compressed. Painfully.

"Where are you?" he said aloud.

There was no answer.

B'taav tested his strength. He didn't have enough to get up. That angered him.

He had another, belated thought.

You're still alive.

Despite the exhaustion, he laughed.

A sharp pain in his chest and sides ended that. He coughed and gasped.

Easy. You're still alive. How about keeping it that way?

B'taav relaxed.

All right. Open your eyes.

B'taav did so. A painfully bright white light came through. He closed his eyes.

After a while, he tried again.

Better.

He stared up at a gray, metallic ceiling, then around.

There wasn't much to the room. It was an empty rectangular cubicle. The Independent was on a cushion. No, a mattress.

Normal people call these things a bed, dummy.

B'taav rolled to his side and grunted. He sat up. The room's walls were painted a military gray. There were no marks on them. The floor and the ceiling were a darker gray. The bed was designed for one. At its foot and side were computer panels displaying medical information.

Medi-Scanner. Very old model.

On it was a complete read out of the Independent's status. All indications suggested B'taav was healthy.

That's an improvement.

B'taav allowed his feet to dangle over the edge of the bed. The Medi-Scanner sensed his departure and let out a final beep before shutting down. There were no alarms.

The machine knew I was ready to go.

B'taav thought about that.

Go where?

The Independent was no longer on the *Xendos*. Unless Inquisitor Cer found yet another ship to dock into, this room was likely somewhere inside the *Argus* prototype.

Where are you, Inquisitor? Why aren't you here?

On a chair at the opposite end of the bed was a set of folded clothing. It was B'taav's dark leather jumpsuit, cleaned and freshly pressed. He slid off the bed and dressed.

There was only one door in the room and B'taav stepped up to it. He did so carefully, checking to see if there were security monitors. For all he knew, Inquisitor Cer and he were prisoners.

B'taav ran his hand across the door's edge. He found nothing.

Satisfied, B'taav stood before the door. It slid open automatically and revealed a very long corridor. B'taav looked both ways. A series of doorways spread out evenly on either side. Like his room, the corridor was gray and bereft of any identification markings or wear. The doors within the corridor, likewise, sported no numbers.

B'taav recognized the corridor's general design. He saw something very similar —no, identical— on the *Argus*.

If this ship is the same on the inside as it was on the outside...

B'taav knew where the elevators were. He could take them to the ship's central computer room or cockpit. He turned right and walked on.

After a half-dozen steps, he leaned against the wall. He grunted.

Come on, old man.

B'taav gathered his strength. This corridor would eventually lead to an elevator. Somewhere beyond it was the hydroponics level and beyond that the central computer system.

If he wanted to learn this ship's secrets, he had to go there.

B'taav reached the closest of the elevators, stopping twice to rest along the way. Beside the elevator doors were a set of stairs. On the *Argus*, B'taav was forced to use them to get to the central computer systems.

Hope the elevators are working, he thought. *I'm in no shape to climb stairs.*

The elevator doors opened as he approached.

"Destination?" a computer voice inquired.

"Let's start at the top," he said. "Take me to the highest floor."

The elevator doors silently closed and the device ascended.

Bright lights poured in from behind the Independent. He turned and was stunned by what he saw.

The elevator traveled along the outside of the spacecraft, giving B'taav a clear view of the ship's side. It stretched out for miles, eventually disappearing into the distance. As enormous as it was, the ship was nothing compared to the gas giant it orbited. Swirls of red and orange clouds –hurricanes the size of planets– spun fast enough on the surface for his naked eyes to see.

Amazing.

Even more incredible was the fact that the planet looked so familiar. B'taav tried to recall where he had seen it before. He couldn't.

So entranced was the Independent by this view that he only belatedly realized the elevator reached its stop. He spun around, expecting the doors to open. They did not.

"Elevator, open doors," he said.

The elevator doors remained closed.

A chill passed through him. The doors were designed to seal tight. It was impossible to pry them open with his hands. He searched for an emergency button. He found none.

B'taav reached for the doors.

You can't open them.

He tried. His muscles screamed from the effort.

"Take it easy," a male voice spoke over the elevator's speakers.

B'taav stepped back and looked up. A security camera stared down at him.

"I'm glad to see you're on your feet," the voice continued. "Please join me."

"Who are you?" B'taav asked. "Where are you?"

"Look straight down and to your left," the voice said.

B'taav approached the rear of the elevator and did as told. He was almost directly over what on the *Argus* was the tinsel glass encased hydroponics level. On this ship, however, the tinsel glass surrounded a great body of water and, incredibly, what appeared to be a sandy shoreline.

"A beach?!" he said.

B'taav pressed his face against the elevator's wall.

Someone was standing on the sandy shore and next to a chair. He stared up at the Independent.

The elevator descended, returning to the bowels of the starship. It made several course changes, at times moving vertically and horizontally before coming to a full stop. The elevator doors opened.

Before the Independent was a rustic wooden platform overlooking the artificial beach. There were old fashioned vending stands on either side advertising refreshments, foods, and towels. B'taav walked to the end of the platform. A large wooden stair led down two floors to the beach itself. The water sparkled dark blue and the sand was pure white.

Sitting on a beach chair was an elderly man. Next to him was another, empty, beach chair.

The elderly man waved to the Independent and said:

"Come join me, B'taav."

41

B'taav held tight to the railing and grimaced as walked down the stairs. The clear blue water beyond the beach was calm, with light waves lapping against the shoreline. If it wasn't for the artificial lights and the gas giant visible past the tinsel glass ceiling, one might think they were on a typical beach at night.

More wooden beach chairs were folded to the side of the stairs and a small cabin housed fresh towels. A computer panel above the towels awaited input. Beside the towel station were large his and hers bathrooms. The sand extended for at least two hundred yards from the base of the stairway to the shoreline, enough to occupy a very, *very* large group of people.

B'taav removed his shoes at the base of the stairs and stepped onto the sand. It was comfortably warm. He approached the old man, examining him along the way. The man was thin and frail. There was little hair left on his head and what there was was gray and stringy. He was dressed in heavy clothing and had a thick towel wrapped around his shoulders and neck.

"You must be tired," the old man said when B'taav reached his side. "Please, have a seat."

B'taav accepted the offer. Once seated he drew a deep breath and took in the fresh scent of sea water.

"You have questions," the old man said.

"Who are you?" B'taav asked. "Where is Inquisitor Cer?"

Before the old man could answer, a small, rectangular robot rolled to B'taav's side. Monitors on the robot's body displayed a list of drinks and foods.

"Can I interest you in something?" the robot asked.

"Go ahead," the old man said. "Don't be shy."

"Water," B'taav said.

One of the monitors on the robot's body slid down and a sealed cup slid out. B'taav took it and the robot rolled away.

B'taav pulled the straw from the cup and took a sip.

"How are you feeling?" the elderly man asked.

"Better," B'taav said. "Where is Inquisitor Cer?"

"She left."

"Where?" B'taav said. He abruptly rose. The effort made him to stumble.

"Easy," the elderly man said. "You still have time."

B'taav's grimaced.

"Time for what?"

"Time to catch up to her," the elderly man said. "If that's what you want to do."

"She took the *Xendos*?"

"No. Your ship wouldn't let her. Perhaps your invisible passengers didn't want her to go alone."

"You know about the nano-probes?"

The old man smiled.

"That and a few other things. Inquisitor Cer was determined to leave but had to take my shuttle. It's bigger and so much slower. You'll catch her before she reaches her destination."

"Her destination?"

The elderly man chuckled.

"Where are my manners?" he said. "I didn't mean to overwhelm—"

"Why were we brought here?" B'taav asked.

"You were brought here because both you and Inquisitor Cer were needed. She should have waited for you to get better but you were so very sick. It's why she went alone. Very noble on her part."

"Where did she go?" B'taav yelled.

The elderly man stared deep into B'taav's eyes. There was deadly seriousness in them and, despite his age and frailty, it was clear he was the master of this craft and had the means of taking care of the Independent, should he become too unruly.

B'taav lifted his hands.

"I'm sorry," B'taav said. "I didn't mean to get so emotional. It's just that—"

The old man waved him off.

"I'm just as concerned as you are about Inquisitor Cer," the old man said. "I was hoping to see both of you at the same time, instead of separately."

"You knew we were coming?"

"Not you specifically," the elderly man said. "I knew someone was coming."

The elderly man extended his hand.

"My name, by the way, is David Desjardins."

B'taav frowned. He reluctantly grasped the elderly man's hand.

"Pleased to meet you."

"Don't be so sullen," Desjardins said. "All right then, here it is: The ship you're on board is the super-juggernaut *Thanatos*. She's a Phaecian craft, a prototype of the *Luxor*, the starship that destroyed Erebus and ended the Galactic War before it began."

"Phaecian?" B'taav said. "But this ship's design is almost exactly that of the *Argus*. The *Argus* was an Epsillon craft. Did the Phaecians steal her?"

"No."

"Then... they stole her design?"

The smile returned to Desjardin's face.

"Or was it the other way around?"

"Neither," Desjardins said. "These ships were made at roughly the same time and by scientists in each Empire that were completely unaware of what their rivals were up to."

"The design similarities can't be a coincidence."

"They aren't," Desjardins said.

"Then, how...?"

"There were those who knew the Phaecian and Epsillon Empires would eventually come into conflict. That's why the super-juggernaut program was initiated. The end goal was always meant to be like what happened at Erebus."

"The Galactic War was anticipated?"

"Yes. Hundreds of years before the fact. The *Luxor* completed her mission and destroyed the Erebus Solar System along with the backbone of both fleets. The two Empires' power was wiped out. Everything but the *Argus*. Years later, you and Inquisitor Cer took care of her."

"How do you know all this?"

"I have access, limited though it is, to what happens behind the curtains," Desjardins said. "Now I'm giving you a peek. You still listening?"

"Go on."

"The Epsillon Empire's first super juggernaut prototype, code named *Blister*, was a disaster," Desjardins said. "There were serious problems with her power core and during her second trial run her engines malfunctioned while she was in the gravitational field of a small star. The ship and all hands were lost. At about that same time, the Phaecians were readying their prototype, the *Thanatos*. She was put together in a solar system as far from the edges of the Epsillon Empire as possible."

The elderly man wrapped the towel tighter.

"Like the *Blister*, the *Thanatos* was built and intended to be used immediately. A test, if you will, of its destructive power. She was to be taken to an even more distant and unoccupied solar system and detonated. That day came and the *Thanatos* was launched. She was escorted to a specially modified Displacer, one capable of fitting a ship her size. On the other end of the line was another oversized Displacer and another group of military escorts. All was clear and ready. The *Thanatos* and her skeletal crew took her out of her metal cocoon and headed for the Displacer. The *Thanatos* sped up, for the energy required to maintain the Displacer was great. She entered the energy field and then, just like that, she was gone."

"At the *Thanatos'* destination, the solar system meant to be destroyed in this test, the Phaecian military waited for her arrival. The *Thanatos* didn't show. Thirty minutes later, the military was in a full panic. They checked and rechecked the Displacer logs but found no anomalies. By day's end, the *Thanatos* was declared lost."

"The existence of this vessel was buried along with the best kept secrets of the Phaecian Empire. Her makers moved on and built the *Luxor*. They planned to test her, but rising hostilities led to her first, and final, trip to Erebus."

"You're telling me the people who designed these ships made sure each Empire had one?"

"Yes," Desjardins said.

"They hijacked the *Thanatos* while making sure the other two vessels were used to force peace between the Empires."

"Correct."

"What... what did Cer think of this?"

"About the same as what you're thinking, I imagine."

"How did you get here?"

"I can't rightly say," Desjardins replied. "I woke up some fifty odd years ago and here I was. My best guess is that I was brought here."

"By who?"

"You familiar with Saint Vulcan?"

B'taav's breath caught in his throat.

"I just came from Pomos."

The elderly man nodded.

"So you did," he said. "Well, she either had me flown here or I was birthed in one of the many thousands of rooms I have yet to explore on this vessel."

"Birthed?"

"I'm not really David Desjardins," the old man said. "At least not the *original*."

"You're a construct?"

"A clone."

"Clones are illegal," B'taav said.

"As soon as we get back to the Empires, I'll make sure to turn myself in."

B'taav shook his head and smiled. The smile faded.

"Clones are also not supposed to last more than a couple of years."

"This body begs to differ."

"Who was David Desjardins?"

"A highly decorated Captain of Saint Vulcan's fleet, way back in the years when she was still considered a Saint."

"He worked for her?"

"As did his –my– wife," Desjardins said. "I was the highest ranking of the twenty starship Captains in vessels around Pomos when it was destroyed. My wife... my wife died with everyone else on Pomos."

"Saint Vulcan had control over your weapons," B'taav said.

"I know," Desjardins said. "Just before initiating that massacre, she contacted the fleet Captains and told us what she was about to do. I was the only one who saw her actions as not only justified, but something which *had* to be done."

A single tear ran down Desjardin's cheeks.

"Though I gave no command and was not in charge of my vessel, I felt just as responsible as Saint Vulcan for killing every person on Pomos, up to and including my wife. Years later, when I was as old as I am now, Saint Vulcan appeared in my apartment."

"So she *is* still alive?"

Desjardins shrugged.

"At this point, I don't know," Desjardins said. "The Saint Vulcan I saw that day hadn't aged at all. Maybe I was talking to a clone of her. She offered me a second chance. A chance to be with my wife."

Desjardins pointed to his right. There, at the far end of the beach, was a small mound of sand. B'taav hadn't noticed it until that moment. The mound, he realized, was a grave.

"My wife and I lived here. We grew old. We were... happy. She passed away in her sleep last year. She had a smile on her face."

Desjardins rubbed his eyes and stared out at the water.

"Saint Vulcan didn't do all this just so you could re-live your life."

"No," Desjardins admitted. "My wife and I were brought here to look after the *Thanatos* while she made her way to her destination. We checked her systems every day and made sure she was ready."

"For what?"

"The one thing this craft was designed for," Desjardins said.

B'taav's blood ran cold.

"Why... why does this solar system need to be destroyed?"

"Because one its planets is infected with an ancient evil. One that needs to be exterminated once and for all."

"Where are we?"

"We are parked in a small solar system in the Ulinda quadrant," Desjardins said.

"The name is familiar it's..."

Chills rose up and down B'taav's spine. Though the Holy Texts were dismissed as fairy tales by the Epsillon Empire, he heard the stories and was familiar with the legends. He knew of the cursed lands and he knew of the Exodus.

"The planet we're orbiting around," B'taav said, recognition dawning on him. "It looked so familiar."

"It should," Desjardins said.

"Jupiter."

"Yes, B'taav," Desjardins said. "But the planet this ship was brought here to destroy lies far closer to this system's sun. The *Thanatos* is here to destroy Earth."

42

B'taav shook his head in disbelief. Desjardins continued:

"'Destruction of the Homeworld was upon us and the means of salvation lay in the stars. Three Arks took us from our home to those stars. The first Ark flowered into the Epsillon Empire. The second, the holy empire of Phaecia. The third Ark was lost...' "

The elderly man chuckled.

"Or so say the Holy texts," Desjardins said. "The scripture, it would seem, wasn't entirely right. Earth was not destroyed. It lies only eight hundred million miles away."

"What happened?"

"It is better I show you," Desjardins said. He pressed a button on his arm rest and a female figure appeared before them. She was middle aged and had black hair accented with gray strands.

"Saint Vulcan," B'taav said.

"Not quite in the flesh."

"How may I help you, Captain?" the hologram asked.

"Tell our companion what this is about."

The hologram nodded.

The glorious view of Jupiter in the tinsel glass roof above them faded and was replaced by the image of a planet, one with sparse clouds and a brown, desert surface.

"Few have seen this," the hologram said. "It is among the last pictures our forefathers took of Earth before the Exodus."

B'taav's mouth hung open as his eyes absorbed the image. The planet had degraded terrain along with choked up cities and desolate interstates.

"Earth's population settled into a dozen large cities while the environment around them died," the hologram said. "The Earth was poisoned and could no longer sustain humanity. This was not the product of overdevelopment and environmental ignorance. It was part of a plan."

"Plan?" B'taav repeated. "You mean Earth's citizens *intended* to poison their world and make her uninhabitable?"

"Not the citizens," the hologram said. "One man."

"One man was responsible for all this?"

"Yes."

"By the Gods, why?"

"It had to do with the question most asked after our ancestors settled and produced the Phaecian and Epsillon Empires: Why, after all these years, have we not found any other intelligent alien life forms? How is it conceivable the human race appears to be the only advanced life form out there?"

The image on the tinsel glass changed. It displayed lakes and forests, animals of all kinds and, finally, human beings.

"The emergence and survival of life forms is subject to adaptation and evolution. Simply put, those who adapt to their environments are the ones most likely to survive while those who don't risk extinction. On Earth, the human race was at the top of the evolutionary ladder. We created mighty cities and harnessed tools to cure illnesses, healing what in previous generations were fatal injuries. The blind, the infirm, the crippled... all benefitted from procedures that not only allowed them to survive, but *thrive*. There were those who theorized humanity had triumphed over evolution itself. Yet millions of years before humanity's first appearance on Earth, reptiles were at the top of that planet's evolutionary chain. Their end likely came from space in the form of one or more asteroids."

The hologram folded her arms.

"Like the dinosaurs, humanity also faced an outside threat. Instead of asteroids, they were targeted by a force so advanced from our own they made humans and their technology look like children's toys."

The glass above them changed again, this time displaying strange alien worlds and even stranger war machines.

B'taav was shocked. They were a vision from a nightmare.

"The aliens had no formal name, though our ancestors eventually called them the Locust Plague," the hologram continued. "Their means of existence lay in pillaging and absorbing entire worlds. They traveled from system to system and planet to planet and stripped each world they visited of its nutrients. They fed off living creatures, intelligent or not, and when they were done, the world left behind was nothing more than a husk. A little over five thousand years ago, they were on the verge of arriving on Earth."

"Precious few knew of this coming danger," the hologram continued. "One, a very clever man, was given this information with the hope he could fashion some kind of response. This man soon realized there was not enough time nor enough resources available to stop the invaders. Humanity would lose any battle against them and Earth, therefore, was doomed. However, this clever man came up with an equally clever plan. As fearsome as the Locust Plague were, they needed to feed to continue their travels. Therefore defeating the Locust Plague was as simple as starving them to death. And the only way to do that was by poisoning the Earth. The Locust Plague would arrive to an already ravaged planet, an Earth they could not feed off of. They would starve. Humanity's only hope for survival was in fleeing their home world."

"The Exodus," B'taav muttered.

The image on the tinsel glass shifted. Images of scientists in laboratories working on an incredibly large machine filled the glass. B'taav instantly recognized the machine.

"That's a Displacer."

"Contrary to what history journals say, we did not develop and refine Displacer technology," the hologram continued. "That same clever man who intended to poison Earth gained access to information the Locust Plague amassed from other alien cultures. With the discovery of the Displacer, he found the means of getting humanity away."

The images shifted. Wars and nuclear explosions were displayed.

"Now with the means to get people out, humanity's savior became the Earth's executioner. He singlehandedly brought the world's powers into conflict and forced them to use their nuclear devices. The Earth was rendered a radioactive, sterile desert while waves of people were simultaneously sent to the space arks."

"He built the arks?"

"No. They were the last remnants of the same alien race that developed the Displacers. It was theorized they built these ships to escape the Locust Plague, but ran out of time and abandoned them."

"The man who destroyed the world –the man who saved humanity– is he the same Unknown Hero the Holy Texts talk of?" B'taav asked.

"Yes."

"What became of him?"

"Exactly what the Texts say: he remained behind while the others fled."

"Why?'

"Because his body was infected with Locust Plague nano-probes. He controlled them throughout most of his life yet feared his control was tenuous at best. He worried the Locust Plague could regain their power over the nano-probes and take over his mind and body. The Locust Plague would learn of his plans or turn him against humanity. That is why he chose to remain behind."

"*He sacrificed himself to save us all.*"

A smile appeared on the hologram's face. Realization dawned on B'taav.

"We're here to rescue him?" B'taav said.

"Yes, B'taav. You are to rescue him before the *Thanatos* wipes this solar system –and the Locust Plague– out of existence."

"This man... what was his name?"

"Spradlin. Paul Spradlin."

43

"It's been five thousand years since the Exodus," B'taav said. "How can Spradlin still be alive?"

The Saint Vulcan hologram continued smiling. It was a programmed human reaction designed to comfort whoever it was talking to. It didn't comfort B'taav.

"When the Exodus began, he was already over three hundred years old," Saint Vulcan said. "The nano-probes within his body kept him young. There is no reason to believe they wouldn't continue doing so."

"For this long? All while trapped in a planet held hostage by this Locust Plague? You must have proof."

The Saint Vulcan hologram motioned to David Desjardins. He cleared his throat and said:

"When the *Thanatos* reached the outer boundaries of the solar system six months ago, we sent a single, microsecond long transmission. It consisted of several questions only Paul Spradlin knew the answer to."

"He replied correctly?"

"Of course," Desjardins said.

"When –if– we find him, how will we know it truly is this Spradlin?"

"I've given Inquisitor Cer two other very personal questions to ask him," Desjardins said. "In case she is unable to ask, I'll give them to you. You must remember these questions."

"Go ahead."

"How old was Jessie when she died?"

B'taav nodded.

"Ok."

"Where was she buried?"

"That's it?"

"Yes."

"Who is this Jessie?" B'taav asked.

Desjardins shrugged.

"Do you know?" B'taav asked the Saint Vulcan hologram.

"I was given the questions and their answers," Saint Vulcan said. "I have no information regarding this person. Clearly it was someone Paul Spradlin was familiar with."

"Clearly," B'taav repeated. "I understand using the *Thanatos* to destroy the Locust Plague threat, but sending us to Earth? Why risk exposing us to contamination?"

"Surely you know Inquisitor Cer and you were designed for this job."

"The immunity?" B'taav said.

"You were also bred to be stronger, quicker, and more intelligent than others," the Saint Vulcan hologram said. "You analyze situations and draw quick, logical conclusions. In the rare cases where you sustain injury, you heal faster than a human being should."

The hologram moved closer to B'taav.

"You and Inquisitor Cer spent your lives walking among humanity yet never felt a part of it. How could you?"

"What exactly are we?"

"The next level," the hologram said. "We ensured the right DNA was passed from parent to offspring for generations."

"*We*? Who are you talking about?"

"The people who created you," Saint Vulcan said. "The Locust Plague aren't the only ones capable of making centuries' long plans."

"By the Gods," B'taav said.

"Humanity's first exposure to the Locust Plague was through their nano-probe Chameleon units," Saint Vulcan continued. "These units watched and interacted with our ancestors and made sure we posed no threat to their master's invasion. Like most their technology, the nano-probe tech was stolen from one of the many races the Locust Plague wiped out. But they didn't anticipate what the technology was capable of. The first group of Chameleons sent to Earth not only observed, but *evolved*. They gained independent thought and, after many years, severed their ties to their masters. It was one of these Chameleon units that found and infected Paul Spradlin with nano-probes. The nano-probes in him are rich with technological data, information that even today could lead humanity into another golden age. Spradlin's a valuable asset. One we intend to get back."

"Who are you people?"

The hologram's face remained passive, yet her tone changed.

"We are those who watch over the rest and ensure humanity thrives."

"Whether we want your help or not," B'taav said. He thought some more. "Even with the right responses to those two questions, this could be a trap."

At this, David Desjardins let out a laugh.

"Inquisitor Cer said the same thing."

B'taav shook his head. He frowned.

"She left *because* she thought it was a trap," B'taav said.

"She knew you were getting better. She wanted to spare you."

"Are you in communication with her?"

"At this point, we cannot risk sending any transmissions. The last thing we want to do is alert the Locust Plague of our presence."

"You said I had enough time to catch up to her. Is that still the case?"

"By now she's a little more than halfway to Earth," Saint Vulcan's hologram said. "At the *Xendos'* top speed, you will reach her just as she nears the Moon's orbit."

"The *Xendos* was damaged in the trip here," B'taav said. "Have the nano-probes had sufficient time to fix her?"

"Yes," the hologram said.

B'taav faced the elderly man.

"Permission to depart, Captain Desjardins," B'taav said.

"Permission granted."

B'taav rose from his chair. He paused.

"Your body is also resistant to the Locust Plague nano-probes, right?"

The elderly man nodded.

"What about the *Thanatos*? Can her computers be breached?"

"It would take a long time, if at all," Desjardins said. "The systems on the *Thanatos* were considerably simplified and insulated. She operates on a series of switches pulled in a certain order. Primitive but effective."

"They created you out of whole cloth yet made Inquisitor Cer and I over several generations. Why?"

"I don't know," Desjardins said. "What I do know is the original David Desjardins was the only Captain willing to destroy Pomos when it was infected. My creators knew he –I– would do the same thing here. As for you, Inquisitor Cer, and Paul Spradlin, I suspect they have other plans."

David Desjardins rose. His feet were unsteady and his arms shook.

"In forty eight hours the *Thanatos'* fusion reactors will be fully charged," Desjardins said. "By then, all I have to do is hit one last switch to set her off." The expression on Desjardin's face hardened. "I will set the switch off at that time, B'taav. I will not linger. I will not wait."

B'taav calculated the *Xendos'* speed and the distance between Jupiter and Earth.

"I'll have four hours once I arrive at Earth."

"Provided you don't make any detours," Desjardins said. "Your only escape from here is through the Displacer unit on the *Thanatos'* starboard side. When this vessel is primed, I will activate the Displacer for exactly five minutes. If you're not through her by that time..."

"Understood," B'taav said. "Please, take me to the *Xendos.*"

44

Desjardins accompanied B'taav through the corridors of the *Thanatos*.

The elderly man's movements were slow and unsteady and he paused to rest a couple of times. As impatient as B'taav was to leave, he didn't rush the elderly man.

They used the elevators to go down to one of the lowest levels on the *Thanatos* and from there made the walk to the ship's central docking bay. They passed several large but empty chambers designed for storage.

"Where exactly was Inquisitor Cer going on Earth?"

"To the location from which Spradlin sent his reply," Desjardins said. "The coordinates are in the *Xendos'* navigational computer."

They reached the last of the double cargo doors, large metallic sheets that stretched over nine floors. Beside the door was a smaller one meant for human passage. It slid open noiselessly. Beyond that door was a large control room. The room's walls were made of tinsel glass and looked into the docking bay. Five hundred feet away and directly in front of them was the *Xendos*. She was parked in the nearest landing pad, her body covered by the glass bubble.

Desjardins motioned to a monitor on the control panel. A timer counted down from forty eight hours.

"This is the time you have to make it back," Desjardins said. He moved to a cabinet next to the control panel and opened it. The small cabinet held a fusion handgun.

"Take it," Desjardins said. "Just in case."

B'taav grabbed the weapon.

"I hope you find her," Desjardins said.

"When I get back, I'm taking you with us."

"Focus on what you have to do," Desjardins said.

B'taav nodded.

"Thank you."

Desjardins activated a control panel beside the door leading to the landing pad. It opened.

"Good luck, Independent," Desjardins said.

"Good luck to you," B'taav replied.

He walked to his ship.

B'taav stepped up to the *Xendos* and examined her.

From outside she appeared almost the same as when he last saw her aboard the *Dakota*.

B'taav wanted nothing more than to board her and leave at full speed after Inquisitor Cer. Instead, he forced himself to carefully check her before taking off. The *Xendos'* surface glimmered in the hanger lights. The last time B'taav saw her up close, the *Xendos'* surface was dull and scratched and showed every bit of her age. Now, she looked better than new. Light reflected brilliantly off her shiny silver surface.

Cautiously, B'taav reached up with his hand and, for a moment, hesitated. The ship's hull was painted with a layer of nano-probes. In touching it –and them– he wondered if he could send or receive some kind of message from them.

B'taav rubbed his hand across the metal panels. They were smoother than ceramic.

"Please help me," he whispered to his microscopic angels.

B'taav pulled his hand back and walked around the ship. He wasn't sure which side sustained the damage from Overlord Octo's sabotage, but both sides were now intact.

B'taav walked to the ship's rear and stepped up to the doors leading into the decompression chamber. Inquisitor Cer's remote computer panel lay beside the door.

"Hope you didn't change any of the codes," B'taav muttered. He snapped the panel over his left arm and pressed a series of buttons. A couple of seconds passed.

Nothing happened.

"Come o—"

The door opened and a stair lowered.

B'taav let out a relieved sigh. He climbed up the stairs and into the chamber. After he was inside, the stairs folded up and the outer door shut and sealed itself.

B'taav placed the fusion gun into a weapons cabinet in the decompression chamber. He then walked past the inner decompression door and climbed two flights of stairs before reaching the ship's cockpit. The controls were mostly how he remembered them, including the few new panels and gauges. He didn't know what they were for and, at the moment, decided it best not to experiment.

Let's leave that for later.

B'taav stared out the front window and at the tinsel glass doors leading back into the *Thanatos*. Desjardins remained in the control room, watching. Besides him was a figure, the hologram of Saint Vulcan.

Or was it?

B'taav squinted his eyes. No, the figure wasn't Saint Vulcan. It was that of a young woman, one B'taav didn't recognize yet knew.

"Peace to you," B'taav said. "And your wife."

He settled into the pilot's chair and flipped a series of switches.

The *Xendos'* engine rumbled. For several seconds they warmed up. All readings were within nominal range.

B'taav clicked the radio on.

"Desjardins, this is the *Xendos*. I'm ready to go."

"Understood."

Within the Docking Bay control room, the elderly man reached for a control panel to his side and keyed in a command. The tinsel glass bubble surrounding the *Xendos* rolled away, leaving the ship free to move within the docking bay.

B'taav gripped the controls and lifted the *Xendos* off the ground. He retracted her landing gear before spinning her around. Her nose soon faced the far side of the hanger. The *Thanatos'* outer doors slid open, revealing the darkness of outer space.

B'taav applied thrust and the ancient Phaecian ship made her way to the exit.

"I'm coming for you, Inquisitor," B'taav said.

45

The *Xendos* flew past the *Thanatos'* outer doors.

B'taav pulled at the controls and the ship rose up and away. Another burst of thrust and she climbed faster, passing hundreds of levels of the ship before sailing over her.

The *Xendos* was like a bug hovering over a large metal table. Beyond it lay the planet Jupiter. Her colors were incredibly vivid and her size overwhelming. B'taav watched in awe as his ship moved past the *Thanatos* and gained speed. He used the planet's gravity to give the *Xendos* even more forward momentum. B'taav regretted this. He could spent days –*weeks!*– examining the wonders around him.

The *Xendos* was past Jupiter. On the rear camera monitors the *Thanatos* and the planet she orbited shrunk and shrunk. B'taav applied magnification until he had a clear view of the top of the ship. He saw David Desjardin's beach and a pair of tiny black dots. They were the chairs he and David Desjardins sat on only moments before.

B'taav's attention returned to the forward view screen. He wondered if that would be the last he'd ever see of the ship.

B'taav settled in his chair and examined the readouts.

He used every one of the *Xendos'* outer cameras to get a three hundred and sixty degree view of the area around him. He commanded the computer to be on the alert for any vessels.

For the next five hours, he watched each monitor intently, looking for any sign of Inquisitor Cer's shuttle.

His energy waned. Though he had kicked the nano-probes from his system hours before, he was tired. Without meaning to, he drifted off to sleep.

B'taav was violently awoken by the discordant blare of an alarm.

It took great effort to pull himself from his chair and focus on the *Xendos'* controls. He scanned the monitors and snapped to attention when he realized a mind-boggling thirteen hours passed since he fell asleep. The *Xendos* was well into the process of deceleration for its approach to Earth. He looked up.

The *Xendos'* cameras caught sight of Earth's Moon and, even more fascinating, the planet she orbited. The Moon appeared intact, but what little he could see of Earth both excited and chilled him. He saw strange structures surrounding her, tentacle-like wires that circled and encased her.

He searched for Inquisitor Cer.

"Where are you?"

Just then, something else caught his attention.

A shadowy object moved parallel to his ship. It was half the size of the *Xendos* and bullet shaped. It was a defensive drone not unlike those he saw on Pomos. A pair of red lights on her bow gave the appearance of bloodshot eyes. Her speed was nearly double that of the *Xendos* and she didn't appear to notice him. She passed his ship and disappeared into the darkness.

B'taav took a deep breath.

Lucky she didn't see—

Another ship, similar in shape and size, flew toward him. She too passed.

They're in a hurry.

A fourth ship appeared in the distance.

Her speed was slower than the others. She was an older craft, her surface pock-marketed and scarred. Unlike the two that came before, she was rectangular in shape and almost as large as the *Xendos*. Instead of two red lights on her front tip, she had only one.

She was coming at him.

B'taav gripped the ship's yoke and pulled the *Xendos* away. His free hand reached for the controls of the fusion cannons.

"How do you cloak?" B'taav muttered even as he activated the ship's only weapon. He drew a bead at the craft's dead center. "*How do you cloak?*"

The alien craft continued her advance.

B'taav's finger hovered over the fusion control, ready to fire.

"Go away, Cyclops," B'taav said.

She drew nearer. Her eerie red eye sparkled.

Do you see me?

B'taav's finger lingered over the fusion cannon trigger. If he fired, he would surely alert the other drones.

"Go—" he began and stopped.

Cyclops continued her flight, passing a very close dozen miles over him.

B'taav let out a relieved breath. He checked the *Xendos'* underside camera. From it, he had a direct view of the lower parts of his ship. Instead of seeing her gray metallic paneling, all he saw was darkness. The thin layer of nano-probes had altered the ship's color to black. She was cloaked.

"Thank the Gods," B'taav said.

The Independent switched cameras and focused on the last of the alien crafts to pass him. Cyclops continued her slow progress, converging on the area the other ships were going.

B'taav activated the *Xendos'* receptors. Strong sensor waves emanated from the alien crafts. They were searching the area for something.

Unlike the *Xendos*, Inquisitor Cer's ship didn't have the ability to hide. This worried B'taav.

"Where are you, Inquisitor?"

B'taav switched the automatic pilot off. He applied thrust and a warning came through the navigation system. It would be difficult to smoothly make Earth's orbit if he didn't continue braking.

B'taav kept pace with the alien craft.

He increased her speed.

For over an hour the *Xendos* followed the one eyed defensive drone. That ship's sensor pings were joined by a dozen others. Before the *Xendos* were a large group of alien crafts. Every one of them converged on a single point in space.

B'taav fiddled with the camera controls and locked on that area. He saw a flicker of light, a flash that lasted no more than a fraction of a second. Something was out there, tumbling away and toward the Moon.

B'taav hurriedly turned to his computers and typed in instructions to calculate the tumbling object's mass and size. The results came in and they were exactly what he feared. The object the drones were pursuing was the shuttle craft from the *Thanatos*.

The object swirled as it tumbled. There were no propellants detected nor any sign of energy coming from within. The ship was out of control.

B'taav re-engaged the *Xendos'* brakes. The alien crafts at his side disappeared into the distance.

The Independent sat in his chair, his mind a blank.

Slowly, ever so slowly, the *Xendos* approached the tumbling shuttle craft.

Alien drones surrounded and rammed the vessel, furiously ripping holes in her side and nudging her out of her original flight plan. Lying just outside the group was the old, one-eyed drone. She kept her distance and appeared to be overseeing the assault.

Cyclops is the leader.

B'taav swore.

The *Thanatos'* shuttle spun around, her sides ripped open. Large quantities of debris pouring out from within. The alien drones continued hammering her.

The whiplash tumbling of the shuttle would surely have crushed anyone aboard.

B'taav's eyes flickered up. The drones ignored the smaller debris falling from the shuttle and focused on the ship itself.

If the Locust Plague's defensive drones go after large objects...

B'taav had the ship's cameras scan the area immediately before the *Xendos*. Following the trajectory of the shuttle craft, B'taav spotted still more debris. He zoomed the cameras in, looking farther and farther ahead of her flight path, until...

There!

B'taav almost jumped out of his seat.

The object's dimensions were standard and she was intact.

It was a Phaecian escape pod.

B'taav aimed the *Xendos* at the pod and checked its speed. The escape craft was moving far slower than the *Xendos*.

Not surprising, B'taav thought.

Escape pods had very limited energy reserves and, given her distance from Earth, Cer was forced to hold back on thruster use in the hopes she could make atmospheric entry and landing. But her speed was so slow that by the time she reached Earth, the entire Solar System, would be rubble.

I have to get you.

B'taav made more calculations. Given the *Xendos'* speed relative to the escape pod, B'taav would overshoot Cer by many miles. There was no way for him to slow enough to pick her up.

At least not yet.

B'taav corrected the *Xendos'* direction. He didn't dare use his communicator to alert Cer he was close for fear the drones would pick up the signal.

Still B'taav wanted her to see he was near. To let her know she would make the trip to Earth in time.

To let her know she wasn't abandoned.

46

The *Xendos* approached the escape pod and in moments would rush by. Even with her forward thrusters at full, a minute later the *Xendos* would be over a hundred miles away.

B'taav inched the ship closer to the escape pod's path. He considered his next move.

The timing is too tight, he thought.

B'taav needed the computer to initiate all actions.

Hope I don't scare you too much.

B'taav sat back. The moment came and passed so quickly the Independent wasn't sure it even happened. As the *Xendos* flew by the escape pod, the ship's starboard lights came on for an instant while her gravitational hook momentarily gripped the escape vehicle.

The energy used was enormous and the *Xendos* shook from the effort. B'taav heard a low electronic buzz, the sound of stressed machinery. He looked at the *Xendos'* underside camera. The ship was once again visible.

Nano-probes have their limits.

The buzz stopped but the camouflage remained off. B'taav checked where the Locust Plague drones were. They continued bashing the *Thanatos* shuttle craft.

"Hope you don't look my way," B'taav muttered.

His attention switched to the escape pod. Her trajectory and speed were altered, though not severely enough to injure her occupant. The escape pod now moved in line with the *Xendos*. In the next half hour she would near the larger craft while it slowed. Eventually, it would be close enough to grab and tow all the way to Earth.

B'taav played back video from the starboard cameras. He slowed the images until they represented fractions of a second. He stopped on one image. Inquisitor Cer was on it, staring out the only window of the escape pod, her mouth open in surprise and the glare of the *Xendos'* lights illuminated her features.

"You saw me," he said.

B'taav killed the video and switched to a real time view of the pod. The Moon approached. Not only were the *Xendos'* thrusters fighting to slow her momentum, they were also fighting the pull of the satellite's gravity. The strain on the ship would be even greater when the escape pod was captured.

The *Xendos* was about to be pushed to her limits.

"Don't fail me," B'taav said.

The Moon grew.

B'taav's worked the computers furiously, testing algorithms and processing flight path data. So involved was he that he barely noticed the motion alarm.

B'taav's attention turned to another monitor. He spotted a flash of light and zoomed in on it. The *Thanatos* shuttle craft was in pieces and the light was likely the last of her propellant systems rupturing. The Locust Plague drones circled the shuttle's remains at wider and wider arcs, as if predators searching for fresh blood.

Several of the drones drifted away, probably returning to millennia old routes.

Two of them moved in the *Xendos'* direction.

One was Cyclops.

The drones drew closer and closer.

They can see me.

B'taav activated the fusion cannon controls. In seconds the systems were green. He locked the cannon on the drone closest to him. Cyclops.

B'taav had his clearest view of her yet. She was indeed a very old vessel. Deep cracks marred her surface and within them were the remnants of asteroids and jagged machinery. Mysterious spires, some bearing fearful peaks while others were dulled with age, rose from her body. At her tip was the single red light. Jutting out beside it was a long, reinforced tip. It was designed to stab its prey.

If they're after objects of a certain size, they'll ignore the escape pod and come after me. But the escape pod is between *them and me.*

B'taav's finger hovered over the fusion cannon's activation button.

The Locust Plague drones gained speed.

B'taav projected their course and breathed a small sigh of relief. They would pass the escape pod. *Very* close, but they would pass.

The *Xendos*, on the other hand…

Each second the drones closed in, their red lights glowed brighter and brighter. Abruptly, the lights on one of the drones shut off and it broke formation and drifted away.

Cyclops remained on course.

Maybe it's just checking you out. Don't fire. Not yet.
B'taav fingers moved away from the trigger.
He waited.

After a while, B'taav jerked forward in his chair.
The drone slowed. Its direction shifted ever so slightly.
B'taav was back at the controls of the fusion cannon.
"Come on," B'taav muttered. "We're no threat to you."
There were no other drones in sight.
Cyclops came in behind the *Xendos*. It matched speeds with the escape pod. Its single light glowed bright. Brighter still.
It's checking the escape pod. What for?
B'taav desperately looked at the monitors and the debris from the *Thanatos'* shuttle craft.
Why is it ignoring debris far larger than the escape pod?
The debris was off their port side and several hundred miles away. Chunks of the shuttle fell, yet Cyclops ignored them as they moved on...
...on toward the Moon.
B'taav's black eyes lit up.
You're designed to protect Earth from falling bodies.
Thanks to the drones, the remains of the *Thanatos* shuttle would fall dead center on the Moon. They were no threat to the Earth.
The *Xendos* and the escape pod, on the other hand, were moving toward the Moon's edge. They would eventually fly around the satellite and toward Earth.
And the drone was figuring this out!
B'taav released the fusion cannon controls and hit the forward thrusters. He altered the angle of his descent while the escape pod continued hurling toward the ship.
B'taav pressed a series of buttons. He slowed enough to get the escape pod within the range of the *Xendos'* gravity hook. The catch would be hard. Hard enough to hurt. But he had to do it now or risk missing her entirely.
"Come on," B'taav said.
The gravity hook was on. The escape pod moved a little closer. A little closer.
Just beyond it was Cyclops. She remained nearby. She was now checking the *Xendos'* trajectory.
"Give us time," B'taav muttered.
The escape pod was only a dozen miles away.

Suddenly, Cyclops accelerated. Other, smaller lights came on her surface. The red light on her spire glowed bright. She gave off high levels of radiation. She was arming herself. She was preparing to attack.

"Come on," B'taav repeated.

The escape pod was five miles away. Four.

The drone gained more speed. It was locked in on them.

The escape pod flew under the ship.

So fast...

There was no time. B'taav slammed his hand over the gravity hook, activating her in full. The *Xendos* locked onto the escape pod and gripped her tight.

The ships jerked wildly. Energy readings spiked as the engine protested. The escape pod was drawn in, closer and closer, until she slammed and locked into the larger craft's underside.

"Got you."

Alarms buzzed. The *Xendos'* engines were redlining.

B'taav ignored the warnings. His attention shifted back to Cyclops.

It continued its steady advance.

Another, different alarm buzzed.

Two other monitors activated. They displayed a group of drones. Twenty. Thirty. Forty five.

They were converging on the *Xendos*.

B'taav bit his upper lip. He used the *Xendos'* side thrusters to alter the ship's course even more.

They'll let me go when they see I'm on a collision course with the Moon.

B'taav continued the craft's sharp turn. Vibrations threatened to pull her apart. Abruptly, they lessened. The *Xendos* and the escape pod were now on course.

The engine warnings remained critical. Sparks shot out of one of the monitors.

B'taav ignored them. He aimed the fusion cannon at a surface crack on Cyclops. Perhaps a well-aimed shot might penetrate the...

All the monitors abruptly shut off.

The cockpit was enveloped in complete darkness.

B'taav couldn't see his hand before his face.

He couldn't do anything...

47

Long, terrible seconds passed.

The drones surrounded them. B'taav saw them through the ship's front window without the aid of his cameras. They circled his craft.

If they still perceived the *Xendos* or the escape pod as a threat, B'taav and Cer were finished.

Suddenly, the ship's lights came back on.

B'taav jumped to the monitors. Energy readings were still red and the *Xendos* remained crippled. B'taav checked the gravitational hook. It was still online and, through one of the cameras, he saw Inquisitor Cer's escape pod nestled below his ship. The drones around them circled a few more times. Slowly, too slowly, they backed off.

"Move on," B'taav said.

A couple turned away. Others followed.

All but one.

Cyclops appeared directly in front of the *Xendos*. She was less than a hundred feet away. Her single red light shined into the ship's cockpit, illuminating her interior in a bloody red.

B'taav was frozen in place as she remained there, eye to eye, hunter to prey. Cyclops waited. Her single light grew brighter, then brighter still, until it was blinding.

She remained before the *Xendos*, her tip practically touching the front of the ship.

B'taav's heart pounded. If he reached out, he could touch her...

Abruptly, the red light dulled.

Cyclops backed up.

She veered off and flew away, disappearing into the darkness.

B'taav took a few seconds to let the tension dissipate.

That was close.

He then focused on the ship's approach to the Moon... and beyond.

The ship rocked side to side, the escape pod moving with it.

B'taav scanned the monitors, searching for any alerts. He examined the outer camera monitors. The Moon filled the forward view screen.

"You've been through a lot," B'taav told his ship. "Hang on for a little longer."

The nano-probes, if they were capable of doing so, didn't answer.

The energy levels within the *Xendos* fluctuated as she and her companion neared the Moon's surface. B'taav kept the ship's path directed at the celestial object. No turns, no deviations.

The escape pod's sole window was dark. What was Inquisitor Cer thinking in there?

B'taav wanted to contact her, tell her what he was about to do.

Any such activity might attract the Locust Plague probes.

B'taav's free hand hovered over the thruster controls. His other hand tightened on the yoke. The Moon's surface, its gray valleys and craters, filled the view screen.

At the last possible second, B'taav acted.

He engaged the *Xendos'* full thrusters while pulling back on the controls.

The *Xendos* and her companion spun to the side, paralleling the satellite's rocky surface.

B'taav kept his hands locked while focusing on the monitor displaying the escape pod. For a second Inquisitor Cer's pod pulled away and looked like she might rip free. The ship's engines groaned and lights flickered. The escape pod snapped back.

Thank the Gods...

The *Xendos* and her companion skimmed the Moon's surface. B'taav switched the images on the monitor and searched for drones. All of them, including Cyclops, were gone.

His gaze returned to the dreary lunar terrain. It passed under him in a blur. Craters and their valleys. Mountains and—

Abruptly, his eyes opened wide.

In the far distance, he spotted a structure. It was a large, flat building.

B'taav swore.

It was too late to turn. Whatever the structure was, he'd pass right over it.

If it was another Locust Plague defensive system...

A second passed. Another.

He spotted a single light shining from a window within the building.

Oh no...

Just like that the ship was over and past her. A moment later the structure was long gone.

B'taav checked every monitor for signs of defensive measures. He spotted none.

Did I really see a light? he wondered.

He thought some more. Was the structure human or alien? He couldn't be sure. He was frustrated there would be no chance to investigate.

B'taav applied more thrust.

Another light shone. This one was at the edge of the Moon's horizon. It grew brighter.

B'taav held his breath. His mouth opened.

The light grew brighter still.

The Independent knew what was rising before him. Inquisitor Cer and he would be the first humans to lay eyes on her in over five thousand—

And there she was.

The Earth rose like a miniature sun. She was a heartbreaking sight. Her surface was almost as gray as the Moon's and a crosshatch of dark metallic tentacles of incredible length extended like chains around her. They lay near the edge of the planet's atmosphere and enveloped its prey.

Over the Earth's southern hemisphere floated the Locust Plague's mother ship. She was a patchwork monster, larger even than the *Thanatos* and made up of odd pieces welded together over thousands and thousands of years. The vessel covered a fourth of the planet and had the shape of a ball split in half. She did not rotate with her captive, instead remaining stationary and gathering sunlight while not allowing it to filter below.

B'taav recognized the ship and her tentacles. They were a vision of a recent nightmare.

The *Xendos* flew away from the Moon. If the drones were to reappear, they would do so now.

Yet B'taav saw no sign of them. Perhaps their patrol area lay just outside the Moon's orbit and they were not programmed to protect the space between the Moon and Earth.

Which meant the Locust Plague's mother ship could take care of anything that made it this close.

B'taav heard a low hum. He frowned.

The *Xendos'* engines were again taxed to their limits.

B'taav checked the ship using the outside cameras. He wasn't surprised to find she was trying to cloak herself.

The nano-probes sense danger.

The energy expended, however, proved too great. After a couple of attempts, the cloak remained off.

B'taav kept the *Xendos* far from the Locust Plagues' mother ship. He approached the metal tentacles, for to get to Earth he would have to pass through the empty spaces between them. Those spaces were sizeable, but B'taav worried there might be sensors that detected his movement.

The tentacles stretched out and around the planet, black jagged metal with cruel, sharp spikes protruding from underneath. At regular intervals were hollow scoops designed to collect whatever the spikes ripped apart.

The crafts fell further and further. Soon, they neared the first layer of these tentacles.

Closer... closer...

B'taav leaned back in his chair. The tentacles were scored with deep cuts. This equipment was well worn, having been used to murder countless worlds.

The *Xendos* was parallel to them.

The *Xendos* passed them.

The interior of the craft was bathed in darkness.

B'taav scanned the monitors, searching for any new threats.

Abruptly, the darkness fell away.

B'taav relaxed, if only a little.

There was another layer of tentacles further below the one he just navigated through. Having successfully passed the first without incident, he was optimistic about passing the second.

The ship shook.

This is it, B'taav thought.

The *Xendos* entered the Earth's atmosphere.

48

The *Xendos* **slowed** as it dipped. B'taav flipped the ship around, using her upper body to protect the escape pod.

The prolonged use of the gravity hook, especially while entering the atmosphere, worried B'taav. He shut down all unnecessary systems and re-directing energy to the engines. Thrusters lit up and attempted to further slow the ship's speed. The crafts buckled.

Light cascaded through the window of the escape pod and B'taav had the *Xendos'* cameras peer inside her. Inquisitor Cer was in her seat, strapped down. Her hair was disheveled and there was an ugly cut on her forehead. She waved frantically at the window, trying to get B'taav's attention. The Independent zoomed the camera on her lips.

Let me go!

B'taav didn't want to. But with each shudder, with each energy fluctuation, he realized it was best to do so. The wear on the *Xendos* was great, especially since entering the atmosphere.

You got her to Earth, which you had to do. Inquisitor Cer can land the escape pod far better on her own. For that matter, it'll make it easier for you to do the same.

B'taav shone a light on the pod, an acknowledgement of receiving Cer's message.

Cer lifted her hand and waved.

Anytime you're ready.

B'taav pressed another button and drew a breath.

Your Gods be with you, Cer.

The gravity hook was off and the escape pod almost instantly was gone. The strain on the *Xendos'* engines lifted.

B'taav followed the escape pod through the ship's cameras and calculated her landing site.

She would drop within five miles of the signals sent by Paul Spradlin to the *Thanatos* and at the base of a series of jagged mountains.

B'taav checked his remote unit and its timer. They had four hours and fifteen minutes to search for Spradlin before they needed to leave.

The smaller craft slowed faster than the *Xendos*. B'taav had to keep his altitude and use the atmosphere to continue braking.

Wait for me.

Once down, all they had to do was investigate the source of Paul Spradlin's transmissions, find the man –if he was still alive and in that place– and get the hell out of here.

A simple enough task.

B'taav looked at the second layer of tentacles. It had even more jagged claws extending throughout its underside.

Four hours and fifteen minutes to find a man and get back to Jupiter sounded simple enough.

In B'taav's line of work, nothing was ever simple.

In time, the *Xendos* slowed enough for B'taav to lower her closer to the second layer of tentacles.

By then, Cer's escape pod was well past them and long gone. B'taav looked for any reaction from the alien artifacts, but they remained still. There was no evidence their arrival was noticed.

The *Xendos* lowered some more.

Her cameras swung around and trained on the Locust Plague mother ship. As with the metallic mesh encircling the planet, it too appeared lifeless.

B'taav relaxed.

A couple dozen miles south of the mountains where Spradlin's signal originated were the remains of a city. The city's area rivaled the largest cities in the Empires, though what was left of her appeared to be no more than rubble.

B'taav's attention returned to Inquisitor Cer's escape pod. It touched down on the desert floor before the dark mountains.

The Independent activated the *Xendos'* thrusters.

In a little while, he would be back with Inquisitor Cer.

No time to lose.

49

The *Xendos* moved across the Earth's dingy gray sky.

B'taav kept the craft steady despite the urge to hurry up and land.

This is it.

The second, and last, layer of tentacles was thinner than those orbiting outside the planet's atmosphere. B'taav eased the *Xendos* past them. Their bodies were approximately a mile in width and, like the first layer of tentacles, their claws were pockmarked with scars.

B'taav spotted gears at their connections. They were designed to loosen or tighten the tentacles. As they moved, so too did the entire wire-like lattice, until it reached the planet's surface. At that point the tentacles and their jagged claws became a mesh garrote, digging into the ground and eviscerating it, exposing the ores, liquids, and elements that lay beneath a planet's surface.

Below the tentacles and on the Earth's surface were thousands of miles of crisscrossing shadows. The shadows barely moved as the planet rotated. If there was any vegetation left, it would surely have been killed by their extended darkness.

The fact that the tentacles were miles above the planet's surface after all these years proved Spradlin's plan worked. The aliens had not fed. Instead, their machinery waited. It *remained* waiting.

B'taav fought back a chill.

He was flying through the graveyard of hungry Gods and the last thing he wanted to do was make them stir.

The radiation monitors clicked.

There were areas he flew over that were heavily contaminated. Others, less so. As he approached the point from which Spradlin's message originated, the counter dropped. This area proved to be one of the relatively few clean ones left on Earth.

Of course, B'taav thought.

The Independent applied the ship's forward and lower thrusters, slowing and leveling the craft at twenty thousand feet. The *Xendos* turned ever so slightly, until she was in line with Cer's landing site.

B'taav flew over the mountain terrain and opposite the city remains.

He skirted the mountain peaks, noting gray valleys that once held forests and streams. Nothing was left of either.

B'taav pulled a readout of surface conditions.

The *Xendos* detected no winds at all and an extremely dry, stagnant atmosphere. There was no evidence of any living things below.

It was as if this world was preserved at the moment of her death.

The *Xendos* flew past the mountain range and was over the coffee colored desert sands.

The escape pod lay only a couple of miles away.

Her side was marred with black streaks. The attack on the *Thanatos'* shuttle craft and the atmospheric entry had almost taken her out.

B'taav re-checked his monitors for signs of movement. None were detected. The hatch to the escape pod was open yet he could not see Inquisitor Cer. B'taav shook his head.

Where are you?

He slowed the ship until she hovered over the pod. Cameras zoomed in and B'taav spotted footprints in the sand. They led away from the escape pod and toward the mountain range.

Why didn't you wait for me?

B'taav had the ship touch down and jumped from the cockpit chair. He ran to the decompression chamber, removed his space suit and remote control unit, put on a jacket and snapped the control back on before activating the chamber's doors. As the doors worked through their cycle, B'taav checked the remote unit and made sure it was properly linked to the *Xendos*. Satisfied it was, he grabbed a medi-kit and the fusion gun Desjardins gave him back at the *Thanatos*.

Dry, dusty air filled the chamber as the outer door opened.

B'taav left the ship.

The Earth's atmosphere was breathable, just as the *Xendos'* instruments indicated, yet B'taav found it lacking.

It was sterile and hot and, as the ship's instruments noted, stagnant.

Looming to the east was the mountain range Inquisitor Cer walked off toward.

B'taav raced onto the desert sands, his feet sinking into the fine grains. He stopped momentarily beside the escape pod and looked inside. There were drops of dried blood on a panel but otherwise her interior was intact.

B'taav left the pod and followed Inquisitor Cer's path. He neared the edge of the mountain's rocky terrain.

"Cer?" he yelled out.

His voice echoed.

Where did you go? Why did you leave the ship? Especially if you knew I was right behind—

There was a loud groan and B'taav spun around.

The sand between the *Xendos* and the escape pod shifted. Something below the surface moved, drawing up closer to him. A few feet away another patch of sand stirred. Several feet from those disturbances came still more movement.

Three dark figures rose from the sands. Their bodies were metal and their shapes roughly humanoid. Their movements were clumsy. They were made of metallic scraps cobbled together, it appeared, by a madman. The largest of the three was at least twice B'taav's size while the smallest was just a little shorter than him.

All three moved in the direction of the *Xendos*.

B'taav pulled up his left arm and spoke into the remote control panel.

"Liftoff," he said.

The *Xendos'* engines fired and the ship rose. It continued rising. Too high.

"Xendos, level o—"

B'taav stopped in mid-command. Five dark forms appeared in the sky. They were attack drones similar to the ones he saw on his journey to Earth. They came from different directions and headed towards the *Xendos*.

On the ground, the three robots stopped. With the *Xendos* out of their reach, their focus turned to B'taav.

The Independent swore.

Ambush.

He drew his fusion gun before addressing the remote control panel. With the ship under attack and so far away, his instructions would be, to say the least, inadequate.

If the *Xendos* was lost, there was no chance either he or Inquisitor Cer could leave this cursed Earth.

The robots' strides quickened. Each move was followed by a metallic groan. The smallest of them raised its arms. Something on it glowed an angry red.

B'taav ducked and fired his fusion gun.

He hit that robot dead center, the fusion blast punching through its chest and blowing a chuck of metal out of its back side.

The creature didn't slow.

B'taav backed up. He fired again and again, aiming each time at his pursuer's midsections. None of the shots significantly slowed them. B'taav stepped off the sands and was on the outer perimeter of the mountain range. He looked up in the sky and the flying forms converging on the *Xendos*.

His ship remained still in the air, an easy target, and there was nothing B'taav could do about it.

Nothing at all.

50

Things happened quickly.

The *Xendos* faded, her dark grey colors changing to match the sandy brown sky. Without the strain of carrying the escape pod while attempting atmospheric entry, she had enough energy to hide herself. In moments, there was little left of her but a faint outline. Seconds after that, she was gone.

The drones pursuing her slowed and circled the area. They were confused by her disappearance but continued their search.

Surprised and pleased as B'taav was by this, his attention immediately switched to the approaching robots. Though the fusion blasts hadn't slowed them, dark liquid spilled from their wounds and, after taking a dozen steps, the medium sized robot stumbled.

I did some damage after all.

B'taav skipped up the rocks and found cover. He took a quick peek at the sky but, like the drones, could no longer locate the *Xendos*. For their part, the drones' moves grew more frantic. If their attention turned to B'taav...

The sound of a fusion blast smashing against the rock he was hiding behind forced B'taav to crouch low. Dust and rock chips fell into his hiding place. That blast was followed by another coming from behind and somewhere above him. This one was directed at the robots.

Is that you, Cer?

B'taav peeked over the rock he was hidden behind. The right appendage of the largest member of the group of three robots fell to the ground. B'taav looked back, toward where the last fusion blast came from.

"Cer?"

"Up here!"

Inquisitor Cer was hiding in an outcrop above the Independent.

B'taav put away his fusion gun and climbed toward her while she covered him. Fusion blasts seared through the smallest robot's legs, causing it to fall. It didn't stop. It used its arms to propel itself forward.

Inquisitor Cer kept firing as B'taav made his way closer to her position.

The largest of the robots passed the others. Once on the rocks, it gained speed. It clanged closer and closer to the Independent. It reached out...

Its claw-like hand nearly grabbed B'taav's left leg. Metal slammed against rock, pulverizing it and sending dust into the air.

B'taav twisted away.

The robot was on the ground. Its head came up and red, shining eyes settled on the Independent. B'taav drew his fusion gun and fired. The blast blew out one of the robot's eyes.

The creature emitted an angry, explosive howl that forced B'taav to cover his ears.

Move.

He stumbled up, climbing as quickly as he could.

The creature's mouth closed and it moved on. Again it reached out, its jagged arm grasping at space only inches away from the Independent's back.

Another fusion blast from above, this one aimed at the ground below the robot, shattered the crumbly rock. The mighty creature stumbled backwards, sliding before falling on its back.

The other two creatures passed their larger brother.

"Hurry!" Inquisitor Cer yelled.

B'taav climbed up, higher and higher. He looked back. On flat surfaces, the creatures moved swiftly but on inclines they slowed considerably and the Independent gained distance from them.

Despite the good news, the Independent grimaced. The heat and exertion, coupled with his recent illness, had weakened him considerably. His energy waned until, after climbing one last pair of ledges, he had to stop and catch his breath.

B'taav peered into the sky. The drones pursuing the *Xendos* were mostly gone. Those that remained zoomed around in ever widening circles.

B'taav activated the remote control on his jacket sleeve.

"*Xendos*, acknowledge," he said.

A short transmission confirmed the *Xendos* was still in one piece.

"Maintain evasive maneuvers," B'taav said.

Despite everything, he laughed.

The ship is doing a pretty good job without me.

B'taav stared back down the rocky mountain trail.

The three metal creatures pursuing him were also gone. Pieces of them lay on the rocky path. They scurried away, possibly tending to their wounds and readying for another attack.

"Cer?" B'taav said.

"Up here," she said. "You see them?"

"No."

"Come on."

B'taav climbed the remaining rocks. By then, his face was covered in sweat.

"Inquisitor?" he called out.

He heard the scraping of boots on rock. He couldn't be sure – not *entirely* sure– if it was Cer who approached.

He lifted his fusion gun.

The noise grew. A pebble rolled away and fell over the edge of the outcrop. It clanged somewhere down below.

Standing before him was Inquisitor Cer.

The left side of her face was bloody from the cut on her forehead. The blood stained her jacket and her left eye was swollen. There was feral quality to her face, a mix of anger and determination.

"You look like hell," she said.

"And you… you've never looked better," B'taav countered.

B'taav reached out.

They hugged.

They spent several minutes resting and recuperating.

B'taav bandaged and dressed Cer's wounds. Her left eye was fiery red but thanks to medication, the swelling was considerably reduced. Her vision, she said, was not affected. After putting the medi-kit away, they split a pair of Nutri-Sticks.

To their west were miles of flat desert. Still further was a patch of darkness, a shadow from the metal tentacles surrounding the Earth. To their north and south were more rocks while to their east the mountain rose higher and higher.

"And they called this place Eden," B'taav said.

The words were greeted with silence. After a while, Inquisitor Cer spoke.

"Why did you come after me?" she asked. "Finding Paul Spradlin is a fool's errand. Bad enough one fool goes, much less two."

"If this mission required a fool, then I should have been the one to go in the first place," B'taav said and smiled.

Inquisitor Cer did not react. The smile on the Independent's face disappeared.

"What happened after the *Dakota*?" B'taav asked.

"I told you."

"What happened to *you*?"

Inquisitor Cer remained silent.

"Please," he said. "I want to know."

Inquisitor Cer drew a sharp breath.

"I've... I've lost a lot these past days," she said.

Inquisitor Cer's eyes were suddenly on B'taav. There was fury in them.

"People I thought were good weren't. The Empire and the Holy Texts I swore my life to were revealed to be—"

The fury was gone.

"—lies."

She was silent for a few seconds before continuing.

"I've witnessed bad things... the worst in my fellow man. At times, it was tempting to just give it up. Yet there was always one thing I could look to for guidance: The Holy Texts and the Word of the Gods. They kept me going, B'taav. For better or worse, it made me what I am. Now, to find so much of it was a... a lie."

For a moment she lost control.

"Easy," B'taav said. "I'm sure—"

"Did you talk to Desjardins?" Cer snapped. "Did he tell you what he was? What *we* are?"

"Yes."

"We're abominations," Cer said. "Created for this very mission by puppet masters we didn't even know existed."

"Cer," B'taav began.

"How are we any different from laboratory mice?"

B'taav was quiet. These words pierced him as deeply as they had her.

"It doesn't matter if we were created by man or God," B'taav said. "We're still human. We have our free will."

The Independent drew his left arm and produced the *Xendos'* remote control panel.

"Say the word and I'll bring the ship down. We fly back to the *Thanatos* and tell Desjardins we're done here. We go home and forget all this ever happened."

Inquisitor Cer wiped a tear from her face.

"We can return home," Cer said. "But how do we forget? Running away doesn't change anything."

"It doesn't," B'taav admitted.

"You've lived an entire life without faith." Cer asked. "I have not. My faith is crumbling away. The Words of the Gods were wrong. According to them, the Earth was destroyed after the Exodus. It obviously was not. The Overlords were supposed to exemplify human divinity, yet they're sinners just like all of us. What else should I question? Is there a final reward? Are there really any Gods? Is there a kingdom above?"

She paused.

"You've lived life without faith," Cer repeated. "How can *I*?"

B'taav thought about that. He spoke.

"When I was very young, I realized I had memories. I know. It sounds like a simple thing, but I was so very young at that time and the realization surprised me. So I thought back. I could remember things that happened the day before and the day before that but there came a point where my memories ended. Beyond that point was a... a darkness. It wasn't a mysterious, scary thing. More like the darkness one feels when falling to sleep. I somehow knew this was where I –where *everyone*– came from. It was also where after a lifetime worth of memories and action we all return. Because this darkness held neither joy nor fear, glee nor sadness, the thought of returning to it didn't scare me."

"What scares you?"

"Accomplishing nothing in between."

Inquisitor Cer thought about that.

"I've done good things and been humbled by failures as I'm sure you have," B'taav continued. "Today, at this moment, regardless of all that has happened before, we have an opportunity to see where we came from. Even if this place isn't what the Holy Texts said it was, we have a chance to meet the man who saved humanity. And when we meet him, we may discover secrets hidden for thousands of years."

"What if Paul Spradlin is just an ordinary, flawed man?"

"Then we'll treat him as such," B'taav said. "There may be no Saints, there may be no heavenly reward. Our faith may be misplaced and everything we do may amount to nothing. We have the choice of closing ourselves off until we return to darkness, or we embrace life and make the best of it while we can."

Inquisitor Cer thought about that. She looked down at her Nutri-Stick and, for the first time in a while, cracked a smile.

"You think he'll like our food?" she said.

"There isn't *anyone* –human or God– who likes this crap," B'taav replied.

They laughed. Their laughter cut the tension and brightened their moods. Inquisitor Cer wrapped what was left of her Nutri-Stick and pocketed it.

"What do you say, Independent? Do we make some history of our own?"

"I thought you'd never ask," B'taav said.

Cer rose and offered B'taav her hand. He took it.

Together, they marched north.

51

For over an hour they walked.

At times they slowed because the terrain grew difficult while at others they took advantage of clear paths and hurried along. Now and again B'taav consulted the remote control panel on his jacket sleeve to get an idea of their progress while making sure the *Xendos* remained intact.

In time they neared the site of Paul Spradlin's communique to the *Thanatos*.

It was then that Inquisitor Cer crouched and pulled B'taav down. They huddled in a shadowy grove.

"What is it?" B'taav whispered.

"Something's in front of us."

"More robots?"

"I can't be sure. It didn't look like them."

"What did it look like?"

Cer bit her lip.

"A woman."

She leaned out of their hiding spot. All was clear.

"Whoever it was is gone," Cer said.

They stepped from the shadows and cautiously drew to the area Cer spotted the female figure. On a patch of sand they found a pair of footprints.

"Boots," B'taav said.

"We have company," Inquisitor Cer whispered. "More company any—"

Inquisitor Cer stopped talking. Both she and B'taav detected movement at their sides. Quick. Silent. Lethal.

B'taav slid to his side. His head scrapped a rock and for a moment his vision clouded. When it cleared he spotted Inquisitor Cer.

She was backing up while a dark, rectangular form came between them. It was the smallest of the three robots. Its destroyed legs had fused together and produced an even smaller, stubbier frame. For a moment the thing paused, unsure of which of its targets to attack. A decision made, it moved.

B'taav spun away just as the machine's claws slammed against the ground he lay on. B'taav drew his fusion gun and fired. The blast hit the creature on its shoulder and momentarily knocked it to its side. Steam rose from the wound.

Another fusion blast, this one from Inquisitor Cer, blew a chunk off the creature's stubby legs.

B'taav didn't linger. He got to his feet and hurried to Cer's side.

"The other two have to be close," B'taav said.

The robot blocked their path forward, forcing them back. It rose unsteadily. The damage from the fusion blasts was great and its moves were much slower.

"Let's end this," Inquisitor Cer said.

Independent and Inquisitor fired a barrage at the creature. Chunks of shrapnel flew in all directions. When they finished firing, the robot was in pieces.

They approached its remains, curious to see how this mechanized thing operated. The pieces of metal, however, proved to be just that.

"I don't see any circuitry or machinery," Inquisitor Cer said. "No gears. No levers."

"How is it moving?"

The answer revealed itself. The metal scraps vibrated. Some remained in place while others came together. A couple of pieces already touching each other fused and formed a new whole.

"Nano-probes," Inquisitor Cer said. "The repair process is just like what I saw on the *Xendos*. Only quicker."

"We tear the metal to pieces and the nano-probes bring this thing back together again. How do you stop something like that?"

They hurried away from the metal fragments, careful not to touch any of them, and were back on the trail leading up the mountain.

"You hear that?"

B'taav listened. He heard a faint roar. The two walked to the edge of the rocky terrain and looked over it and to the west. Far in the distance they spotted a small dust cloud.

"Is that a storm?"

"The *Xendos* detected no measurable winds in the atmosphere."

"The Locust Plague must have started the storm," Cer said. "If that's the case, they must be controlling it."

"For what reason?"

B'taav keyed in a command on the *Xendos'* remote control panel.

"*Xendos*, I need a visual close up, west 20 degrees, approximately fifty miles from my location."

B'taav and Cer examined the remote control's small monitor. On it was an overview of the dust cloud.

"Enhance and magnify," he said.

The image cleared up. Despite the clarity, there was little to see beyond the dust cloud itself.

"She's about a mile across," B'taav said. "Wind speeds are sixty miles per hour. Sixty five. A tornado?"

Inquisitor Cer noted something at the corner of the monitor. Small black figures rushed into the swirling dust.

"What's that?" Inquisitor Cer said.

"Magnify lower edge," B'taav said.

The image magnified.

"By the Gods," Inquisitor Cer said.

The black pieces were metal beings similar to the ones that attacked them. A few had wheels while most moved on limbs. They penetrated the dust cloud and disappeared within.

"What are they doing?"

"I don't know," B'taav said. "Could they be cobbling up, making something bigger, more powerful?"

"Cobbling up into a storm?" Cer said. "That doesn't make much sense."

B'taav nodded.

"Well, whatever they're doing, it can't be good."

"How long do we have before we need to leave?"

B'taav checked the remote panel's timer.

"Two hours and fifty minutes."

"The storm isn't that strong," Cer said. "At least not yet. We need to find Spradlin before that's no longer the case."

They rushed up the rocks, climbing higher and higher into the mountain range.

The path narrowed. There was less sand and the air felt even drier.

The dust storm continued its growth. Its clouds grew darker.

"Winds are at ninety five miles," B'taav said.

Inquisitor Cer grabbed B'taav's shoulder and spun him around.

Some two hundred feet away and almost hidden in the rocky shadows was a woman. She had long black hair and stared directly at the two. She was dressed in a worn black jumpsuit and her arms were exposed. They were made of flesh and metal.

"What is she?"

"I don't know. Perhaps she's one of them—"

What followed was a blur.

A rusty metallic arm, cold and gritty with age, slammed B'taav's side. The blow sent his fusion gun sliding away. Inquisitor Cer fired at the creature but the robot, the largest of the three pursuing them, took the blasts far better than its smallest brother.

The thing stood directly over B'taav. It lifted its leg.

Inquisitor Cer yelled and tried to distract it, but the creature's focus was on its helpless captive.

The creature's leg was directly over B'taav's head. Sharp, rusty spikes protruded from under its foot.

Inquisitor Cer fired her gun with her right hand and grabbed B'taav's side with her left. She tried pulling him away.

The creature's free arm swatted her aside before she could. Its leg slowly lowered. The hideous spikes drew closer to B'taav's head.

B'taav frantically reached for anything he could use to defend himself. He spotted Inquisitor Cer on the ground, stunned by the robot's blow. She looked at him and he at her.

"Please don't leave me," she said.

The spikes were inches away. They touched the side of B'taav's head. The pressure grew. The robot was taking its time, making the Independent suffer.

"No," Inquisitor Cer whispered.

There was nothing she could do but stare in horror as B'taav slowly died.

The spikes broke skin and blood dripped down the side of the Independent's head.

"Let him go."

The voice was female but didn't come from Inquisitor Cer. The woman's speech held a strange accent yet her words were clear.

Inquisitor Cer spun around. The dark figure they saw moments before stood only feet away.

She was indeed a woman. Barely.

She was tall, muscular, and held an ancient rifle in her right arm. On that arm, human flesh merged in a grisly fashion with metal. The left arm was in better shape, though the union of metal and flesh was just as gory. The woman was in her mid-forties but from the way she carried herself, she appeared considerably older, if not at all fragile.

She aimed her weapon low. She fired.

The projectile burst seared the robot's lower leg at its joint. The rusted metal fell to the side and crashed on the ground. The appendage let off a cloud of steam before turning black.

"Move!" the woman yelled.

Inquisitor Cer pulled B'taav away.

More shots were fired. The projectiles slammed into the robot, ripping out large chunks of metal. The smell of gunpowder was heavy and the noise from the weapon deafening.

B'taav and Cer ran.

They reached B'taav's fusion gun and the Independent grabbed it. The two fired upon the robot but their fusion blasts did only a fraction of the damage of the woman's shots.

"Save your ammo," another voice, also female, said.

She stood on a rock formation above them and was shorter than the metal and flesh woman. She had black, shoulder length hair and wore sunglasses that barely hid a trio of blue rectangular tattoos over her right eye. Unlike her companion, she looked completely humanoid. In her arms was a black blade.

The woman silently dropped to the ground before the robot. She held the blade in front of her.

Incredibly, the creature hesitated at the sight of this even more primitive weapon. It took a step back.

"I don't think so," the woman with the blade said.

The robot turned. It hurried to the edge of the cliff.

Before it could escape, the woman rammed her weapon through its midsection. She released it and jumped back. Instantly, a flash of brilliant electric sparkles showered the area.

Both B'taav and Inquisitor Cer covered their eyes from the blinding lightshow. In moments the steam and energy crackles dissipated and revealed what remained of the robot. It stood as before, just feet from the edge of the cliff and escape. Its metal body turned to black ash. The ash crumbled and formed a pile of dust.

B'taav and Inquisitor Cer looked for their saviors.

They were gone.

"Stay still," a hidden voice –the first of the two women– whispered.

B'taav and Cer did as told. After a few seconds, they heard the sounds of footfalls. The mysterious women reappeared from the shadows. They circled the area, checking for other attackers before again disappearing.

All was completely silent.

And then there was another footfall. This one was metallic.

"Easy," the woman with the sunglasses whispered.

B'taav and Inquisitor Cer pointed their guns in the direction of the noise.

Their last pursuer was at least fifty yards away. It too hid in the rocky shadows and considered whether to attack. All was still for a while. Silent. Eerily so.

Until...

"We haven't got all day," the woman with the sunglasses yelled out.

There was a loud groan followed by a metallic creak.

The sound faded.

"Is it gone?" B'taav whispered.

"What do you think?" the woman with the sunglasses replied.

She emerged from her hiding place and drew a second blade from the sheath around her belt. She held it before her and crouched.

"Come on," she said. "I'm right here."

All remained quiet. The woman with the sunglasses smirked.

"Fucking coward," she said.

There came a mighty rumble. The third, medium sized robot erupted from its hiding place and charged at the woman. B'taav and Inquisitor Cer aimed low and fired their weapons. Fusion blasts hit the creature's legs, sending chunks of metal in all directions.

Just as it was almost on her, the woman with the black blade swung her weapon. The creature barely avoided it by the rolling out of the way and to the edge of the mountain.

It was back on its feet and leaped high over that edge before falling. It crashed down, down below.

The group of four hurried to the cliff's edge and watched as it slammed hard against the rocks and lost bits and pieces of its body before landing with a thud at the bottom. The creature remained still for several seconds before, incredibly, crawling into the shadows and out of sight.

The woman with the stringy brown hair and metal appendages leaned as far as she could over the ledge. For the first time B'taav and Inquisitor Cer had a good look at her eyes. They were silver orbs.

"What do you see?" the woman in the sunglasses asked.

"Give me a second," her companion said. She stared hard for a while before shaking her head. "It's gone."

The woman with the sunglasses and tattoos nodded. She pointed to the west, toward the growing sandstorm.

"What about out there?"

"Still building," the metal and flesh woman said.

The women faced B'taav and Inquisitor Cer.

"Looks like you two brought along quite a party," the woman with the sunglasses and facial tattoos said.

"Who are you?" Inquisitor Cer asked.

The woman with the tattoos pointed to her companion.

"She's Becky Waters. My name is Nox. Nice to meet you, Inquisitor Cer and... B'taav, right? The hell kind of name is that?"

"You know us?"

"Weren't expecting any other visitors," Nox said. She faced B'taav. "You're the Independent?"

"Yes," B'taav said.

Nox shook her head before addressing Inquisitor Cer.

"Lady, you could do so much better."

"You were in touch with the *Thanatos*," Inquisitor Cer said.

"Bright girl," Nox said.

"You're with Spradlin? You know where he is?"

"Better than anyone," Nox replied. A weary smile worked its way onto her lips. "It's a bit of a story. How about we get out of the sun before I tell it?"

Cer and B'taav weren't sure what to make of the women. Nonetheless, they lowered their weapons.

"Lead the way," the Inquisitor said.

52

The Earth spun on, ensnared in a metallic spider's web...

They walked through the increasingly rocky terrain, their bodies exposed to tremendous heat. They climbed higher and higher up the trail and into the mountains until they found themselves among the remains of ancient structures. They were no more than a series of rusted metal beams whose shape indicated they were once part of a building.

They climbed on until the rocky ground leveled off. Becky Waters, the woman-machine hybrid, took point. Nox followed a few feet behind, her back to Inquisitor Cer and B'taav. This, they realized, was intended to build trust.

The group moved into what looked less and less like part of the mountain and more like that ancient building. Finally, they reached an opening and, past it, a dark cave.

"This way," Nox said.

The air within the cave was even more stagnant than that outside. B'taav and Cer hesitated before walking several feet into the darkness.

"Hang on," Becky Waters said.

Inquisitor Cer and B'taav heard the sounds of tumbling switches. Lights came on and revealed the ruins of a metallic corridor. At its end was a large vault door.

A red scanner activated. It bathed the group in its light before shutting off. Afterwards, a series of latches whirled and clicked. The vault door swung open.

Becky Waters stepped through the door and disappeared into the darkness beyond. Nox motioned to Inquisitor Cer and B'taav.

"Let's go," she said.

"What's in there?" B'taav asked.

"Shangri La," Nox said.

"What?"

"We'll explain in a moment," Nox said. She grinned. "Don't worry, we won't keep you past your time limit."

B'taav and Inquisitor Cer looked at each other.

"Yeah, we know about that too," Nox said.

With that, she followed her companion into the darkness.

They stepped past the vault door. It silently closed behind them and all was momentarily dark.

A series of dim lights came on. They illuminated the sagging walls of another metal corridor.

B'taav and Cer followed that corridor to its end before stopping in front of a metal door with even more armor plating than the vault door they just entered. There was evidence of corrosion on parts of it, a patina of extreme age that was unmistakable. A computer panel to the door's side lit up and Becky Waters put her metallic right hand over it.

The door noiselessly swung open.

B'taav and Inquisitor Cer followed Nox and Becky Waters past this door. More lights came on and the duo found themselves on a circular balcony overlooking what appeared to be countless floors stretching down into the heart of the mountain.

"A hidden base?" Inquisitor Cer said.

"Pretty common way back when," Becky Waters said. "Rich technocrats had dozens of places like these hidden away in the deserts and, as you see, mountains. It was how they kept their research secret."

"Who did this base belong to?" Cer asked.

"Doesn't matter all that much anymore," Nox said. "The important thing was that it was closest to the city and Spradlin prepared it for us."

"How?"

"You'll see."

The group walked around the circular balcony and to an elevator. It took them down a couple of floors. When they exited, they found themselves in a medical observation room. Glass panels separated them from hundreds of rows of rectangular containers. The two closest to the glass divider were open.

Recognition dawned on Inquisitor Cer.

"Stasis chambers," she said. "Though bulkier than the ones I'm familiar with."

"We call them Cryo-Med units," Becky Waters said. "They were designed to heal while keeping one's body suspended. Perfect for our long wait."

"You've been in them since the Exodus?"

"That's what you guys call it?" Nox said. "Nice name. Becky and I call it the day everyone took the fuck off and left us to fend for ourselves."

Becky Waters noisily cleared her throat.

"To you, over five thousand years have passed," Becky Waters said. "To us, it's been little more than a year."

"How's that possible?"

"We're here, aren't we?" Nox said.

"That's hardly proof," B'taav said. "How do we know you're human and not one of those things?"

Nox approached the Independent and offered him her arm.

"You want to take a sample of our blood?"

"We're wasting time," Cer said. "And that isn't something we have much of."

She pointed to the unopened chambers.

"Are there more of you?"

"We're it," Becky Waters said.

Both Inquisitor Cer and B'taav were confused by her words.

"What about Paul Spradlin?" Inquisitor Cer asked. "Where is he?"

"Dead," Nox said.

"What?" Inquisitor Cer said. "The signal sent to the *Thanatos*... it was verified as coming from—"

B'taav gripped Cer's hand. He pulled her behind him.

"When did he die?" B'taav demanded. "*How* did he die?"

"When was a long time ago," Nox said. "As for how, he was captured, tied down, and cut to pieces."

"Who did this?"

"A group of his ex-soldiers," Nox said. "I was among them."

B'taav reached for his fusion gun. He was about to pull it from the holster when another hand grasped his. It held him tight, preventing him from moving. The hand was Becky Waters'. Despite her bulky metallic parts, she moved like lightning.

"Easy," Becky Waters said. "You'll have to forgive my partner's blunt manners. They leave more than a little to be desired. Even when she is telling the truth."

Inquisitor Cer sidestepped B'taav and Becky. She drew her weapon and aimed it at Nox.

"Let him go," Cer said.

Nox raised her hands.

"Some bodyguard you are," she told Becky Waters.

"I took care of one of them," Becky said. "You're more than capable of taking care of the other."

"That's going to be rather difficult," Nox said. Cer's finger tightened on her fusion gun's trigger. "Now."

"Then I suggest you do something really outside your comfort zone," Becky Waters said. "Be polite and reasonable."

"Enough," Cer said. "What happened to Spradlin?"

"He's dead," Nox repeated. "But you use that weapon on me and he's gone forever."

"What are you talking about?"

"General Spradlin died an hour or two before the start of the... the Exodus, as you call it," Nox said.

Inquisitor Cer frowned and stole a glance at B'taav. He was just as confused –and curious– as she.

"His remains are dust but there's plenty of Spradlin left—" Nox pointed to her head. "—up here."

The frown on Inquisitor Cer's face disappeared, replaced with a sudden awareness.

"His nano-probes?"

"Ask me the two questions," Nox said. "You know the ones."

Inquisitor Cer held her gun steady. She again looked at B'taav. The Independent nodded.

"How old was Jessie when she died?"

Nox was silent for several long seconds. And then, a transformation occurred. Her face grew darker, her body tensed. She spoke, but her voice was no longer her own. It was deeper, masculine.

"Eighty five," Nox said.

"What is this?" B'taav said. "Some kind of—"

"Ask the second question."

"Where is she buried?"

"Outside the Blue Mountains, next to her mother."

The darkness on Nox's face abruptly disappeared and she stumbled back. Becky Waters released B'taav and rushed to her companion's side.

"Are you OK?"

"Yeah," Nox replied. Her voice was her own.

"Were those the right answers?" Becky Waters said.

Inquisitor Cer lowered her weapon.

"Yeah, they were."

The group of four sat at a table, facing each other. They were in a conference room and before a window that looked out at the desert. In the far distance were the remains of the large city. Farther still was the growing sandstorm.

"Spradlin comes to me, now and again, in visions and whispers," Nox said.

"He answered those questions?" Cer asked.

"Of course," Nox replied. "I have no idea who this Jessie was or where she was buried."

"You heard the questions?"

"Spradlin was in control but I'm never completely out of the picture," Nox said.

"So he's alive in you?"

"Just enough to make a real asshole of himself."

"We know what Spradlin did," B'taav said. "How he poisoned Earth and sent humanity away on the Displacers. Where do the two of you fit into this?"

"I first met General Paul Spradlin nearly three hundred years before the Exodus," Becky Waters said. "It was before the rise of the Corporations, when we still had nations. He was military, of course, but very much a free agent. Back then I was more... human. Spradlin knew of the coming invasion but at that point he still thought there was a way to defeat the Locust Plague without sacrificing Earth."

"What happened to you?"

Becky flexed her machine and flesh arms.

"Many years after we first met, we found ourselves on a mission in the forests of the Amazon," Becky said. "Like most everything else on Earth, it's a place that doesn't exist anymore. I won't bore you with the details, but we were attacked by alien agents and I was badly injured. Spradlin used his knowledge, and those damn nano-probes within him, to save me. Shortly afterwards, he came to the realization that we stood no chance against the invasion and my just completed treatment, it turned out, inspired him. I became a prototype for his next generation of soldiers. Using nano-probes in humans and programming them for battle allowed him to hide his real plans from the invaders."

"I was part of that next generation of soldiers," Nox said. "Spradlin took a couple thousand babies and infected them –us– with nano-probes. When we reached our teen years, we were programmed war machines. We were shipped off to fight in a war Spradlin fabricated just for us. While in our minds we killed hundreds of thousands of civilians, in reality, Spradlin used the war and our manufactured memories to test his Displacer. Every person we thought we killed was actually sent away. The culmination of Spradlin's experiment was to have nukes strapped to our backs. We were then marched into the enemy's biggest cities and simultaneously detonated our payloads, killing ourselves and, the world and the Locust Plague thought, millions in the process. Like all the other supposed kills, those millions thought dead were in reality sent to the Arks just seconds before the nukes detonated."

"A couple thousand child soldiers died so that millions could live," Becky said. "In Spradlin's mind, quite a bargain."

They were quiet for several seconds.

"The problem was that Spradlin's programming never quite took in me and a group of child soldiers deemed –ironically enough– too dangerous to be sent to the war," Nox said.

"They were the failures," Becky Waters said.

"Those failures, the ones like me, were retired from the battlefield," Nox continued. "Most were sent to asylums or prisons. I wasn't quite on that level of dysfunction which is why I was on the battlefield when the nukes went off. I survived and Spradlin didn't even know that was the case."

"How did you survive?"

"I dropped my nuke and ran the hell away," Nox said.

"You were a deserter," B'taav said.

"I was fourteen years old and could barely think," Nox shot back. "Between Spradlin's programming and my attempts to kick it, I was a mess. But I was fortunate. An allied tank found me. Their crew cared for and hid me until I was well. They brought me to the Big City and I did my thing for twenty some odd years until the remaining soldiers awoke. They attacked. Their target was Spradlin. They sensed me through their nano-probes and tried to gain control. I held off as best I could but in the end they took me as well. Because of this, Spradlin had to alter his master plan. With the Exodus about to happen, he allowed himself to be caught by us and, as I said, we ripped his body to pieces. I awoke to find Spradlin's blood all over me. Blood rich with his nano-probes. He programmed them to kill the other soldiers, but not me."

"Why?"

"Because he knew that I, more than the others, was capable of retaining my free will until… until I couldn't anymore," Nox said. Her voice rose as she spoke, the anger within threatening to burst. "Either that or the mother fucker wanted to make up for all the shit he put me through."

Becky laid her hand over Nox's.

"By the time Spradlin and his one-time soldiers were dead, the only two people left on this planet were Nox and I," Becky Waters said. "We picked up as many weapons as we could and headed here, to sleep."

"What about all those other stasis chambers?"

"They were there in case of emergency," Becky Waters said. "If the Displacers didn't work quite as well as was hoped, they were meant to hold as many people as we could bring to them."

"But the Displacers did work," B'taav said. "On the *Thanatos*, Captain Desjardins told me Spradlin didn't go on the Arks because he feared losing control of the nano-probes in his body. You have those same nano-probes in your bodies. Is that why Spradlin didn't send you away?"

"Yes," Becky said. "Spradlin worried we might be susceptible to the aliens' commands as well."

"If that's the case, what's changed?" B'taav asked.

"You mean other than five thousand years' worth of time?" Nox said.

"We were sent here to bring back Spradlin," B'taav said. "Instead, we find the two of you. We could bring our ship down right now and take you away from here, but why should we? Seems to me Spradlin had a damn good reason to leave you behind. Seems to me those reasons still apply."

"Still?" Nox sputtered. "We saved you, you son of a—"

"Thanks for that," B'taav shot back. "I assure you your actions are much appreciated. But it doesn't change the fact that your blood is infected with alien devices."

"What are you saying? You going to leave without us? You're going to leave us here to die?"

B'taav didn't reply. Nox's face grew red.

"What kind of fucking—"

"The choice is theirs," Becky Waters said.

Nox was incredulous.

"What?"

"You heard me," Becky Waters said.

"Fuck this," Nox hissed. "Fuck all of you."

"What do you propose we do, Nox?" Becky said. "Overpower our guests and bully our way onto their ship? What then? We can't fly their craft so we'd have to force them to do it for us. Where do you think they'll take us? How long before they figure a way to get rid of us? Even ignoring all that, where would we *want* to go? We don't know the Empires. We barely know anything about the worlds and cultures out there."

"The least they can do is—"

"The choice is theirs," Becky repeated. She faced B'taav and Cer. "I'm sure they'll choose wisely."

With that, Becky Waters leaned back in her chair and turned until she faced the window.

"But before you do, there's something you need to see," she said. She pointed toward the city remains. "Look over there."

Cer and B'taav followed her instructions and stared out the window.

"That's what's left of the Big City," Becky said. "Our last home. Back when the ruins were a living, breathing place, Spradlin's people numbered in the thousands, if not the hundreds of thousands. He had his own shadow army filled with soldiers, scientists, and politicians. They were sent away with everyone else in the Exodus and have been doing his bidding ever since. If you were to look closely at your Empires' records, I'm sure you'll find his agents were behind many key historical events. I know for certain they were behind the building of the solar system killers."

"What?" B'taav said.

"I saw the blueprints of those ships long before the Exodus," Becky Waters said. "For a while, General Spradlin thought building such a ship and using it against the Locust Plague was our only hope. Doing so, of course, was an impossibility. We were trapped on Earth and there would be no way to create such a vessel without massive amounts of material and personnel. When Spradlin decided to poison the Earth, he knew it would trap the Locust Plague here, but he wasn't sure it would kill them. He ordered his army to manufacture the solar system killer and bring it to Earth so that we could finish the Locust Plague off once and for all."

"By the Gods," Inquisitor Cer said.

"Paul Spradlin had his hands in everything," Becky Waters said. "*Everything.* Spradlin's people flew the solar system killer here without the use of a Displacer to ensure maximum secrecy. He had the two of you genetically modified over generations to resist the nano-probes, making you prime candidates to come here and see what the situation was without the risk of nano-probe infection."

"He probably named the *Thanatos* after his favorite fucking dog," Nox injected.

"As long as the Locust Plague exists, it's a danger to all humanity," Becky Waters continued. "You weren't sent here just to find Spradlin. You were sent here to make sure the *Thanatos* does its job."

"How do we do that?" B'taav asked.

"I'm not sure, but I have an idea," Becky Waters said. She again pointed out the window. "Look toward the southern end of the Big City. Keep your eyes open."

They did and, after a while, they saw it. A faint yellow light came on and shone directly at them. It lasted for a few seconds before turning off. B'taav was absolutely riveted by the sight. He couldn't take his eyes off it.

"The light's been coming on every fifteen minutes on the dot," Becky Waters said.

"When did it start?" B'taav asked. His voice was low, almost a whisper.

"Right after we received the *Thanatos'* first transmission. The ship's arrival activated the signal, which means Spradlin's behind it. That means it's very damn important to us."

"The *Thanatos* will wipe everything out," Cer said. "I don't understand the need to—"

"After all you've seen and all we've said, do you still doubt Spradlin's plans?" Becky Waters said.

"What could possibly be out there?" Cer said.

Becky Waters shrugged. Cer turned to B'taav and realized he was still staring at the remains of the Big City.

"What do you think, B'taav?"

B'taav didn't answer.

"B'taav?"

As if emerging from a trance, B'taav reached up and rubbed his eyes.

"I think," he began and stopped. He put his hands down. "I think Becky's right. If Spradlin's behind that signal—"

B'taav paused. His eyes were suddenly very alive.

"We don't know what the Locust Plague's ship is capable of withstanding. For all we know, she might be strong enough to survive a supernova. The *Thanatos'* payload might not be enough to..."

Again he stopped talking. His eyes returned to the Big City's remains. They did not waver.

"We have to have faith in Spradlin," B'taav said. "We have to investigate that signal."

The Independent checked his watch. They had two hours and ten minutes left.

"And we better make it quick."

53

They readied their gear and moved to a lower level chamber.

It was a large garage that smelled of oil and gas and was filled with antique land cruisers. Almost all of them were dismantled, some more so than others.

"Over there," Nox said, pointing to the chamber's far end.

Two vehicles were parked there, a large, sturdy desert truck with a highly reflective silver surface and, next to it, a motorcycle. Both had oversized tires designed for desert driving.

"We're going in these?" B'taav asked.

"Yeah," Becky Waters said. "We've been fixing them in preparation of our trip."

"It would be quicker to use the *Xendos*," Cer said.

"It would," Becky Waters said. "But it wouldn't be wise. I saw your ship come in and fade away when the drones appeared. She possesses some kind of invisibility?"

"Camouflage."

"The Locust Plague nano-probes weren't ready for that kind of tech but they're nothing if not adaptive. Expose your ship to them a couple more times and they'll figure a way around her camouflage and attack."

"How's using this truck any better?" B'taav asked.

"It may not be invisible, but it has a stealth coating," Becky said. "The nano-probes will have a hard time locking onto her. At least for little while. Either way, we keep your ship out of their reach."

B'taav rubbed his hand over the truck's hood.

"You sure it drives?"

"What's the matter, Independent?" Nox said. "Don't trust the primitives and their old technology?"

B'taav turned away from the truck and examined the motorcycle. Despite its age, it looked pristine.

"She's a beauty," the Independent said.

Nox was taken aback by the comment.

"If nothing else, you've got taste," she said.

"Before this is over, maybe I can take a—"

"Fuck no," Nox said. "No one rides her but me."

"I'd say the same if she were mine," B'taav said. "You're quite a mechanic, Nox."

"Last of a kind."

"We leave in five minutes," Becky Waters said. She faced Nox. "Get everything you need. We don't come back."

Becky Waters and Nox retreated to the other side of the garage and grabbed their gear.

Inquisitor Cer entered the desert truck and examined a computer mounted to its dashboard. Like everything else in the base, it was an ancient terminal which Inquisitor Cer doubted could compete with even the simplest such devices back in Phaecia. She pressed a button and it turned on. She checked the information within.

Cer was surprised to find the computer held a robust history of Earth complete with images and sounds from the planet's distant past. She scrolled through some of that information, confirming much of what Nox told her about the years leading up to the great Exodus.

B'taav entered the truck. He looked over Cer's shoulder.

"Would you really leave them behind?" Cer asked.

"I don't want to, but if Spradlin—"

"Forget Spradlin," Cer said. "They saved our lives."

"They did," B'taav acknowledged. "But what they've got inside them could threaten the lives of everyone in the Empires."

"Not if the *Thanatos* does its job," Cer said. "With the Locust Plague gone, there's no reason to think the nano-probes within them will act up."

"How do you know?"

Cer sat back in her chair.

"I don't." she said. "But... but something tells me I can trust them."

"Even Nox?"

Cer smiled.

"Yeah, even Nox," she said. "It's you I'm worried about."

"Me?"

"What happened back there, when you saw that light signal?"

"What do you mean?"

"You looked like you were in some kind of trance."

B'taav thought about that. He shrugged.

"There was nothing—"

"Don't say that."

Lines of worry filled Cer's face.

"Just before I left the *Dakota* and while in the company of Overlord Octo, I had a... a premonition. There's no other way to describe it. I knew Octo was about to do me harm. I shook the feeling off, thinking it was my imagination. It wasn't."

"You think I might harm you?"

"No," Cer said. "Not at all. I just feel there's something you're keeping from me."

"I'm not," B'taav said. "What you saw back there... maybe the mission's importance finally hit me."

He managed a smile, but Inquisitor Cer saw something hidden behind it, something she knew he wouldn't tell her. At least not yet.

Cer's attention returned to the truck's computer.

"So many people and places and events," she said. "It's fascinating to see where we came from."

She scrolled through the images before clicking on the search function. She typed in two words and on the monitor appeared a grainy black and white photograph. It was of a handsome, athletic looking individual who appeared to be in his early forties. His short hair was dark but graying. His eyes were remarkably clear and steady.

"General Paul Spradlin," Cer said. "The man who poisoned a world to save the universe."

"You mean the man who irradiated—"

B'taav abruptly stopped talking.

"What is it?" Cer asked.

"Spradlin irradiated Earth so that the Locust Plague couldn't feed off her," B'taav said. "On Pomos, I saw machines that cleaned radioactive waste. It didn't mean all that much to me at the time, but it meant a lot to Latitia."

"What are you thinking?"

"I don't know," B'taav said. He shook his head. "What would the Locust Plague give for that knowledge?"

54

The desert truck drove out of the cave just as the sun slipped toward the western horizon. It wouldn't be long before nightfall and darkness.

"How much time do we have?" Becky Waters asked.

"An hour and a half," B'taav said.

"It'll take us at least forty minutes to get to the city," Nox said. "We're cutting it close."

The air outside remained as stagnant as before, lifeless and controlled, for what it was worth, by the Locust Plague's machinery. All was not still. High in the sky buzzed a group of drones. They hadn't tired in their pursuit of the *Xendos*. Off to the west, the dust cloud was much larger.

Nox drove with her sunglasses in place and her attention fully on what lay ahead. Next to her and on the front passenger seat was B'taav. Behind her, in the rear seats, were Inquisitor Cer and Becky Waters.

"The storm's moved," Nox said.

It was much closer to the city.

The truck followed the last ridges of the mountain before reaching the soft sands of the desert plain.

They spent the next thirty minutes of the drive staring out their windows and at the bland scenery.

Eventually, they approached the city ruins. By then, dusk settled over the land and the light from the sun was rapidly dying.

"I'll be," Nox said.

Becky Waters leaned forward to look out the front windshield.

The ancient city's buildings crumbled over time, leaving rusty hulks and glassless windows. Despite being built with metal and mortar, the areas still standing looked like they were melting into the ground.

"The Big City, in all her glory," Nox said.

She recalled the many times she cruised the long lost highways and roads while taking on urgent, sometimes life-and-death missions. Now, thousands of years later, every single one of those missions amounted to nothing. Everyone she knew, everyone that laid foot here, were long gone. All their struggles, all the problems they had that she helped them with, all their desires and hopes...

All of it was gone.

If not for her memories, forgotten as well.

"I didn't think I'd ever see her again," Becky Waters said.

Nox aimed the vehicle in the direction of the city's center and, ten minutes later, approached its outer edges. She stopped just inside the border.

Off to the west, the storm cloud was lit up by the last rays of sunlight. It was large enough to take out most of the west ward view.

"Wherever Spradlin's light came from, it has to be near," Nox said.

Nox shifted the truck into gear and moved into the dusty remains of asphalt roads.

They drove down what was left of the Big City streets, inching their way block by block deeper and deeper into the ruins. Nox swiveled the lights on the front and roof to get a clearer look at what lay around them.

They spotted strange mechanical devices on rusted girders at the sides of the road. They saw the shells of once mighty buildings and architecture laid to waste. Patchwork robots similar to the ones that attacked them on the mountain littered the streets. All were frozen in mid stride.

The truck moved along, dodging the fallen ruins and avoiding the robots' bodies.

"They're alive," Nox said. Her voice was low, masculine. "Don't mistake slow motion for *no* motion."

Becky Waters laid her hand on Nox's shoulder and the Mechanic shook.

"What?" Nox said. Her voice was back to normal.

"He was talking through you again," Becky Waters said. "You know what he said?"

Nox nodded.

She pressed the accelerator and the noise from the engine drowned out any other conversation.

The truck rounded a corner and passed a field of debris.

The passengers gasped when they saw another robotic figure, this one as large as a building and carrying a strange metallic box, frozen in mid-stride. It was headed west. Their eyes followed its path. It was walking toward what was once the center of the Big City. There, and barely visible in the darkness, were thin metallic wires that reached up from the ground and disappeared into the sky. They came from one location. Once every few minutes, a crackle of energy ran across their body.

The truck stopped and her passengers gazed at what lay ahead.

There was an army of metallic beings between them and the city's center. Many of the robots faced away from that center, staring in all directions as if on the lookout for intruders. Many of them carried fearsome looking weapons.

Nox pointed to a larger field of debris that lay beside the still figures and stretched out into the distance.

"We have to go through there," Nox said.

"Very conveniently," B'taav said.

"A trap?"

"What do you think?"

"I think I agree with you," Nox said. "For once."

Nox faced her fellow passengers.

"We've got two choices. I use the motorcycle and take one of you with me to find the source of the signal or we use the truck and all of us go through the debris path. If we use the cycle, we'll be detected for sure but save time. If we use the truck, we have whatever remains of our stealth but it'll take longer to get there."

B'taav checked his watch.

"We're down to fifty three minutes."

They mulled their choices and were about to make a decision. Before they did, a scraping sound was heard coming from the side of the truck. To the passengers' surprise, one of the robotic figures' rusty hands was on it.

Realization dawned on them quickly.

Several of the frozen robots were indeed moving. Though their motion was almost imperceptible, they were gradually speeding up. The Locust Plague' security forces were activating.

"They're still weak and vulnerable," Becky said. "They won't be for long."

55

The desert truck lurched forward.

Nox allowed plenty of space between them and the approaching debris field. As they moved, the Geiger counter on the central control panel clicked.

"Radiation levels are increasing."

"Swell," Nox said. Her voice grew deeper. She said: "Hurry."

Becky Waters pressed down on Nox's shoulder. She pressed *very* hard.

Nox let out a faint grunt.

"Stay with us," Becky said.

Nox shook her head.

"That fucker's getting real chatty."

Nox moved the truck even closer to the debris field. Just before reaching it she hit the brakes and skidded to a sudden stop.

"What is it?" B'taav said.

"It's a trap all right," Nox said. She pointed to the ground.

Thin metal rods emerged from the debris. A couple of them sported faint red lights.

"Charges," Nox said.

"How do we get around them?"

"We don't."

They backed up a hundred yards and parked the truck near a pair of rusted figures.

"What's the plan?" B'taav asked.

"I'm going out," Nox said.

"Won't the nano-probes detect you?" Cer said.

"They will," Nox said. "But we're not getting through until I clear us a path."

Nox opened her door. Inquisitor Cer did the same.

"I can do this alone," Nox said.

"It's not wise to split up," Inquisitor Cer countered. "Especially when you're not always yourself."

"Hear that, Becky? Everyone wants to babysit me." She gazed at B'taav. "Well, not everybody."

Nox exited the vehicle and walked to its rear. Inquisitor Cer drew to her side.

"I have Spradlin under control," Nox said.

"Then my company won't matter one way or another."

"What the hell," Nox said. "Enjoy the fresh air while you can."

Inside the desert truck, B'taav and Becky Waters watched their companions walk away.

"You surprised me back there," B'taav said.

"How's that?"

"Nox is right to be angry," B'taav said. "Given what I said, given what I'm sure you're capable of, you could have easily..."

"Killed you?"

"I don't think there's anything I or Inquisitor Cer could have done to stop you."

Becky said nothing. B'taav frowned.

"I spoke out of turn," B'taav said. "I shouldn't have."

"It was the truth, wasn't it?"

"Yes."

"You're wise to be suspicious," Becky said. "Especially with what's at stake. The fate of humanity is in your hands."

B'taav was startled by what Becky said.

"What's out there?" he asked. "What's that signal for?"

"I don't know," Becky said. "You don't have any ideas?"

B'taav shook his head. Too vigorously.

"I suppose we'll find out soon enough," he said.

Becky's silver eyes betrayed no emotions.

"Soon enough," she repeated.

Nox and Inquisitor Cer stepped past the rusted figures. Nox looked around for a flat spot. While doing so she said:

"Are Inquisitors like Independents?"

"Not at all," Inquisitor Cer said.

"Then you're the good guys?"

"You're implying Independents are bad?"

Nox didn't say. Cer frowned.

"I was raised to hate all things related to the Epsillon Empire and Independents are an integral part," Cer said. "Not all Inquisitors are good and not all Independents are bad. Coming from me, that's is quite an admission."

"Are you talking about Independents in general or B'taav specifically?"

"Maybe a little of both," Cer said.

"How did you two wind up sharing space together?"

"You don't know? I thought you and Becky knew everything about us."

"Not everything," Nox said.

"It's a long story," Cer said. "Perhaps afterwards."

"Fine."

"Why do you hate Independents so much?"

"They're competition. Competition, by definition, is the enemy."

"I was taught to appreciate competition," Cer said. "It forces you to work harder and do better."

"There is that," Nox acknowledged.

"You were an Independent?"

"Hell no. I'm a Mechanic."

"Is there a difference?"

"Of course," Nox said.

"You work for money?"

"Yeah."

"Spying, detection? Merc?"

"If needed."

"Strong arm?"

"Sure."

"So how exactly are you different?"

Nox thought about that for a few seconds. She opened her mouth then closed it once again. Finally, she shook her head.

"Why exactly did I let you join me?" she said. "All right, Inquisitor, Mechanics and Independents are not all that different. If I catch you telling anyone I said that…"

"My lips are sealed."

"What do Inquisitors do?" Nox asked.

"We live by the Holy Laws and make sure others follow," Cer said.

"How?"

"Policing planets, preaching…" The smile on Inquisitor Cer's face disappeared. "…preaching the words of the Sacred Texts. For all that was worth."

"Never was all that religious," Nox said. "Then again, other peoples' beliefs didn't bother me so long as they didn't push their shit my way. Was that part of your job?"

"Yes," Inquisitor Cer said. "Only now…"

She paused.

"The Holy Texts were filled with stories of the Exodus. Of Earth's destruction and humanity's saviors. Spradlin was the Unknown Hero, the man of legend. The Texts say that without him we would have all died."

"That much is true," Nox said.

"He's considered the First Saint."

Nox laughed.

"You guys think Spradlin's a Saint?"

"If what's left of him is within you, there will be those who consider you a Saint as well," Cer said. "Only you don't look or act like much of one."

"What do I act like?"

"Someone with a hell of a temper."

"Back in the good old days we called it an attitude."

Cer was silent a few seconds.

"We'll take both of you with us," she said. "B'taav wouldn't abandon you."

"You sure your boyfriend will allow it?"

Cer was taken aback by that characterization.

"Boyfriend?"

"Yeah," Nox said. She stared into Inquisitor Cer's eyes. "Come on. You haven't noticed the way he looks at you?"

"How... how does he look at me?"

"The same way you look at him," Nox said. She shook her head. "Five fucking thousand years gone by and people still haven't figured out love."

Nox finished setting up her rifle and motioned for Inquisitor Cer to get behind her. Nox got down on her knee and pulled the rifle up. She set its stock against her shoulder and peered through the telescopic view.

"You may want to shield your eyes."

Nox pulled the trigger and a blast of heavy compressed air burst from the weapon's barrel. Cer spotted a small metal spike fly across the length of the debris field. In a fraction of a second it hit the ground and embedded itself into muddy soil.

"Here we go," Nox said.

She pressed a button on the side of the rifle and a burst of electricity sprang from the metal spike. It flowed through the objects planted below ground, in turn causing them to spark and smoke.

The electrified objects blackened before crumbling into dust.

"That's that," Nox said.

She aimed and fired several more spikes, embedding them roughly every twenty feet along a straight path. When she was done, she pressed the button on the rifle's side and each of the spikes erupted. The charges disabled the line of buried objects.

Satisfied her work was done, Nox picked up her rifle.

"Let's go," she said.

The two jogged back to the truck.

Cer followed closely behind, her eyes on the terrain. She detected motion to her right, from behind their vehicle, and abruptly tackled Nox to the ground.

Something sharp and metallic flashed before them, whizzing by only inches from their heads. The thing disappeared into the distance. A whirl was heard, then the sound of metal scraping against metal.

"It's over there," Cer said, pointing toward the columns of frozen metal warriors.

The warriors remained rigid, though at least one of them wasn't as frozen as the others.

"Look," Inquisitor Cer said.

There were three drones in the air.

They were circling closer and closer to them.

Inside the desert truck, B'taav and Becky Waters saw the object fly past their companions.

Becky Waters also spotted the drones in the air and, along with B'taav, made the same guess regarding their presence.

"They've been detected," B'taav said. "We have to get them back inside the truck."

"I'm on it," Becky Waters said.

She rushed out of the vehicle and moved toward her companions. Her prosthetic limbs dug into the withered ground and propelling her forward at incredible speeds.

B'taav slid into the truck's back seat and reached for its cargo hold. He shoved aside the material there, looking for a weapon. As he did, he accidentally pressed the screen of an ancient computer tablet stored alongside Nox's gear.

The tablet's screen came on. On it was the image of a wounded woman. Bandages covered her head and her right eye was a swollen mess. She tried to say something but couldn't. Tears ran down her good eye.

So shocked was B'taav by the image that he momentarily forgot what he was looking for. The woman on the tablet spoke.

"Hello Nox," she said. The tablet's speakers were damaged and the woman's voice was garbled. "I hope... I hope you're doing well..."

Despite his shock and intense curiosity, B'taav shut the tablet off. The woman's image, however, shook him to his core.

"By the Gods," he muttered.

Below the tablet was a handgun. He grabbed it and exited.

B'taav used the vehicle as cover and worked his way to its front. He gazed over its hood and in the direction from where the attack came. He couldn't see much beyond the immobile rusted metal figures. He looked away, towards Inquisitor Cer and Nox.

"Come on," B'taav said.

Another couple of drones joined the trio already in the sky.

B'taav kept his finger over the gun's trigger. First Nox, then Inquisitor Cer made their way to his side. They covered the vehicle's rear while B'taav covered the front.

"See anything?" Inquisitor Cer asked B'taav.

"Nothing," B'taav said. "Where's Becky?"

"I don't know," Nox said. Despite her gruff exterior, there was concern in her voice.

A sudden blast of electrified light appeared in the near distance. Sparks burst from the ground and rained on the transport vehicle. The groan of metal destroyed the silence and was followed by an even stronger screech.

B'taav, Inquisitor Cer, and Nox were on their feet as one, rushing toward the source of the noise.

They stepped past the rusted figures, all eerily silent and unmoved by the spectacle happening around them. They trained their weapons while the acrid smell of burnt metal and cordite floated around them.

Becky Waters stood before them, holding a bent and scraped metal tube. Lying on the floor in front of her was another metal figure, the third of the robots that pursued B'taav and Inquisitor Cer from their landing site.

The remains of the figure were twisted and broken. Sparks rose from its midsection and a dark fluid drained from its head.

Becky Waters dropped the metal tube. As she did, the group of four felt the wind rise up. Unsettled dust stirred momentarily before dying down. The wind returned seconds later with renewed strength.

Up in the sky and for the first time since their arrival, the Locust Plague's enormous metal tentacles showed signs of life. Faint lights appeared on their dark forms and with each passing moment more and more of them came on. The tentacles, the group of four realized, were moving. They were slowly rotating against the Earth's orbit.

After thousands of years, the planet killing machines were coming to life.

"Oh, shit," Nox said.

56

They returned to the desert truck and got in.

Nox turned it on and drove through the cleared debris path while Inquisitor Cer checked Becky for wounds on what remained of the flesh on her arms. She had several scrapes along with a pair of deeper cuts.

"Does it hurt?" Cer asked.

"A bit," Becky replied.

Inquisitor Cer reached into the cargo hold and found the medi-kit B'taav brought from the *Xendos*. She removed crème from the kit and applied it to the woman's wounds before binding them.

"Whatever that is, it works well," Becky Waters said. "But you shouldn't have bothered. There's so little of me left."

"There's enough."

The desert truck left the debris field and approached the western end of what was left of the Big City. The Geiger counter continued to click, displaying progressively higher levels of radiation.

"If this continues, it will be too dangerous for us to exit," B'taav said.

The truck moved on and her passengers were quiet. After a while, Nox stiffened.

"What is it?" B'taav asked.

Nox faced Becky Waters.

"You know where we're going?" she said. There was a mix of surprise and fear in her voice.

"Yes," Becky replied.

They drove over a large, sandy hill and there, in the valley below, saw it.

It was a nine story building which, incredibly, was relatively intact. Its surface was square and worn down. Its color was dark brown and her surface sported neither identification nor signs. From its roof extended a series of thin, almost invisible wires. They rose up into the sky until disappearing into the far distance.

Upon seeing it, Nox's face turned pale.

"It can't be," she muttered. "I saw it blow up."

"Are you sure?" Becky Waters asked.

"I was... I was a couple of blocks away. It blew up."

Nox shook her head. Anger welled within her. She slammed her fist into the steering wheel.

"*Fuck!*"

"Easy," Becky said.

"Spradlin gave me false memories of killing people in Arabia," she said. "And I saw this fucking place blow up!"

Becky pointed to the side of the building. The ground there was ripped up and charred.

"Maybe you did," she said. "Something exploded all right. Oscuro itself."

"What is Oscuro?" Inquisitor Cer asked.

"The place where Spradlin made his soldiers," Nox said. "It was where he made me."

"And obviously much more," Becky said as the movement of the wires on the roof increased.

At the wires' base and on the building's roof, a light came on. It flashed for a few seconds before shutting off.

"Right on time," Becky Waters said. "There's the source of our light signal."

Becky Waters looked out of the window, her metallic eyes following the trail of the thin wires up and up.

"They go on for miles," she said. "They must be directly linked to the Locust Plague tentacles. They might even reach up to the mother ship itself."

"When did Spradlin arrange this?" Nox said.

"Why don't you ask him?" Inquisitor Cer said.

Nox was silent for a few seconds. She shook her head.

"Bastard only talks when he wants to."

"Could it be another trap?" B'taav said.

"We won't know until we get inside," Becky Waters said.

As they approached the Oscuro building, the wires on the roof continued their vibration, swaying as if pushed by the rising breeze.

In the air, still more drones buzzed by. There was a crack of lightning. The dust cloud bearing down on the city was momentarily lit up.

"By the Gods," Inquisitor Cer said.

The cloud was *enormous*, covering many miles of territory.

B'taav checked his watch.

"We're down to forty minutes."

"Let's move," Becky Waters said.

Because of layers of ancient debris, Nox was forced to park their vehicle behind a hill and fifty feet from the building. Becky Waters checked the Geiger counter.

"Not so bad around here," Becky Waters said. "Which means we shouldn't stay a second longer than we have to."

The passengers grabbed their weapons and exited the truck. Becky Waters took a set of flashlights and affixed them to the others' jackets.

"You don't need one?" B'taav asked.

Becky pointed to her silver eyes.

"Got my own flashlight."

Above them, the drones kept their distance.

"They're avoiding the building," Inquisitor Cer noted.

"After years of getting their asses kicked by Spradlin, they have a healthy distrust of all things touched by him," Becky said.

The four moved on, walking past layers of broken concrete and mortar. Nox took point, her burly arms cradling a shotgun. She spotted a crumpled sign on the ground and kicked it.

On it and barely legible was written: *17th Avenue and James.*

"We're really here," Nox said.

They continued moving toward the building. B'taav kept close behind Nox while Inquisitor Cer and Becky Waters brought up the rear.

Above, the Locust Plague's tentacles gained speed while more of her lights came on. Strange, electronic buzzes were heard coming from within the Oscuro building. Joining the noises were other, even stranger sounds. They came from farther away and deep within the ruins of the city. They were the sounds of movement. They were the sounds of primitive engines.

"The party's starting," Nox said.

They broke into a run. B'taav passed Nox to lead the group on. They kept their distance from the gaping hole by the building's base before reaching her outer wall. The windows, the few that were left, were dark. The lobby doors were large and extra-wide. They were designed to allow the passage of trucks.

B'taav hesitated and, behind him, the others did as well. For several seconds, he remained frozen in place.

"What is it?" Cer asked.

B'taav shook his head.

"Nothing."

"We have to do this," Becky said.

B'taav nodded.

"Let's go," he said.

They entered the building's lobby and, apart from a thick layer of dust, found it completely empty.

It was very dark, though the Desert truck's lights offered some illumination.

The group moved to the lobby's rear. There, they found stairs.

"Up or down?" Becky asked.

Nox shone her flashlight down the stairs.

"There can't be much left of the basement," Nox said.

"The basement was where Spradlin kept his tech," Becky Waters said. "We need to check out what's there."

"The wires and the light signal are upstairs," B'taav countered.

"One or the other," Becky said. "We don't have time to explore both."

"Unless we split up," B'taav said.

"I know what's down there," Nox said. "I'm going up."

B'taav faced Cer.

"You and Becky take the basement," he said. "I'll go with Nox."

"You sure about that Independent?" Nox said.

"I'm sure," B'taav said. "Consider it an opportunity to bond."

B'taav removed the *Xendos'* remote control panel from his jacket sleeve and handed it to Inquisitor Cer.

"Take it," he said. "We've got more ground to cover."

Inquisitor Cer placed the remote panel over her forearm, snapping it into place.

"Come back in one piece," she told B'taav.

They stared into each other's eyes.

"Don't worry," Nox said. "I'll bring him back. If only for your sake."

B'taav motioned to the stairs.

"What are we waiting for?"

While B'taav and Nox climbed, Becky Waters and Cer headed down the stairs. Eventually, they reached the basement level and found a large metallic door. It was torn from its hinges and covered in dust. Beyond it was a hallway and several enormous rooms. Overturned metal desks lined the floor.

"Looks like a war broke out," Inquisitor Cer said.

"It did."

They moved on, passing long silent monitors and burnt out computers. Inquisitor Cer was surprised by the look of these primitive machines, and even more surprised by how much of it survived.

B'taav and Nox climbed the stairs and quickly looked over the building's second floor.

Like the lobby, the area was empty and deathly quiet. At one point, it might have housed a large office. Now, it was completely deserted.

"You have any idea what's upstairs?" B'taav asked.

"I never had the chance to check the upper floors," Nox said. "Last time I was here I was under a pretty tight deadline."

"The more things change," B'taav said.

They returned to the stairs and climbed past the third floor. B'taav bypassed the fourth and fifth floor and rushed toward the sixth. The Independent's pace increased as they moved along.

"Don't you want to search the floors?" Nox asked.

"What we're looking for is at the top," B'taav said.

Nox felt a chill. B'taav moved as if he knew where he was going.

Inquisitor Cer eyed the disheveled desks, broken monitors, and computers. At times she outran Becky Waters, her eyes taking everything in while stopping and checking each piece of wreckage.

Becky Waters held back. Rather than the old and broken equipment, her interest was on Inquisitor Cer. It took a while before Cer realized this.

"There's nothing here," Cer said. "I had a feeling..."

"A feeling?"

"It was more than that," Cer said. "I *needed* to come down. I needed to come down with you."

Cer's eyes opened wipe. Her face was filled with apprehension.

"What aren't you telling me?"

Becky Waters lowered her weapon.

"What are you feeling now, Inquisitor?"

Cer opened her mouth and was about to say something. Instead, she thought. She felt.

"Something strange... yet familiar," Inquisitor Cer said.

"You've felt it before?"

"Yes."

"A premonition?" Becky asked.

Cer was startled by the words.

"You... you know?"

"It's nothing mystical."

"Implanted memories," Cer realized with a start.

"If Spradlin's agents could create a person whose body can fight nano-probes, they could surely implant a few thoughts into their head."

Cer's hand came to her mouth.

"How much of what I'm thinking is my own? How much of it comes from Spradlin and his agents?"

"Spradlin is many things," Becky said. "He's a first class manipulator and he has no problem sacrificing lives for the greater good. I worked with that bastard for years and there were times I couldn't tell if he was a hero or a fucking villain. But he saved humanity and now he's making sure we stay saved. It's why he left Nox and me behind. It's why he sent you two here. But sending you does not ensure you complete your mission. Those premonitions you feel are gentle nudges designed to keep you on task."

"Do you have them?"

"I don't know," Becky said. "I don't think so. Not anymore."

"Are you willing to sacrifice yourself for Spradlin's cause?"

"I'm willing to sacrifice myself to destroy an evil that has no place in this universe," Becky said. "Now, think. Is there anything else you feel?"

"There is something," Cer admitted.

"What?"

"I feel we're not where we should be," Cer said. "Not exactly. And we're not doing what we should be doing."

"What should we be doing?"

"Guarding the building's entrance," Inquisitor Cer said. "Making sure none of the machines make their way inside. Give them... give B'taav and Nox time."

Becky Waters' eyes shone in the darkness.

"If you feel we need to guard the building's entrance, we guard the building's entrance," Becky Waters said.

Inquisitor Cer lowered her weapon. She knew Nox and B'taav had to do their work.

So too did Becky Waters and she.

57

Inquisitor Cer and Becky Waters returned to the lobby.

For a second Cer thought of continuing up the stairs. Nox and B'taav were up there, somewhere.

B'taav.

As much as she didn't want to, she needed to leave the building. She had to go outside and...

Wait for them.

Inquisitor Cer checked her watch.

"We're down to twenty five minutes," she said.

Upstairs, B'taav climbed faster and faster while Nox strained to keep up. If it wasn't clear to her before, it was obvious now: B'taav knew where he was going.

They were past the seventh floor, then the eighth.

At the ninth and final floor, B'taav abruptly stopped.

The Independent and the Mechanic stood at the end of the staircase and before a large double door.

"This is it," B'taav said. "Can you feel it?

Nox was silent for several seconds before answering.

"Yes."

B'taav opened the door.

Outside, Inquisitor Cer and Becky Water looked into the night's darkness and at the ruins of the Big City.

"What do you see?" Inquisitor Cer asked.

"Plenty of movement," Becky replied.

In the distance, she spotted enormous black shadows rising from the ground. The earth rumbled as the creatures emerged from it and stood fully erect. Desert sand and debris rolled off their bodies. Some of the creatures were as large as the buildings that once filled the area.

"It's an army," Becky Waters said.

The creatures flexed. They checked their limbs and stretched their joints.

They took their first steps.

"They're moving in."

Inquisitor Cer heard the sound of the howling wind and knew the dust storm just behind the creatures had grown into a hurricane. Dust and sand whirled around them. Above, the metal tentacles that encased Earth were almost all lit up. They spun around faster and faster. It wouldn't be long before they were fully powered.

Suddenly, faint lights came on from the army of robots. For the first time Inquisitor Cer saw what until that moment only Becky Waters could. The robots were indeed an army. On the front lines were the smaller units. Behind them were a second, taller group and behind them the giants.

"They waited for us to guide them here," Cer said. "They couldn't see the wires, they didn't know what Spradlin left behind. Now they know. Now—"

Cer's eyes opened very wide.

"If they get hold of B'taav or me they'll learn everything about the Empire," she said.

Becky Waters checked her weapon.

"After that, they'll no longer need your ship," she said.

B'taav and Nox walked through the doors leading to the ninth floor.

They found a large, empty hallway. At the end of it was a metal double door.

"We have to go through it," B'taav said.

The stairway exit closed behind them. They kept their weapons at their sides for they knew they weren't needed. At least not here.

They walked to the doors and paused. B'taav raised his hand and laid it flat on the door's surface.

"Ready?"

Nox nodded.

B'taav grasped the door's handle.

Nox felt a surge of energy, a feeling that things would soon be over, one way or another.

We're here, General Spradlin. Why don't you show yourself?

His voice, usually a whisper from somewhere deep in her psyche, was remarkably still. Whatever he had planned, whatever he intended, it was going to happen here and now.

B'taav applied pressure to the door's handle and felt a latch click. The door's hinges groaned as if a soul wailing in pain. The door opened.

What they saw beyond it made them gasp.

58

Inquisitor Cer ran to the desert vehicle and climbed onto its hood.

Becky Waters' silvery eyes took in the sights around them and silently made calculations as to how long it would take before their position was overrun. The clouds of dust continued growing. Incredibly, the largest of the metal beings was followed by a group even larger than them. They moved slowly, gaining speed as they progressed, until the mass of rusted metal was a violent sea.

"We can't stop this," Inquisitor Cer said.

The metal warriors, the muscle of this long dormant alien race, moved as one. Inquisitor Cer looked up, at the sky. She couldn't see any of the drones.

"We have to call down the *Xendos*," Inquisitor Cer said. "We have to get out of here."

"How far away is your ship?"

Inquisitor Cer checked the remote panel on her sleeve. She shook her head.

"It's close but..." Inquisitor Cer bit her upper lip. "Fifteen minutes. What about Nox and B'taav?"

"We have to make time," Becky Waters said.

"You got nukes hidden in the trunk of this thing?"

"Order the ship down," Becky Waters said. "We'll do what we can."

The room beyond Nox and B'taav was enormous and very, very cold.

Lights came on.

They revealed walls filled with ancient computer equipment that hummed with life.

B'taav stepped deeper inside and Nox followed closely behind. She felt the vibration of ancient fans.

Was it all here before? she wondered.

Though still active, some of the machines were damaged. Parts of their outer cases were melted and strange, multi-colored cables snaked through them, leading up and into the ceiling.

"Parasites?" Nox said.

"Could be," B'taav said.

"Maybe the aliens hacked into these machines."

"Or maybe Spradlin hacked into the aliens," B'taav said.

Nox stared at the other side of the room. There, a large glass panel opened into an equally large room. Or did it?

Nox walked to the panel. The room beyond it looked to be on a different plain. It was as if they were staring into a funhouse mirror or—

"It's a monitor," Nox said.

The image on it was incredibly sharp. The room displayed on this monitor was filled with what appeared to be funeral caskets. They were lined up and spread out into the distance. There were a staggering number of them.

"Where is the image coming from?" B'taav asked.

"No place I'm familiar with," Nox said.

B'taav lifted his hand. He pressed it against the monitor and strange symbols appeared. They illuminated every one of the caskets. B'taav pressed one of the graphics and the screen changed. It displayed an image taken from directly over one of the caskets. They realized it was a dark cryogenic unit not unlike the one Nox and Becky Waters used during their millennia long sleep. This one was significantly larger, created to contain something at least eight feet in length.

B'taav again pressed his hand against the monitor and the image zoomed in on the casket's side. He slowly pushed his finger up and, as he did, the image shifted until they were looking at the casket's upper half. On it was a rectangular window and, beyond that, a shadowy form. Inside the casket was an alien creature.

It took a moment for them to realize what they were seeing.

"It's them," Nox said. "The actual Locust Plague aliens. Can we get a closer look?"

B'taav pressed down on the monitor and the camera zoomed in even more while compensating for the darkness. The skin on the creature's face was emaciated and its eyes withered away and gone. It had long black hair and a slender build.

"A female," B'taav said.

Her bony arms were crossed in front of her chest.

"A dead female," Nox added.

B'taav slid his hand and the monitor's image changed back to the initial, more distant view of the room. B'taav pressed the symbol over another of the caskets and the creature within was displayed. It was just as withered as the previous one.

"Another," Nox said.

B'taav moved to other caskets. Every one of the aliens within them were dead.

B'taav tapped on the monitor and navigated the camera to the end of the room and out into a long corridor. The corridor walls were illustrated with colorful alien designs. There was no sign of movement and poor lighting. B'taav guided the camera further down until it reached another door. He moved past it and into another large room filled with stasis chambers. He visited the one closest to the camera and found the creature within was also dead.

B'taav pulled the camera back into the corridor. He took a sharp right turn and entered yet another corridor. A dim light came from the end of it. B'taav guided the camera toward that light and was shocked by what he saw.

Before them was a large docking bay filled with alien space craft. At its far end was a crystal wall looking into outer space. Beyond that wall was Earth.

"These images are coming from the Locust Plague's mother ship," Nox said.

The Independent moved the camera past the docking bay and into other corridors. In a matter of seconds they sped past a series of frustratingly empty rooms. They found at least two more stasis chambers and more dead crew.

B'taav moved on, quicker now, as the passage of time weighed on him. He moved to a clutter filled corridor. Debris was laid in a heap, as if to form a barricade. There was evidence of fire and violence.

"What is this?"

B'taav drew the camera close to the debris. He spotted another camera on the wall beyond that debris and tapped on it. Instantly, he had a view from that camera.

"By the Gods."

Lying on the floor on the other side of the debris and cradling what appeared to be a weapon were the withered remains of several alien creatures. The creatures were enormous and their mummified bodies still had the ghosts of powerful, sinewy muscle. The aliens' faces were twisted into a terrifying grimaces. In many of them, sharp metal teeth were exposed. Charred black blast marks were visible on many of their bodies.

"They died fighting," Nox said.

B'taav moved past the aliens and continued jumping from camera to camera while moving deeper into the alien ship. More bodies were spotted. Most were barricaded in their quarters. All died violently.

"They're so emaciated," B'taav said.

"They were starving," Nox said. "Just like Spradlin planned."

B'taav moved on, passing the individual quarters before entering a very large corridor that was a picture of chaos. Dark scorch marks, the result of heavy weapon fire, lined the walls.

"I've seen this before," B'taav said. Memories of the *Argus*, of the desperation of its crew as they realized they were trapped and doomed, filled his thoughts. When the rations were gone, the crew resorted to cannibalism to survive.

The Locust Plague were also trapped. Once their food ran out...

"Look at the stains on the floor," B'taav said. "It's where they did the butchering."

Skeletons were carefully laid out, perhaps in honor of those who fell... or perhaps to remind themselves of their desperation.

"Without food, they were forced to feed off each other," Nox said.

B'taav hurried on.

He found quiet, untouched sections along with others filled with incredible damage. He moved through them before finally reaching a central control room. It was enormous and faced an equally large and impressive glass panel overlooking Earth and the metal cage the aliens crafted around her.

In the dead center of this room was a very large and elegantly decorated chair.

"Get a closer look," Nox said.

B'taav navigated the camera to the chair. There were a series of buttons around the armrest and gold flourishes at its side. As the camera came around, they saw the chair's inhabitant, an alien creature much like the others lying about the ship.

Like all the rest, this one was also dead.

It was dressed in a solid black robe. What appeared to be medals hung from the creature's chest. Its arms were splayed to either side. One of them held an alien handgun.

As a final act, the creature used it on himself.

"The Captain goes down with the ship," Nox muttered. "He knew all was lost. Everyone under his command, the entire race..."

"They're all dead," B'taav concluded.

"If that's the case, what are we fighting?"

"Isn't it obvious?" B'taav said.

"Their machines."

"The nano-probes are doing what they were last programmed to do," B'taav said.

The wind outside grew more intense as the figures in the distance closed in.

Becky Waters laid out a line of crude explosives in a circular area around them while Inquisitor Cer kept her weapon trained on the incoming hoard.

After Becky returned to her side, she reached for a very bulky weapon stored in the desert truck's trunk. It looked like a rocket launcher.

"What is this?" Inquisitor Cer asked.

"Energy weapon," Becky Waters said. "It fires in a wide burst and should take out a couple of these things."

"That'll buy us –what?– a second or two?" Inquisitor Cer said. "How long before the *Xendos* arrives?"

"Seven more minutes."

"That's *really* cutting it close."

Inside the ninth floor, Nox stepped away from the monitor and leaned against a wall. She felt a tingling inside her, a feeling she had once before, a very long time ago.

The room around her blurred. She felt as if she was looking through a foggy haze. The room receded before turning gray. She closed her eyes tight and tried to clear her head. She couldn't.

"What is this?" she muttered before opening her eyes.

Nox's vision was now clear.

She was standing in the middle of an Arabian desert village. It was here that General Spradlin's plans first came to fruition so many years before under the Desert Brigades.

The village appeared empty.

"Where are you?" Nox called out.

A shadowy form stepped out of one of the buildings and approached her side. His body was lean and muscular, his walk clipped and exact. He wore green military fatigues. Unlike the first time they met, he had both eyes. The right side of his face and his right arm were intact. A small smile formed on his lips.

"Hello Nox," he said.

"Hello General," she replied.

For the first time since the Exodus, the man who defeated the Locust Plague by destroying Earth stood before her.

The Unknown Hero.

General Paul Spradlin.

59

A wave of metal beings roared over and past the building. They had rusty, bulky bodies and didn't appear aerodynamic enough for flight, much less the speeds attained. Strange contraptions at their base swiveled and focused on the desert truck and its two guardians.

"Scouts," Becky Waters said. "They're hesitating. Seeing if we're hiding any surprises."

"Hate to disappoint them," Inquisitor Cer said.

Both were huddled behind their vehicle, weapons in hand.

The cloudy tide of moving metal continued its approach while the winds behind them howled. It was as if an entire city and mother nature herself were coming after them.

Despite everything, Cer and Becky worried about their companions, both of whom they had yet to hear from...

General Spradlin looked Nox over.

"You haven't changed much," he said.

"I got plenty of rest," Nox said. "Is this all happening in my mind or am I out there in the real world talking to myself?"

"If you were?"

"I wouldn't want my companion to think I'm crazy. Well, *crazier.*"

"The Independent?"

"His name is B'taav. But you knew that already."

"He's a handsome fellow. Your type?"

"Independents aren't my type."

General Spradlin chuckled.

"Don't worry. Our conversation is within the confines of your mind. When we're done, only moments will have passed in the outside world."

"Long enough to look like I spaced out."

"Did you bring it?"

Nox stiffened. She reached into her shirt collar and grabbed a string necklace. She snapped it off her neck and pulled it out. Tied to the now broken string was a black, rectangular object. It was an ancient microchip.

"Lemner's passkey," Spradlin said.

"What's left of it," Nox said.

"Is the microchip...?"

"It's fine. I took care of it."

"Good. We'll need it."

"For the nano-probes?"

"Of course," Spradlin said.

"You suspected the aliens were dead, didn't you? You figured we'd be fighting their nano-probes."

"An educated guess," Spradlin said. He shook his head. "Too bad."

"The aliens that were hell bent on wiping Earth out are dead and all you have to say is that it's 'too bad'?"

"Not all of them were out to destroy us. There was one small group that actually helped. They provided us with Intel and, at one time, even gave us one of their most sophisticated chameleon machines."

"Why would they do that?"

"They retained a sliver of the race they used to be," General Spradlin said. "Many eons ago, the Locust Plague were not unlike us. Curious, intelligent, outgoing. One day, they took their first steps into space. Soon they left their nest and traveled from solar system to solar system, expanding their knowledge and gaining a remarkable understanding of the Universe. By the time Earth cooled enough to allow the first microbes on her to flourish, the Locust Plague was an ancient race. But what started well was corrupted."

The surrounding village dissolved. Around them were images of astronauts, planets, and starships.

"Pushing into the unknown meant taking risks. During one of their trips and while their fleet was between solar systems, their food stock and nutrients were spoiled. Ironically enough, an alien parasite was to blame. The Locust Plague barely made it to their destination and when they did, they were quite literally starving. The system they arrived at had one habitable planet populated with a race of primitive humanoid creatures on the verge of entering an industrial age. The Locust Plague contacted them. The planet's politicians were overwhelmed to discover there was life outside their world and only too eager to help. They offered what they could, but the quantities were inadequate. The Locust Plague needed *everything* the planet had to survive and make it to their next destination. They thanked the planet's leaders for their help and withdrew their diplomats and cargo ships. Safely in their mother ship, they made a decision that would change them

284 GHOST OF THE ARGUS

forever: They would take what they needed, the humanoid race be damned."

The image changed. An alien world surrounded by Locust Plague fighter craft was displayed. The fighter craft raced into the planet's atmosphere. Fearsome weapons ignited and destroyed primitive cities. Masses of city dwellers ran along the streets while the Locust Plague machines swooped down on them. Some of the city dwellers fought back. Their weapons were pathetically ineffective.

"The Locust Plague decimated the planet and took what they needed. In the process, every living thing on it was killed and converted to food stock. Afterwards, the Locust Plague's elders swore that if they were ever in a similar situation they would do all they could to seek nutrients from systems that held no intelligent species. It was a noble promise but they had already taken their first step. When similar situations arose as they inevitably did over the centuries, it proved easier and easier for them to take what they needed. It wasn't long before they fed off whatever lay in their path. The Locust Plague no longer created. They no longer explored. They no longer advanced. They conquered. They stole. They fed. All civilizations were their enemies. Evolution, adaptation, and the passage of time turned them into parasites."

The alien planet disappeared, replaced with an image from within the Locust Plague mother ship. A group of aliens converged.

"At least *most* of them. There existed one small group within the larger whole who suspected their actions were wrong. They could not put their feelings into words and spent years searching their data banks to learn what they could about their forgotten past. In an ancient section of their ship they found answers. Texts, many written on brittle paper, told of their race's evolution. These few members of the Locust Plague now understood why they were filled with such a strange loathing when attacking other planets. Their hands, just as their brother's, were far from clean yet the knowledge of what they once were gave them hope. Their race changed over the millennia. Could they not change back? But they were cautious. These rebels quietly sowed the seeds of their knowledge and gained followers. Unfortunately, they were discovered. In one bloody week, their ranks were decimated."

The meeting dissolved and the scene switched to a dark corridor filled with alien machinery. Hidden in the shadows was a single alien figure. It looked over information on a monitor.

"The purge was so brutal and so ...absolute... that the few rebels left realized the old ways were truly gone. Fortunately for us, some were still alive when the Locust Plague made their journey to Earth. They offered us help in the form of snippets of lost technologies. They implored us to prepare for the coming onslaught, though they didn't think we had much of a chance. You know the rest. Now, all that's left for us to do is stop the Locust Plague machines."

Nox held the microchip firmly.

"With this? You think your solar system killer isn't enough to take those machines out?"

"It probably is," Spradlin said. "But in war, you make sure your enemy isn't just defeated, but completely, mercilessly, *obliterated*. Otherwise, they might just come back."

"What exactly will the program do?"

"It'll enter the nano-probes' logic web and compromise their functioning, at least for a while. Infected nano-probes will no longer be able to latch onto you, your companions, or your ship. The *Thanatos* will do the rest."

Nox eyed the memory chip.

"Back before the Exodus, when I was staring at your corpse, I felt the need to take this with me. Was that your doing?"

Spradlin nodded.

"I planted that need as surely as my agents planted the need for B'taav to come up here with you."

"What are you talking about?"

"The *Xendos* is a Phaecian ship and Inquisitor Cer's more familiar with it than—"

"What about B'taav?"

"He will take this chip and enter the room on the roof of this building and at the base of the wires. He will insert it into a computer there and the computer will load Lemner's passkey into a massive amount of Locust Plague nano-probes trapped inside that room. The infected nano-probes will be released through those wires and link up to their brothers from here to the Locust Plague mother ship. In a matter of minutes, all of them will be infected."

"The room is filled with nano-probes?"

"Several trillion of them."

"They'll attack his organs. They'll cut his veins. They'll—"

"His body was built to fight them," General Spradlin said. "He will resist the nano-probes long enough to upload the virus and in so doing, he will ensure humanity's survival."

"How does he get out of there?" Nox asked.

"He doesn't."

60

Nox was silent. She was silent for far too long.

At first, B'taav thought she was in deep thought. Then he was concerned.

"Nox?" B'taav said.

He tapped her shoulder. She didn't react.

"What is it?"

Still nothing. B'taav grabbed the Mechanic and, gently at first, shook her. Her eyes, hidden behind her dark sunglasses, were barely visible. B'taav removed the glasses. The Mechanic stared forward, her eyes glazed.

"Nox?" he repeated, louder.

His grip on her shoulders tightened. He shook her harder.

Nox blinked and let out a moan.

"What happened?" B'taav asked.

Nox rubbed her head.

"Sorry...I was..."

She stopped talking and stared deep into B'taav's black eyes.

"Hello B'taav," she said. Her voice was deep, masculine. "There is a room upstairs filled with Locust Plague nano-probes. There is a large computer on the right side of the room. On that computer is an eye level slot."

Nox reached up and snapped a string from around her neck. She pulled it out and, at its end, was an old memory chip. She offered the chip to B'taav.

"Insert this memory chip into that slot. The computer will do the rest."

B'taav took the memory chip.

"Am I talking to you, Spradlin?" B'taav asked.

"You are."

"That room... I knew it was there. I knew I had to go to it. Cer called this a premonition." B'taav paused. He drew a deep breath. "I had another... another premonition. I won't be leaving that room, will I?"

Nox said nothing.

"Of course," B'taav continued. "There's no such thing as premonitions. Whoever put those instructions into my head, was kind enough to tell me this was a one way trip. Tell me Spradlin, why am I the only one that can do this?"

"For five thousand years my machines have trapped Locust Plague nano-probes there. When you enter, they will attack. Your body will fight them, but only long enough for you to do your job."

"One life to save billions," B'taav muttered. "Quite the bargain."

Nox put her sunglasses back on.

"It was a pleasure knowing you, Independent."

"Please tell... please tell Inquisitor Cer I'm sorry I couldn't take the ride back."

"I will," Spradlin said through Nox. "Go. There isn't much time."

In her dream world, Nox continued her conversation with General Spradlin.

"You created generations of people increasingly resistant to the Locust Plague nano-probes with the sole purpose of having them here just for this day?" Nox asked.

"Yes."

"You knew the one who entered that room would die?"

"Sacrifices must be made."

"I've heard that before," Nox snarled. "I won't let you do it."

The memory chip in Nox's hand vanished.

"You're too late to stop it," Spradlin said. "I'm sorry it had to end this way. But it is for the best."

The image of General Spradlin disappeared.

B'taav climbed the stairs leading to the roof of the building. A gale-like wind slammed him and dust filled the stairwell.

He gazed ahead, at an open air parking garage. Lightning flashed and thunder roared. What B'taav saw beyond the roof was a vision from a nightmare. Surrounding the building was a huge black dust cloud. Just before it was an army of metallic giants moving ever closer.

At the other end of the garage was a glass encased room. It glowed an eerie white. From it rose the thin metal wires that disappeared into the sky.

B'taav drew a sharp breath.

Move.

The Independent ran past a line of rotted vehicles and reached the glass room. Beside the entry door was a hand print scanner. He pressed it. A door to a small cubicle in front of the nano-probe filled room slid open. It was large enough to fit only one person.

In his mind, B'taav pictured Inquisitor Cer. Her touch. Her smile. He held on to those thoughts.

"You're so beautiful."

B'taav stepped into the cubicle and the door closed behind him. Once the small room was pressure sealed, the cubicle's inner door slid open.

B'taav was immediately exposed to what lay inside the large glass room. The heavy concentration of Locust Plague nano-probes swarmed his body. He immediately itched and found it increasingly hard to breathe. He could feel the microscopic creatures in his nose and ears and on his eyes like sandy grit. In seconds they were inside him, attacking his lungs, his stomach...

B'taav hurried into the room.

Though his body's immune system fought off the invaders, their mass quickly overwhelmed him. He could barely see. He could no longer breathe.

B'taav reached the right side of the room and the computer. He looked up. The outside wires came down into this machine. B'taav rubbed his eyes. Blood dripped from his nose and ears. He retched but nothing came out. He was in agony.

B'taav desperately felt along the computer's panels. Each passing second brought a fresh wave of nausea and pain.

His body was shutting down. He only had seconds...

He found the slot.

B'taav slumped against the computer. His legs were useless.

He let out a moan and, with the last of his strength, pulled his hand up. He could barely hold the microchip. He pushed it against the computer, hoping it would enter the slot.

It didn't.

B'taav fell to knees and let out another moan.

Blood flowed from his mouth.

B'taav knew this would be his last attempt.

He thought about Inquisitor Cer. He pushed hard...

The world around her abruptly changed.

Nox was no longer in the desert village nor on the ninth floor of the Oscuro building.

Instead, she was standing in its lobby, facing the door leading out.

Inquisitor Cer and Becky Waters were outside and next to the desert truck, weapons in hand. Inquisitor Cer's attention was on the remote control panel on her arm. Heavy dust swirled around them and an army of metallic beings were only feet away. Beyond them and in the distance, the edges of the mighty black storm was just arriving.

Nox ran out of the building and approached the two women. Despite the madness around them, Inquisitor Cer said:

"Where's B'taav?"

"He's inside," Nox replied. Her voice fluctuated, growing deeper and deeper. "Our time is up. We need to leave. Now."

"What about B'taav?" Inquisitor Cer insisted.

"He's gone."

"Spradlin?" Becky Waters said. "What did you do?"

"We must leave."

"We can't. The ship isn't here yet," Becky Waters said.

Nox looked at the machines surrounding them.

"You must get out of here. We only have... only have seconds—"

Nox let out a roar. She slumped to the ground and slammed her fists into the dirt.

"Son of a *bitch*," she yelled.

Inquisitor Cer checked the readout on her remote computer panel.

"We've got three minutes before the *Xendos* arrives," she said.

"Such a short amount of time to wait," Becky said. "Yet too much."

The robot army would overrun them in a matter of seconds. The storm would follow shortly afterwards.

"What happened to B'taav?" Becky asked.

"He's infecting the Locust Plague nano-probes with Lemner's passkey," Nox said. "To do so, he had to enter a chamber filled with them. Spradlin said he would resist them longer than we could, but that there was no way he would survive."

Above them, the sky lit up. The Locus Plague tentacles were spinning faster. They countered the rotation of the planet and, with enough speed, would rip what was left of her atmosphere apart.

The giant robot army was almost on top of them. The largest of these creatures reached forward, its rusty metal arm the size of a high rise.

Inquisitor Cer turned away. She looked up, at the roof of the Oscuro building.

"B'taav," she whispered.

The creatures' footsteps shook the ground. The roar of the storm was deafening. The tentacles surrounding the Earth moved faster and faster.

Over all this, Inquisitor Cer heard a beep. She looked down at the remote control computer panel on her arm. A timer read zero. They were past the point when they needed to begin their journey back to the *Thanatos*.

"Time's up," she whispered.

All hope was gone.

61

Inquisitor Cer's head came down.

Nox looked past the desert truck and to the advancing army of machines. She raised her gun.

"Fuck if I'm going down without a fight," she muttered.

Something far above caught Becky Waters' attention. She stared up at the Locust Plague's tentacles. Past them.

She frowned.

Her silver eyes shined in the darkness. The frown grew, then disappeared.

"Cer, Nox!" she said.

"What?"

She pointed up.

"Look!"

Beyond the tentacles and somewhere between the Earth and the Moon was an incredibly large object. Its side was illuminated by the sun and its shape, even from this distance, was familiar. Chills rose up and down Inquisitor Cer's back.

"It's the *Thanatos*," Inquisitor Cer said. "Desjardins brought her here! He didn't wait for us at Jupiter!"

Bright red energy flares flew out of the super-juggernaut. They slammed into the Locust Plague tentacles and burst into fireballs.

"She's firing on them!" Cer said.

One of the missiles shot past the tentacles and roared into Earth's atmosphere. A gigantic sonic boom was followed by the explosive sound of missiles smashing into the ground nearly a mile away. The resulting fireballs knocked most of the advancing metal creatures to the ground.

"By the Gods!" Nox said.

Even as the robots hit the ground, another series of missiles, these smaller and laser directed, sliced through their bodies and ripped them to pieces.

More missiles rained down, this time creating a perimeter of fire around the Oscuro building. The still standing machines slowed. They could not fight this attacker.

"What about the *Xendos*?"

"Two minutes," Inquisitor Cer said. Her gaze shifted from her remote control panel to the Oscuro building and its roof. Toward where B'taav was...

Nox looked at Inquisitor Cer and followed her gaze. She saw the pain of loss in Cer's face and very familiar feelings hit her.

Hard.

The Mechanic looked around and spotted a cement ramp at the rear of the Oscuro building. It wound up and around, floor by floor, before reaching the building's roof. Her gaze returned to her companions.

"Do you have something that can track my movements?"

Becky Waters reached into the vehicle's trunk and pulled out a microchip. She handed it to Nox.

"This will do the trick," she said.

Nox pocketed the device. She ran to her motorcycle and pulled at the straps that held it to the back of the desert truck.

"I spent months restoring this baby," Nox said. "I'll be damned if I'm not going to ride her."

"Where are you going?" Cer asked.

"Where else?" Nox said. "To get your boyfriend."

Becky Waters lifted the heavy bike off the truck's frame and gently laid it on the ground.

"You've got a minute and a half."

"Way more time than I need," Nox said.

She mounted her bike and turned the key.

"Start up," she muttered.

Nox kicked the ignition and the cycle roared to life with a vigor she didn't expect.

"Right on!" she yelled.

Nox hit another button and the blare of music was heard.

"What is that?"

"Heavy fucking metal," Nox yelled.

Nox's motorcycle roared past the entrance ramp and up the garage floors, its tires squealing with each sharp turn.

Dust filled the ramp while the howls from the enormous storm and the roars of the *Thanatos'* missile attack were nearly drowned out by music. In less than a minute's time she was on the tenth level of the garage and, at its end, spotted the glass enclosure and within, the slumped figure of B'taav.

This is a mistake. Go back.

"Spradlin, why don't you shut the fuck up," Nox said.

B'taav was covered in what appeared to be a layer of dust. Nox knew it was actually a layer of nano-probes. He was so very still. So—

He's dead already, Spradlin said. *Go back!*

For a moment Nox hesitated. How was it possible for him to—

B'taav's body shook. He tried to lift himself up. He fell back down.

"He's still alive!" Nox yelled.

He is! Spradlin's voice said. He was as surprised as Nox. *Well, what the fuck are you waiting for?*

Nox revved the motorcycle's engine and the rear tire squealed. The cycle rushed toward the glass room.

Be quick, the familiar voice inside her head said.

"Got any more great advice?"

Lemner's passkey is in the room and within the wires. Might as well release the rest of them into the air.

Nox pulled her handgun from its holster and aimed it at the room's glass walls. The wind kicked up, almost wrecking her. She fired the gun and the glass panel shattered.

The heavy winds whipped the dust. The infected nano-probes were freed from their cage and dissipated. Over the sound of explosions and thunder alarms blared.

Nox hit the accelerator and roared through the broken glass. She felt the sting of nano-probes around her. As with B'taav, they attacked her body.

The nano-probes can't hold on.   They're dropping away. Lemner's passkey did its work.

Nox's motorcycle skidded to a stop beside the Independent.

The Mechanic reached down and grabbed him. The dust covering his body fell away in clumps as she pulled him up and into place behind her.

"You still alive, Independent?"

B'taav groaned.

"Alive enough," she said. "Hang on."

Despite their weakness, the nano-probes continued their attack. Nox felt them in her eyes and throat. But with each passing second, their sting lessened. Nox checked her watch.

Time's up.

She reached for her communicator and pressed it.

"I have him!" she yelled.

Nox bit her lip and revved the motorcycle's engine. They were ten floors above ground and the hurricane storm and the metal militia were at the Building's doorstep.

There was no time to drive back down.

"Fuck it," Nox said. She clicked on her communicator. "I hope you see us because we're coming out the west side. The hard way."

Nox raised her handgun and fired at what remained of the room's outer glass walls. She looked out into the darkness beyond and the ten story drop.

"Catch me," she said.

Nox released the motorcycle's brakes and the vehicle sped toward the shattered glass.

They passed it.

Nox, B'taav, and the motorcycle were airborne.

Gravity took hold and they dropped. The ground, so very far below, rushed up toward them.

Nox released the cycle and grabbed B'taav. The cycle fell down and down, with Nox and B'taav just feet away.

Then, a miracle.

The cycle continued its fall yet Nox and B'taav slowed.

They were two feet away from the cycle. Five.

Ten.

Twenty.

Nox watched in wonder as her beloved motorcycle smashed into the ground beside the desert truck and shattered into pieces.

By then, Nox and B'taav were no longer falling.

Instead, they were lifted higher and higher, as if in the grasp of invisible hands.

Nox caught the shadow of something very large camouflaged in the sky directly above them.

A hatch opened in mid-air and the two fell into it. Their bodies slammed against a cold metal floor.

The dim light from outside was extinguished. In the few moments of consciousness left to her, Nox realized they were inside Cer's airship. Its outer hatch closed.

She felt a blast of air. The mass of infected alien nano-probes fell from her body and were whisked away.

Lemner's passkey had done its work well.

62

Becky Waters was at the door leading into the *Xendos'* decompression chamber.

Next to her and on the floor was an overstuffed duffle bag, everything she and Nox packed to take with them from Earth. She pushed the bag aside and gripped the door's handle. The veins remaining in her arms throbbed as she put all her strength into prying the door open.

"How are they?" an anxious voice called out over the intercom.

"I can't open the door," Becky yelled back.

In the cockpit of the ship Inquisitor Cer sat at the controls.

She arrived moments before and was still breathing hard. She checked the area around the ship. The *Thanatos'* missile attack stopped as the storm closed in on them. It swirled faster and faster and threatened to rip everything around it to pieces.

"Brace yourself, I have to fly through hell itself," Inquisitor Cer said.

She pulled at the craft's controls and the *Xendos* rose straight up. As it did, they entered the storm's outer edges. The ship lurched back and forth.

A flash of lightning illuminated the sky and Inquisitor Cer gasped. A wave of metal approached at the speed of sound.

"By the Gods," she said.

Just as the words left her mouth, a piece of metal the size of a transport truck slammed into the *Xendos'* view screen, cracking the tempered glass before her and sending the craft deeper into the storm.

Alarms blared and circuitry sparked.

The ship's camouflage was gone.

Becky Water pressed harder against the door. It didn't budge. The *Xendos* shook, throwing her to the floor. She looked up at the door's handle. It bore her handprints.

She placed her face against the door's window to look in on Nox and B'taav. She frowned.

"Inquisitor Cer," Becky called out over the intercom. "The decompression chamber is filling up with a white gas. What the hell is it?"

"No idea," Inquisitor Cer said. "Could it be a fire?"

"That's all we need."

Inside the airlock, Nox stirred. The microscopic assault on her body was over. She felt her skin was cooling.

Cautiously, she opened her eyes and expected to be blind. Instead, she could see, though her vision was blurry. Or was it?

She waved her hand before her. Her vision wasn't blurry. The chamber they were in was filled with gas.

They.

B'taav lay next to her. His pale skin was ruby red and raw, as if he suffered from extreme sunburn. His eyes were closed and a line of dried blood ran from his nose and mouth.

"Aren't you a mess," Nox said.

She reached over and felt for a pulse.

He had one. Barely. He was also having trouble breathing.

Nox pushed down on his chest.

"Come on," she said.

B'taav gasped and Nox sat back. The Independent coughed. He coughed again, louder, before spitting out a bloody blob. Once exposed to the air, it turned white, dried, and became ash. The ash was whisked into the ventilation systems.

The Independent opened his eyes. He looked around.

"N...Nox?" he muttered.

"Yeah," Nox said.

"How...?"

"I never liked the idea of leaving anyone behind."

B'taav smiled.

"That's a good philosophy," B'taav said. "I should follow it."

B'taav and Nox laughed. She got to her knees and offered B'taav her hand.

"I shouldn't have survived the chamber," B'taav said. "How did I?"

"I wish I knew—"

As the words left Nox's mouth and at the very moment B'taav took Nox's hand, the decompression chamber disappeared.

Nox was back in the Arabian village and, to her surprise, B'taav was there with her. They still held hands. B'taav rose to his feet and was about to release their grip.

"Don't let go," Nox said.

"What is this—?"

"You're inside my head," Nox said.

A lean, muscular figure appeared before them. B'taav recognized him from his picture.

"Spradlin."

The figure nodded. There was a troubled look on his face.

"How are you, B'taav?" he asked.

"All things considered, pretty good."

"How about that, General?" Nox said. "B'taav survived your nano-probe room. You thought he couldn't. You were wrong."

"I wasn't wrong," Spradlin said. "B'taav shouldn't have survived. The only reason he did was because his immune system was much stronger than it should be."

"One of these days, you're going to admit—"

Nox stopped talking. The troubled look on Spradlin's face was something she had never seen on him before. It was the look of fear.

"To build up your immunity, generations of your bloodline were exposed to progressively stronger nano-probe viruses," Spradlin said. "But they were artificial creations that didn't – *couldn't*– have the potency of the real thing. There's only one way your immune system could have strengthened to the point where you survived that room. B'taav, you were exposed to something very close, if not identical, to the real Locust Plague nano-probes."

"When could that have happened?" Nox said. "He was in our sight his entire time on Earth."

"Back in the Empires, shortly before coming here, I was attacked," B'taav said. "One of my attackers scratched my neck. I felt very sick but recovered before the flight here. Do you think it was...?"

Spradlin nodded.

"The Locust Plague nano-probes may already be in the Empires," he said.

Spradlin turned away from Nox and B'taav.

"Our work is far from done."

As the words left his mouth, Spradlin and the village faded away. B'taav and Nox were back in the fog filled decompression chamber. B'taav stared at Nox and she stared at him. She released his hand and a sharp noise came from behind them.

At the entry to the decompression chamber stood Becky Waters. She held a bent metal tube and was surprised the door automatically opened.

"What the hell?" she muttered before running to Nox and B'taav's side.

The gas in the chamber was all but gone.

"I thought there was a fire," Becky Waters said. "That gas—"

Becky thought hard. She noticed the traces of ash on B'taav's clothing.

"It was some kind of purification process," she said. "It destroyed the remaining nano-probes on you. Are you two ok?"

"I think so," Nox said.

63

The redness on B'taav's skin faded.

"Did Lemner's passkey work?" he asked.

"I'm not sure," Becky Waters said.

Both she and Nox held B'taav between them and hurried through the *Xendos'* lower corridor and up the stairs to the top level. The ship rocked side to side, sending them against the walls and slowing their progress. Finally, they reached the cockpit and found Inquisitor Cer there, fighting the controls.

The storm continued swirling around them. More lighting flashed and another wave of metallic fragments slammed against the craft.

"*Thanatos*, this is the *Xendos*," Inquisitor Cer said. "We're nearing orbit."

There was no response.

"*Thanatos*, do you read me?"

"Hello, Cer," B'taav said.

For a moment, Inquisitor Cer's face lit up. She struggled to remain in her chair and not jump up and hug the Independent. Instead, she said:

"Take a seat."

B'taav slipped into the co-pilot's chair.

Another flash of lightning illuminated the storm. It was followed by a burst of wind that pushed the *Xendos* sideways.

In the distance and held up by the winds flew one of the largest of the metallic creatures. It swirled in the air as if a marionette on a string, moving closer and closer to the craft. Behind it was another robot. And another. They closed in…

"Hang on!" Inquisitor Cer yelled.

Just as they neared the *Xendos*, the winds caused the robots to slam into each other with incredible force. The colossal beings were ripped to pieces by the impact and their remains rained down on the *Xendos* like confetti.

The passengers of the *Xendos* couldn't understand what they just witnessed. They saw other metallic figures, both large and small, swirling around in the storm. They too were ripped apart by the winds.

"We were wrong about the storm," Inquisitor Cer said. "It's not working with those creatures. It's destroying them."

Cer checked the sensor readings.

The metal storm released another intense flash of lightning. Through it Cer saw their way out.

"Here we go!" she yelled.

The *Xendos* picked up speed, rising while a mountain of metallic fragments rained down on the remains of the Big City.

Directly below them, the Oscuro Building was pelted with this debris. The nano-probe filled room was smashed and the wires that extended from the room into the sky were severed. The building lasted only seconds more under the metallic assault before crumbling.

"Goodbye... and good riddance," Nox said.

"Approaching upper atmosphere," Inquisitor Cer said after a while. "Shouldn't be long now."

Inquisitor Cer trained the ship's cameras on Earth as they rose. The passengers were dead silent, witness to a sight they would never forget.

The mighty storm enveloped all of Earth.

"By the Gods," Nox said. "What is happening?"

"Maybe Lemner's passkey didn't work," B'taav said.

Becky Waters pointed to the tentacles around Earth. They had slowed to a near stop and their lights were rapidly dying out.

"It worked all right," she said.

"But this storm?"

"I don't know," Becky said. "I just don't know."

Within the clouds they spotted oddly shaped forms. Some were angular and others were straight. With a start, they realized they were witnessing titanic structures being created at a furious pace.

"*Xendos*, this is the *Thanatos*," came a voice over the communication system. "Do you read me?"

Inquisitor Cer hit the communication system switch. A monitor lit up and on it was David Desjardins.

"Thank the Gods!" she yelled. "We read you, David."

"You did your job well," Desjardins said. "The Locust Plague's mother ship was almost at full power until a few seconds ago."

"What's the status of the *Thanatos*?" Inquisitor Cer asked.

"I've had to swat away a bunch of drones," Desjardins said. "Otherwise, we're ready for detonation."

"Ready? What happened to the time we had to fly back to Jupiter?"

"Little white lie," Desjardins said. "There was no way of knowing if you'd be captured and forced to reveal everything you knew about this ship. Better the Locust Plague search for me around Jupiter than in their back yard. Now, can you make it?"

"We'll do our best," Inquisitor Cer said.

The *Xendos* passed the two layers of Locust Plague tentacles. They saw the enormous form of the *Thanatos* before them. A light as bright as a small star shone on its side.

"He's activated the Displacer," Inquisitor Cer said.

"Look," B'taav said and pointed to a monitor. "Defensive drones!"

"David, there are more drones heading toward you," Inquisitor Cer said.

"I see them," Desjardins replied. "Hurry, Inquisitor."

The *Xendos* passed low orbit and drew closer and closer to the Locust Plague's mother ship. The first time they passed it, the ship was lifeless. It had life now, but it was dwindling. Less than a fifth of it was lit up, and what lights were on were quickly dying. The still ship moved, if very slowly. As it did, a wave of fusion fire erupted from her and a series of Earth-shattering blasts slammed against the *Thanatos'* starboard side. Mountains of debris were sent into space. The *Thanatos* answered in kind, its hellfire missiles lighting the top of the alien craft and ripping her upper decks. Smaller missiles and fusion blasts took on the waves of drones between the two ships.

The *Xendos* rushed by the mother ship and found herself between the enormous crafts.

Another wave of missiles and fusion blasts emerged from the rival vessels, lighting both ships up with even more explosions. The chaos was incredible.

"Desjardins, we're only seconds away from the Displacer," B'taav said. "How do we get you out?"

"Get me?" Desjardins replied. He smiled. "You don't."

"There's still time to save you!"

Desjardins shook his head.

"No there isn't," Desjardins said. The smile remained on his face. "I've lived two full lives, B'taav. One more than everyone else. Make yours count."

The *Xendos* flew over the *Thanatos* and was shielded from the barrage of Locust Plague fusion blasts. This side of the *Thanatos* was remarkably calm. It was as if it was part of a completely different vessel.

Inquisitor Cer banked the *Xendos* so they could see the *Thanatos'* upper deck. In moments they had a clear view of her tinsel glass roof. They stared in wonder at the beach encased within the *Thanatos'* uppermost level. Even from this extreme distance they spotted a single dark form sitting before the crystal clear blue water.

"Goodbye," Desjardins said.

The man on the beach waved.

In another second he was gone. The *Xendos* was past the tinsel glass and nearing the rear of the ship. The small Displacer the *Xendos* had flown through to arrive in the Solar System was ready for them.

"Oh no," Inquisitor Cer said.

Three defensive drones appeared at the *Xendos'* side. They were moving quickly toward her.

"We can't deviate," Inquisitor Cer said. "We don't have the time!"

B'taav reached for the ship's defensive systems. He used the targeting system to zoom in on the drones. He instantly recognized one of them.

"Cyclops."

The ancient drone was behind the other two. It tried to pass them, as if eager to be the first to attack.

"The *Xendos* doesn't have enough firepower to take them all down," Inquisitor Cer said.

B'taav hit the trigger.

A beam of fusion energy flew from the *Xendos'* single defensive cannon. It struck the lead drone, shattering it into pieces. Pieces of it rained against one of the two remaining ships, momentarily sending it away. Cyclops closed in.

"They're behind us," B'taav said. "They're coming around."

"We'll make it," Inquisitor Cer said.

The tiny ship closed in on the Displacer but Cyclops and the remaining drone gained on her.

"Faster," B'taav muttered.

"A lot faster," Nox added. The second drone gained more speed. It was beside, then just in front of Cyclops.

"Come on," Becky Waters said.

They were nearly there...

...they were nearly there...

Within the *Thanatos*, David Desjardins faced the beach and the placid water before him.

He felt a distant rumble. The other half of the ship was taking enormous hits.

At his side appeared Saint Vulcan's hologram.

"You've done well," she said.

"Could I see her one last time?"

"Of course."

In the water appeared two forms.

It was a young David Desjardins and his wife. They frolicked in that water, impossibly young and so painfully in love. They wore no clothing and passionately embraced. They kissed. They made love.

He remembered that day. All those days.

"Thank you," Desjardins said.

"Thank you, David Desjardins," the Hologram replied. "Are you ready?"

"Yes."

The Hologram took a step back. Desjardin's attention remained on the images. He reached out, his frail hand shaking.

"Holly," he said.

So young and so beautiful. She reached out to him. She smiled and in that moment he was so very, very happy.

Desjardin's other hand felt along the side of his beach chair. He found the switch.

He pressed it.

And then a light millions of times brighter than the Solar System's sun obliterated all that surrounded it.

The *Xendos* hit the outer boundaries of the Displacer's energy field and rocked as it entered the slipstream.

A blinding light filled the energy arc.

"The *Thanatos*," Inquisitor Cer said.

"Goodbye, David," B'taav muttered.

The Displacer's aperture abruptly closed behind them, dissolved by the extreme energy from the *Thanatos'* destruction. The *Xendos* thrashed to and fro, its hull heating to the point that alarms blared through the ship's speakers. Inquisitor Cer fought the energy tides and checked for system failures.

"We've got company," Becky Waters said.

Behind them were the two defensive drones. Cyclops was just behind her younger counterpart.

"How did they get in?" Inquisitor Cer said.

"Doesn't matter," B'taav replied. "They're gaining."

"Can we take them out?" Nox asked.

B'taav got to work on the fusion cannon controls. He clicked on a sensor and noted the rising radiation.

"What's wrong?" Nox asked. "Why aren't you firing?"

"The radiation in the slipstream messes with the targeting systems," B'taav said. "As long as it's there, those systems are compromised."

"At what point does the radiation drop?" Nox said.

"Toward the end of the journey," B'taav said. "That's how we know we're about to arrive at our destination."

"We can't fire without the targeting systems?" Becky Waters asked.

"We can," B'taav said. "Hitting something, on the other hand..."

B'taav motioned to Nox while continuing to work the cannon's controls.

"Help me," he said and pointed to the yoke before him.

Nox grabbed the device. On the monitor over it was displayed a view of the incoming drones. At the center of the monitor were crosshairs.

"You want me to line up the crosshairs?"

"Yes," B'taav said.

"Just like a vid game."

Nox aimed until she had the drone closest to them in the crosshairs. But its image fluttered and at times it was nothing more than a ghostly apparition.

"Am I lined up?"

"Only one way to find out," B'taav said.

The Independent hit a button and a fusion beam roared from the *Xendos'* cannon. It dispersed wildly, its energy diffused by the strange physics found in the slipstream. Parts of her beam held together long enough. They hit the nearest drone's side, splintering it into pieces. Just as the fusion blast was fired a strong energy feedback sent sparks through the fusion cannon controls. The fusion cannon monitor went dark.

"Give me the rear camera!" B'taav said.

Inquisitor Cer pressed a button and another monitor lit up. It displayed the ship's rear view. The two drones were on it. The one closest to them shattered. Most of its pieces fell to the side, leaving the slipstream corridor and vanishing forever. A large chunk blew off and moved directly toward Cyclops.

"Come on!" B'taav said.

The chunk fell faster and faster toward the ancient drone.

"Come on!"

The chunk slammed into Cyclops, causing it to deviate. The drone was hurt. Badly. Sparks and smoke emerged from her. She fell away, farther and farther. She was almost gone...

And then she managed to correct her course. Despite her injuries, she sped up. She was once again behind the *Xendos*.

"Damn!" B'taav said.

"She's no longer trying to ram us," Inquisitor Cer said.

"She's hurt," B'taav said. "Hurt enough to want to wait us out."

"Wait us out?" Becky Waters repeated. "What for?"

"For you to get to the end of the line," Nox said. Though the Mechanic spoke, it wasn't her voice.

"Spradlin?" Becky said.

"The drone knows your fusion cannons are fried. She's following you to the Displacer's end. In regular space, she will attack without fear of getting lost in the slipstream and there won't be a damn thing you can do to defend yourselves. When you're gone, she'll move on. She'll find shelter and replicate, maybe create an army of Cyclops drones and—"

Nox's body shook. She doubled over.

"*Fuck!*" she yelled.

Becky held her. Nox nodded.

"I'm fine," she said.

"How much longer before we leave the slipstream?" Becky Waters asked.

"I don't know," Inquisitor Cer replied. "It took us nearly six minutes to go from the Empire to your Solar System. I don't know where we're being sent, but the trip back might take just as long."

"We can't let that drone reach Empire space," Becky Waters said.

"How do we stop her?"

Becky Waters examined the radiation display. It had reached a maximum level and was no longer climbing.

"By doing something crazy," Becky Waters said.

"You have a plan?" Nox asked.

"Yeah," Becky replied. "You strong enough to join me?"

"Of course," Nox said. "How crazy is this plan?"

"Plenty."

Nox smiled.

"Count me in."

Inquisitor Cer spun in her chair.

"What are you—?"

She didn't finish her question. By then, Becky Waters and Nox were gone.

They ran out of the cockpit, down the corridor, and down the stairs until they were before the door to the decompression chamber. Becky Waters opened the faded green duffle bag she left there and pulled out a large black blade.

"What are we doing?" Nox asked.

Becky Waters grabbed a space suit from the charging rack and handed it to Nox.

"Get dressed," she said. "Quickly."

Becky grabbed another suit for herself. They dressed and entered the decompression chamber.

"You can't go outside," Inquisitor Cer said over the suits' communication systems. "You saw the radiation readings!"

"Are they dropping?"

Inquisitor Cer was silent for a second. Then:

"Yeah," she said. "Slowly. Check the readings on the monitor to your right."

They did.

"By the time we're ready to step out, those levels will be much lower," Becky Waters said.

"You'll still be poisoned," Inquisitor Cer said.

"This body is barely human," Becky Waters said. "It's also fought off radioactivity for over five thousand years. It can take a couple more minutes."

"What about you, Nox?"

Nox smiled.

"I'm Blue Brigade. It's been said nothing stops us."

64

Warning lights came on and they heard Inquisitor Cer's voice over their communication system.

"Radioactive readings at half," she said. "We're maybe two minutes from exiting the slipstream."

Becky Waters and Nox checked the reinforced metallic rope tied to their suits and took a step closer to the decompression chamber's outer door. In Becky Waters' right hand was the black blade.

The outer door opened, revealing a cascade of bizarre violet lights.

Becky Waters whispered something, then, along with Nox, stepped out of the ship.

In the cockpit, Inquisitor Cer and B'taav were captivated by what they saw.

A monitor displayed Becky Waters and Nox exiting the decompression chamber. Their magnetized boots stuck to the ship's ladder. Some seventy feet away from them was the ancient defensive drone.

Becky Waters clicked the communicator.

"How do I maneuver?" she asked.

"The directional guides are in your belt."

Becky Waters' free hand reached for them.

"Up, down, left, and right," Becky Waters said. "Couldn't be simpler."

Nox shook her head.

"You weren't kidding when you said this plan was crazy."

In the silence of the slipstream, Becky Waters heard her breathing. Behind her was Nox, holding on to the rope. Cyclops remained in position, its single outer light glowing a bloody red.

Nox patted Becky Water's helmet.

"Come back," she said.

"I will," Becky Water replied. "As long as you don't let go."

She took another step and was gone.

Becky Waters' body floated out, farther and farther, her tether to the *Xendos* held by Nox. She closed in on Cyclops and adjusted her movements to bring her directly to it.

Inch by inch Becky Waters lined herself up. As she did, the radiation gauge continued dropping.

"How much longer before we're out?" Becky Waters asked.

"Seconds," Inquisitor Cer replied.

She was right in front of the drone yet still a good ten feet away.

"I need more slack," Becky Waters said.

"That's all I've got," Nox replied.

Cyclops was so close. Close enough for Becky Waters to see its weathered surface. Her single red light flickered, an angry eye staring at its victim, waiting so very patiently to attack.

"I can't reach her," Becky said.

She shook her head and clenched her teeth. There was only one thing left to do.

"Cut the rope."

Nox didn't immediately answer.

"You heard me, cut the rope."

"The hell I will."

"Radiation is near normal," Inquisitor Cer said. "We've got maybe twenty seconds!"

"Do it. *Now!* "

"I can't let you go," Nox said. "I won't—"

"If you don't, billions may die. *We* certainly will!"

"Fifteen."

"Please..."

The tether gave.

Becky Waters fell.

For a moment Becky Waters felt the quiet horror of being completely on her own.

She forced it out as she closed in on the drone.

Becky Waters released the controls of her suit and pulled at the black blade. She took aim at Cyclops.

Despite it all, she smiled. If her last action saved humanity, then her life was easily worth the sacri—

Cyclops' red light sparkled. The drone abruptly shifted its position, taking Becky by surprise.

She grabbed at the directional controls of her suit, but by then Cyclops was past her. It sped up.

"No!" Becky Waters yelled.

She was all alone and floating into the void. She spun around helplessly, her mind seized by the terror of failure.

And then, abruptly, her line was taunt.

Nox held the line with one hand while grasping Cyclops' nose with the other. She pulled at it, bringing Becky Waters back.

Inside the *Xendos*, B'taav and Inquisitor Cer watched in silent dread as Nox pulled Becky Waters towards her. Cyclops realized the danger it was in. Solid metal converted into liquid, bubbling up and enveloping Nox's arm. The liquid nano-probes moved toward her helmet.

"Hurry," Inquisitor Cer muttered.

Radioactivity readings were almost normal. The slipstream corridor dulled. In the distance they saw darkness and small lights.

Stars.

Becky was at Nox's side. Cyclops moved from side to side, trying desperately to throw the stowaways off.

"Do it!" Nox yelled.

"We'll be fried," Becky said.

"*Do it!*"

With a violent thrust, Becky slashed forward with the black blade and penetrated the drone's body. In that second, Nox released her grip on Cyclops while simultaneously applying her suit's thrusters. As she flew away, she grabbed Becky Waters and held her tight.

Thick electric arcs enveloped Cyclops. Her metallic skin darkened and the liquid that made up much of her surface bubbled before growing still.

Nox and Becky Waters tumbled away, their view of the drone coming and going with each revolution.

Cyclops' straight arrow movement stalled. The electric arcs grew and grew, flashing wildly, before abruptly stopping. By then, her body was black.

The slipstream was gone. With a start, Nox and Becky Waters realized they were floating in outer space.

The dead drone's charred body lay before them. It left ashen pieces in its wake.

"You two still alive back there?" a voice came over their comm. It was Inquisitor Cer.

"Yeah," Nox replied.

In the distance was the *Xendos*. For the very first time they had a clear, close up view of the ship.

"That's the most beautiful starship I've ever laid eyes on," Becky said. "Not that I've seen all that many."

"You will," Cer said. "You will."

Nox and Becky Waters spent several hours in the decompression chamber.

Their space suits protected them from most of the slipstream radiation and were quickly discarded. Afterwards, Becky Waters and Nox were given powerful medicines to combat any lingering effects from their exposure. Thanks to the medication and the nano-probes inside their bodies, they quickly recovered.

While they did, Cer and B'taav checked the *Xendos* and made sure it didn't sustain any serious damage from the prolonged flight from Earth. The crack on the view screen glass and a few minor problems notwithstanding, it appeared all vital systems were functional.

With the checkup finished, they focused on where they were.

"The Displacer we emerged from is a Type 1," Inquisitor Cer said.

The Displacer lay before the *Xendos*. It had considerable scarring yet her identification numbers were visible on her side.

"She's Phaecian," Inquisitor Cer continued. "Old. *Real* old. According to her serial numbers, she was part of the first generation of automated Displacers sent by us. She was thought lost over a thousand years ago. Her last communication was an emergency signal. She said she was hit by a meteor and her hull was compromised."

"I don't see any sign of meteor hits," B'taav said. "Given her age, she looks pretty damned good."

"There's more," Inquisitor Cer said. "When she sent that signal, she said she was over three hundred light years from here."

"The ship faked her status?"

"Looks that way."

"How is that possible?"

"I don't know," Inquisitor Cer said. "But she's been right here ever since, waiting."

"For us?"

There was no answer to that question.

At the end of the day Nox and Becky Waters were deemed sufficiently recovered to be freed from the decompression chamber. They joined Inquisitor Cer and B'taav in the cockpit.

"Where are we?" Becky Waters asked.

"In Phaecia," Inquisitor Cer said.

"Are we near any habitable world?"

"We're two light years away from a solar system. It contains three planets, one of which is habitable."

"Are you familiar with the system?"

"No," Inquisitor Cer said. "According to my records, we will be the first people from either Empire to explore this area. And yet..."

She pressed a button on the panel before him. A buzz came through the ship's speakers.

"Hear that?"

"What is it?"

"A distress signal," B'taav said. "It's old, universal. It's coming from that planet."

"But if no one's been here before, how is that possible?"

"I don't know."

"Should we answer?" Becky Waters asked.

"The signal's been repeating for at least a thousand years," B'taav said. "Whatever emergency they had I'm guessing is long over."

"We were dropped here on purpose," Inquisitor Cer said. She addressed Nox. "Has Spradlin any idea of why?"

"When I get the chance, I'll ask him," Nox said. "If he's willing to talk."

"In the meantime, we have to consider what exactly we're going to do from this point on," B'taav said.

"Can we still use this Displacer?"

"Yes," B'taav said. "We could activate it right now and reach any number of well-populated inner worlds. Unfortunately, neither Inquisitor Cer nor I will be welcomed on any of them with open arms. As for you two, if either Empire finds out who you are and what you've got inside your bodies, there'll be an army of people eager to get their hands on you. I doubt you'd want them to."

"So for now we go to that planet?"

"Yes. It'll take us a week at full impulse to reach her."

"Time enough to prepare," Becky Waters said.

"Quite a bit of time," Nox added.

Inquisitor Cer and B'taav eyed the monitor and, after a while, each other.

"It'll also give us time to rest," Nox said. "You have cabins in this craft, right?"

"Second level," Inquisitor Cer said.

"Showers?"

"Yeah."

"Excellent."

Nox tapped Becky Waters on her shoulder. The two walked to the door leading out of the cockpit. Nox paused before exiting.

"B'taav?" she said.

The Independent eyed the Mechanic.

"Kiss her already."

Nox stepped out of the cockpit, leaving the Inquisitor and the Independent alone.

EPILOGUE ONE

HELIOS – Deep Within the Phaecian Empire

The *Cygnusa* entered the orbit of Helios shortly after 1500 hours.

Merchant and repair scowls approached the craft and locked onto her body. A refueling ship emerged from a distant star base and neared the ship's port side.

Other, smaller service vessels also approached, every one of them intent on doing their individual job.

After the second hour of orbit, a single shuttle craft emerged from the enormous ship's landing bay. It passed the service vessels and descended into the atmosphere of Helios.

From there it made a straight line to the planet's capitol.

"Overlord Emeritus, Inquisitor Raven has arrived."

The chamber was large and bare. Her black walls had no windows to provide light nor any pictures to offer comfort. Overlord Emeritus, the senior most member of the Overlord staff, sat in his chair at the head of a large wooden table. The Overlord was gray and withered. His body was frail to the point when he walked, he did so with a noticeable limp. Yet his eyes, pale and green, were ever alert and displayed a feral intelligence.

The table he sat before was made from one of the largest, and last, of the planet's Greenwood trees. This particular one was at least three thousand years old at the time she was cut down.

Overlord Emeritus checked the computer display before him, making notes where appropriate and crossing out items already dealt with. Finally, he reached the last item on his list.

He grabbed his communicator and pressed a button on it.

"Please send Inquisitor Raven in."

Overlord Emeritus pale eyes were on the door leading into the room.

From it emerged Inquisitor Raven. The Inquisitor bowed.

"Your grace."

Overlord Emeritus nodded, barely acknowledging the man's arrival.

"Your mission was a failure," the Overlord said. "Explain."

Inquisitor Raven bowed a second time and said:

"I stationed the fleet along the Longshore Shipping Lanes, the last known location of the *Xendos*. We had the area surrounded."

"Not well enough."

"No," Raven admitted. Despite his granite exterior, the old warrior shuddered. "We did not find the *Xendos*."

"And?"

"We assume Inquisitor Cer is still alive and in hiding."

"How did this happen?"

"I cannot explain, your excellence," Raven said. "No ship entered or exited the Shipping Lanes without our knowledge. Yet she somehow escaped us."

"Your report states you found human remains?"

"Yes sir. Those of Overlord Octo and his two guards."

"There is no chance Inquisitor Cer's remains might still be out there?"

"I wish that were the case, your Eminence," Inquisitor Raven said. "But the debris we found was minimal. I'm certain Inquisitor Cer jettisoned it along with the three corpses to buy time."

"You were not deceived, Raven?"

"No."

"Not even for a moment?"

"No."

"You're frustrated?"

"Yes."

"Angry?"

"Yes."

"You should be," the Overlord said. "Inquisitor Cer made a fool not only of you, but of the Law and every one sworn to uphold it. Your failure is a mark of shame. Shame requires restitution."

"Your Eminence—"

Overlord Emeritus pressed a button hidden in a panel on the side of the table. The wall behind him, black as the other three in the room, lit up and became transparent. Revealed was a room behind them. In it were a woman and her two young boys.

Inquisitor Raven's wife and his sons.

Overlord Emeritus pressed another button and a pair of Inquisitors stationed themselves at either side of that room and between the mother and her children.

"In 5303, my predecessor was faced with a rebellion in the Pollox sector," Overlord Emeritus said. "To quell the rebellion, he sent a fleet of ships under the command of his most trusted Inquisitor, Morre."

"Sir—"

"Morre was a loyal servant to the Overlords and could be counted on for any job the Overlord asked, no matter what. Yet in the face of this rebellion, Inquisitor Morre faltered. You see, he was from the Pollox Sector and familiar with many of the people involved in this rebellion. With each passing day doubts grew regarding Inquisitor Morre's... resolve."

"Overlord Emeritus—"

"The Overlords brought Inquisitor Morre before them. They asked him why the rebellion had not yet been put down despite the overwhelming military forces at his disposal. Morre offered explanations. Excuses. He tried the Council's patience. In the middle of the inquest, my predecessor brought Morre's wife and children to the tribunal floor. Inquisitor Morre was told he would have one more chance to succeed where so far he failed. But his failure to this point required punishment. Morre was told to choose who among his immediate family would pay for his failure."

Overlord Emeritus laid his hands on the table.

"Inquisitor Moore was stoic," the elderly man continued. "He chose his wife and she was executed on the spot. When Morre returned to the Pollox sector, his resolve was strong. The rebellion was quelled in two days."

Overlord Emeritus' gaze settled on Inquisitor Raven.

"Who do you choose, Inquisitor?"

EPILOGUE TWO

After two days, all remaining *Xendos* repairs were completed. The ship floated among the stars, her engine running healthy.

Nox and Becky Waters kept mostly to themselves. Becky Waters spent time in the ship's cockpit going over all the information she could about the rise of the Phaecian and Epsillon Empires as well as the technologies available in this new day and age. There was much to learn and, it was clear, she was only too eager to do so.

B'taav and Inquisitor Cer spent their free time in their quarters, laughing and talking and caressing. It was a new and welcome experience for both. Toward the evening of that second day, Inquisitor Cer fell asleep in B'taav's arms.

The Independent gently pushed Inquisitor Cer aside before quietly rising from their cot. He dressed and exited the room.

B'taav found it eerie to walk the *Xendos'* corridors in peace.

He made his way down to the crew cabins and silently walked past several doors, stopping before Nox's room. He knocked on the panel beside the open door.

"Come in," came his response.

B'taav stepped inside. Nox was in B'taav's old room, the one he used while searching for the *Argus*. It had no window and was Spartan in its décor. Nox sat on what was now her bed. She held the computer tablet B'taav found in the desert truck back on Earth.

"You could have taken a room with a view," B'taav said.

Nox pressed the tablet's screen and set the device aside.

"What's on your mind?"

"Two questions," B'taav said. "Has Spradlin contacted you since we've arrived?"

"No," Nox said. "He's been unusually quiet. What's your second question?"

B'taav pointed to the tablet.

"Back on Earth, in your desert truck, I accidentally turned that device on."

A flash of anger appeared on Nox's face.

"You were snooping on me?"

"It was an accident," B'taav said. "I had –*have*– no interest in prying into your personal affairs."

"Yet you did."

"And I'm afraid I must do so once more. My second question is this: Who is the woman on that tablet?"

Nox allowed her anger to subside. She tapped the tablet's monitor and the woman's image appeared. She froze the playback.

"Her name is ...was... Catherine Holland," Nox said.

"She was special to you?"

"Very. Why do you care?"

"Because I know her," B'taav said.

Nox's mouth hung open.

"What the hell are you talking about?" she demanded.

"She's alive, Nox."

"That's not possible," Nox said. "She was sent on the arks thousands of years ago. She can't—"

"She is," B'taav said. "When I met her, she used a different name, but it is her."

B'taav approached a computer panel beside Nox's bed. He turned it on and pressed a few buttons. An image of a woman appeared on the computer's monitor.

"She goes by the name Latitia," B'taav said. "She's an Independent."

Nox stared at the image and read the data alongside it. It painted a picture of a ruthlessly efficient, even bloodthirsty, Independent.

"It can't be," Nox insisted. "She just looks like Catherine. It can't *actually* be her."

"Latitia got me to the *Xendos* and Inquisitor Cer, which in turn got us to Earth and to you," B'taav said. "What are the odds that someone who looks this much like Catherine Holland would be the one to send me to get you?"

For several seconds both the Mechanic and Independent were silent. Finally, Nox removed her sunglasses and rubbed her eyes.

"We were sent to this part of the Phaecian Empire for a reason," B'taav said. "Maybe we'll find some answers here."

"Maybe," Nox repeated.

Despite herself, a single tear rolled down Nox's cheek.

For now, neither could guess what lay before them.

For now, there would be no answers, only many, many questions.

For now.

THE END

Atomic Rocket

The Works of
E. R. Torre

Available
now

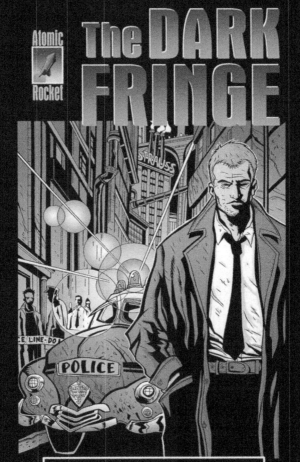

From the grittiest corners of a dark metropolis...
...to the coldest reaches of outer space...
...and all those uneasy places in between...
SHADOWS at DAWN
E. R. Torre
Fourteen tales of Mystery, Suspense, and the Fantastic.

Visions of a dead actor haunt a lonely young man...
Fate leads him on a journey to the man's home town...

E. R. TORRE

HAZE

It started with Blood...

...see how it ends.

Return once more to the world of
The Dark Fringe.

COLD HEMISPHERES

E. R. Torre

An elderly Hitman's most dangerous job
Is the one he can't complete.

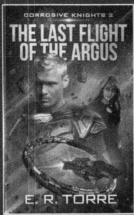

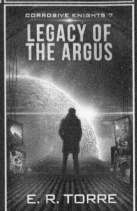

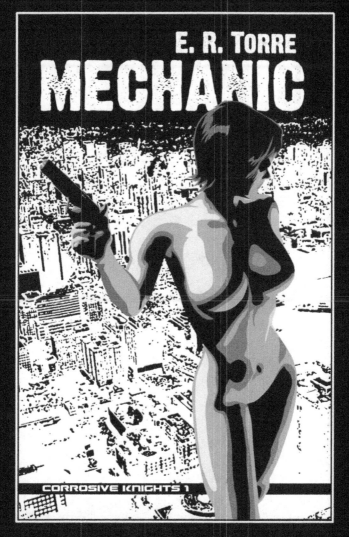

For over two hundred years a deadly secret has been kep[t]
A secret that could shatter the delicate peace between tw[o]
galactic empires and result in the death of billions...

CORROSIVE KNIGHTS 2

THE LAST FLIGHT OF THE ARGUS

E. R. TORRE

That secret is about to be revealed.

Arizona, 1925: A Sheriff makes a discovery in the fiery desert that changes everything.
Bad Penny, the Present: On an idyllic island army base, a hidden menace is about to be unleashed...

CORROSIVE KNIGHTS 3

CHAMELEON

E. R. TORRE

For the seven passengers of a military transport helicopter, the next twelve hours could signal the end of mankind.

Nox the Mechanic is back and this time she faces a threat that could destroy all of mankind...

CORROSIVE KNIGHTS 4

NOX

E. R. TORRE

A threat she carries in her own blood...

Centuries ago, an unstoppable enemy
forced humanity to flee to the stars.

CORROSIVE KNIGHTS 5

GHOST OF THE ARGUS

E. R. TORRE

Today, humanity will take the fight to *them*.

A scavenger on a lost planet
carries a terrifying secret...

CORROSIVE KNIGHTS 6

FOUNDRY OF THE GODS

E. R. TORRE

What lies beneath the desert sands
within the Foundry of the Gods?

The Corrosive Knights series comes to
its explosive end...

CORROSIVE KNIGHTS 7

LEGACY OF
THE ARGUS

E. R. TORRE

ertorre·com

Atomic Rocket

Science Fiction, Mystery, and Suspense

Made in the USA
Coppell, TX
11 March 2021